# EMERGENCE

# PRAISE FOR EMERGENCE

"Hicks writes like Philip K Dick and Robert Crais combined, making for clean, exciting prose. He focuses on the story and never lets go."

— Lucas Bale, author of the award-winning
Beyond The Wall series

"It has all the gritty cyberpunk of the first book plus a more fully-realized world in which to immerse yourself. Excellent."

— SciFi365.net

"Excellent, fast-paced thriller with fantastic world building. Mesa is a troubled yet strong heroine that captivates you from the first page."

— E.E. Giorgi, author of *Chimeras*

# PRAISE FOR CONVERGENCE

**An Amazon Breakthrough Novel Award Finalist**

"[A] smart splice of espionage and science fiction. ... frighteningly realistic. Well-drawn characters, excellent pacing, and constant surprises make this a great cautionary tale about technology and its abuses."

— *Publisher's Weekly*

"From the opening page of Convergence I was hooked. The dystopian world building is well done and the descriptions are vivid. The technology is imaginary and different...great characters and plenty of suspense/action."

— Nicholas Sansbury Smith, author of *Extinction Horizon*
and the Orbs series

"Convergence is fast-paced, full of action and a thrilling ride from start to finish. There is violence, depth of feeling, explosions, car chases and tenderness. The book has everything and is perfect for those who like their SciFi gritty, edgy and realistic."

– J.S. Collyer, author of *Zero*

"A cyberpunk thrillride through a future America under Chinese rule. The conflict between the humanity of the main character, Jonah, and the things he has had to do to survive in this harsh new world makes 'Convergence' an absolute pleasure to read."

– SciFi365.net

# PRAISE FOR REVOLVER

"Wow. Just... Wow. *Revolver* aims at the world we live in and blows its head off."

- Edward Lorn, author of *Bays End* and *The Sound of Broken Ribs*

"*Revolver* ... takes the 'shocking' gold medal. A classic example of social science fiction ... most gripping."

- David Wailing, author of *Auto*

"[A] truly gut twisting, heart wrenching, sphincter squeezing tale of lossand abandonment that stuck with me long after the last page."

- Anthony Vicino, author of *Time Heist*

"*Revolver* is a brave, powerful piece of writing... It's unapologetic, visceral, and the kind of story that would probably have sent the Clean Reader app into cyber meltdown. Give it a read if you like your stories to take you to the edge of your seat."

- Tommy Muncie, author of *Shadow's Talent*

"A lot of what happens in this story resonates with what we see and what we read in our very lives today. *Revolver* is a great story, bristling with tension, unflinching with its descriptions and thoughtful. I get the feeling that people who misunderstand this may need to perhaps take a long hard look at themselves in the mirror."

- The Grim Reader

"*Revolver* is a perfect short story/novella to read right now. The political extremists are gaining more and more power and they aren't easily ignored anymore. *Revolver* tells the story of what would happen if we let this extremism go too far. And wow was it good. ... *Revolver* is a big "what if" book that will leave you feeling raw and full of emotion."

- Brian's Book Blog

"Hicks has written a seminal political – psychological thriller that packs a massive punch in a short space. ... I think it's a piece of fiction that will stand the test of time."

- Steve Stred, Kendall Reviews

# ALSO BY
# MICHAEL PATRICK HICKS

## DRMR SERIES
Convergence (A DRMR Novel, Book 1)
Emergence (A DRMR Novel, Book 2)
Preservation (A DRMR Short Story)

## THE SALEM HAWLEY SERIES
The Resurrectionists (Book 1)

Broken Shells: A Subterranean Horror Novella
Mass Hysteria

## SHORT STORIES
The Marque
Black Site
Let Go
Revolver
Consumption

# EMERGENCE
## DRMR SERIES, BOOK 2

MICHAEL PATRICK HICKS

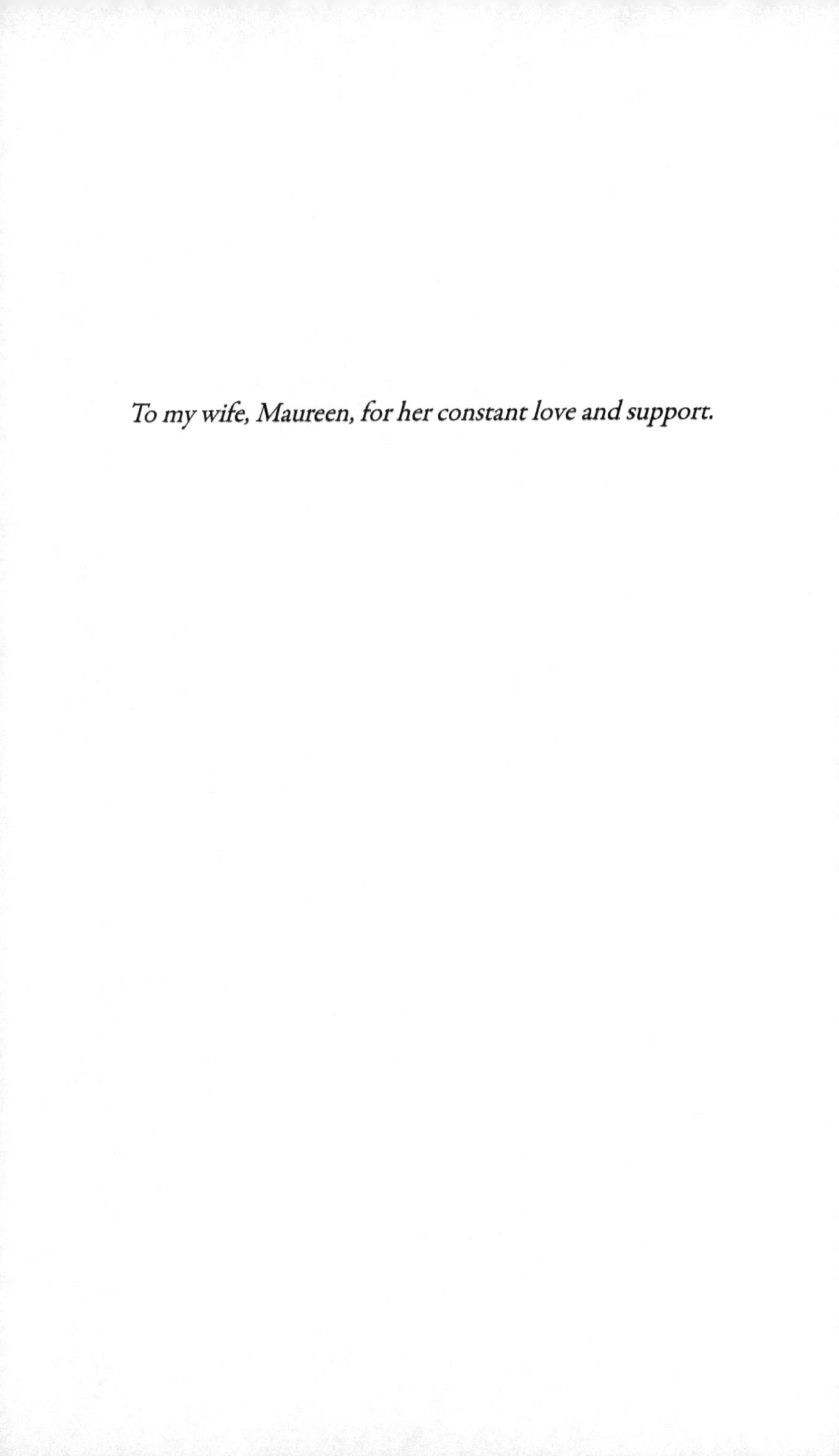

*To my wife, Maureen, for her constant love and support.*

# CHAPTER ONE

S EX AND DEATH FLOWED FREELY, amped up across the nightclub's bio-fi. The emotions and sensations were intoxicating. The music was loud; the bodies, sweaty. Strangers ground against one another, riding the waves of euphoria.

Mesa Everitt felt a body press against her, and she tilted her hips back, swiveling her waist, waving her hands above her head. The response was instant, and she smiled, leaning her weight against the handsome stranger. With a sloppy-drunk grin plastered on his face, her boyfriend, Kaizhou, watched Mesa dancing. Eyes wide, pupils small, he enjoyed the show. Then he stepped up and embraced her, stealing her back from the strange man.

"This is amazing," she said.

His tongue flicked against hers, nearly in sync with the

strumming pound of an electric cello and the blasted riff of a synthetic piano. She locked her arms around his neck, staving off a wave of dizziness. Strange hands moved across her hips, but she didn't care. Couldn't care.

Watching, their friend Jade danced with an easy rhythm, her skin glistening under the pulsating lights. She disappeared briefly as a wave of artificial smoke crossed over her. Moving bodies generated air currents strong enough to part the foggy vapor before it could fully enshroud her. In those few seconds of her slight disappearance, she had found a companion.

Center stage, on a large floating platform above them, Muzyakimo Aki sang. His voice was powerful for such a slim, meek-looking man. He wore thick black frames, and his hair had been dyed multiple colors—purple, yellow, and red—against his natural black. His eyebrows were bushy, nearly a unibrow, and his gaunt face was pockmarked. But his voice... the rich timbre lulled listeners, ensnaring them in a rapture that demanded attention and seriousness. Like Aki himself, his music was a study of contrasts. Every verse, every chorus, each solo, and the chords themselves meant something different to each listener.

The DRMRs on the dance floor were transmitting freely, their lithe figures awash in the experiences of varied pasts. For the last hour and a half, Mesa had been submerged in the lives of others. Aki's music pulsed through her, and she swam through the crowd's associated memory cues streaming across the bio-fi. The sadness and joy of more than a hundred strangers pushed through her DRMR implant. She mourned the loss of a beloved pet then was caught up in the throes of a first orgasm and the loss of virginity. She felt the pride of a first A in school and the crushing defeat of a first F after the tedium of studying for a complex exam. She remembered the first time this particular Aki song came across the entertainment comm, but only a snippet had played before Mom interrupted with a list of chores. Then she shared outrage over illegal whale hunts and fishery raids by corpo suits, and Aki's music was very nearly a call to arms.

She soaked up the experiences and memories, none of them hers.

Onstage, the synthetic dancers bumped and ground, dancing against one another. They were older models, appearing human in only the most superficial ways. With slender arms and legs, as well as jointed fingers and toes, the dancers were clearly artificial. Inhuman. Their skin was shiny egg-white plastic moldings, and a cool electric-blue ring encircled their cybernetic eyes. Facial features were barely defined. Their designer had instead opted for the subtle impression of a face pressed into smooth, flat planes. The aesthetic was both undeniably beautiful and disconcerting. The dancers were logged in to the bio-fi feed, and their mimicry captures were set to resemble movements of people in the crowd. They danced with cybernetic abandon but with a computerized off-set that forced a stutter to their steps.

For a brief, halting moment, Mesa rose above the crowd, her mind soaring higher than those around her. She could see the flashes of memory, the pattern of convergence that roped through each individual soul, tying one to another. The sight was electrifying and beautiful. Their thoughts jived against the laser-light show. Bodies slammed against one another; others held embraces. Slick human machines slid against one another, exchanging kisses and sweat, running fingers through the hair of strangers. Their subconscious echoed against the synthpop of Aki's performance, the wails of electronic guitars, and the random interruptions of found noises turned into hyper-idealized artificialities. Mesa floated, briefly ethereal, long enough to see the man at the center of the convergence. Like a hollow void, he was disconnected from those around him. A black ember burning brightly, Muzyakimo Aki united everyone around him, yet stood apart from them all. Nothing flowed from or through him. He was a jetty, an interjection in the center of the convergence.

Hands slid up Mesa's flanks, and her mouth pressed tightly against Kaizhou's, their tongues exploring one another's. He held her with a promise to never let go. Discerning the flow of his memories from the tangled current of everyone else's was impossible.

She had tried posh a year ago and marijuana the year before that. Neither was remotely similar to the rush of hundreds of souls and thousands of memories amplified through the bio-fi's feedback loop. She'd been high before, but the euphoria she felt at that moment was... exciting. She was truly high.

Jade had joined them at some point. Mesa blinked with languid slowness, taking Jade's arm and pulling her closer, so that both Jade and Kaizhou hugged her. Mesa enjoyed being between them, and she laughed as Jade's companion pressed his way in, nuzzling at Jade's long, glistening neck.

The percussions drove on, deeper and deeper, pulsing harder and harder. The concussive shockwave of sound slowly degraded into a shrill siren before giving way to pure silence. A thin skein of fog blanketed the crowd as the lights powered down, plunging the club into darkness. And then the crowd exploded in cheers, screams, and applause. The dim houselights slowly warmed up, and beneath their soft glow, Aki waved at the crowd and nodded. He turned sharply and strode offstage without a word.

"That was amazing," Mesa said again. She wiped a bright-red streak of hair away from her eyes, pushing the trails of natural black behind her ears.

She was sweaty and high, and her heart was hammering. She'd been dancing for two hours, and her throat was tight and sore from screaming along to the music and cheering for Aki. Her words were a harsh whisper, difficult to edge past her lips. She was exhausted and energized to the point of being hyper.

Fingers danced up her arm, and she met the smiling face of Jade's companion.

"Cool tattoo," he said, his index and middle finger slicking away the sweat as his digits traced the curve of a thick green dragon tail as it wrapped around a Gaelic cross.

"Thanks," she said, her throat constricting against the word in painful defiance. It came out husky and hollow. She tilted her body slightly away from him, leaning into Kaizhou enough to make it clear she didn't want this stranger touching her. More, she didn't want to discuss the tattoo.

Her arm was a sleeve of color, but she didn't remember getting the tattoo. She didn't know why she had it or what it meant. And the why of all that was a whole other story she didn't want to go into. Not there, not after Aki's performance. She was already feeling the come-down, and she knew the stranger's questions would make things worse and leave her uncomfortable.

Her fingers laced between her Kaizhou's, she said to him, "Let's go."

Jade was lost in the attentions of her companion, but Mesa nudged her anyway and tugged at her fingers.

"You coming?"

Jade's free hand was lost in the long hair of the man suckling at the joint of her neck and shoulder. She smiled and promised, "I'll catch up later." She gave Mesa's hand a squeeze goodbye then turned to face the man behind her to continue their familiarization.

The crowd was slowly thinning, but the bar and dance floor were still crowded. The club stank of sweat, spilt booze, and reefer. The floor was tacky. Mesa and Kaizhou jostled their way to the exit, shimmying between couples, gently pushing around others. Cold air blasted their hot bodies as they stepped outside. The physical force drew their breath away and frosted it in the early morning air.

In the clear sky, bright stars and a full moon illuminated Mount Rainer in the distance, and closer, the Space Needle and the Seattle skyline glowed.

"That's fucking beautiful," Mesa said.

Kaizhou followed her gaze. Neither ever tired of the view. He took her in his arms and kissed her bare shoulder. She tilted her head so that their temples touched. A small sigh of happiness blossomed into a white puff before her lips.

"You OK?" he asked.

She slipped her hand into the back pocket of his jeans, warming her palm against the curve of flesh beneath the thin fabric. "Yeah, I'm good."

She traced the outlines of the stars, making imaginary constellations, connecting them across time and distance. She was the center of that convergence, with Kaizhou beside her. Somehow, some way, she imagined it all connecting back to Muzyakimo Aki, drawing him into her web and unraveling his secrets. Onstage, the man had been an inspiring enigma, and standing in the middle of the sidewalk outside the club, she dreamed of connecting with him, pouring her hopes into him, and pulling from him all of the details of his life so that she might wrap herself in his purpose and find an aim in life.

"You sure you're all right?"

Her gaze, far-off and distant, snapped back into focus. Her eyes drew a bead on Kaizhou. She gave him a smile that washed away the troubled expression on his face, forcing a grin out of him.

Playfully, she squeezed his bottom. "I'm fine," she said.

He leaned close, nose to nose with her. Their smiles widened, and for that evening at least, she found purpose.

Later, she quietly disentangled herself from sodden bedsheets. Warm air blew from the ducts, but by the time it reached her, it felt cool against her bare, sweat-slicked skin. She wrapped herself in a chenille blanket and curled up in the plush leather chair in Kaizhou's living room, hugging her legs close and resting her chin against the peaks of her kneecaps. She could make out the muffled sounds of his snores through the thin walls of the small apartment.

The emotional ecstasy from Aki's concert was dissipating, and she was crashing back to the baseline of normalcy. The emotional low bordered on depression simply because the highs of the night had been so far above. Such was the risk one bore for attending an Aki performance with guards willfully down to allow the bio-fi amplifiers unrestricted access to the DRMR enhancements. The memory was a powerful, jolting surge, exhausting in its exactness, and she didn't risk replaying it.

No matter how well one's memories were stored and replayed, they never captured the lived experience exactly due to the lack of amplification. Anybody who'd been to one of Aki's shows understood that risk, and all others were befuddled. The memories were a one-off, stored for enjoyment and reminiscing, but never replayed because the replay was hollow and untrue, cheapening the individual experience.

She wiped away a tear, grateful for the memory and its freshness. The memory was truly her own, even if she lacked a wealth of experiences from which to draw cues and associations while lost in the throes of Aki's music. She cried softly, but the tears were not of sadness.

She knew she couldn't go home in her wrecked state. Her nerves needed to settle, and the jitters needed to pass.

Sporadic traffic passed below, separated by long intermissions. The dull rhythm was enough to make her eyes heavy then lull them closed.

"Hey, wakey-wakey," Kaizhou said, squeezing her shoulders. His thumbs made slow, long circles along the muscles above her collarbones. The massage was enough to wake her and pleasing enough to keep her eyes shut.

"But I don't wanna," she said, mumbling the childish mantra and exaggerating her sleepiness. The daylight surprised her. Kaizhou stood next to her, still naked. She kissed his hipbone and buried her face against his belly, breathing in his scent.

Slowly, Mesa unfolded herself from the chair, keeping herself wrapped up in the blanket, adoring its soft gentle comfort against her body. She gave him a peck on the cheek as she passed then began rounding up the trail of errant clothes.

She frowned at the previous evening's mini-skirt and halter top. The outfit was fine for a late night of clubbing but not exactly appropriate morning wear if she wanted to avoid the walk of shame.

"I'm borrowing some sweats," she called out as she pulled the drawstrings tight. Then she lost herself in one of his baggy University of Washington sweatshirts.

In the bathroom, she combed back her hair and let it fall over her shoulders. She studied her reflection, pleasantly surprised by what she saw. The smart-mirror flashed a quick "GOOD MORNING." Then the default presets loaded unobtrusively along the side and bottom: the weather forecast—cloudy, fifty-six, seventy percent chance of rain after 6 p.m.—stock reports, and a news ticker accompanied by a talking head who delivered the top news stories. Mesa turned on the water faucet, and the sink's biometrics measured her temperature and pulse rate. The data presented itself on the bottom-right corner of the mirror, next to a pulsating, bright-red heart icon. It told her she was in excellent health for a woman in her early twenties.

Emotionally and mentally, she had reached her baseline of normalcy, and she felt surprisingly good. Her earlier breakdown after the high was fading, clouded over by the memories of better feelings. A fullness had engulfed her and made her content. The only thing missing was coffee.

The door of the flat opened with a protesting squeal. The noise was enough to wake Jonah from his stupor. Mesa met his frown with an apologetic smile.

"I was getting worried," he said, pushing himself into a seated position on the sofa. "You didn't call."

Mesa felt her cheeks flush with guilt. "I'm sorry. I got wrapped up in my night out."

"You know I worry about you, right?"

"Yeah, Dad, I know. I'm sorry."

"You need to be careful out there."

"I know. I said I'm sorry." She talked over her shoulder, moving into the kitchen, both hands wrapped around a cup of Morning Java blend.

"You need to call me when you're going to be out all night."

"Look," she said, "I told you I'm sorry. Move on."

She tossed the plastic lid in the recycler then took a deep breath of the coffee's aroma, letting the steam warm her face.

"I needed a night out. That's all. Needed to have some fun." She sat next to him, tucking her legs beneath herself.

"I get that," he said. His hunt for the next words was plainly difficult.

Mesa's therapist had suggested they learn better communication skills and encouraged them to be open with one another. Open lines of communication would be difficult for both of them, the doctor had said, but being honest about their feelings and speaking freely without worry of judgment was necessary. Jonah had taken the message to heart. Still, it never came easy. He was a buttoned-up sort.

"It's just that... before, I mean. You used to disappear a lot. You'd come and go whenever you wanted, and I don't want you to feel like a prisoner, but—God, am I making any sense?"

She rubbed his back with the palm of her hand and gave him a quick peck on the forehead. "It's cool, Dad. I get it. I screwed up."

On the coffee table were curled e-papers. Jonah's drafting pencil had rolled to the floor. She recognized the woman emerging from the thin lines and rough markings. The prominent cheekbones were defined with light shadows. Mesa knew her mother's face only from her father's drawings and the rare mem recording she kept in her bedroom.

She took a deep breath then continued. "I wasn't thinking about you. I was focusing on myself."

"You should be able to do that, though. You deserve your own space, time to yourself, whatever. Call next time, OK?"

She gave him another quick peck then pushed herself up. "I need to study."

"You're doing great, you know."

She beamed. "It feels like it. I think I'm finding my groove."

A smattering of data chips were splayed across the desktop in her bedroom, along with empty coffee cups, which she dumped into a small trashcan. Her clubbing outfit went into a hamper filled with the last few days' worth of pending laundry.

She fished the DRMR pad from a desk drawer and uncoiled the thin black cable. She scooped back her hair behind her ear and plugged the male end of the cord into the port that lay flush with her skin. An electronic chill bloomed inside her as the devices in her skull mated with the peripheral device and queued up the menu. The display came alive, splayed across her retinas. She gave the play button a mental tap, and the data began synchronizing with the installed REMINDER software.

Developed by DARPA to help brain-damaged soldiers recover from trauma, REMIND mimicked the hippocampus and aided long-term memory storage. DRMR, an earlier DARPA invention that had expanded into the civilian market, relied heavily on the hippocampus. Because that segment of her brain was severely damaged, DRMR was largely useless. However, with the addition of the REMIND prosthetics and some rewiring, her DRMR became a natural delivery system for the REMINDER protocols.

Three years earlier, she had been abducted and suffered severe trauma at the hands of a madwoman, Alice Xie. Mesa had woken in a hospital with no memory, no identity. A stranger had been beside her. Her father. He'd done everything he could to help, but any hope of recovering her lost past had vanished. Her life prior to that reawakening was gone forever.

She'd relearned many of the skills she had once had through a series of progressively difficult learning modules. With the REMINDER downloads came homework—lots of it.

The last three years had been grueling but progressive. Mesa was a quick learner, and her degree of determination, commitment, and achievement astounded her doctors and private tutors.

Her tutors believed that in another year, she would be able to pass the GED and start hunting for colleges. She wasn't sure what she would study, and she rarely thought about that aspect of her future. Although she couldn't remember her past, the void of things forgotten clung to her like a shawl. She was more interested in unearthing her previous life and learning more about her own history than worrying about what might become of tomorrow.

By the time the first tutorial was finished, her coffee was cool. Still, the acidic bitterness set off a spark of pleasure. She shut her eyes briefly, smiling to herself. She interrupted the dataflow and dislodged the chip before hunting through the rest scattered on the desktop.

She swiveled the chair around, propped her feet up on the edge of the bed, and leaned back. Mesa plugged in a new chip and let a scrap of the unremembered past wash over her.

Mesa was two years old, running barefoot through the grass. She wore purple pants and a T-shirt with a big yellow flower on it, her full belly poking out beneath the fabric. Her face was chubby, and she was constantly laughing. A smile stretched so widely across her face that her cheeks nearly pushed shut her eyes. Large and black, those almond-shaped eyes tilted upward, the clearest mark of her Japanese heritage from her mother.

Her laugh was infectious. She clung to Selene's index fingers as she and Mesa twirled around the lawn. A slight breeze ruffled their long black hair.

"Ashes, ashes," Selene sang.

Mesa's laugh built into excited shrieks. Her head tilted back toward the sun as she spun. Her favorite part was coming up.

"We all fall down!"

Mesa let go of Selene's fingers and flung herself back, squealing as she fell. She gyrated on the lawn, kicking her arms and legs in the air, laughing and laughing. Then Selene was on top of her, tickling her ribs and grabbing playfully at Mesa's little feet, her fingers drawing more excited bouts of laughter from the child as they drew across her soles. Mesa was laughing hard, out of breath, her cheeks rosy. She stuck her tongue out between her tiny, perfect teeth.

"Ashes," Mesa said, the word too large for her mouth. "Fall down!" she shouted, rolling about in the grass, grabbing clumps of green in her tiny fist.

In her bedroom, Mesa could feel the heat of the remembered sunlight warming her. A flush of joy bloomed deep in her core, imitating the original. The memory wasn't hers, nor was it Selene's. The memory belonged to Jonah. He'd given Mesa a bag of these chips—his collection of memories from her childhood. Cherished recollections. He'd lain in the grass that day, watching his wife and daughter enjoy a perfect moment, and more than twenty years later, he'd shared that moment with his daughter, who had no recollection of him or herself. Although Selene had died years before Mesa's problems, the woman's affection for Mesa's youthful counterpart had endeared her greatly. Her mother's love swam across the ages to her, and Mesa wished for some way to thank her.

A few dozen more memories littered the desk and its drawers. Even more were scattered across the web, archived in deeply buried caches of sites such as MemSpace and Episodic. She'd found a few, posted by Selene more than a decade ago, but the search hadn't been easy. More were out there, she knew. There had to be.

She finished the coffee and unplugged, calling it quits for the day. She felt antsy and confined, stricken with a hard-core case of cabin fever.

"I need to take a walk, get out and stretch for a bit," she said.

Still dressed in Kaizhou's clothes, she said goodbye to Jonah and promised to call, but she didn't think she would be out late.

Even as the door closed behind her, she wondered how it would be to leave and never come back. To disappear. It wasn't the first time she'd had the errant thought. But she knew how much irreparable pain that would cause Jonah, and as she had before, she dismissed the idea before it could fully form. Even though her psychiatrist suggested keeping an open line of dialogue with her father and sharing her thoughts and feelings with him, she kept that secret to herself.

That and one other.

# CHAPTER
# TWO

COFFEE WAS THE LIFEBLOOD OF a memorialist, Mesa thought.

Time was fleeting, and sleep took up too much. Hence, caffeine.

Jonah would have gone batshit had he known. Thinking of sharing her thoughts with her father, Mesa had asked him about memorialists once. Instead, she'd gotten a lecture on how they were a cult of crazies who cooped themselves up in basements and overloaded their brains with other people's lives instead of having lives of their own. She'd learned this was a common stereotype, and she rarely spoke of her activities to non-memorialists. She held the secret close, maintaining a private world she could escape to.

The movement had its share of critics who denigrated the memorialists, calling them nothing more than memory addicts. The accusation, while not necessarily untrue, always carried a heavy weight of condemnation.

There were memory whores who joined up simply to ride the DRMR-amplified highs. They got off on the voyeuristic aspects of others' sexual experiences or the by-proxy euphoria of drug use. Others, including Jonah, thought memorialists were simply another brand of religious zealots.

Many tried to find God in the memories of the masses. They believed God was in the details and his invisible hand guided each interaction, rolling the dice on every occurrence. The God seekers thought that somewhere, deep within these associations, sparking to life in the unseen chemical reactions of memory, was the key to unlocking the mystery of his existence. Mesa, a skeptic, considered that to be nonsense. DRMR was a powerful tool, and the brain was a bioelectric machine built through millennia of evolution. Science had advanced to the point where it allowed mankind to not only record these electro-chemical reactions but also replicate them exactly in the minds of others. That ability was a staggering achievement. Those replicative powers interested Mesa the most.

Kaizhou was one of the few who knew Mesa's history as intimately as she did. He knew of the chemical assault against her brain by Alice Xie—the attack three years prior had left her mind a blank slate—and her on-going efforts toward recovery. He'd tutored her in the more difficult math assignments. Then eventually, their slow affair had grown into something more, and he'd worried about a conflict of interest. Somewhere along the way, he'd admitted to being a memorialist and suggested she try it. Despite her reluctance, the idea had taken root and grown into a quiet certitude.

Joining his group had been a means to an end that gave her a particular standing among her fellow memory hounds. She was an aberration because much of her mind was a void. The others had greeted Mesa with awe then respect and a shared common interest. They helped navigate the memory caches and built a convergence web around her.

Constructing the web was slow. Jonah's mem chips provided focal data points, as well as points of reference to expand upon. Selene had become another reference point, a fragmentary construct built from Jonah's experiences. Mesa's mother had been active on various social networks, but digging deep enough to recover pertinent information from the historical layers was grueling. New data constantly buried older information deeper and deeper.

When Mesa arrived at the coffee shop, Jade and Kaizhou were already there. She'd hit them both up over the commNet and asked if everyone was still meeting. Ashita, Sri, Rameez, and Doris were there, too, plugged in and carrying the blank stares of an engaged DRMR, caffeine at the ready. Other than their group and the PetHuman server bots, the cafe was largely empty.

"Where's your boy toy?" Mesa asked.

Jade let out a noise and made a jerk-off motion. "He was a tosser. Had a thing for feet. No thank you."

"How was the concert?" Ashita asked.

"It was amazing," Kaizhou said, beaming. Kaizhou was Aki's biggest fanboy. His music populated an enormous amount of data sectors in Kaizhou's head, to the point that Mesa had once told him she was worried it would spill over and corrupt his actual memory banks. He was a purist, though, and felt the risk was worth it. Aside from a live, bi-fi-fed performance, the native digital releases were the best way to experience Aki's scriptures. And that was how obsessed Kaizhou was; he never called it music, always scripture.

"I'm sorry we missed it," Sri said, her arm slung around Ashita's shoulders, leaning into the woman.

"What were you doing, Rameez?" Jade asked. "Saving the whales or some such?"

Rameez frowned, which only served to make Jade laugh. The Pakistani gent had a deep affection for marine life, which Mesa appreciated, but Jade never understood it.

"Hey," Kaizhou said, holding a data tablet toward Mesa, "I got you something."

Mesa looked at him expectantly, practically tearing the pad out of his hand. She plugged in before he could even tell her what it was.

"Oh, wow," she said. The clip was short, the briefest of instances, and she replayed it.

She recognized the Japanese woman with long black hair. Selene was sitting on concrete steps, with Jonah beside her. Mesa was four or five, eating popcorn.

She slowed the playback, trying to absorb the details. Selene was in mid-laugh, and Jonah was smiling. Mesa was turning back to watch them, her small hand raising a large chunk of caramel popcorn to her lips. Her black hair stuck out in stubby pigtails on either side of her head.

Whoever had recorded the scene was in a hurry, walking fast. His head darted around as he weaved through pedestrian traffic. The mem was nothing more than a quick glimpse of her family, but it was enough.

She played it again.

She wrapped her arms around Kaizhou and kissed him. "Thank you," she whispered.

"It's not much," he said.

Mesa unplugged, handing the tablet back to him. "It's more than I had before. It's another piece, another connection."

"Does it help at all?" Jade asked. "I mean, do you ever remember anything?"

"No," Mesa said. "But I don't expect to." *I only hope I will,* she didn't add.

Rameez shifted his bulk, turning to face Kaizhou. His eyes were large. "Have you seen the newsfeeds?"

"No. What's up?"

"Seven memorialists were killed in Los Angeles. Police think it was the whole sect. News is calling it a massacre."

"Holy shit." Jade straightened up, curling her long fingers around her white paper cup.

News out of LA was rare following the PRC takeover and the cease-fire, unless the story was sensational or gory, preferably both. PacRim military kept a tight filter over the government-run news services. Mesa quickly realized that the news had originated from local citizen sources and filtered out of California by way of pirated newsfeeds across the hacker satellites.

"PRC is keeping mum, but some anonymous police sources are confirming the story to legitimate outside news agencies," Jade said, scrolling through the feeds on her tablets.

"Any idea who's responsible?" Kaizhou asked.

"Nothing concrete, but lots of speculation to pick from. Either some of God's warriors"—her voice dripped with derision—"or some psycho off his meds."

"This is crazy," Doris said, his Greek accent thick, his eyes downcast and somber.

"And it's also an isolated event," Kaizhou said. "It sucks, but there's no need to panic."

He met Rameez's worried eyes and waited for his friend to absorb his words. Finally, Rameez nodded, and his face cleared. Doris also seemed to have taken the words to heart.

"Keep an eye on the forums," Mesa said. "If anybody made it out of there, they could reach out for help."

"I'll keep Somnambulist up and running and refreshing for news. There's already a lot of posts coming in," Rameez said.

Somnambulist was a private memorialist forum, and users were scrutinized at registration prior to being allowed access. Hierarchy was based on the amount of interaction and number of posts. Lurkers were monitored and allowed access to more basic, generalized postings, while the regular users were granted unrestricted privileges but were still a level below the mods who supervised for compliance to the site rules.

"Anything useful?" Jade asked.

"We've got a lot to sort through. There's a lot of data coming in through the sats," Doris said.

"Two were plugged in at the time of their death. They were actively transmitting."

"Oh, shit!" Mesa closed her eyes.

"Those snuffs are going to be everywhere," Kaizhou said. His face blanched, his features turning into a sour scowl.

The coffee in Mesa's stomach suddenly turned against her, sending bile up in a thick gorge. She clamped her mouth shut and forced it down.

"I don't want any part of that," Jade said.

"No, but somebody needs to," Ashita said. Her hair was cut into a cute bob and dyed a dark purple. She wore ties with men's button-down dress shirts along with hoop skirts. Nobody ever mistook her for a death fiend.

"You volunteering?"

She crossed her arms, her hands squeezing the opposite biceps. "I was just saying," she said lamely. "I mean, there could be evidence on there."

"It's a good point," Rameez said hollowly.

"What about all their data?" Sri asked from her rear-corner table.

"It's pouring in," Jade said, a blank glaze on her pale features. "Our hacktivists are raiding their servers, doing a massive, rapid backup and purge. Somnambulist is getting flooded hardcore."

"This is insane," Doris said.

"This is why we have backups and protocols," Sri said. Her eyes flickered across the retinal display that only she could see.

"The work will continue," Kaizhou said. "But we lost seven people here."

"'This is crazy," Doris said.

"We heard you the first time, dude," Jade said, then muttered, "Fucking broken record."

"Other sects are pinging in," Rameez said, "taking work orders."

"We raffling it?" Ashita asked.

"I'm getting reports that twelve people were in that cell. We've got five unaccounted for."

"We'll handle the outreach," Mesa said. All eyes turned to her. She shrugged. "The Frenchies can't handle it alone."

"Raffle it," Kaizhou said. "Put in some dibs for the snuffs. The more eyes working on this, the better."

"We've got support on the outreach," Jade said.

"Snuffs are rolling in," Rameez said. "Swiping 'em over to you, Ashita."

"Keep the safety filters on," Kaizhou said. His gaze went blank as he turned inward to his retinal display. His head bounced a bit, in tune with music Mesa knew he had playing in his skull. Kaizhou loved rhythm and pulsing beats, and he tapped his foot in time with what was no doubt an Aki album.

"We've got six sects on seven snuffs," Rameez said. "We'll cross-reference the convergence."

"Their data history is being redeployed across the satband."

"We'll slot it in where we can," Kaizhou said.

"This is—" Doris began.

"Shut the fuck up," Jade said, cutting him off. He gave her the finger. She gave him a raspberry.

"Send me profiles on the missing five," Mesa said. "I've got the wide-band assist notice out there." She gulped coffee, careless of the heat. She was too focused on the data to even notice.

"Let's hope they see it," Sri said. She and Mesa locked eyes and nodded, being strong for one another. *We can do this,* their eyes said. Mesa squeezed her hand, waiting for the profile to collate.

Five faces hung in the air before her, floating above the table on her retinal display. The data was for her eyes only, leaving only dead space between her and the group in the physical world. She quickly reviewed their bios as the pertinent details crossed the right side of her vision.

Jacob Kessler, a 22-year-old high school dropout.

Lisa Kessler, 25, Jacob's sister. An undergraduate at UCLA.

Chenfang Liu. 19. PRC-born immigrant. UCLA freshman.

Matthew Ritz. 33. The oldest member of the sect. Divorced.

Mariann Korgan. 24. Waitress. Red hair and freckles.

They were out there somewhere, and their lives were likely in danger. They might not even know what had happened. The massacre could have been a one-off, or the killers might be hunting them at that very moment.

She pinged the five of them, sent them a brief summary of events, and let them know her sect was ready to support them however necessary. The ball was in their court. All Mesa could do was wait for them to make contact.

"The data's gone loose," Sergeant Samuel Kaften said.

Wind beat against the tent, and the unzipped entry flapped against the interior. He closed his eyes, enjoying the sudden cool of the draft, despite the dust that blew in from the middle of nowhere. Another six hours, and sats in orbit overhead would start moving. He planned to be gone long before then.

"We knew that was a viable risk." The disembodied voice came through the commNet, rattling around the inside of Kaften's skull. He hated the prissy tone of the suit. *Fucking Schaeffer.* "Probability estimates expect the potential damage to be inconsequential the further removed it becomes."

"Meaning what?" Kaften asked. He broke down and cleaned his semiautomatic H&K handgun while they spoke, needing to give hardly any attention to the maintenance of the recently used firearm. He could perform the simple process in his sleep, so Kaften was still able to give Schaeffer the undivided attention he expected.

"Meaning, by the time anybody figures it out, you'll have the op wrapped up, and our IP will be secured. Meaning no more fuck-ups on your end."

"We've got five in the wind."

The sigh shook through the connection, loudly. Kaften grew more irritated. "Identities?"

"Patching them out to you now," Kaften said, popping loose the data packet.

"We'll run it through local resources. I want your team to move north and engage phase two."

"Copy that." He disconnected the transmission.

He hated cleanup details. The operation was three years late—something about proof of concept and cohesion rates. Whatever, the reason didn't matter. The job was far above his pay rate. Naturally, it had gone sloppy because the suits and geeks were involved. They were so far removed from ground operations as to be utterly clueless, but orders were orders. And money was money. His team hadn't been able to purge the data, and some of the memorialists had been live-transmitting, which made for even further complications. But if Schaeffer didn't care, neither did Kaften. The higher-ups weren't making it a problem for him, so it was time to move on.

"Boyd, Crassen, prep for a rapid exfil and redeployment. We're moving out."

They set about breaking down their camp and packing away equipment. In half an hour, they would be on the road. Two hours after that, they would be across the border and on a flight north.

Kaften hoped he never set foot in California again.

Three men clad in black stood before Mesa, guns raised. Darkness surrounded them, a tunneled void of empty pitch.

Mesa stared down the barrel of a gun, her eyes wide. She tried to plead, but the eyes that glowered down upon her were blank and uncaring.

She raised her arms before her, fingers outstretched. "No, please, wait a minute—"

A flash of bright light and heat blasted against her face. The skin around her eyes billowed out from the concussive wave, bursting open flesh, crunching and cracking bone. The high-velocity frag bullet shredded her face and splattered the wall with the back of her skull. Tiny chunks of meat and flecks of red splashed against the desk.

As she lay there dying, the final spark of brain activity flickering away, a hand reached for her. She saw whiteness, and beyond the reaching fingers, long black hair. The fingers reached ever closer as the world faded to gray then darker and darker.

Mesa shot up, her eyes springing open. One hand went to her chest, trying to calm the rapid beating of her heart. She flung the bedsheets away, too hot. Beads of sweat peppered her forehead.

"Jesus," she said, breathless.

Rain tapped at her bedroom window. She flicked on

the small nightstand lamp, unsurprised by the knock at her door.

"Yeah, Dad?"

Jonah pushed open the door, his eyes puffy from sleep. "You OK?"

She shrugged, pulling the blanket tighter against her. "Bad dreams," she said. "That's all."

He came into the room and sat beside her. "You screamed."

"Did I?" She watched him studying her then said, "I don't remember."

Jonah swept back her sweaty bangs. "Want to talk about it?"

She closed her eyes and turned her face into his palm, enjoying the roughness of his hand against her smooth cheeks. "Nah. I'll be all right. The dream's already fading."

He watched her closely for a moment then nodded. He leaned in to kiss her forehead and said goodnight. "Love you, kid."

She smiled. "Love you, too, Dad."

With her eyes closed, she listened to the click of the door shutting and his soft footsteps down the hall. She knew sleep would be hard to get back to, and feeling too hot, she kicked free of the covers and padded into the bathroom.

The T-shirt she'd slept in was ringed with dark stains of sweat. Her whole body felt wrung out and exhausted, as if she'd endured a marathon workout. She ran the cold water and washed her face, slicking the water back through her hair. The red highlights stood out against her natural black, but they would need freshening up soon. Maybe she would get purple streaks, but not nearly as extreme as Ashita's. That woman didn't dare sport a single strand of natural color.

Mesa brushed her teeth, trying to clean out the funky taste the nightmare had left behind.

*Never should have watched that fucking snuff,* she

chided herself. *Too late now.* Her curiosity had gotten the better of her. The mem was horrifying and powerful, and she was grateful to have at least had the foresight to keep the safety filters on. She didn't think she would have been able to handle the pain or the chemical overload as her brain reproduced the narcotic trip of death and the psychedelic rush of DMT into her system.

She hoped Ashita was being responsible and that she wasn't having similar nightmares. The smart-mirror said her heart rate was normal, but she still felt off. Shaken.

She spit, rinsed, and spit again. She tried to meet her eyes in the mirror but gave up after seeing the dark bags racooning against her pale skin.

The pillow and sheets were sodden. She decided to sleep on the couch, if she could even go to sleep again that night.

Normally, she focused on the REMINDER studies until the dataloads lulled her back to sleep. All she could see were dark, compassionless eyes staring down at her and the large black barrel of a gun being leveled upon her. She wouldn't be getting any work done.

She stripped off her panties and T-shirt, stepped into the shower, and let the hot water wash over her. She closed her eyes, waiting for the steam and pelting blasts to relax her. Standing under the showerhead, she opened the Sheffield program, her psychiatric AI.

"Hello, Mesa," Dr. Sheffield said. "Are you OK?"

"Bad dreams," she answered.

Sheffield's face was blank, but he had an underlying note of warmth and compassion. Mesa preferred running the program with her eyes shut while her mind's eye broadcasted his face against the dark emptiness inside her closed eyelids. He was a surprisingly pretty man, and she wondered, not for the first time, whether a real Dr. Sheffield existed or if he was simply a programmer's fantasy.

She gave him a brief rundown of her day and what she

remembered of the nightmare. "I saw her again."

"Your mother?"

"Yeah," Mesa said. "I mean, at least I think so. I never really 'see her' see her. You know?"

"But you think about her. You've been trying to find out as much as you can about her. I know she's important to you."

"Well, yeah. Of course."

"It's natural you would dream of her. She's at the forefront of your mind. That's bound to carry over."

"I guess, but..."

"What?"

"I mean, I know what she looks like, right? How come I never see her in my dreams? I can never make her out. Like, tonight. She was disembodied. Her hands were reaching for me, and I saw her hair, but that was it. Where was her face? It's weird. I can never see her face."

"Dream interpretation isn't really my specialty. Sometimes they mean something; sometimes they don't. What do *you* think it means?"

"You're the AI, doc. How the fuck should I know?"

He smiled, a clearly artificial tic. "You never knew your mother. Or at least, you don't have memories of her, would be more accurate, yes? Maybe you never see her in your dreams because it represents that you're afraid of what you might learn about her."

Mesa rolled her eyes. "Real profound, doc."

"Well, sometimes a cigar is just a cigar."

"Now what the fuck does that mean?" she asked.

They both laughed.

"I'm signing off doc. Thanks for the chat."

"Mesa, would you send me tonight's dream?"

She spliced together a memory file and sent it off. He thanked her and said goodnight. Enveloped by the steam, she felt marginally better.

"I've got eyes on subject," Crassen said. The apartment's window shades were drawn, but thermal vision broadcast the occupants clearly.

"Clear shot?" Kaften asked.

"Negative."

Kaften was craving nicotine. Two ops in one day, nearly twelve hours apart. He was drained.

He and Boyd climbed the stairs, guns drawn and at the ready. Tactical masks woven from spider silk covered their faces. The fabric was stronger than the black Kevlar shirts and cargo pants they wore.

Four flights up, they crossed the landing and moved down the hall swiftly and silently.

"Status?" Kaften asked.

"Still stationary. No shot."

Once it became clear that the subject was up and moving about, they deployed quickly. They'd been observing from an apartment directly across the street. The renters hadn't objected to his team's use of the space at all, not after two silenced rounds punched through their foreheads.

A lit display identified apartment 456. Boyd and Kaften took up positions on either side of the door and readied for breach. If Crassen had a clear bead on her, then he could take her out silently. That left one other target, who, according to the thermals, had been asleep and stationary for several hours.

Boyd hacked the door locks with an illegal master override. Police, fire, and rescue had a universal electronic skeleton key for emergencies. Boyd had dummied up the software, and after a few seconds, the locks disengaged with a quiet snap.

"She's moving," Crassen said. "Coming out of the

bathroom now."

Kaften waited.

"I have the shot," Crassen said.

Hand on the doorknob, Kaften said, "Take it." Then he flung the door wide and led the way inside, gun at the ready.

H ER UNDERWEAR MISSED THE HAMPER. Mesa bent down to pick them up, heard the glassine pop, and felt plaster fall against her wet hair. She dropped flat to the floor, quickly crawling away from the point of attack. She glanced up and saw the bullet hole in the wall, exactly where she would have been standing if she hadn't gotten clumsy.

Soft thumping noises peppered the mattress, sending puffs of foam into the air. They were trying to draw her out, get her to panic and run.

She cursed Jonah's paranoia—only because he'd been right.

She reached for the go bag beneath the bedframe, snagged the loop across the top of the shoulder pack, and dragged it to her. She unzipped it and pulled out a pair of clothes that had been packed away for years. The jeans were snug but good enough. The top, too. She half-rolled onto her side to lace up her sneakers quickly, making sure she didn't rise above the mattress and provide an easy target.

Inside the bag were a knife and gun. She'd been trained to use both, hoping that she would never need them. Her tutoring hadn't been limited to math, science, and literature. She'd been drilled to fire everything from the Heckler & Koch HK4 that was in her bag and cleaned weekly to an AR-15 assault rifle. She could break down, clean, and reassemble firearms blindfolded. All because of Jonah's paranoia.

She realized she hadn't heard from him. Mesa queued up the commNet and sent the panic alert to him.

"They're here," she said. Her heart was racing, but her voice was calm. The HK4 was loaded and ready to go. The pocket pistol fit snugly in her hand; the sheathed knife clipped to the waistband of her jeans. With her free hand, she zipped the bag then put her arms through the shoulder loops. Inside were cash, ammo clips, and two more sets of clothes.

Jonah was on his feet and moving. She heard his heavy steps in the hallway. Her dresser was beside the door. She moved fast, and the sniper's bullets missed her by a hair. Crouched against the wooden face of the dresser, she tucked up close to the wall.

A wet breeze drafted in from the ruined window. Glass shards glittered in the rain-soaked carpet. She reached for the doorknob and pulled the door open a crack.

Dark shadows swept through the living room, and Jonah was on top of them quickly. He wrestled with a figure covered head-to-toe in black. A second shadow moved toward her.

A whisper of a gunshot punctuated the air, and she saw a cloud of red explode from Jonah's belly and out his back. The shock choked his scream, and he stumbled backward, a single hand going to his belly.

Her shout died in her throat as the door was pushed open. A shadow moved across her, and a dark, almost-ethereal hand reached for her.

Keeping the HK4 close to her body, nearly invisible in the inky shadows of the night, Mesa fired three times. Despite the panic that threatened to overwhelm her, Mesa's aim was true. The bullets hit center mass in a tight configuration, rocking the intruder back on his heels, but that was not enough to drop him.

He was caught off guard, and she sprung up at him. She grabbed a fistful of his Kevlar shirt and turned him around, toward the window. Pushing him forward, she used his body as a shield. No shots came from outside.

She risked a quick glimpse back over her shoulder, out the bedroom door. A tall, dark-clad man stood over Jonah and fired twice. The fragmentation bullets tore apart his skull. Tears stung her eyes, blurring her vision, but she couldn't allow herself the moment of sadness. Or weakness.

The soldier tried to reassert himself and regain control by stopping his forward momentum, but she was pushing hard, amped up by adrenaline. His hands hit the window ledge, and she crashed into him with a lung-jarring oomph, toppling them both through the window.

Glass stabbed at his Kevlar, but the material was too tough for the glass to do any damage. Mesa wasn't as lucky. The shards tore at the sleeves of her blouse, slicing open skin. Her arms were bleeding, as was her face, from a shallow cut atop the curve of her cheekbone. Her shin snagged on a long sliver, and the glass knifed its way along the bone, cutting through the jeans and breaking off against the tongue of her sneaker.

They hit the metal landing of the fire escape hard, knocking the wind from both of them. On top, she knew she was a clear target. She had fractions of a second before the sniper took a shot.

The soldier heaved up and threw her off him, bulling his way to his feet. He turned, but she was already recovering, rolling onto her side. A powerful kick connected solidly with his knee, and his leg jutted backward painfully, in a way nature never intended. Tendons snapped, and his leg buckled under the weight of his two hundred-plus pounds. He hit the slick metal grating hard. He reached for Mesa, trying to snag one of her ankles, but she was moving quickly down the metal steps to the landing below.

Sniper's bullets pinged the metal around her, coming rapid-fire. She ducked, letting herself half-fall down the winding stairs. Her feet hit the landing on the third floor, and she pivoted, throwing herself forward and down to the second. Sparks flew as the bullets hit the support struts of the fire escape surrounding her, as she tumbled to the second-floor landing, and bounced down the steps to the first.

The ladder was too risky. Even if she slid down it, she made for an easy target. When her feet landed on the first floor, she turned heel lighting fast and launched herself over the railing, hoping the move was unexpected enough to surprise the shooter and give her the lead time she needed.

She let her body go loose, fell into a tumble, shoulder-rolled across the wet concrete of the alley, and found her feet again. She sprang up into a dead run. Her sneakers splashed through the puddles, loud and quick.

No shots followed.

The glass lodged against her ankle bit through the thin shoe leather, stabbing deeper with each footfall. She ran—running through the bloody hurt, through the sawing pain, and into the rain-soaked street and the dying nightlife as the bars of Pioneer Square emptied.

Before she made it to King Street and the edge of her apartment building, a door burst open. A black shape launched forth and tackled her to the ground.

The HK skipped out of her fingers and skittered away against the cold concrete, stopping out of reach.

A fist collided with her face, rocking her head back. Her skull crashed against the floor of the alley, sending silver glints exploding across her vision. He punched her again, and the world went hazy, crazily out of focus. He pushed back, sitting up, straddling her, pinning her body to the ground. He reached for the gun at his waist.

She flicked open the buttoned hasp and drew her knife, blinking to clear her eyes. They were gummy with rain-washed blood. Icy cold drops of rain prickled her skin. She turned the knife in her hand then stabbed it up, launching herself toward him. The knife worked its way between the hem of his Kevlar shirt and the waist of his pants to puncture the thin weave and stab into flesh.

He howled, and she took a moment's satisfaction. The screams of heavy boots smashing against steel stole her pride. The sniper was clanging his way down the fire escape, fleeing his shooter's perch.

She kicked backward, tearing the knife out of her attacker, then kicked him roundly in the chest with both feet. He toppled backward. She scooped up the gun and ran, firing at him as she went, not caring if she hit but hoping she at least gave him a few things to think about.

The HK4 got tucked into a hip pocket, the knife went back into its sheath, and she pulled her shirt down to cover both.

She knew she looked hellacious, soaked and bleeding. Even the half-cognizant drunks stared.

She pushed her way into the crowd and pounded through the rolling hills of the streets, her legs complaining with exhaustion, until she hit Yessler.

She joined the ranks of a cluster of people waiting for the last bus of the night. Glancing back the way she had come, she waited for a glimmer of recognition to pass across somebody's face as they spotted her. She waited for her black-clad gunmen, but none came. No faces locked onto hers. Those who did get catch a glimpse quickly averted their eyes, not wanting her problems to become theirs. She was ignored. Invisible. Exactly as she wanted.

Bus 71 pulled to the curb with a gassy stomp and the hydraulic hiss of the doors pulling apart. She pressed her thumb against the biometric reader, fully aware that she was leaving a trail. Then she hopped back off before the doors closed and pushed her way through the small group coming up the stairs behind her. She ignored their confusion and shouts.

She took in her surroundings, moving quickly away from the bus stop, her head swiveling back and forth over each shoulder. She stopped and scanned for tails every few blocks as the streets emptied. She suspected anybody following her would be easy to spot.

But there was nobody.

She ducked into the opening of another alley and pulled the glass free from her shoe, slicing open a finger in the process. Relief from the pain in her ankle was immediate, but her sock was soaked through, and the interior of the shoe was a mushy, squelching mess.

She shut her eyes and took a deep breath, trying to re-center herself. All she saw was Jonah's face being blasted apart as he died in their living room. Every time she blinked, she saw it all over again.

With a mental tug, she brought the commNet online and sent an encrypted shout to Kaizhou. He was still awake.

"What happened?" he asked, his voice spiked with a frightened edge at the sight of her.

"I need your help," she said. "Come get me. Warn the others. I don't think any of us are safe."

He nodded, knowing better than to ask for details. "I'm on my way."

She'd warned Kaizhou about this day a while ago. After he'd admitted to being a memorialist, Mesa had told him of her father's paranoia and confided in him about the weapons training and self-defense classes. A part of her thought it was crazy, but he'd disagreed.

"You don't know what you went through before," he had reminded her. "He does. Maybe it's for the best. For your own good."

Since then, they'd both hoped this day would never come. But it had, following closely on the heels of the murders of their Los Angeles counterparts. A part of her hated Jonah for not being more open with her about her past. He had kept too many secrets, too much history buttoned up, thinking her too fragile to handle the full, unvarnished truth. She wondered if any of that history would have helped her spot the threat ahead of time. If they could have, she might have prevented the whole mess.

She allowed herself a moment of recrimination and then sealed off those emotions. Shifting the blame and finding excuses wouldn't help.

Wincing and shivering as the exhaustion hit her hard enough to nearly knock her back down on her backside, she stood, favoring her injured foot. She was walking with a limp, but at least she was walking.

Moving down East Yessler, she made her way to Kobe Terrace Park. Again, she kept a careful watch and studied her surroundings, keeping close to the clusters of people wandering the streets as their own nights unwound. Nobody paid her any particular attention.

She hid among the shadowed terraces and dug around in the backpack. Her fingertips brushed crinkling cellophane, and she pulled out the pack of stale cigarettes. She popped the lid, shook loose a smoke, worked the lighter loose, and lit up. That first hit of nicotine made her dizzy, and she held the smoke in her lungs for an extended moment, slowly letting it escape. Enjoying it.

She tried not to close her eyes for long.

50 MICHAEL PATRICK HICKS

# CHAPTER
# FOUR

KAFTEN KEPT PRESSURE ON THE knife wound, pushing the pain out of his mind. The medichines that coursed through his body would be going to work soon, and the wound would be just another memory. The bleeding was already slowing as the medichines repaired broken vessels and initiated cellular repair. Another half hour, and the deep gouge would be a faint line across his abdomen.

He brought up the team's health assessments. Only Crassen had come through unscathed. Boyd's diagnostics had flooded his system with morphine, knocking him out. The knee would take longer to fix, but he would be back on his feet by morning.

The bus was a non-event. They'd arrived ahead of the 71 and staked out the stop from across the way. When Mesa didn't get off, they followed it to the next stop then maintained the trail through to the end of the bus's late-night service. It had emptied, and the girl was nowhere to be found.

Maybe that was a good thing, he thought, taking stock of this clusterfuck of a mission.

"Hack into the local services," Kaften ordered Crassen. "Get us eyes and find her."

Crassen nodded, then his eyes dulled as he focused on the electronic dirty work. He was searching out a secure avenue to sneak into the local surveillance drones and the city's monitoring networks. An image of Mesa Everitt would be uploaded, along with hidden lines of code that would hijack the Seattle security services and flag Kaften's team if the electronic eyes across the city captured her image. Because they did not want the local services picking her up on a false all-points bulletin, they had to keep everything as low-key as possible.

Kaften shifted, keeping his prosthetic hand pressed tightly to the wound. The pressure was unbearable, but he needed a few more minutes before the medichines kicked in. Sweat beaded across his forehead. He debated the merits of waiting to call Schaeffer and deliver his after-action report, but he decided it wouldn't matter. Hell, maybe his injuries might even make the suit sympathetic. *Fat chance*, he thought.

*Hell with it.*

"Status?" Schaeffer asked. He appeared on Kaften's retinal display then took a moment to observe his subordinate. Kaften watched as Schaeffer's eyes crinkled at the corners briefly then dismissed whatever ounce of humanity he possessed in favor of being obstinate. His eyebrows lifted with impatience.

"Status?" Schaeffer asked again, clearly annoyed.

"Jonah Everitt has been eliminated."

"And the girl?"

Kaften let out a slow, pained breath. "We lost her."

"And how did this happen?"

"We underestimated her."

"You were warned about them. In fact, if I recall correctly, you warned us."

"Yes," Kaften said. "I did warn you. Three years ago. To take them out when you had the chance. Not fuck around and wait."

The suit took a deep breath, his face reddening. The corners of his jaw jumped as he fought down the anger.

"Three trained soldiers against an old man and an amnesiac. This is ridiculous."

"We underestimated the situation. And the old man is dead."

"A failure is still a failure."

Kaften lowered his eyes. Arguing was pointless.

"And this is your second failure in a single day. Thankfully, we've been able to... hmm... secure three of the memorialists you allowed to escape earlier."

"We're in the process of tracking Mesa down."

"She needs to be eliminated immediately."

"Has she made contact?" Kaften asked, his eyes narrowing.

"No. Not yet. We cannot allow it. You need to find her. Now."

"I understand."

"Kaften?" Schaeffer said, making sure he got the man's attention before the commNet was disconnected. "You have two strikes against you. I do not expect there to be a third."

"I understand," he repeated. He let his eyes close as the call terminated, then he settled his head back against the seat rest.

Mesa felt queasy, the strong stink of stale urine mingling with her own sweat and blood. The auto shop's bathroom was a greasy mess. The grout between the wall-to-wall floor-to-ceiling tile was stained black. Rameez's uncle had let them set up shop in the sub-basement sometime back, and they'd gathered there for what felt like their last meeting. The rest of the group was waiting on her to emerge, waiting for answers, ready to pepper her with questions. She pushed all that to the backburner and shut it out of her mind. The whine of the electric razor blotted out the world for her.

With a fresh cigarette dangling from her lips, Mesa met her eyes in the mirror. The razor was set to its second-lowest setting, and she shaved off the right side of her head. Kaizhou did the back, baring her scalp from the peak of her skull to the nape of her neck. Other than the long strip of hair that ran across the top of her head and down to her left shoulder, her skull was covered in downy peach fuzz.

She colored the buzzed portion purple, a brighter shade than Ashita's, and streaked the jet strip with neon-green highlights. She braided a few fingers' worth at the front and let it to dangle alongside her cheek.

Hair and cigarette ash collected in clumps in the bathroom sink. She flicked the smoking nub into the pile. "What do you think?" she asked.

"Different," Kaizhou said. But he didn't seem displeased.

Earrings were the next step. She hated the idea of needles stabbing through her face, but eyebrow rings, a nose ring, and large hoops through each earlobe would help fool the superficial facial-pattern-recognition cameras. It wouldn't do shit if she had to pass through body scanners, nano security clouds, or X-ray imagers, but she wasn't planning on going through the high-security areas of airports or harbors. She needed to change up her appearance so that she no longer resembled the Mesa everybody was familiar with—the Mesa on her ident card, passport, and online profiles.

*Maybe some lip rings,* she thought, adding more bling to the list. She dropped the lid on the toilet, took a seat, and nodded at Kaizhou. *Ready.*

She squeezed her eyes shut tight, sending up purple flares behind the sealed lids. The ice against her eyebrow numbed her, but she still let out a groan as Kaizhou pulled the skin taught and slid a long needle through. Her knees knocked together, but the operation was over fast.

"Take a look," he said.

She blinked, surprised that part was finished. The tiny red hoop stood out against her inky eyebrows. Mesa smiled, approving, but she was glad to not have to repeat the job on her already-pierced ears.

In the go bag were black-market contacts that would alter her retinal patterns enough to fool eye scanners. The contacts would not interfere with her DRMR implants and communications software since the retinal displays interfaced directly with the optic nerves rather than the eyes themselves.

Old-fashioned, thick-framed, non-prescription glasses helped complete the disguise. With the piercings and change of hairstyle, her surface appearance was markedly different. She had shoes with tall heels and flat-soled sneakers with lifts to mask her true height. Jade or Ashita could make a run for her and buy bras with additional padding and support cups to help round out her features and change her bustline. Most people who saw her wouldn't recognize her. The big question was whether or not it would fool the city-wide security feeds. A street test was the best way to find out for sure.

She rotated her injured foot, happy with the medichines' progress. The bleeding had stopped, and the only sign of injury to her shin was a thin, jagged white line. It didn't hurt much, but the bone felt bruised, and her knees ached. Her elbow smarted a bit, too, where she'd banged it on the fire escape.

Looking down at her arm, she realized one last alteration still needed to be made. The dragon tattoo that wrapped around her arm was one hell of a distinguishing feature. Unless she wore long sleeves, the colorful design was bound to standout. One look at her arm and all of her efforts at disguise would unravel in a blink.

She shut her eyes and took a long, deep breath. Aside from a handful of mems, the tattoo was her only connection to the Mesa of old, her prior self. That sleeve of ink and vibrant hues connected her to her heritage. The Japanese icon—a massive, long-winged creature that wended its way around her from wrist to elbow—acknowledged her mother's side. It sat atop a Gaelic cross, an icon of her father's heritage. This symbol of family had meant a great deal to her former self, whom she constantly lived in the shadow of and hoped to, one day, bring into the light.

But it was too much of a risk.

She set the medichines to work on breaking down the ink that stained her flesh. She watched the dragon's tail unravel in a cascading wave. The dark green was replaced with a yellowish hue of her mixed parentage. Cell by cell, the tattoo disappeared, leaving clean, raw flesh a shade lighter than her normal complexion. The color would settle as the medichines completed their task.

Letting the medichines toil away, she focused on the next step—her clothes. Her blue jeans were a total loss. One leg was shredded, soaked in blood and embedded with pinpricks and shards of glass. Her blouse hadn't fared any better.

After rummaging around in the backpack, she came out with a fresh pair of black jeans and a gray tank top.

"Let's see if you pass muster," Kaizhou said, opening the bathroom door.

As she strode into the cement-and-metal expanse of the auto body shop, Rameez gawked. He wasn't subtle about it, letting his eyes travel up and down, lingering.

"Wow," he said, his Pakistani accent over-inflecting the vowel.

"You look fucking awesome," Jade said. "I want to loan you my checkered skirt."

"I'm not playing dress-up here, guys. This isn't for fun."

Her words shook some of the triviality out of her friend.

"No, you're right," Jade said.

"Are we all in danger?" Ashita asked.

Mesa stared at the assemblage before her. They stood, clustered close. Ashita and Sri were holding hands, leaning on one another for support. Sri's doe eyes were red-rimmed, her cheeks puffy. She was dazed and lost, and seeing her that way broke Mesa's heart.

Doris licked his lips, his mouth opening and closing, but he said nothing.

"I don't know," Mesa said. Leaning against the hood of a rusty early-twenty-first century Camaro, she crossed her arms over her chest. "But we have to presume you are. We need all of you to be safe. Go underground, get off the grid, back up everything, and destroy what's left. Stay off Somnambulist. Keep a low profile. Whatever. Just be safe."

"What are you going to do?" Rameez asked.

Jade chewed on her lip, not liking any of her options. "Honestly? I have no clue. But we've got five of our own in the wind after that thing in LA. Try to find them, I guess."

"You think it's connected?" Sri asked.

Mesa shrugged, going for a coolness she couldn't quite muster. "I kinda have to think that it is. Nearly a whole sect wiped out, now they're after me. Maybe after all of us. It's not a coincidence."

"Who are they?" Doris asked.

Mesa shook her head. "Guys, I wish I had answers for

you. I don't. I'm completely lost here. I don't know what the fuck's going on. I can't tell you where I'm going or what I'm doing…"

"Right, in case they kill us and chip our skulls," Jade said. Her crooked smile wobbled as her eyes went glassy.

Mesa wrapped her arms around her. The woman's tears splashed on her shoulder, wetting the sides of their faces. Jade was her sister, not by blood but family, nonetheless. Her best friend. She was in danger, and Mesa couldn't even tell her why. She had no answers to give, but she sure as hell was going to find some, for all their sakes.

"You be careful, honey," Jade said. "I love you, OK?"

Mesa squeezed tighter. "I love you, too. We'll relink once all this over."

"We better."

"I need to finish backing up," Rameez said, breaking away from the group. The repair shop belonged to his uncle, and Rameez worked the day shift. In a sub-basement below the service bay was an office with a smattering of tablets and mem chips—their secret outpost for their memorialist enclave. After tonight, none of them were likely to return. In another hour, all the data on their local servers and storage devices would be erased.

Slowly, the rest of the group broke off with hugs and goodbye kisses until Mesa and Kaizhou were the last ones left.

"You don't have to do this for me," she said.

"Fuck that noise," he said. "We do this together."

"Love you, Kai."

He took her in his arms, and she tried to clamp down the tears. She allowed herself that moment, savoring the warmth of his body and the security of his embrace. Gently, she pushed away, telling him she needed to use the bathroom and get her stuff.

She closed the door behind her and rested against its

cool steel, trying to resolve herself for what came next. In three years, she had worked hard at building a life for herself, worked at trying to reclaim herself, a self she didn't even really know. She tried to figure out what kind of a woman she was, and she'd let Jonah guide her toward the woman they both wanted her to be.

Her tears smeared the thick layers of mascara. The mirror gave her a glimpse of her appearance. She looked like a disheveled raccoon or a stoned, drunken, troubled rock star. She tried to laugh but couldn't.

At the bottom of the go bag was a data plug. A kill stick. She inserted the male connector into the port behind her ear and brought up the menu.

*I can't do this.* She gave a mental tap to the Proceed box.

A warning symbol flashed, asking her if she was sure. YES floated before her left eye, NO on the right.

If she hit YES, the kill stick would disconnect her immediately. She would be completely off the grid. Lines of code would shut down her cybernetics and dismantle the entirety of the DRMR delivery system that wrapped around her hippocampus. The REMIND programs would cease to be. She would walk out of the bathroom with her memory intact, but she would be utterly alone. She could never use another memory chip or never dream of her father with anything other than her own memories. The kill stick was a last resort, one more layer of security.

In three years, she had never been disconnected. She didn't remember a single day of her life before waking up in the hospital, already connected to the world around her. She hadn't spent a single day outside the cool embrace of modern technology, with information nothing more than a simple thought away. She'd been constantly plugged in to an entire web of instant gratification—sports, news, shopping, research, learning opportunities, the Somnambulist boards, MemSpace, and all the other DRMR addicts she could instantly connect to.

If she hit YES, her world would promptly collapse down to a single party of one. She would never have Kaizhou in her head again, never get to share her thoughts on the most intimate level imaginable. The neuronal interface would cease to be, and the bioelectric wiring that ran through her brain would eventually shrivel and dissolve from disuse. The medichines would break it down and carry it away.

The tears came freely, and she collapsed under the weight of the evening. On the bathroom floor, her back pressed against the door, she let it shake loose.

She tapped NO and tore the kill stick loose then flung it across the small, confined space. It hit the floor and skittered back to her.

Palming away the tears, she shoved herself back up, wincing at the various aches and pains. She stuffed the kill stick back into the bottom of the bag, buried beneath loose mem chips, ammo clips, food packets, and her last change of clothes. Shouldering the bag, she stepped into the empty bay and followed the chattering of rain against the building. Kaizhou was waiting for her.

"Ready?" he asked, squeezing her hand and drawing it to his mouth. He kissed her knuckles.

"No," she answered.

# CHAPTER
# FIVE

MESA WATCHED AS THE WIND whipped hair across the woman's face, obscuring her features. The inky strands gleamed with a mercurial shine in the dying embers of the passing day. With the certitude of dreamscape knowledge, Mesa knew this was Selene, just as she knew the enflamed city behind her was Los Angeles. The fire-ravaged cityscape was unfamiliar to her, yet recognizable. Long, skeletal fingers stretched toward her, and as the wind died down to reveal the woman's face, her body turned to ash and collapsed with a puff before the strong thermal currents of approaching flames carried it away.

She emerged from sleep, feeling disoriented and lost, her body tightly cramped in the confines of the passenger seat. Passing headlights washed through the cabin of their parked Trans Am, obnoxiously bright. Beyond the windshield,

Nickelsville brightened and dimmed in the waves of light. She pushed herself up in the leather seat and rubbed her eyes, scratching away the pointy, gritty carbuncles glued into the corners.

Outside, bent forms shuffled as they organized their belongings. Others huddled over rusty barrels and burning wooden pallets, warming themselves over the fire. A group of children sat in collapsible lawn chairs, doing their homework by the light of the flickering flames. There were tents and wooden shacks, and some of the homeless, dressed in bulky layers of thick clothes, slept in sleeping bags or covered themselves with dirty newspapers. A hand-written poster was staked to the ground, illuminated by the headlights of passing motorists: "I see less rats! Keep up the good work, Nickelodeons!" A cluster of ratty blue tents formed a loose cul-de-sac, and somebody had crafted a sign adorned with glued-on cartoon cats, proclaiming the small area Kitty's Korner.

A few other families were packed away in their own vehicles, many of which were unwashed and banged up. Kaizhou's ancient car blended in nicely. As far as the Nickelsville residents were concerned, he and Mesa were just another down-on-their-luck couple. Nobody had greeted them, but none had discouraged them from parking and keeping to themselves. Nicklesville itself was a large tract of city-owned land that had been turned over to the city's homeless.

Unlike the rest of Seattle, the politicians and police didn't think it was worth keeping watch over. Nicklesville was a small black hole in the web of surveillance that reached across the city. It had no cameras, no securiclouds, and little to no police presence. After all, what were the lives of non-taxpayers worth? The Nickelodeons, as they called themselves, policed their own. Occasionally, they got some outside help, and every Thanksgiving, kind-hearted folks from the Vietnamese Cultural Center gifted them with food, haircuts, fresh clothes, and pleasant conversation. Other than that, they were on their own and forgotten until a well-fed suburbanite mom got uncomfortable with their presence being too close to home.

Jonah had called it King County's answer to Tent City, the derisive name of the refugee camp he and Mesa had lived at following the Pacific Rim Coalition's invasion of California. Of course, she didn't remember anything of those days, and her father had rarely spoken of it. When she'd asked, he'd been vague and turned their discussion to other topics.

Her eyes burned, and she felt haunted by the unpleasantness of her dreams. She knew little of her mother. Still, she found herself unsettled by the nightmarish vision of Selene's disintegration. When she closed her eyes, all she saw were the fatal shots to Jonah's chest and the way he'd folded in half. The despair in his eyes was etched into her soul.

When she'd woken up in the Harborview Medical Center three years ago, he'd been at her side. His face was the first to greet hers; his warmth was a thing she could cling to. There had been an odd sense of familiarity, despite his stranger's presence, and she'd absorbed the mems of their lives together. Memories were all she had left of Jonah, she realized. She pressed her knuckles into the corners of her eyes and sniffed back the mucusy gorge compressed in the center of her skull.

Kaizhou began to stir. He reached over and scratched at her fuzzy scalp.

"We can't stay here," she said.

"Where do we go?"

"I don't know," she admitted. Staring out the windows, she watched children finish their schoolwork beneath rain-soaked hoodies. "They'll come here soon, though. Looking for me."

She pictured the dark, empty void in Seattle's securiweb that was Nickelsville, and she knew it was only a matter of time before the hunters stalked her there. She eyed her stark reflection in the passenger's window and wondered if her old life at Echo Park had been the same—one day passing into the next, waiting for the horrors to find her.

Kaften woke up annoyed. *Those fucking suits.*

The more he thought about the botched op, the more annoyed he became. They could blame him for that crap in LA. That was one thing. But he would not take the blame for Mesa Everitt being in the wind. It was not how he would have run it if he'd been given free rein on the planning.

The suit had called him as they were setting up. He told Kaften to carry out the mission right away, don't wait. "There's no time for observation," he'd said. "Get in and get it done."

And that was what Kaften and his team had done. And half of their quarry had gone missing in a city of more than half a million people.

Kaften would have waited and followed her around a bit, learned who her friends were, where she went, and what she did. He would know if she had a job, had a boyfriend, or did a lot of partying. He wondered who would miss her. If he'd been given op control, he would have an answer to all those questions.

But the suits—they sat on high and spat out their commands, entirely ignorant of the subtleties of fieldwork. They had no appreciation for planning. Too often, they insultingly mistook Kaften and his team as nothing more than hired guns.

If they'd had eyes-on, maybe they would have learned

enough about Mesa Everitt to avoid underestimating her. Would have learned she was a scrapper with shooting experience. Would have learned, maybe, that her daddy had taken things to heart and trained her.

If, if, if. All kinds of ifs.

Ifs were pointless. Kaften closed his eyes, drew in a deep breath and let it out very, very slowly. Then he took in another slow, deep breath and spent several seconds exhaling.

Again. Inhale, exhale. In, out. The aggravation was lessening, and the muscles in his shoulders began to unstiffen and relax. He rolled his head from side to side and rotated his shoulders in small, smooth circles, his eyes closed all the while, his breathing steady. He still had a job to do, and there were ways to carry it out.

While waiting for the 71 bus, Crassen had kept them apprised of law enforcement activity. Surprisingly, nobody had called to report their activity or seemed to have even taken notice of the evening's earlier violence. He knew the sound suppressants and noise-camouflaging software had gone a long way toward keeping their own gunshots whisper quiet, but he had presumed Mesa's wild gunshots in the alley would not have gone unnoticed. He chalked their good fortune up to the joys of living in a desensitized modern world.

Unconcerned about a heavy police presence, Kaften and Crassen returned to the Everitt apartment while Boyd slept off his injuries in the van.

The door was unlocked, and they entered cautiously. The apartment stank of cordite and gore. In the living room lay the dead man.

Kaften had known Jonah in another life, back in Los Angeles. Mentally, he shrugged it off. Their association had been superficial at best, a means to an end. No love lost.

The frag rounds had not been kind, and his skull was

brutally misshapen. Kaften knelt and studied the data port behind Jonah's right ear, surprised to find it still intact.

*Poor bitch.* After making it out of LA, starting over, preparing—none if it had mattered. He'd found Jonah's go bag, and Mesa... well, she was a spitfire, to be sure. Years of preparation and training. The corpos should have taken care of Jonah sooner; Kaften had warned them. He let out a noisy breath as he stood.

He pushed up and waved his partner over. "See what you can collect. Maybe the backup's in good shape."

Crassen nodded, already unspooling the data cable and pulling a tablet from one of the many pockets on his black pants.

"And hey," Kaften said, meeting Crassen's eyes. "Find me something happy in there, huh?"

Kaften left him to it and went about the search. He gave the kitchen a cursory review then went back into the living room, where he ran his hands between the couch cushions, flipped through a small collection of old, well-worn books on the coffee table, opened up drawers, and closed them when he was finished. Gently, he lifted a collection of e-papers and swiped through the digital drawings. He recognized much of it—the Echo Park camps, Chinatown, Mesa. He carefully refolded the documents and placed them back atop the table. He swiveled his head, making sure he got a good mem capture of the area for future analysis. If needed, he could physically go back through the place further, but he didn't want to leave a giant footprint of activity.

His primary concern was Mesa, and he figured the information he needed would be found in her bedroom. He passed photos of Jonah and his daughter—some showed her as a child and a few were more recent—hanging in the hallway, forced smiles on their faces, as if the photographer had coaxed them into being happy. Some of the photos were nice, and a few even approached honesty. Kaften didn't have any photos in his place—he considered them too old-fashioned. The ones on Jonah Everitt's wall were relics of much better days, and Kaften felt that helped prove his point all the more.

Mesa's room was neat and orderly. Her dirty clothes were sorted by color. Clean clothes hung in the closet; socks and underwear, folded and put away in the dresser. Her desk was the busiest part of the room. The fake wood was stained with rings of coffee, and a sheaf of e-papers and mem chips vied for space. The drawers held more chips, an odd assortment of doodles, and torn pieces of recycled paper with notes scrawled across them in a tightly controlled print. He recognized some book titles and names of authors, but the others were obscure. He didn't think any of the notes were important or useful. He certainly wouldn't be able to lure her out with an ancient Stephen King book whose title had interested her enough to actually write down—certainly not after killing her father, at least.

He slid the center desk drawer closed and scooped the mem chips and e-papers toward the edge of the desktop, dumping them all into the plastic bag he'd brought from the kitchen. Having physical backups would make data sorting easier in the immediate, while his crew spent valuable man-hours hacking the Everitts' cloud storage. Chips were becoming a rarity, but he knew many mem addicts and memorialists preferred the hardware and the process of preparing their high. His crew would have time to sift through the data and glean whatever might be of importance.

Standing in the hallway, Kaften debated going through Jonah's room. After a moment's indecision, he decided to let sleeping dogs lie. He wanted primary sources of information. If they got some stuff out of the man's brain, then great. The last time he'd rooted around Jonah's skull, he'd learned some very interesting things. Lightning rarely struck twice in the same spot, though, and the chips in the bag he carried were probably his best bet.

"You done?" he asked Crassen.

"Yeah, I think. The frags scrambled his noggin, but we might be able to get something out of him."

Crassen wound the data cord around his fingers, pocketed it, then stuffed the tablet into a pocket on the opposite thigh.

Kaften wasn't looking forward to another conversation with the suit. The higher-ups were expecting a status report in an hour. Grimly, he wondered if he would be out of a job before breakfast time. He shrugged off the thought, took a deep breath, and convinced himself to be unconcerned. His skill sets were always marketable, suits be damned.

# CHAPTER
# SIX

JONAH HAD ONCE TOLD MESA that a good defense was a good offense. She had questioned the need for all her training, including the months on end of firearm safety courses, practicing at various target ranges. Although she had enjoyed the martial arts courses, she doubted it was a practical necessity. Jonah had been right, though. And it still hadn't been enough.

Sitting on a scarred wooden bench at the periphery of Nicklesville, she'd spent much of the morning hatching a plan with Rameez and Kaizhou. She wanted both of them to lie low, and both had refused. She worried less about Rameez, who had boarded a ship headed to a seastead community in the Pacific.

"I've got safeguards in place," Rameez said. "You do not need to worry about me."

Thinking he would be safely hidden in an independent oceanic nation-state, he was only too happy to help from afar and provide technical support. He assured Mesa that he could roam the netscape freely, using a collection of false idents and ping bots that would obscure his online trails.

"I spent all night coding," he said, a grim smile on his face and large black circles beneath both bloodshot eyes.

A few seconds later, she and Kaizhou both received data packets filled with custom security apps: a personal firewall, private IP masks, and geotag clones that would randomly synch with any one of the world's billion-plus users and obscure both their digital footprints and mask their real-world trails.

That was the first layer of security. Higher-level masks hid all three of them behind backstopped false identities carrying composite hacks from various bank accounts and bitcoins, each further encoded with its own unique set of personal IPs that would shield both Mesa and Kaizhou's current IP assignments.

"You've muddled the waters nicely," Kaizhou said, sounding impressed.

Rameez smiled and gave them a mock salute. "Thank me after I've wreaked havoc with the city cams."

"Can you find out if anybody else has been rooting around in there?" Kaizhou asked.

"Of course," Rameez said bluntly.

An hour later, he was able to determine that local authorities were unaware of the attack on the Everitt's apartment and that they were not actively searching for Mesa.

"But," he said, the word pregnant with peril, "there is a passive search in place."

"Can you disable it?" Mesa asked.

"Whoever coded it has some high kung-fu. He's got self-replicating backdoors and tripwires all over the place."

"So you can't disable it," Mesa said, thinking, *It's a good thing I changed my look.*

"If I tried, it'd probably make a dozen more doors as a deterrent."

"Awesome," Kaizhou said, sounding defeated.

"The good news is, it's all sourced to the same batch of images. They found some pretty pictures of you, Mesa."

"Terrific," she said, lobbing him a smile.

"I thought you said this was good news," Kaizhou said.

"It is," he said. "Because I can go into the sources and make subtle changes, enough to force the filters to re-project and develop an altered image of you. Raise your cheekbones, curve your nostrils a bit. Nothing that would be too obvious unless they did a direct side-by-side comparison, but enough to make the computer think it's a non-match to your actual appearance."

"Awesome," Kaizhou said, perking up a bit.

"I sense another *but*," Mesa said.

"To be sure it works, you need to field-test it."

"No," Kaizhou said immediately.

Mesa's "Yes" overpowered his objection. She glared at him and said, "It's the only way to be sure."

"And if Rameez is wrong and this doesn't work, you end up dead."

"If I stay here, I'll wind up equally dead. Kai," she said, gripping his hand, "I have to do this. I can't hide forever."

Kaizhou rolled his eyes and frowned, but the determination in her eyes was plain. He knew arguing was a lost cause and threw his weight into supporting her instead.

"What can I do?" he asked. He squeezed her hand reassuringly, letting her know he was still on her side, no matter what.

They left Nicklesville and headed for an underground parking garage. She was wearing one of his hoodies, the hood pulled up and hanging loose around her face. Her eyes were hidden behind large, dark sunglasses that gave her a bug-like appearance. Casually, she turned away from the cameras before their car rolled across the sloping drive, pausing for the ticket. Once inside, Kaizhou parked in the cameras' blind spot, and Mesa hopped out. She joined a cluster of businessmen and their female coworkers, keeping her head covered and slung down, her shoulders slumped forward.

She crowded into the elevator with them, rudely pushing her way into the center, trying to hide herself among their collective mass and consciously hiding her face from the overhead security sensors. When the door parted at street level, she saw no police were waiting to arrest her. So she steeled her nerves and stepped out, forcing herself to be casual.

Walking the rolling hills of downtown, she let the hood fall back and pocketed the glasses. She spent hours on foot, blending in with tourists and worker bees, letting herself be seen.

"You're doing good," Rameez assured her over the commNet. "No spikes in the image captures, nothing unusual."

Kaizhou maintained a roving patrol, driving aimlessly around the city streets and circling blocks. After a half hour, he parked and went into a convenience store for bottled water. Another half hour later, Rameez rejoined them via conference.

"I'm pulling some randomized images from your walk and running them against the sourced image on this surveillance alert."

"Do it," Mesa said.

"If the authorities didn't set up the alert," Kaizhou said, the sound of his fingers tapping against the steering wheel piping in across the CommNet and into each of their heads, "then who did?"

"Well, the people trying to kill her," Rameez said.

"No shit," Kaizhou said. "But who are they? Any way to tell?"

Mesa and Kaizhou watched Rameez tap his fingers against his lap, lost in thought. "OK, so, some simple deductions. They had to hack into the cityweb and build backdoors. Obviously, they're somebody without legitimate access, and they don't want any official agencies interfering. I think, then, we can rule out police or government, yeah? Their clothing and artillery and training seems to indicate some kind of military background, either a corporate or maybe a covert government entity. Or private security."

"Awesome. My girlfriend has trained military assassins after her. Great."

"It does make me pretty damn desirable," she said.

"The images are running clean. I think you're free to roam without any worries," Rameez said.

She crossed with the pedestrian traffic at the light then spotted the white front and the rust-colored sign with orange lettering of Wild Ginger. "I need a drink."

The Kickin' Mango Martini lived up to its name. Heat spread through Mesa's mouth, opening her taste buds with a delightful burn. The slender, bright-red Thai chili sat at the base of the glass, providing a vibrant splash of color against the sunny-orange concoction. She'd watched the bartender muddle two other chilis among the mango, wearing rubber gloves as he prepped the drink to keep the chili's burning oils off his fingers. Then he'd tossed it all in an ice shaker to infuse the rum.

The bar was crowded. A throng of people pressed against one another. The main dining area was filled to the brim, and the waitstaff shuffled carefully and rapidly between the shifting clientele. Waiters spun with balletic grace away from an impending collision, raising heavy trays above their heads with ease.

Nobody paid much attention to Mesa, and that was fine with her. The buzz from the drink was loosening her up, but she knew not to get too comfortable, or too drunk. She was on a trial run, after all.

The cosmetic changes she'd made at the auto body shop should have been enough to fool the dummy filters of Seattle's basic surveillance efforts, and Rameez's additional hacks spoofed the filters even further. The security grid was largely a deterrent, rather than an active, preventative measure.

Conceptually, people were meant to be instilled with the knowledge that they were being observed and to act accordingly. If crimes were committed, investigators would eventually unravel the footage back to the point of time in question. The recorders were simplistic capture devices that could be filtered, but they were limited to superficial facial matches.

If the recorders had skin-penetration efforts, it would have been hard to fool the smarter bone-deep levels of authentication. Though there were ways to physically alter her bone structures, she couldn't afford the redrafting. So despite the superficial efforts she'd taken, if roving security bots that relied on unique hard-structure mappings captured her image, she would be hard pressed to avoid detection.

From her spot at the bar, she was able to keep an eye on the main entrance. She hoped the thick crowd would deter any threats from reaching her long enough for her to disappear into the crowd and haul ass to an emergency exit.

The plan wasn't ideal, but, then again, nothing about her current situation was. Her dad was dead; his killers were on the loose and chasing her, apparently hell-bent on killing memorialists. And she was getting drunk and flippant.

*Shape up, kiddo.* Then she wished the drink wasn't quite as harsh against her tongue so she could throw one back and let the dizzy spins hit. But she had to keep her cool, take her time, and try to relax.

She ordered a second martini and decided to stretch her luck by ordering the Rama Setu for dinner. She wondered if she would live long enough for dessert, keeping the chocolate torte in the back of her mind.

Twenty minutes later, she was picking her way through the red curry dish and the heady aroma of lemongrass. The eggplant had a nice bite, but some of the flavor had been drained by the heat of the martini. Still, she couldn't complain.

And nobody had tried to kill her, yet.

Halfway through the meal, she realized she was too full for dessert, and she'd probably risked her safety enough for the day.

Stuffed, she pushed the plate away but continued to nurse the martini. In short order, probably eager to free up her spot at the bar, the bartender swiped her plate.

"Would you care for dessert, miss?"

"No, thank you."

The bartender quickly wiped the counter and put down a fresh napkin for her drink.

"Mesa?" Rameez said, pinging her gently across the commNet.

*Oh no.* "Yeah?"

"I think you need to see this. Keep your safety filters on." With the A/V protocols running, Rameez's face and voice were broadcast into her skull. Furtively, he looked around, and she could make out his troubled expression. She tried to prepare herself for the worst. "They got another one."

*Oh no*, her brain repeated. The Rama Setu made a hot lump in her belly. A DRMR file transmission blinked into the air before her, and she gave it a tap.

*I don't want to watch this.*

She swallowed a cool drink of the spice-infused rum. The chili seared her mouth, sending flames tap-dancing across her tongue.

She clicked Play and found herself standing in the center of a deserted, ruined cityscape. The buildings were blackened and half-leveled. Jagged broken spires rose from crusty, heat-glazed earth. She knew the city was Los Angeles because the recorder of this memory, Lisa Kessler, had known that, and she recognized the destruction from other, similar mem files.

A hand tugged hers along. Its owner screamed, "Let's go!"

She recognized the boy—a nicely muscled Caucasian with a lantern jaw and crisp, neatly combed hair—as Jacob Kessler. The high school dropout turned memorialist.

Her own dread of this memory's inevitable outcome ran parallel to Lisa's high-strung fear in the moments before her death.

Lisa ran, lungs burning, dry throat aching, clinging to her brother's sweaty hand.

"C'mon," Jacob said over and over, his voice strained with panic.

The hollowed corpses of shattered buildings around them offered little protection. The air was still, and the sky was a rich blue, dotted with puffy white clouds. A low whine from above interrupted the disparate tranquility. Mesa's POV shifted as Lisa glanced up, spotting the gray body in the sky. Slim wings flanked the slender rounded spine of the drone, which tapered off to the pointed shell of the long aircraft's head. It turned with precision, angling down toward them, then launched its payload.

"Move," Jacob screamed, pulling painfully at her arm. She jerked with surprise, tripping over her feet. She fell to the ground but in hurried fear, Jacob dragged her along. The rocky ground dug into her thigh, and a rock tore through her nylon stocking, biting roughly into the skin beneath.

Her yelp was lost to the shrieking noise of artillery cutting through the air. The missile hit the ground, exploding where they'd been standing. A hot blast of air pushed over her. The inside of her skull compressed against the shockwave, which ruptured her eardrums. Jacob was pushed down, and she saw in his face a mirror of how she felt: bloodied nose and ears, a dazed expression, and unfocused eyes. His feet worked at the earth while his arms weakly tried to push himself back up. Both of them were covered in a thick layer of dust. The impact crater smoked, and she thanked God they were still alive. Lisa could not hear the drone retracing its trajectory above them, locking in on their new positions.

She thought it a miracle they hadn't been in the data center. She and Jacob had received warning of the attack from their fellow memorialists, some of whom were in their death throes, struggling to sound the alarm in their final moments. They had watched as the state-run news covered the aftermath of the assault, speculating on the possibility of an attack by Liberty's Children, although the terror-militia had yet to claim responsibility. Lisa and her brother had disregarded that idea—if LC had been responsible, they would not have kept quiet about it.

The attack was something else. The drone proved that. Who had sent it, though, they had no idea.

They'd fled into the ruins, scared but intent on staying low and off the grid. Mesa absorbed the surface level details etched into the mem, understanding Lisa's fears all too well. Being in the city meant being under constant surveillance from PRC security forces and random checkpoints. Their decision to flee had been easier once their faces started appearing on television, where the news labeled her, Jacob, and three others as persons of interest who were wanted for questioning.

That had sealed it.

Two hours later, they had passed the limits of the reclamation zones and were in the wild, mostly through sheer force of luck. They hadn't even thought of the drones.

Mesa closed her eyes as the power of that realization jolted Lisa. Shutting her eyes did nothing to block out the mem sequence unraveling in Mesa's brain, imprinting her neurons.

Walking side-by-side, Lisa and Jacob picked their way through the ruins, trying to find a safe place to hide. They found a suitable campsite far enough away from the homeless that hid in the ruins and tried to settle their nerves.

Then she saw it—a grayish speck flying above them, slowly turning for another pass.

"Oh, shit!" She grabbed Jacob's arm.

Surprised, he followed the length of her gaze, and then they were off. All of the surface details doubled over the primary mem stitch, creating an immersion loop of causation and depth.

Losing the drone on foot was useless.

Lisa had managed to roll over and get her scraped-raw knees under herself when Jacob wrapped his arms around her waist and pulled her to her feet. She clung to him, one arm around his neck, her legs refusing to move. He dragged her, and she kept trying to get her legs to cooperate, but they were sluggish and clumsy. Her feet kept catching on one another.

Jacob's chest was rising and falling rapidly. Lines of sweat cut deep swaths through the dirt streaking his face. Clinging to him was like riding on a rough sea. She made the mistake of glancing up at the sight of a black cluster of sky falling toward them. Not falling. Raining.

She got her feet under herself and pulled free from Jacob. Her brain was disconnected. The images her eyes transmitted were confused muddy thoughts she couldn't piece together.

Jacob tried to grab at her again, but he was too slow. They were both too slow, and he was injured.

She hadn't even noticed. His shirt was shredded and blackened, revealing a burned torso. She saw now that his every step drew a pained wince. He cradled his belly, and she wondered how long he'd been doing that. She couldn't even remember.

She shut her eyes against the black clumps of rain coming for her. Her hand found Jacob's as the earth shook and the sky grew warm.

Mesa was shaken back to reality. Her arm flicked out in reflex, knocking the martini aside. The orange fluid spilled against the bar, and the glass rolled away then crashed to the ground.

"Miss?" the bartender asked.

"Sorry, sorry," Mesa said. "I'm sorry."

The bartender frowned at her then offered her the bill, clearly ready for her to leave. She dug around her pocket for a hundred dollars, more than enough to cover the bill and leave a tip large enough to sooth the bartender's impatience.

She broadcast a simple thought through the CommNet. "Rameez?"

"Yeah, Mesa?"

"Watch out for drones, sweetie."

He blushed and nodded, a bashful grin crossing his lips. "You, too."

# CHAPTER SEVEN

KAFTEN WAS FEELING REMARKABLY UPBEAT. That state of mind was dangerous, he knew, and he tried to keep it in check. No need to get cocky, especially after their earlier screw-ups.

Hours ago, Kaften had squeezed Crassen's shoulder in congratulations. It had been a good op. As far as the PRC's drone operator was concerned, a software glitch had led to a weapons malfunction. No lives were lost. The ordnance had simply fallen into the ruins, no harm no foul.

*Should make that suit prick happy. Two less things to worry about.*

The data recovery from Everitt's apartment had led to a rich trove of information, and he was confident that they would have the girl soon. Mesa was a diligent memory recorder, which made sense, all things considered.

She was proving difficult to locate. Crassen speculated that she had gone off the grid, gone completely dark, and buried herself under layers of smokescreens. He was probably right. That didn't bother Kaften in the least. If Crassen was correct, Mesa would have needed experienced help in doing that. If the mem chips were anything to go by, he guessed she would have turned to Rameez for help.

They had a whole list of subjects to locate now, in addition to Mesa. Kaizhou, clearly her boyfriend. Jade. Doris. Sri and Ashita. And, of course, Rameez.

Crassen had updated their backdoor search bots, throwing images of Mesa's friends into the mix. They were bound to get a hit on at least some of them, sooner or later. From there, Mesa would be a stone's throw away.

A tight little convergence web. Kaften had to smile at the irony.

He figured Kaizhou would be the jackpot. But Jade... there was certainly something about her, and Kaften anticipated meeting her. She was a firecracker, a Japanese Brit with spiky hair and attitude to spare. She was the one to break. She and Mesa had a clear affection for one another, which gave him immediate leverage. He never relished an enhanced interrogation, which some would call flat-out torture, but he knew it was a necessity of the job. Another day, another dollar.

Within minutes, their data trove grew all the richer. Rameez was captured on over fifty securiclouds as he passed through Seattle Port to board the passenger ship *Meridian*. Local authorities had no idea he was traveling under a false identity, but that was just one of the problems of standard security protocols.

Securiclouds, body scanners, and Transportation Security officers were all an illusion. They existed largely to make people feel safe, rather than to provide actual security or preventive measures. The number of security breaches that occurred on an annual basis was a staggering indictment on the failure of these illusions.

Ironically, the security protocols operated on the assumption of human honesty. When Rameez presented an identity for Abdulrahman Sufi, the security terminals ran the name and matched it to a photo ID. The picture matched Rameez, which matched the ID of Sufi, so Rameez was allowed to proceed without any trouble. If the facial-recognition scanners had been set up to act as a deterrent, security may have caught the multiple images of Rameez and the multiple identities he had uploaded after hacking into the city's security system. The security web's AI should have freaked out over the multiple return vectors and triggered a warning, but Rameez had been careful, and a little care was all that was needed to fool the system.

Kaften couldn't help but laugh at the incompetence and the staggering failure of relying on cheapest-bid civilian contractors to provide illusory-enhanced security. That was the problem with illusions, though; watch too closely, and they fall apart. From behind the scenes, it was all ridiculously fragile. *No wonder Liberty's Children operated with such impunity down south.*

For the moment, Rameez-slash-Abdulrahman was in the wind, and the transit authority was none the wiser. He'd walked right through a billion dollars' worth of security and boarded *Meridian* with a one-way ticket to the seasteaders.

*Welcome to fucking amateur hour in Seattle, British Columbia. Good job, boys.*

Doris hadn't surfaced anywhere yet, probably keeping to his parent's basement, dicking around in some MMORPG with a masked IP to keep him hidden from local radar. He would turn up eventually.

But Jade... she was clearly relying on her own natural state of belligerence to see her through her friend's absence. She'd been radio-silent, but at around ten thirty that evening, Kaften got a ping when she resurfaced. They were able to track her in real time.

Dressed in a loud blouse busy with dragon prints, a plaid miniskirt, fishnets, and calf-high boots, Jade had spiked her hair into a faux-hawk and adorned one arm with thick leather cuffs. Kaften watched the hacked city-cam feeds live-track her as she marched down Yesler, took Occidental to Washington, and joined the line waiting to pass through nightclub security. She fist-bumped a bouncer and went through the nano-securicloud without any hesitation, head already bouncing to the music, her palms bouncing against her thighs in rhythm.

As far as he could tell, everyone was dressed as a reject from an ancient 1980s retro-punk historical holo.

"How's the knee, Boyd?"

"Doing better."

"Think you're up to some dancing?"

Boyd eyed the hacked feed from the nightclub, watching the writhing bodies, the fake smoke, and the flashing laser light show. He sighed, his distaste for clubbing apparent.

"What do you need me to do?"

"Pretend you're a young, dumb anti-establishment guy and score a hottie to bring back here." Kaften tapped the holo, his fingernail causing Jade's image to flicker and warp around the digit.

Crassen chuckled, but Boyd was clearly up to the task, regardless of how little he enjoyed the undercover crap. Fortunately, plenty of guys at the club weren't playing along with the night's theme, and Boyd wouldn't appear entirely out of place in his black tee and tactical pants. Waiting around for a snatch-and-grab could be too complicated, especially if she scored a date while inside the club or left with a group of people. By taking the initiative, he could enter the club, and Crassen could mask him from the security protocols and clean up his digital footprints. If local authorities ever got interested enough to trace back as far as the club, Boyd wouldn't even be a speck on their radar.

"OK, let's do this," he said.

Jade's direct approach sometimes intimidated men. Other times, it gave them the wrong idea about what they could get away with. In those instances, she was quick to correct them, oftentimes forcefully. Those encounters typically ended in predictable slurs that equated her to a singular female organ in the crassest possible verbiage or a socially inappropriate comparison to a female dog.

Such was the case with the blond boy who'd bought her a drink and tried to dry hump her on the dance floor. When she refused to repay him with a hand job at the booth his friends occupied, she suggested several colorful ways he could get himself off instead, all them anatomically impossible.

"Fucking cunt," he said.

Then he tried to put his arms around her waist, utterly clueless. She stomped on his instep with the steel-lined heel of an army boot and threw a quick jab with two stiff fingers into the hollow of his throat. His scream died on a sudden choke, his face empurpled. He was far too distracted by trying to breathe to even notice her lifting his wallet in the process.

She worked her way back to the bar, her heart racing. Hands shaking, she snatched the cash and dropped the billfold. *Rich ponces, always thinking they're so much better than they are. Always so fucking entitled.* He could afford the loss, and she knew the money would be far more useful in her pocket than in his. Stealing didn't bother her in the least, but she hated physical confrontations and the cold sweats they always brought. The adrenaline was already flushing out, leaving her shaky and in need of a drink.

"JD," she said, "straight up."

The bartender gave a brisk nod, and she slapped some of Blondie's cash on the bar. The bartender slid the whisky over, and Jade finished it in two quick swallows.

"That was nice work over there," a man said from beside her. Politely, he squeezed between her and the crowd, signaling the bartender. "You want another?" he asked, shouting over the noise.

Jade loved free drinks and hoped this asshat didn't try to leverage his generosity into something more. Her fingers were sore, and she didn't feel up to clocking another douchebag in the throat if she could avoid it. Her fun evening out was starting to leave a stale taste in her mouth, as if her tongue were coated in the ashes of funky old cigars.

"Sure," she said, nodding. She folded her stolen currency in half, then halved it again, and stuffed it into her skirt's tiny hip pocket. The bartender poured out the two rounds of Jack, and she waited for the guy to make small talk. When he didn't, she wondered what his deal was.

"Cheers," he said, holding up his glass.

She said cheers back, clinked her drink against his, then shot it back.

He caught the bartender's eye and held up two fingers.

"I should warn you, I'm a violent drunk," she said.

His laugh was surprisingly buttery. She took a good look at him, suddenly more interested. He had a solid, muscular build but wasn't egotistical alpha-male, muscle-head big. The black tee fit nicely, and his brown hair was trim and precise. She pegged him for a law dog or something similar but didn't dismiss him outright. Cuffs could be fun when used properly.

"I'm Ben." He held out his hand.

She introduced herself and took the proffered hand. His skin was warm and callused. The web between thumb and forefinger was a rough patch of taut skin. She'd dated gun enthusiasts before, and his hands were definitely those of a shooter.

All of a sudden, Jade regretted leaving her flat for a quick romp around town. Alarm bells were going off, loudly. That was the other thing she hated about getting into confrontations—they left her paranoid afterward. And this guy was starting to seem all kinds of wrong, even if his smile was warm honey, all sweet and inviting. Even two shots in, she started to realize his smile didn't quite reach up into his eyes.

"Hey, it was nice meeting you," she said, taking the fresh drink and detaching herself from the bar. "My friends are probably wondering where I'm at, though."

"You should stick around," he said.

She shrugged. "They worry. I'll come find you in a few, if that's cool."

Nodding, he pursed his lips. "Sure, that's cool." He turned his back to her and nursed the whisky.

She wondered if she'd overreacted, but went with her gut. It was time to leave.

"She's moving," Kaften said.

"Alone?" Crassen.

"Yup. Poor Boyd. Him and that nice-guy act."

"When's he gonna learn, huh?"

Kaften laughed and fist-bumped Crassen. Boyd was a nice guy, but he had an innate ability to dry up girls that always marveled Kaften.

"When the fuck are *you* going to learn?" Kaften asked. "Pay up."

He held out his hand, waiting for Crassen to lay the ten-spot down.

Getting serious, he said, "All right. We go for the bag and tag. Let's hussle."

Kaften started up the van and maneuvered into traffic, spotting Jade before she got to the mouth of the alley. He cut the wheel sharp, stomping on the brakes. She took a small, surprised step back, swinging to turn around and run as Crassen slid open the side door.

When Jade turned, her shoulder collided with Boyd's chest, and he was wrapping her in a bear hug, lifting her off her feet, rolling his head into her shoulder, and covering her mouth with one hand. She kicked and flailed, jerking her head back. She clipped his ear but didn't do any damage.

Taking one step forward, he threw her inside. After a second step, he was inside, sliding the door shut.

Crassen jabbed a shock stick into her belly, turning her screams of protest into a gurgle of pain. She threw up on the floor then gagged on the dry heaves. Her face was red, her eyes watering.

Kaften continued down the alley, rejoining traffic on Occidental.

Jade's belly burned with an acidic heat, and she felt as if a thick, heavy vise encircled her skull. The combination of light and movement made her wince, and the plush mattress surprised her even as she pushed up into a sitting position.

The room was a study in whites: white bed linens, white tile floors broken by thin lines of white caulk, and smooth white walls. Even the noise was white, muffling any outside sounds. She searched for a door, but the seam was hidden, and she couldn't find the entrance. Someone had taken her clothes, left her barefoot, and redressed her in white hospital scrubs. Her short black hair and tanned skin were the most colorful aspects of the tiny cell.

Her head felt heavy, but the sensation was strangely disconnected from the painful tension wrapping the upper half of her torso. DRMR was down and the OS frozen. She reached behind her ear and felt a large metal disc clamped over the port, flush with her skin. She probed the inhibitor with her fingers, sending spikes of pain through her neck. The disc wasn't simply plugged in; it was embedded in her. The skin surrounding the device was encrusted with scabs, and her brief ministrations left her fingers red and sticky. She noticed the rust-colored stains on the pillowcase.

*Where the fuck am I?* she wondered, with a rising sense of fear.

Heart racing, she felt the shakes coming on. She wanted to panic but bit down that response—and choked on it. She refused to let the terror engulf her and fought to own it. Her ribs ached, but she tried to inhale deeply, sending shiny splotches across her field of vision. She squeezed her eyes shut, which made the headache more violent and, in turn, quickened the sickening churning within her stomach. Bile rose, and she choked that down, too, grimacing at the foul, bitter taste. It hurt, but she worked to keep calm, forcing her breathing to be steady and rhythmic. She tucked her face down, between her knees, and sat there, hunched over, waiting for the awfulness to pass.

She needed to calm down. Being distraught was useless. She needed to be rational, to examine her situation and figure out a way to escape. Although she was physically confined, she could not allow herself to become a prisoner to her own out-of-control emotions.

Counting to one hundred, she methodically relaxed her muscles one limb at a time, working her way up from her toes to her waist. After a second one hundred count, she willed her stomach muscles to loosen, and she mentally massaged her torso and arms, up to the crown of her head, demanding the tightness in her scalp to release. By the time she hit two hundred, she felt better.

Then she threw up between her bare feet.

# CHAPTER
# EIGHT

MESA HAD BEEN SHAKY SINCE leaving the restaurant. Kaizhou drove, circling through downtown in an erratic pattern, both of them watching for tails and studying the skies for drone reconnaissance. They spent forty minutes making sure they were safe before blowing out sighs of relief.

Despite the safety protocols, the death of the Kesslers had rocked her to her core. She couldn't imagine experiencing the snuff in its purest form or riding the highs of the chemical reactions of a life being extinguished. In its dying moments, the brain flooded the system with DMT, a powerful psychedelic that made those final seconds much less lucid.

Jonah, she knew, had been a DMT junkie and a recovering addict. He'd been brutally honest and afraid that the admission would drive her away. She also knew that he'd stayed clean for her, and that whatever had happened in her previous life had scared him straight.

For his sake, she hoped that his final moments had been peaceful and that the chemical rush had helped him escape this life free of pain.

The windshield wipers squeaked as they rode over the tough plastic shell, where the thick layer of mist resettled instantly.

"We can't stay on the road," Kaizhou said.

"Nickelsville is out the question." Going back was too much of a risk because the black-hole nature of the homeless camp made it an obvious hiding place. They'd gotten lucky once, but pushing their luck would be foolish. Plus, the havoc those drones were capable of… If the drones were in play, Mesa refused to put all those lives in jeopardy.

After a half hour of driving, they found themselves alone on a single-lane forested route, debating the merits of finding a motel to hole up in and wondering how watertight Rameez's false-ident packets were.

"They'll log your plates on check-in," Mesa said, nixing the hotel idea soon after her boyfriend mentioned it. "We shouldn't even be using this car."

"So far, being fugitives isn't all it's cracked up to be."

"I don't think we're very good at this," she said, scraping her fingernail over a small stain on the leather accent beneath the passenger window.

"Running around with false idents and cloner masks, driving around in a car registered to me, which is probably flagged by psychotics who want to kill us, and on our way to becoming car thieves."

"Been a heck of a day," she admitted.

The laughter felt good and broke up the tension, even if for but a moment.

"Where are we gonna go?" Kaizhou asked, his voice cracking under the strain.

Mesa shrugged, staring absently out the window.

Oregon had pretty open borders, but they were still more than one hundred and fifty miles away from Portland, over eight hundred miles away from the Sun Belt provinces and the rough-and-tumble outlaw territories of the Southwest Conclave. Given her current appearance and Kaizhou's ethnicity, stepping foot in Texas would probably guarantee a slow and painful death. Her punk appearance would probably be enough to have her burned at the stake as a witch or a lesbian. The good old boys would probably show Kaizhou some traditional Christian love and have him drawn and quartered then fed to the pigs. And the Corn Belt region, where they could probably find a measure of safety with the eastern Alliance states, was roughly two thousand miles away.

"An entire country of bad options," Kaizhou said.

"We have to do something. We can't just sit around and wait to die or spend the rest of our lives in hiding."

"What are you thinking?"

She bit her lower lip. Then she let out a long, defeated breath and shoved her skull into the headrest, rubbing her face with her palms.

"I don't know," she said. "I don't know how we do it, but we need to get proactive. They know who we are. We need to figure out who they are."

Kaizhou had taken his foot off the gas pedal and let the vehicle coast to a stop. The deserted road was as good a place as any to ditch the ride. Hoofing it wasn't an attractive proposition, but the car was one more link in their data chains, which were liable to strangle them to death.

Kaizhou pushed, she steered, and in a few minutes, the car was lost in the forested shadows, far enough off the road that it could easily go unnoticed for quite some time.

Halfway between Seattle and Tacoma was Des Moines, once a close-knit seaside community on the East Bay of

Puget Sound. War, as it often did, changed all of that.

Even after all these years, the damage wrought by the PRC invasion was apparent. The marina was a ruined shell of crumbling structures. The docks were rotted, on the verge of collapse. The storage yards and yacht club were nothing more than scorched husks. Sailboats were beached along Redondo, their hulls dulled by sun and surf, scraped raw by sand.

They followed Marine View through the suburbs, seeing no signs of life. Dark, empty houses lined the street. The lawns were unchecked wilderness that threatened to overtake the homes. Des Moines had been among the first areas evacuated as officials scrambled to respond and withdraw the non-combatants from the conflict. None had returned, and the city was nothing more than a forgotten ghost town.

Mesa gazed past the blasted-apart walls of one residence and into the remains of a young girl's bedroom. Rubble littered the twin-sized bed. The pink comforter was stained with black mold; vines and weeds spread across the dirty floor and interior walls.

The sight brought on an eerie recollection, a déjà vu that left her disquieted. Even more troublesome were the sudden flashes of phantom memory and the fleeting, scolding moment of familiarity.

"Maybe we can hunker down in one of these places for a bit, get out of the rain," Kaizhou suggested.

She didn't trust the soundness of her voice, and when she spoke, her tenor was flat and quiet. All she said was, "Sure."

Hand-in-hand, they looped through the empty neighborhoods, seeking a relatively safe and secure shelter.

Mesa was chilled to the bone and ready to get indoors. Most of the structures, including office buildings, had been severely damaged during the PRC bombing runs, and even a lot of the homes that looked sufficient were marked with x-codes deeming them structurally dangerous and warning people away. After more than an hour of circling through the blocks to find a suitable house, they found one that still had four walls and a roof. As an added bonus, the door was one of the few they'd seen whose markings bore a measure of good news.

Kaizhou deciphered it for her and explained the compass-like markings of the X, starting at the upper wedge and moving counter-clockwise. "The top is the date"—he moved his finger to western portion of the *X*—"looks like a rescue team of volunteer firefighters from Vancouver entered the structure."

She followed his finger to the eastern side as he explained, "The only hazards present were food or water. We're lucky the rats didn't take up residence."

"What does the zero-zero mean?" she asked.

He tapped the southern quadrant, a small smile on his face. "No survivors, no corpses. House was empty."

"This is as good a place as any."

He studied the ruined neighborhood surrounding them. "It's better than any."

The jamb was a splintered affair. The door was a sheet of plywood that had somehow gone unmolested in the years following the volunteer team's search. All of the windows were busted; shattered glass littered the ground. They walked around the perimeter of the house, tramping through overgrown weeds and unkempt grass, seeking an entry point.

Kaizhou explained that most of the remains of Des Moines had been picked over by scavengers. At the rear entrance, the wood had been pulled away for entry, leaving the rear of the house exposed.

"Feels good to get inside," Mesa said, unplastering a long swatch of hair from her face.

"Long as you don't mind the smell," he said, his face crinkling in disgust.

The house stank of mold and decay. The food had gone past rotting long ago, but the stench clung to the stale air. Their feet crunched the occasional insect corpse and the soft bones of once-furry critters that had decomposed into nothing more than skeletons and fuzz.

They worked their way around the toppled kitchen chairs and a kitchen table marred with old food, black stains, and deep knife marks. The kitchen sink was busted up, and the floor around it was missing where scavengers had torn it apart to get at the piping. They had taken sledgehammers to the interior walls so they could steal pipes and electrical wiring.

In the living room, more walls were broken apart, down to the studs. The sofa was intact but heavily soiled and pungent with mildew. The carpet was caked in dirt and excrement.

Keeping his voice low, Kaizhou said, "We should check upstairs, but we'll stay down here."

She nodded, following him to the stairs. He kept his feet close to the wall, in an effort to avoid creaky boards.

Upstairs, the walls were marred with water damage, and liquid dripped steadily from the ceiling of the master bedroom. The bathroom was torn apart, the ceramic tiles shattered. If not for the total absence of scorch marks, she would have thought a bomb had gone off in there.

They checked the closets and under the bed in both rooms but found nothing more than filth, repulsive odors, and the signs of scavengers.

"You can have the couch," Kaizhou said.

"I don't know if you're being chivalrous or punishing me for something."

He laughed, and she took him in her arms.

"I don't even know if I can sleep." She was exhausted,

and despite her words, she yawned into his shoulder then rested her face there. He rubbed the knots in her back, drawing a pleasant moan from her.

"God, that feels good," she said, forcing herself to relax. After a long moment, she pulled away and sat on the couch. She wanted to take off her shoes, but her feet were swollen from walking, and she worried she would never get them back on. She didn't want to risk being barefoot if they had to make an emergency exit.

She pulled her hood up and lay on the musty couch, trying to get comfortable on the ruined, swollen foam pads.

Kaizhou dragged in a couple of chairs from the kitchen and set them up across from one another so he could sit in one and put his feet up on the other.

"What was it like?" she asked. "The war?"

He sat quietly for a moment. A cloud passed across his eyes.

She'd never asked him before, at least not with the expectation of a deep answer. He never brought up the topic, but she knew the basics of the invasion from the history recall programs. Jonah never really talked about the war, either. Sitting there, in the center of a prime staging area for a battle that had destroyed Washington, she felt compelled to ask.

"It was bad." After a pregnant pause, he took a deep breath and went on. "After the PRC invaded, the US Army started rounding up Asians. Soldiers broke into our home and arrested my father and me. They hit hard and fast, you know? Beating any resistance out of us before we even knew what the fuck was going on. Then they pinned us to the ground and handcuffed us, forced us out of our home and into vans that were filled with our neighbors, our friends, people we didn't even know but who had slanted eyes.

"One day we were Americans, and the next day, we were enemies because of how we looked. The EMPs went off, the attacks started, and we were all rounded up and tossed into prison camps because maybe one of us might have been a traitor or a sympathizer. It didn't matter that I wasn't, that I'd never even been to China or Japan or Korea or any of the Coalition lands. Hell, I've never even been outside this state. They didn't care, though. My dad and I, we wound up in Topeka. I guess that was our first family vacation."

Mesa knew that his mother had died from ovarian cancer when he was a small child. His father had died in the prison camp, but Mesa didn't know the specifics.

"They didn't demand anything of us. They let us keep the clothes we were wearing, gave us some prison garb, three squares a day, and stuck us in these overcrowded huts surrounded by barbed wire and watchtowers. They installed inhibitors on those of us with DRMR, cut us off from the world. No online access, no commNet, no nothing. There was no Miranda, no lawyers.

"The US fell apart before the Supreme Court got around to deciding that maybe this wasn't exactly legal. The jihadists took care of DC," he said, referring to the dirty bomb attacks along the Eastern Seaboard that had irradiated the nation's capital and killed millions.

"Whatever government officials were left went into hiding and started trying to figure out the conditions of their surrender. Canada worked out their deals with the PRC and redrew their borders. Eventually, our guards all just kind of walked off the job and disappeared, leaving the door unlocked behind them."

He stretched in the chair and put his stiff legs down. He bent forward, resting his elbows on his knees, and wiped away the tears streaking his face. The contrails wound down his cheeks and jawline, shiny in the moonlight that reached through the cracks between boards.

"The first winter we had at the camp was a rough one. This polar vortex came through, dropped us into, like, negative sixty degrees. A lot of the old folks died off pretty quickly, froze to death outside. Nobody helped them. The guards didn't care, and the rest of us were afraid we'd get shot or something, or freeze to death ourselves.

"My dad lived long enough for the thaw to come around, and then he had a massive heart attack. Even if anybody had tried, nobody could do anything for him. He just dropped dead, you know?"

"I'm sorry," Mesa whispered, regretting her question.

"No, no, it's OK," he said, balling his fists in his lap. "All this was a while ago now. The soldiers took his body away, did whatever they did with those who died there. I remember him clutching his chest, his eyes going huge, and then he was falling. I didn't even know what to do. I held him, screaming for help loud enough to pull something in my throat. The guards, though, they threw me off him and dragged him away, and that was that. Last time I saw him, he was being dragged away."

She got off the sofa, intending to hold him, comfort him, and dry his face, but he stopped her.

"You should sleep," he said.

The wires bit into Mesa's neck, strangling her. She tried to wedge her fingers beneath the plastic coating, but they were drawn too tight. The cords, slick with her blood, were slicing into her skin. Her nails fought for purchase, but they bent and broke.

Standing, her attacker leaned back, trying to pull her off her feet. She elbowed him and was rewarded with a painful grunt and a brief slackening of the wires. Her throat burned, and beneath her, she saw, for the first time, herself—her other self. Laid out on a slab, her porcelain skin was bare. Her eyes were wide open, staring up aimlessly as if unaware of the violence surrounding her.

She slammed her foot down into his instep and elbowed him again. A tacky wetness warmed her skin, and she delivered another sharp elbow blow. He let out a small cry, then she was carried off her feet as he fell backward, landing on top of his body. The impact was solid, and the last bit of air blasted from her lungs. Her vision was dimming. A mad ocean pounded in her ears as the world turned black.

Her fingers reached toward the table, scrabbling for the girl's—for her own—hand. Trying to reconnect. Trying simply to *be*. She kicked at the form beneath her. Without even realizing it, she was trying to pull the wires away again. Her face was burning from the trapped blood pooling in her skull. Her lungs were on fire. Her whole torso ached, and her limbs felt too heavy.

The wires dug deeper, as if trying to burrow inside of her despite her flailing, clumsy grasps.

The cables cinched tighter. Her tongue protruded from her open, gasping, dying mouth, lapping at the air while her fingers tried to work. She tried to find the peace of her other self, of that empty shell bathed in light across from her.

Mesa woke with a start, heart hammering.

Dust motes glittered in the thin shaft of sunlight beaming through the wooden boards. It would have been filmic if her thoughts weren't glued to her mortality.

Kaizhou was snoring, slumped in his chair, his long legs splayed out across the seat of the other, arms crossed over his belly.

Her first instinct was to grab her pack and quietly sneak out. To leave him.

*That's what you were really good at before, wasn't it?* a dark voice said. The vicious snake curled up in the recess of her mind struck quickly. *Running away.* The sneer in her inner voice stopped her. The violent recrimination of her tone made her lie back down and left her feeling guilty.

She closed her eyes, but sleep was impossible. Mesa listened to Kaizhou snoring. In the still dawn, the noise was an ugly ripping that eroded her guilt into an angry shine. She snapped the pillow out from under her and lobbed it at him, her aim true.

Startled awake, he kicked out of the chair and sent it toppling. A thick puff of dust heaved out around it.

"Get up," she said. "We're leaving."

"You OK?"

"Fine. Let's go. C'mon." She shrugged the backpack on, taking stock of her dusty clothes. She brushed off what she could from her arms and pants legs then shook her hair loose. Kaizhou was a bit cleaner, but his ass was covered in thick, tan-colored grime from the dirty chair.

They set off with no clear destination in mind, knowing only that they had to find a vehicle. She wondered what their odds of success would be.

When the war began, evacuations were hasty and disorganized. Abandoned vehicles had clogged the thoroughfares for months after people had decided they would rather risk escape on foot than be bombed or shot to death while sitting in traffic. Plenty of people hitched a ride out of town with National Guard rescue caravans or in Army Humvees.

Lots of cars would have been left to rust in the residence's garages, and therein lay the real problems. If Mesa and Kaizhou did find a car, it might not even work. Odds were, they would open up a garage and find that scavengers had stripped the car for parts. If the vehicle was an old gas guzzler, fuel was yet another problem. A smart car with an ignition coded specifically to the owner's thumbprint—and it probably would be—would also be a problem. Granted, hacking a car was easier than finding gas and oil. She shoved aside the thoughts. First, they had to find a car, period. Then they could worry about the rest.

They loped through the neighborhood, going up and down driveways, peeking through filthy garage windows, and trying doors. Most of the entries were locked, and the roll-up garage doors were impossible to budge without a manual override from inside the structure. The few units with windows revealed darkened interiors—some neat and organized, others messy—but each had typical garage things: paint cans, lawnmowers, and garden tools.

In the early morning air, their soft footsteps and the noisy chittering of insects and birds broke the silence. Kaizhou hung back a step. Mesa hadn't spoken to him since they'd left the house.

As they made their way up a drive, a low rumbling cracked through the air, growing closer. Mesa's eyes went large, and she took his hand. They ran down the side of the garage and ducked behind it. She peeked around the corner, and he did the same on the opposite side.

The large, bulky front end of an ancient, rusty Jeep slowly rolled into view. Despite the noise, it was an electric unit. The engine generated a digital idling noise so that drivers and pedestrians knew the car was running, giving it that spark of life people had grown accustomed to. Somebody had hacked the audio, though, and given it a more resonant bass and a deeper growl. It sounded loud and intimidating, and the earth vibrated under the pounding noise.

Four men, equally large and bulky, rode in the open-air cabin. Scavengers. Then she noticed their weaponry. Well-armed scavengers.

To a T, each man wore stained, dirty undershirts and frayed carpenter pants. A sidearm was holstered at each waist, along with a knife. They carried tools—axes, sledgehammers, saws, large wrenches, and blowtorches.

One had a rough-hewn leather vest with a complete set of screwdrivers pocketed along both breasts. They were filthy, sweaty, and unshaved.

*Don't stop, don't stop. That's it, keep going.* Mesa willed the Jeep on, keeping herself tucked away from view.

*Keep going. Don't stop here.*

The false noise of the engine rumbled on, vibrating the pavement as it continued its slow march forward. One of the men stood and leaned over the roll bars to spit, and then they were past her field of view.

She exhaled slowly, relaxing a small fraction.

Kaizhou was on the verge of collapsing, his face pale and damp with fear.

"We should hang out here for a bit. We don't want to run into them by accident," she said.

"Maybe we can try cutting through the yards, put some distance between us."

"If they're working a grid, we might cross paths with them. If we stay behind them, it might be easier to hide."

He shrugged, his eyes darting around. Still clearly shook up, he licked his lips and tentatively touched the doorknob then gave it a twist. It turned easily, and he broke into a sloppy grin.

Mesa smiled. Their first success.

"Let's see what's behind Door Number Fourteen," she said, slapping Kaizhou's shoulder good naturedly and pushing him through the doorway.

After her eyes adjusted to the dark, Mesa realized lots of stuff filled the garage, but none of it was of any use to them. The toppled cans, the empty light socket, the corpses of mice and bugs, useless electrical outlets, and the peeled-back fire-stop boards were all pretty good indicators that the scavengers had already been through the house.

"They'll work until nightfall," Kaizhou said.

"We can't wait that long."

"There were four of them," he said. "Probably, they'll split up—two men to a house—work fast, and move on."

"Then we wait until they're hard at work and scoot on by."

"I can still hear their car."

Mesa nodded, straining to listen for the cessation of the noisy idling.

"With all the noise they're making," Kaizhou said, nodding toward the street, "it shouldn't be too difficult to avoid them."

"Maybe we do it your way," she said. "Once we know they're occupied, we'll cut through the yards and work our way around them."

"It's not going to be easy to find a car," he said.

She shook her head. "I think we're on foot for a while."

He leaned against the door as if trying to get the weight off his feet. "It's about twenty miles to Tacoma. We should be able to find something along the way."

She nodded, taking his hand. She needed to hold him, to hold on to what they had. Her anger had swung back around toward guilt, and she felt bad for snapping at him earlier and ignoring him afterward. He gave her a weak smile, clearly conflicted by a jumble of different fears and worries.

Tacoma or the smaller towns in between were options. She doubted the security networks were tightly entwined with Seattle, but she worried that whoever was tracking her would have had the foresight to widen the search after she escaped the apartment. Just because she'd made it out of the city safely, she had no reason to think she could go unnoticed for extended times elsewhere. Hundreds of thousands of intelligent crawler bots could be trawling the digital ether, hunting for her, capturing and scanning information, and running their data troves against any permutation the bad guys could think of or their AI could concoct. She wondered how many hairstyles they would have to sift through before homing in on her old-world punk. Then she laughed. She let out the first real laugh she'd had in a while.

Finally, the trembling reverb halted, and the echoes of the Jeep's engine died away. They gave it a few more minutes before Mesa opened the door.

"OK." She took a deep breath, hoping for the best. "Let's do this."

# CHAPTER NINE

MESA STEPPED OUT THE DOOR, turned the corner of the garage, and walked right into a gun leveled at her face.

Without thinking, she screamed, a high-pitched ear-splitting cry. As time slowed to an infinite crawl, she saw the scavenger's eyes widen in surprise. His friend took a quick step back. With her left arm, she pushed the gunman's extended limb away from both their bodies and, using her forward momentum, curled the fingers of her right hand. She launched the protruding knuckles into the hollow of his exposed throat. She heard and felt a rewarding crunch as his trachea collapsed.

His face went red as he struggled for air but was unable to force any through his open mouth.

Still moving forward, she brought her left knee up

into his groin, driving his pelvis backward. This caused his torso to bend, and in one fluid, continuous movement, she grabbed the sides of his head and brought his face down on her still-rising knee. She felt his nose shatter then heard the gun clatter to the concrete.

Through it all, she had noticed the shocked expression of his bewildered colleague. She was operating on full automatic, instinctually knowing that neither man had been expecting the sudden, propulsive violence. Both had relied too heavily on the threat of implied danger in their bearings and their large frames—they were soft. If they had possessed intent, she would have been dead as soon as the door opened. Instead, she'd quickly stripped them of any control. Mesa was younger and faster. She had trained. They had not.

She twisted her gunman around, using his hunched form as a temporary shield, and shoved him toward his friend. While he stumbled forward, she dove for the gun and rolled to the opposite end of the driveway then scrambled for cover against the corner of the house.

The friend was more worried for the safety of the choking scavenger than he was about the girl or for his own safety. His eyes darted around wildly, hoping for help.

Mesa knew two more men were out there somewhere, and she couldn't risk being outnumbered and out-gunned. She had to level the playing field further.

She leaned out from the corner of the house, presenting the thinnest part of her profile as she assumed a basic shooting stance, and aimed for the second gunman. He tried to bring up his own gun, but he was too slow.

She fired once, twice. The shots clustered closely around center mass. A dark-red stain blossomed against his dirty white undershirt and sent him to the ground.

Turning quickly, she sought out more targets but saw none. She approached the fallen men and fired twice more, once into the skull of each, instantly muting their cries.

"Holy shit," Kaizhou said. He stared at her, his mouth agape. "What the fuck?"

"Get back. Stay inside until I come for you."

She wondered at the sudden steel in her voice, at the still bodies at her feet, and her capacity for violence. The onward march of time caught back up with her, and she realized that, even though it had felt much, much longer, no more than a handful of seconds had passed.

Kaizhou scrambled to get back into the garage, and she ducked back behind the house, heading in the opposite direction. She kept low, walking half-crouched as she passed the deck. Using the large, imitation-wood platform as cover, she crossed the yard, moving away from the driveway and toward a thin strip of grass that wound around the western side of the residence.

Mesa moved quickly but quietly. If the third and fourth gunmen popped around the corner and opened fire, they would be aiming higher, expecting a standing target on level with their own height. She crouched and kept ducked down as she reached the far end of the house and peeked around the corner.

And there was the Jeep. It had reversed back down the street, its audio silenced. They'd known she and Kaizhou had been there, hiding in the garage. Clearly, they'd expected to take them unawares, to rob them, and who knows what else.

The driver was still seated in the car, his head moving around. He was plainly concerned but not willing to risk his life in order to check out the gunshots. Probably, he thought somebody would radio in if there was trouble and was using that small consolation as a balm to soothe his cowardice.

She edged back around the corner of the house, crossed back to the deck, and glanced around the structure. The two dead men were still where she'd left them, but a shadow was moving toward them.

*And there's number three.*

He was a large man, heavily muscled and clearly well fed. He went pale as he approached the fallen scavengers, quickly looking around for the source of violence. He couldn't see her, but as he turned in her direction, she could make out the plainly cosmetic nature of his eyes. They were enhanced by an expensive upgrade package, and it wasn't a subtle one, either. He wanted to broadcast his upgrades to the world.

Slowly, he looked back toward the garage. Mesa questioned her assessment that she'd gone unseen. He could have been sporting any number of different ocular implants, from heat sensors to night vision to sonar guides or infrared. He knew she was there, tucked away behind the deck. He also knew that one more person was hiding in the garage. The split was fifty-fifty on which one of them he would choose to target.

The man looked at the prone forms on the ground. He quickly assessed their firearms, swearing softly to himself. He no doubt realized that at least one of his quarries was now armed. Finding none, he stood again and moved slowly and quietly, his gun forward in a two-handed grip. He took a long time working his way along the side of the garage, pausing at the filth-covered window for a look inside. Then he checked back toward the deck and the far end of the house.

Mesa had kept the gun tucked close, hoping that her body heat would prevent his upgrades from sussing out the weapon. She kept herself hidden by the deck skirting, watching him through the square picture-framed lattice. She cursed silently when he crossed the garage window and edged closer to the entry.

*What are the options here?* Would he shoot first or use Kaizhou to bait her out? She questioned whether she could cross the yard quickly enough to take him out before he did any damage to her or Kaizhou.

She crab-walked back to the corner, took a quick glance, then fell back behind the deck skirting. The fourth man was still in the Jeep, apparently useless. Staring through the lattice, she could make out the blur of his companion as he moved past, out of sight. Around the edge of the skirting, she watched as he rounded the corner of the garage and stopped at the door.

Taking a deep breath to steady herself, keeping the gun tucked close to her center of gravity, she squared the sights on her target.

He kept his gun waist-high as he reached across the door to turn the knob. He eased it open, peeking through. Very slowly, he opened the door farther then glanced at his rear, and—

She fired just as he was turning, as if to meet the bullet. The slug pounded through his cheekbone, and he stumbled back into a clumsy fall.

Hoping the element of surprise was on her side, Mesa launched out of her hiding place, pushing herself off and away from the corner of the house and into a quick run toward the Jeep.

The man started and fumbled for his gun, too slowly. Two rounds to the skull rocked him in his seat, sending a smattering of red pulp and shards of bone across the roll bars and onto the street beside him. The Jeep, fortunately, was in park.

Mesa slowed to a walk, watching as the corpse slumped against the doorframe. She reached the driver's-side door and opened it, letting gravity pull the collapsed figure onto the street. He landed in the puddle of his own mess.

Her new ride wasn't as sloppy as she had feared. She grabbed at the collar of the man's work shirt and pulled hard, tearing away a long, wide strip of fabric. Using the cloth, she wiped the gore away from the roll bar and window ledge then folded it over and cleaned the headrest where a small amount of blowback dirtied the dark, fake-leather interior. She cleaned a few drops from the door trim, too. When she was finished, she gave the ride a quick once-over and was satisfied.

Once the threats had been eliminated, the veil slowly lifted from her mind. Her heart was racing, and a slight tremor had sprung to life in her hand. She had never killed before. In fact, she was fairly certain she'd never done anything with such cold deliberation before. She closed her eyes and fought to focus her thoughts and still her hand. When she reopened them, it was to take things one step at a time. Get in the vehicle. Get Kaizhou. Get out.

The ignition was a hacked start button, and she was grateful she didn't have to worry about thumbprint encoding. The scavengers had already silenced the false-ignition noise, giving her one less thing to worry about.

She climbed in, pulled the shifter into drive, and rolled slowly toward the mouth of the driveway. She looked around, feeling oddly good about herself, and gave the horn a quick tap. Its weak, ill-sounding gasp was disappointing, but Kaizhou got the message.

He poked his head around the corner of the garage, surveyed the damage around him, and ran toward the Jeep. He was pale and sweaty. The stink of fear boiled off his skin, and he took a moment to figure out the door latch. Clumsily, he climbed into the seat, where he then fumbled with the seatbelt. She really hoped he wouldn't throw up inside the vehicle.

Mesa drove for more than an hour before Kaizhou broke the silence. "Did you want to talk about what happened back there?" he asked.

Without taking her eyes off the road, Mesa said, "No."

The truth was, she did want to talk about it, but she had no idea how to. She had killed four men. Executed them. Despite the three years of training Jonah had insisted on, that automatic level of precision was beyond her. Those three years of training had brought her peace, built up her confidence, and helped instill a sense of self that was still largely absent. For three years, she'd been to gun ranges, learning to shoot with skill and capability, but she'd been up against paper targets. Back there, she had murdered with thoughtful deliberation, with ease, and for the last hour, she had been wondering if that was who she was.

*This is who* I *am*, a cold voice assured her. The slithery voice carried the texture of rough-hewn concrete. It spoke with a melodic softness, undercut with a knife-sharp edge.

The doctors had told her that even though her memories had been destroyed beyond recovery, her natural personality could possibly begin to resurface over time. She had reflexes that were ingrained in her body with muscle memory, natural capabilities that her body had become accustomed to over time and could carry out without any conscious need for learned ability. This included things like walking or handling kitchen utensils.

Something was buried deeply inside her. That being was slowly beginning to awaken and resurface—a being that she was and that she wasn't.

*And how in the fuck am I supposed to talk about that?*

"We should talk about it," Kaizhou said, his voice insistent enough to draw her eyes toward him. She was glad to see the color had returned to his face.

"You killed them," he said.

"We needed a ride." Her voice carried an exaggerated cool that she didn't feel, as if she were pretending to spout a line from an old cheesy holovid.

"Christ, don't you feel anything?"

She wanted to scream. She wanted to stomp on the

brakes and swerve the vehicle off the road, kicking up a violent plume of dust behind them. She could scream at him until he shut up and understood, until he stopped being so goddamned self-centered with his bullshit morality, as if he knew anything at all about what she was going through. She felt her face burning, but she bit back the invectives.

Instead, with an incredible detachedness, and remembering the years of frustration and helpful pointers her REMIND therapy had instilled in her, she calmly said, "Of course I do. And I'm working on trying to figure it out. I need time to process all this. We can talk about it but not right this second. Okay?"

The answer seemed to surprise him. His mouth opened and closed a few times, but no words came. Finally, he shook his head, as if to clear the board of his thoughts.

"Yeah, OK," he said. "You're right. Let me know when you're ready."

His understanding and the clear sympathy in his voice bled her of her anger. She was grateful she hadn't lashed out at him and that the REMIND software had helped her stay cool. He was the last person on earth she wanted to hurt.

"I'm sorry," she said, not really sure why.

"You saved our lives, you know?" he said.

"I don't even know how I did it."

"It was a surprise. That's all. Seeing you like that."

"I'm still trying to process it myself."

From the corner of her eye, she watched as he spaced out for a while, his fingers tapped against his jeans in rhythm to the music she couldn't hear. Eventually, the beat he was tapping out on his leg slowed then stopped. At some point, he nodded off for a good twenty minutes. He startled awake, and she felt the press of his gaze before he shifted and stretched.

Looking out the window, Kaizhou asked, "Where are we?"

"The four-ten," she said. "I thought it might be best to avoid Tacoma."

"Good idea."

More commonly known as Chinook Pass, the two-lane blacktop cut through the mountains. They had a steep, hilly incline to one side and rolling banks of fir trees on the other. Ahead, the white-capped points of Naches Peak and Mount Rainier were obscured by a thick layer of grayish clouds.

"That's amazing," he said, absorbing the view.

"I want to stop in a few and check the Somnambulist feeds."

"You think that's wise?"

"I won't be diving in unmasked," she said. "Should be fine. We've still got some of our LA peeps loose in the wind, and if any of them keyed on my offer to help, then... well, we have to help. I need to check."

"Seems as good a place as any to stop then. Get out and stretch."

"It is nice," she agreed. "Perfect, really. We'll have to come back for pictures when we're not wanted fugitives."

"Is that what we are?" he asked, the implication dawning on him as if for the first time.

She shrugged, letting the question dangle.

After putting a few more miles behind them, she pulled off onto the shoulder of Sunrise Park Road and parked the Jeep alongside the shrubs and firs. She didn't know if she'd ever seen such vivid greenness in her life.

Kaizhou let out a long loud breath and let his head fall back against the headrest. He watched Mesa as she dove deep into the feeds, embracing the digital realm fully and putting reality on hold for a few.

Once she'd synched up with the Somnambulist board, she lurked with a calm satisfaction. She owed Rameez big time. The masking software and the cloned pIP were genius moves, and they saved her a lot of hassle and anxiety.

Unfortunately, as she delved deeper into the postings and browsed the updated feeds, her unease grew.

Several private messages were waiting for her, and she recognized the handle of one of the senders. It belonged to Mariann Korgan, one of the missing LA memorialists, and she was responding to Mesa's offer of assistance.

Shell-shocked, Mesa moved on to other, more pressing posts. Others had initially caught her eye, but she had avoided them in order to assess the totality of her waiting messages. Three messages were aimed directly at her, from an unknown handle.

The name was a random mix of letters and numbers, with no matching profile, no geotag, and no associated IP. The lack of information and the tone of his message made him a goblin, and even without any identifiers, she knew exactly who he was.

The kill crew hadn't been able to find her in the physical realm, and they were trying to draw her out through the digital world with a fake Somnambulist account.

The first message was simple. TURN YOURSELF OVER. IT WILL GO EASIER.

Below that were the other three messages. The first header said simply "DORIS." The second said "SRI," and the third was labeled "ASHITA." The two women were inseparable, and before she even opened the messages, Mesa's heart ached for the lovers and for what she had inadvertently brought to their door.

She gasped in surprise upon seeing Doris's battered face. Both eyes were swollen. His lips were cracked and puffy, and his nose was clearly broken. Gloved hands pulled at his hair, yanking his head back, while a knife opened his throat from ear to ear.

There were no words, no demands, no warning. Only murder. Then Mesa's tears. She squeezed her eyes shut and took a deep breath, knowing she had to continue. She didn't want to. Their suffering and pain was her weight to bear, and she owed it to her friends to witness their sacrifices. She could not simply ignore it, no matter how badly she wanted to.

The DRMR files for both Sri and Ashita were composites, but both carried the same gist and the same inevitable outcome.

Mesa knew better than to put herself through the trauma, but she did it anyway. She needed to suffer the agony they had felt and to take their suffering as her own.

Within seconds, she realized how her friends had been discovered and mentally raged against herself for her own culpability. Their killers had found them because Mesa had known where they were. She'd abandoned her cache of private memories in her apartment, where the killers could find them.

The opening moments of the composite were proof enough. They were straight from her own memories.

On a bright and sunny day, she and Jade were holding hands as the pretty Brit introduced her to the Pakistani girlfriends. Mesa remembered it well, even without the digital support and electrochemical encoding being pumped into her hypothalamus. Three days went by before her flirtatious experimentations with Jade dissolved under the weight of mere friendship and an obviously insurmountable challenge to something deeper. Although Mesa had no idea who she, herself, was as an individual, her gender preferences were clearly firmly engrained.

Sri and Ashita were hand-in-hand, their smiles as bright as the late afternoon sun. Their warmth and friendliness quickly disarmed and won over Mesa, welcoming her into their small group.

The heat of their common bonds was violently disrupted. The jump splice was jarring as a masked face jolted into view, her mouth covered by a heavy, leathery hand. She felt a coldness against her throat then a surge of liquid warmth. And then searing pain. Her throat convulsed, choking on itself as air escaped her severed windpipe with a whispery hiss.

The weight of the man atop her eased, and in her dying moments, she turned toward her partner and watched Sri suffer a similar fate. She felt the spray of her lover's blood against her face then watched the pool of darkness expanding around her, even as the world itself shrank away and lost all color and familiarity.

Mesa felt them die, the memories layered one atop another, a stereophonic murder. And as the girls faded away, a rough-hewn voice, distant in their dissolution from life, said, "Mesa, Mesa, Mesa." Her name was issued forth with a tone of disappointment. Scolding her for her transgressions. Blaming her for their murders.

She couldn't deny it, and she accepted the accusatory tone as a base truth. Their deaths were her fault.

And while the damage was beyond repair, she promised to repay their killers a thousand fold. She could not bring them back, but she could exact vengeance.

Mesa returned to her waiting messages and the plea for help. Mariann Korgan was a twenty-four-year-old waitress with a scattershot of dark freckles against pale skin. Thick red hair fell in long, wavy kinks, making her already-slender face seem small and impish. Her tiny upturned nose helped accentuate that impishness. Her big, toothy grin failed to disguise the sorrowful surrender in her jade eyes.

The message held a mnemonic subtext, a chemical encoding that let Mesa in on the girl's personality, enough to know first-hand that Korgan had become a memorialist simply for the eclecticism of the experience. Also attached was a straight-up mem.

She saw glimmers of Korgan as a younger woman, a brash teenager who'd once had a headful of metal studs and pierced cheekbones, before the necessity of a job to pay the growing bills and fund the essential basics of life. Tiny flecks of healed-over holes still marked Mariann's skin, but the freckles were a natural camouflage. Though the skin-deep level of rebelliousness was history, a firm contrarian streak ran through her marrow. With the memorialists, she'd found a home.

And then she'd learned that her friends had been gunned down and massacred, with a small handful scattered to the wind and cut off from contact.

While their small basement-level enclave was under attack, Korgan had been delivering a stack of flapjacks, a side of bacon, one order of scrambled eggs, and another over-easy to Table Twelve. Multiple memorialists used their last moments on earth to push out a warning to the few not on-site. Mariann had nearly lost her grip on the orange carafe of decaf when the last-ditch emergency alerts hit her hard.

Dazed, she put the carafe back on the burner and asked Steve to cover her tables. He was sweet on her, and when she started to lie and tell him she was having female troubles, he blushed and said not to worry. When she offered him a small smile, it came off more like a wince. She'd received not only the alert but a glimpse at the violent affair as well. She supported herself against the counter as she walked into the small staff area in back, trying not to lose it.

She pulled her purse and a light jacket from her locker. The restaurant did not have a standard uniform, but employees were asked to dress neatly in black jeans, a black polo, and black shoes. Stepping outside, she squinted in the daylight and tried to remember the burn protocols she'd been taught years ago.

The mem was Korgan's attempt to sell herself to Mesa

and establish credibility. Mesa appreciated the effort, still chilled by the DRMR files of her friends' final moments.

Different memorialist groups had similar burn protocols, but they varied in how strictly the group followed them and instructed others to adhere to them. Mostly, they included the basics: leave your car, your apartment, and your personal belongings. Stay off the web. Stay hidden. Find some place secure you can hide and stay there. Don't tell anybody where you were or where you were going. Don't ask for help; don't offer help. Mesa had ignored the last. Mariann was glad for it. In the end, their humanity and desire to live had won out, but Mariann lacked the safeguards that Rameez had deployed for Mesa.

Mesa copied the data codes and software bundles that Rameez had given her then sent them off to a secure, private back-channel in a datafarm they'd hacked years ago. She gave Mariann instructions on how to access it. She disconnected and waited for the woman to reconnect and verify her secure, falsified creds.

Minutes passed, which she spent chewing on the inside of her cheek. A short time later, Mesa accepted a CommNet alert from Janet Dopplier and was pleased to see Mariann's face.

Korgan had attempted to quell her riotous hair into a high-up ponytail, but multiple strands had gotten loose. She was pale and clearly afraid.

Mesa found herself unsure of what to say or how to proceed. Korgan was equally oblivious once their hellos were done with.

"Where are you?" Mesa asked. "Are you safe?"

"For now," Korgan said. "I'm out in the desert with some friends."

"Whoever is responsible for all this could come after them. Are you sure it's safe?"

Mariann let loose a jagged smile, one that was far more

natural than her usual canned pleasantry. "They're off the grid. I think it's as safe as I can manage for now."

"We can come get you, band together. Maybe it'll be safer?"

"They're hunting us down," Korgan said. "I think maybe I'm the last of the LA bunch."

Mesa recalled the Kessler mems, wondering about the others. She swallowed. "Why do you say that?"

Mariann shrugged, staring at some far-off point, lost. Mesa wondered if she was high or on some kind of depressant.

"You're the only one I heard from," she said. "The only one who posted. I took a risk logging on, you know."

"Reaching out was brave of you," Mesa said, recognizing the undercurrent of her words, the unspoken message. She alone had broken the burn protocols and reached out to put her own life at risk. At the time, she'd felt risking contact was more necessary than stupid. She wasn't sure anymore.

"I lurked on some of the hidden deep sites, too," Korgan said. "There's rumors out there that others are dying. That everyone in LA is dead." She paused, stabbing at an eye with a knuckle. "Well, everyone but me, I guess."

"We've lost a lot of people, too," Mesa said. For a brief instant, she watched Jonah die. She saw Sri lying next to her, a red tide surging from a large smile that had been carved into her neck.

"Do you know who they are?"

"Do you?" Mesa asked, with a bit more bite than she'd intended. She hated feeling useless. Hated feeling watched. Hated that lazy, half-hearted shrug Mariann used to answer her question.

"I might," Korgan said. "I pulled up other mem feeds, from other enclaves. Some of the memorialists are starting to recognize how big this is and are working to piece things together. I have some information, but I can't risk putting it online. Not yet."

"You should be safe with those creds," Mesa said, determined to move forward. "Kaizhou and me, we're as good as cloaked. We can meet. We should meet."

"I can't come back," Mariann said.

"We'll come to you."

Silence echoed in her skull while she waited for the girl to decide. Then a small ping notified her of a GPS marker, showing Mariann's location.

"We meet there. Just you, just me."

Mesa closed her eyes, bowing her head in relief. "That's good, Mariann. We'll meet tomorrow night."

A nod of agreement. "Ten o'clock."

Mesa assured Mariann she would be there and disconnected. Then she took a deep breath, trying to center herself and study the map. She closed her eyes, practicing the relaxation breathing techniques the REMIND program had advised her on, and put the car into drive.

She pulled back onto the four-ten, anticipating twelve hours of road-time.

"Well?" Kaizhou asked.

She told him, and he pulled the seat belt across his body, clicking it into place. He played with the seat controls, lowered the back, and shut his eyes. They had a long ride to Elko, Nevada.

# CHAPTER
# TEN

THEY DROVE ALONG INTERSTATE EIGHTY-TWO across the open border on the eastern side of Oregon, into the lower reaches of Idaho, where they switched over to US-93 South and crossed into the northern edge of Nevada to I-80.

After twelve tedious hours of driving, they found themselves in Elko with Kaizhou behind the wheel. They'd made a point of stopping every few hours to stretch, take bathroom breaks, and get coffee or fast food. Dawn was breaking across the grubby sky, met with long yawns. Mesa was in desperate need of caffeine, despite the coffee and soda she'd had along the way.

Elko was a tiny town hidden in the dessert. During the ride, Mesa had used her cloner creds to do some anonymous research, and she couldn't help but laugh when she came across a quote from Hunter S. Thompson. The gonzo journalist had said, "The federal government owns ninety percent of this land, and most of it is useless for anything except weapons testing and poison-gas experiments."

Seeing it in person, she struggled to come up with an argument against his claim. The Shoshone called it *Natakkoa,* literally "rocks piled on one another." That, too, seemed a fair assessment.

They'd seen very few people, but the day was early. The only signs of life came from the bright displays of the abundant casinos. Driving past, she stared out the window at the large white polar bear adorning Commercial Casino, at its parking lot packed with the cars of gamblers pulling all-nighters, and the empty lot of the Thunderbird Motel across the street.

They passed a cluster of bored prostitutes dressed in skimpy outfits, their bare skin already baking under the early morning heat.

From Idaho Street, they navigated the one-way lanes around the block at Sixth, made the right at Railroad, and passed the old Pioneer Hotel on Fifth. Mesa spotted a sign and asked Kaizhou to pull into a vacant spot.

The small block was a combination of vacant buildings and a bar. In between were a bright-green awning and a black metal sign of a coffee mug wearing a cowboy hat. Beneath that, in red neon was the word *espresso.* He looked at the Cowboy Joe Coffee sign with a lopsided smirk, and Mesa was out of the vehicle before it had even come to a full stop.

Mesa was surprised by the size of the coffee shop. It was tiny, barely large enough to hold more than a dozen people. She was grateful the place was nearly empty. Kaizhou ordered a regular coffee and grabbed a couple of brownies. Mesa requested an extra shot in her fuel and a bagel with cream cheese. They tipped the barista well, hoping to buy her silence should anyone come searching for them, and took their food and drinks back to the Jeep.

Mesa was happy with Mariann's choice of Elko as a meeting spot. The town was low-end, and the modern world had passed it by almost as soon as it had been settled in the late 1800s. The lack of jobs and industry and the threat of warfare across the state's borders had left Elko on its last legs. The town was practically a black hole, surrounded by desert and dry scrub that threatened to turn into a wildfire without any warning. The few people Mesa had seen all had the same bored, far-off void in their eyes. With its collection of inns, motels, casinos, and brothels, Elko was the definition of a transient town. Taking an interest in anyone was pointless, because they would be gone and replaced with yet another itinerant.

It was perfect.

After refueling, Mesa and Kaizhou walked hand-in-hand down the block and crossed the street to the Esquire Inn. The motel billed itself as the best in Elko and featured a micro fridge as the prime amenity.

Mesa's go bag had carried a few slips of universal currency, which she had discreetly transferred to her hip pocket. Inside the small lobby, she passed over a folded collection of twenties, enough to cover the week. The shaggy gray-haired woman licked the tip of her index finger then meticulously counted out the bills and squinted at the validation markers. Satisfied, she gave them two small plastic cards to Room Twenty-seven.

"Y'all have a blessed day," the motel clerk said, the words nearly an automatic, bored sigh.

Mesa nodded, equally bored, before turning heel. She stepped back into the blistering heat. Even before noon, the temperature was already an inhuman one hundred twenty degrees.

After walking around the side of the main building, past an ancient, banged-up vending machine, and up the flight of stairs, they found Room Twenty-seven. The card reader seemed to be the most modern feature in all of Elko and was perhaps what made the Esquire Inn the city's best motel. With an electronic *click-buzz-whir*, the light flashed green, and the door popped open.

She welcomed the arctic blast of air conditioning, smiling as she stepped inside, unconcerned about the lackluster accommodations.

A king-sized bed covered by a garish seashell-themed comforter, in which clashing pinks and purples vied for supremacy, dominated the small room. A framed faded print of the Taj Mahal hung above the thin wooden headboard. The carpet was clearly heavily trafficked and was worn thin in spots; in other areas, it rolled with the fury of an angry ocean. Crossing the thin aisle between the foot of the bed and the dresser was practically a dare. Sure enough, the micro fridge was there, right next to the bathroom door.

She passed the accent wall—she guessed the sickly pale mucus color would have been inappropriately named cool mint or some such similar misrepresentation—to check out the bathroom. The WC was surprisingly modern and neat but unsurprisingly tiny.

Elko's finest. Nothing but the best.

"I need to shower," she said, pulling off her shirt. Kaizhou nodded and plopped down on the bed, watching her undress. She wiggled out of her jeans then playfully tossed them at his face as she headed into the bathroom.

She twisted the dial for cold then let the arctic blast cool her warm body. She hadn't spent much time outside, but geographically speaking, she was half-convinced Elko resided in the crook of Satan's taint. When her teeth began clattering together, she raised the water temperature to a milder setting.

Eyes closed, she stood under the light rain, willing her body to relax and working the tension from her muscles. Her neck and shoulders ached from the long car ride, despite the regular breaks.

Thoughts of the dying scavengers intruded on her attempts to achieve a clear head. Even in the aftermath of the recent violence, she'd felt calm—full of adrenaline, but calm. In control.

Killing squared away with the rest of her too easily, but even that felt wrong. Was this a natural trait of her personality that she had somehow failed to recognize? Was this who she was before her memory was destroyed? A killer, a woman accustomed to violence and death?

She should have felt more, should have been more psychologically and emotionally wrecked, and she was angry she wasn't. Her flashes of violence had felt too natural, as if somebody else had taken charge and propelled her forward, subduing her conscious will in order to exact the tolls of death. Yet that wasn't quite right, either. Her movements, her finesse with weapons, her calm collectedness while in danger-they all felt reflexive. Instinctual.

*Who the hell am I?*

She wished she could talk with her therapist, but even running the REMIND software was a dangerous idea, and she didn't want to answer the sure-to-be-asked questions regarding her false identity and faked credentials. No, that bit of software was quite off-limits.

And Kaizhou... he was sweet, but the last few days had clearly taken a toll on him. Mesa worried that he was afraid of her. He tried to hide it, but maybe the fear was justified. She couldn't even begin to guess how he would react if she opened up to him about this, regardless of how much she, or he, needed to talk about it. He had tried to talk to about it, but she'd shut him down and weaseled out of facing it. A distance had erupted between them.

During the ride, he'd lost himself in his music, and they'd settled into an uncomfortable lull of silence. When she tried to take his hand, he'd flinched ever so slightly. Trying to recover smoothly, he had given her a dry smile and wrapped his fingers around hers, but he was hesitant in a way he never had been before. Or at least she thought he was. After a brief moment of connection, he'd broken away and gone back to his life's soundtrack while staring blankly out the window. Even when she knew her own gaze must have been burning into him, he'd failed to turn toward her.

He could have been putting distance between them because he was afraid of her cold-bloodedness or maybe he was being distant because she was acting distant. *Or the distance might be all in my head. Fuck!* There would be time for it later, she decided. *Take things one step at a time, that's all. There's a time and place for everything, and now is not the time.* Or so she told herself, pressing her forehead against the cool ceramic tile and letting the cold water run down her scalp and along the curve of her spine.

She tried not to think of dead men, of the corpses of scavengers, or her gut-shot father falling to the floor, torn apart by bullets. She failed. Her body felt rubbery as the tears consumed her, but she wasn't sure whom she was crying for. Were the tears for them or for her?

Damp and naked, she laid her towel across the bed and lay next to Kaizhou. Her eyes burned, and she felt raw and cold, her energy pent up and electrifying her past her own exhaustion. She needed to move, to run, to crash and burn. More than anything else, she needed human contact. After a too-long moment, he put his arms around her and held her close. Her fresh tears soaked through his shirt to the skin beneath.

She could taste the salt on her own lips when she pressed her mouth to his, and she was gratified to feel him return the kiss. She felt ravenous for affection, for the closeness of their bodies, to entwine and become a singular, writhing creature, a proof of life. She needed to feel something other than pain. She needed to feel something other than damaged.

Later, their bodies slicked with sweat, they slept in one another's arms. The exhaustion of the last few days caught up to her, forcing her under.

When she awoke, she was surprised to still see daylight streaming through the window shades. Gently, she broke away from Kaizhou to rinse off in the shower and use the toilet. As she dug the last change of clean clothes from her backpack, he began to stir, his eyes gummy with sleep and unfocused.

"What time is it?" he asked, too lazy or too tired to check the chrono app on the DRMR dash.

"After five. Sunset is still a few hours away, but we need to scope things out."

"I thought you weren't meeting until ten?"

She nodded. "Better to be early. I don't want any surprises."

She'd spent the last few minutes thinking over a plan for the evening. She wanted to trust Mariann Korgan, but blind trust was a good way to get killed. The way things had been going of late, being prepared was a necessity. If things went well, then great. If they didn't, she didn't want to be caught unawares without at least a fighting chance.

"We'll drive around town for a bit, get a lay of the land," she said. "I want to be inside the church by eight, at least, ahead of Korgan."

Kaizhou nodded.

Korgan had sent directions the night before to meet at the Lighthouse Christian Fellowship, one of the last few churches left in Elko. As Mesa studied the map, a sense of dread tickled across her spine over the ironically named Last Chance Road. *Too fucking perfect*, she thought.

According to the map, the drive was five minutes, down Fifth Street to Last Chance. She wanted to see the area while there was still some daylight, but the satellite views didn't show much. Last Chance lied at the clearest demarcation of Elko's borders before they gave way to the vast stretch of dessert and scrub of the pointy Elko Hills, the mountain ranges beyond, and the surging currents of the Humboldt River.

"What do you want to me do?" he asked.

"Drive around, keep your eyes open. If anything goes wrong, I want you nearby."

She slipped into a pair of cotton panties with an image of a cartoon cat grinning across the front of it and pulled on a jogging bra. Her last pair of jeans were a bit loose, but the gun tucked into the waistband helped take up the little bit of slack. The black T-shirt fit, and she briefly admired herself in the mirror then set about fixing her hair. She used the long strands to partially shield her left eye and cheekbone. Elko was unlikely to have sophisticated security image protocols, and the way her hair broke up and obscured half her face should be enough to fool the dummy software and confuse the programming. Dark eye shadow and bright rouge across her cheeks would further disrupt and confuse the surface metrics. She smiled at the urban camouflage, congratulating herself on a job well done. *I actually look pretty hot.*

Kaizhou must have thought so, too. She caught the rising bulge beneath the thin top sheet and gave him a wry smile.

"Later, bud," she said. "Get your pants on. We're going."

The sun had been baking Elko all day, and she regretted the jeans and black tee almost immediately, despite the dearth of choices she'd been left with.

Fifth Street took them across the narrow banks of Humboldt, leaving the bright, flashing lights of the gaming parlors and brothels behind them. Civilization died out completely before long. They passed the tiny burned-out remains of small suburban outposts, and the husks of looted and destroyed ranch houses flickered past the windows.

God hadn't bothered to do anything to save the Lighthouse, much like Elko and the rest of the US surrounding it. The structure was long and squat. Dirty white doors hung off their frames, and the windows were busted out. The white sign advertising the church and the lighthouse logo were broken and askew. The desert winds had sandblasted the blue-and-purple siding into faded ghosts. Still, the sun beat down upon it, threatening to whiteout all sense of color as the years went on.

"We'll stay linked up over the commNet," Mesa said. "Be each other's eyes and ears in case anything goes wrong."

"I'll drive around a bit," he said.

She kissed him, darting her tongue across his before she quickly withdrew and hopped out of the Jeep.

The smell was the first thing to hit her as she passed through the church doors. The building was rank with the earthy scents of mold and rotting wood. The walls were deeply stained with water damage.

A community posting board held yellowed, wrinkled papers. She couldn't help but groan at the flyer, whose author must have been struck with a divine pun, which advertised Wednesday's "Pot Luke" dinner.

She passed through the metal frames of what had once been glass doors before somebody had taken a chunk of concrete to them. Glass crunched underfoot as her eyes adjusted to the dim light filtering in through the stained-glass window.

Walking down the aisle, she noticed the pews had been seriously disrupted. Some were toppled; others had been shifted to form a circle around an old, soot-stained barrel.

Faded paint on the wall showed where Jesus had once hung, but he, too, had fallen and lay on the floor with a cracked skull and a missing arm. His face was contorted with pain. The broken body was cast between a jeweled beam of sunlight shining through stained glass and the empty shadows of the nave.

The priest's office and the administrative quarters were through another door beyond the rectory. A colorfully decorated classroom had fallen into disrepair, a poster depicting the trains of animals boarding Noah's Ark hanging to the wall by a single corner. The whiteboards were spray-painted with obscenities and crude genitals. Somebody had used the entire back wall to spell out FUCK U, and Mesa wondered which author had been more creative, him or the Pot Luke guy.

Content with her explorations, she slowly worked back toward the front doors. Kaizhou pulled up a minute later.

"Everything seems OK," he said.

"No surprises yet," she agreed.

They still had a few hours to kill, and her stomach grumbled for attention. They decided on dinner at the restaurant in Commercial, whose main selling point seemed to be the giant polar bear above the main entrance.

Walking inside, they were greeted by noise, smoke, and White King, allegedly the world's largest taxidermied polar bear. Mesa was surprised by the high-quality oil paintings of gun fighters. They looked expensive, which was an anomaly in Elko.

Even more surprisingly, the ten-dollar prime rib dinner was entirely edible, and the coffee was delicious. She watched the men in cowboy hats and boots quickly scarf down their food before returning to the slots and tables. The cheap music and *ding-ding-dings* of the gaming machines multiplied and echoed, their chorus ringing throughout the floor.

She'd been worried about keeping the gun hidden in her waistband, but that concern had been foolish. The men and women around her were unabashed open-carry fans, and guns were slotted into hip and shoulder holsters of nearly every individual in the casino. Men bullshitted one another, resting one hand on the butts of semi-automatic while the other held cans of beer. Still, she kept the tail of her loose T-shirt over the gun.

The food came and went, and despite the pleasant taste of the meat, the grease left her with an unsettling bit of indigestion. After her fourth cup of coffee, Mesa's nerves were jittery, but she blamed that more on what lay ahead than the caffeine-laced adrenaline that was building in her as the meeting ticked closer.

Kaizhou settled the bill with cash, and they delicately pushed their way through the crowds and back outside. Elko was dark, save for the bright neon of casinos and motels.

By eight, Mesa was back inside Lighthouse, sitting in a pew facing the door, hidden in the shadows, waiting.

She and Kaizhou kept an open optic feed between them. She watched in a small window broadcast across the lower right corner of her field of vision as Kaizhou parked in an alley halfway down the opposite block. Tucked away in the darkness, the position made him difficult to spot but gave him a clear view of the church and its main entrance.

With the commNet live, Mesa watched through Kaizhou's display field as Mariann Korgan approached the building, casually observing her surroundings and checking behind herself. She was dressed in ragged, cut-off blue-jean shorts and a purple tank top, an oversized pink purse hooked over her shoulder. The point of view shifted slightly as Kaizhou scooted farther down the driver's seat, letting the steering wheel obstruct his full line of sight. Korgan disappeared behind the building then came back around the front a few minutes later.

At quarter to ten, Mesa listened to the loud crackling noise of glass underfoot. The darkness shifted as Korgan stepped into view, carefully moving into a shaft of prismatic moonlight.

"You're early," she said, seeing Mesa immediately. She gave the gun in Mesa's lap a long stare but said nothing.

After a long, pregnant silence, she said, "How do you want to do this?"

Mesa shrugged. In truth, she didn't actually know how things were supposed to proceed. She said, "Tell me about LA."

"What, you looking for tourist tips?"

"You know what I'm talking about."

"OK. Fine. No small talk. Mind if I sit?"

Mesa used the gun to point to the pew across from her, and Mariann nodded, sliding onto the wooden seat kitty-corner from her.

"I'm not sure what you know about the LA branch."

"Presume I don't know anything at all. Tell me everything."

"OK. So. Our enclave was small but well-funded. We were supported by a woman named Alice Xie, who was the head of an organized crime syndicate." She paused, making sure Mesa was still with her.

"What use did a gangster have for memorialists?" Mesa asked.

Korgan nodded with approval. "Good question. Most memorialists see the convergence web as a system of unity, something that connects mankind, right?"

"Sure."

"But it can also be used for exploitation, blackmail,

murder. It's amazing how much information people put out there freely on a daily basis, you know? Entire memories that they don't even think about, just surface stuff. Superficial memories. But memories have layers, and most don't even stop to recognize that, or realize how easy it can be to peel back those layers and glean information. So, like, you ask what good a convergence web would be for a gangster, and I'm telling you it's a treasure trove for exploitation."

"And what you're saying beneath all that is, there's a pretty good reason for people to want you dead." Mesa's eyes flickered around the church, seeking any signs of movement. The feed off Kaizhou's sightlines was clear, but she was starting to worry about the implications of Korgan's line of thoughts.

"What I'm also telling you is, people who think memorialists are harmless"—Korgan leaned forward, her elbows on her knees—"they're way wrong."

"You said you know who's responsible for these attacks." Mesa's finger tightened on the trigger, her palms slick against the gun's grip.

"Did I?" Korgan seemed surprised.

Mesa smiled slightly, remembering Korgan's half-hearted shrug when pressed for details the previous evening. "You said you had heard rumors."

"Rumors, sure. Solid intel? Nah."

"Tell me about the rumors, then."

"You mind if I smoke?" Mariann gestured toward the large purse she'd been clutching in her lap. "Some water, too. I'm parched."

"Go for it."

Mariann angled the bag toward Mesa, allowing her to see the contents. Slowly, she fished out a pack of smokes and a bottle of water. The contents inside the purse shifted and jangled as they resettled into the new crooks and crannies. Korgan tapped a cigarette and a lighter from the pack then took a long, slow pull. Tilting her head up and away from Mesa, she let out a long, smoky breath. She closed her eyes, contentment settling on her face, instantly calm and serene.

After giving her a minute to collect herself, Mesa prodded her with, "So these rumors?"

Korgan smiled, unscrewing the bottle cap, and took a swig of water. She took her time screwing the cap back on, apparently enjoying Mesa's impatience. She held the bottle between her knees and tried to find a more comfortable spot for her ass against the wooden seat. "LA wasn't the first hit."

Her words drove the impatience out of Mesa and replaced it with stunned disbelief. "What?"

"Over the last two years, five memorialists were murdered in various locations across the US. At first, their deaths were thought to be totally random. Other enclaves picked up the workflow and filtered the data. Eventually, somebody got curious enough to run a convergence on the victims. One guess where they all came from."

"LA."

"And the girl gets a prize!"

"They're targeting Alice Xie's memorialists," Mesa said. "What is it? Some kind of gangland retribution or something?"

"Well," Korgan began, "that's where it gets a little bit trickier. Each of the vics were recruited by Alice, but each one also had some interesting data packets that got filtered out and rerouted back home to the LA enclave."

She let her words hang in the air, luring Mesa out.

Annoyed at being forced by the prompt, Mesa asked, "What kind of data?"

"What do you know about body-shifting?"

"What? What the hell is that?" A hollowness opened in Mesa's belly; a cool tickle worked down her spine. She'd never heard of body-shifting before, but the term immediately raised the hair on the back of her neck. She knew it could not possibly be good.

"Huh," Korgan said, seemingly thrown. "OK, well. It's like this. Each of the murdered memorialists were data hounding the work of a PRC general named Jiang Yuan. Apparently, before becoming a general, he was a researcher in California. His work revolved around memory formation and replication. He never finished his PhD, because of the war I guess, but he started developing an experimental technique to transfer host memories into a surrogate. Meaning he was transferring an entire life of one thing into another thing. He was doing this on cats or rats or something, lab animals."

"Jesus Christ," Mesa said.

"Hey, c'mon now, we're in church," Korgan said.

Mesa wasn't sure if she was being sarcastic or not.

"And these memorialists," Mesa said, "they were what? Body-shifters or something?"

"No, no, nothing like that. At least I don't think so. They just had the knowledge in their head."

"And that's why they were killed." Mesa's heart raced. Indigestion bubbled up again as acidic bubbles burst in her belly.

"I think so."

"But then whatever they knew got filtered back into the other enclaves and directed back to LA."

"Putting big ol' target signs on each of our foreheads."

"Shit," Mesa said. "After we found out about LA, we picked up the slack. There were other enclaves, too, but we jumped in to help right away."

"You've probably taken notice of a rising body count since then."

Mesa nodded, deflated. Jonah. Sri. Ashita. Doris. "Jesus," she said again, too beaten down for the slur to carry much invective.

"How much do you know about Jade Mori?"

The name hit her as if she'd been punched with a metal weight in the belly. This wasn't going at all as she had expected. "Jade?"

"She came up in the convergence. When the other enclaves started mapping out the data, they found out that Alice Xie had recruited six people. Jade Mori is the one soul unaccounted for. She went north, to Washington. You know her, don't you?"

*Oh, Jade...* "She's a friend."

"Those five who got dead? They got dead because they were stupid. They didn't do much in the way of operational security. No fake credentials, no masks, not like you. You've been real good, careful. You've stayed well hidden."

Mesa felt dizzy. The world around her was spinning out of control. Korgan's voice carried a peculiar tone that reverberated in her eardrums. She felt sick, and her dinner turned leaden, like a smoldering, rising gorge.

Mariann leaned in close, pursing her lips to blow smoke up and away between them. She caught Mesa in an intense stare, her eyes searching hard, as if she could pierce Mesa's soul. Eventually, she seemed to have found a flicker of recognition and spoke. "Hello, Alice."

Mesa's mouth went desert dry. "What?"

"They were lazy. And you killed them. You, Alice, you did that."

"What the hell are you talking about?" Mesa asked. A darker voice, tucked deep in her mind said, *Kill her.*

"You see," Korgan said, "they were killed because they possessed proprietary information. Top-secret developmental research. Technology that some people would much rather be kept off the streets and limited to a very, very select few.

"You'll be happy to know, Mesa, that body-shifting works. Isn't that right, Alice?"

"What the fuck are you talking about? Why do you

keep calling me Alice?"

"I'm not talking to you, stupid girl. I'm talking to Alice."

*Kill her.*

"She is in there, isn't she?" Korgan asked. The question was clearly rhetorical.

*Kill her.*

Mesa raised the gun, but Korgan was fast. She dived in the seat, slinking low and pushing forward. Torpedoing her body into Mesa's, she sent them sliding off the pew, onto the dirty floor.

Korgan delivered a fast punch to Mesa's face, smashing the back of her skull against the metal barrel, keeping her gun arm pushed off to the side.

Mesa was dazed. Flashes of silver speckled her vision. She tried to get a knee between them, but Korgan was in too close for her to get any leverage. Her skull throbbed, but maybe she had enough room to make the pain worse. She flung her head forward, sending the top of her forehead crashing into Korgan's nose, shattering it.

The head-butt was enough to force Korgan away and put some distance between them. Blood poured freely down her face, over her mouth. In reflex, one hand went to her nose, and Mesa was able to pull her gun hand loose.

She brought the pistol forward, too slow. Korgan punched Mesa again, and Mesa's lips cut on her teeth. In the dazed confusion of recovery, Korgan brought a knife out and slashed forward. Mesa whipped her head back, but the blade cut a shallow groove across the bridge of her nose and below her right eye.

While Korgan's bladed fist swung high, Mesa's gun arm pulled low. She jabbed the barrel of the pistol into Korgan's belly, flush with her kidney, and pulled the trigger twice. She jerked a leg free, kicking Korgan off as she rolled away.

Hunched over, an arm wrapped around her waist in an effort to staunch the bleeding, her face a mask of pain,

Korgan was intent on fighting to the end. She held the knife between them, still threatening Mesa with it.

The scene brought back the memory of an old holovid she had watched with Jonah—an old cowboy flick that he'd been excited to rewatch, something from before his own childhood that he'd watched with his father. "Never bring a knife to a gunfight," the cowboy had warned.

Mesa raised the gun, ready to end her. Korgan flashed a red-rimmed smile, a dare in her eyes.

The doors burst open, and booted feet crashed over the broken glass strewn across the floor. Mesa recognized Korgan's look for what it really was—not a dare, but a promise.

The distraction was enough. As Mesa looked up at the three men storming into the room, clad head to toe in black, guns raised before them, Korgan hunched low and ran forward, using the sudden surprise to tackle Mesa.

Though distracted, Mesa caught the flash of movement and turned in time to avoid taking a stabbing blow to her belly. The knife glanced off her hipbone, but Korgan's weight pushed her off her feet. They fell in a clumsy lump, limbs akimbo, wrestling each other for their weapons.

Mesa decided she had no time for finesse. In a snap judgment, she let go of Korgan's arm and sent a cross-hook into her cheekbone. The blow twisted Mariann's face away, but she recovered quickly and stabbed downward. Flaming hot pain shot through her shoulder instantly as the blade slashed through tendon and ground against bone. Mesa howled then punched Korgan again. The woman falling off her, Mesa scrambled backward, trying to get her feet under her, but her hand slid on the dirty floor.

The men fanned across the room, leveling their guns at her.

Mariann was on her knees and elbows, blood gushing from her belly and staining the ground in a spreading pool.

Quickly, Mesa fired but not at the men. She was outgunned, outmanned, and surrounded. They had the entrance covered, which left her only one viable alternative.

The stained-glass window shattered, raining glass across the ledge and onto the pew beneath it.

Reacting to the gunfire, the men took aim, but she was already moving. Bullets stitched the ground behind her as the men swung to follow her. She tucked the pistol into her waistband, screwed her mouth shut, and got ready for a world of pain as she wrenched the knife loose, nearly blacking out. Her arm went numb as a tacky wetness spread from her wound and down her chest.

She forced her arm to move, but the limb was slow to respond, and—*Christ, the pain*. She grabbed a fistful of Korgan's hair and hauled her to her feet. Before Mariann could react, Mesa buried the knife in her throat, driving the blade upward. She felt it stab through the woman's soft palette then gore sliding down the blade and across her fist.

Using the dying woman as a shield, Mesa pushed Korgan forward and shoved her into the nearest gunman. While the man grappled free, Mesa ran to the shattered window and the pew that was pressed up against the wall.

Bullets struck the pew, splintering the wood as Mesa's foot connected. She leapt, grabbing onto the window ledge, her shoulder howling in agony. Broken glass bit into her hands, and she cursed the pain. More gunfire echoed in the rectory, and she could hear the semi-automatic rounds pocking into the wall. She pulled herself up, then glass cut across her belly, slicing her T-shirt to ribbons as she slung herself through the window. She screamed as a bullet struck her thigh, then she was falling.

She landed on packed dirt, desert scrub, and broken glass. She forced herself to move. The shards cut her hands, knees, and forearms as she worked to get her feet back under her, her thigh protesting.

In all the commotion, she hadn't even noticed that Kaizhou's commNet feed had gone dark.

Mesa forced herself to run. Each step made her wounded leg quiver with a pain that threatened to fell her. Her racing heart sent angry throbs and shooting lancets through her shoulder. Despite the more serious injuries, the shallow cuts across her hip and nose fought to make themselves noticed. Glass was embedded in her palms, but she did not have time to worry about that. She ran.

Her slow plodding strides must have resembled something from a horror movie—Frankenstein's monster being chased by well-armed, well-armored village folk or a shuffling zombie fleeing its inevitable massacre. Lights splashed across her, and she could clearly see the men taking aim. The sudden illumination surprised them, and the throaty growl of the Jeep sent a resonant, booming bass through the quiet stillness of Last Chance Road.

Mesa wanted to feel joy, but she hurt too much to rejoice. The Jeep crashed forward, scattering the men, and hurtled toward her. Kaizhou mashed the brake to the floor, turning the wheel hard, and skidded into a one-hundred-eighty-degree turn, facing the gunmen.

"Run," he yelled. "Go!"

*Oh, no.* She tried to protest, to get the words out, but a darker voice overruled her and rallied her to move. To go forward was suicide.

Kaizhou gunned the Jeep forward. The side of the vehicle clipped one of the soldiers who was too slow to move out of the way. The maneuver was a distraction, an attempt to draw the men toward him and away from Mesa.

*Go!* the voice screamed at her, but beneath the pounding inside her skull, she couldn't be sure who the voice belonged to. She followed the command, though, and ran.

Kaizhou threw the Jeep into reverse, backed up enough to get the solider in his high beams, and launched forward again. The grill caught the man's face, and the Jeep rocked as its wheels rolled over the prone figure. Throwing the Jeep into reverse once again, Kaizhou slammed on the gas and maneuvered the rear wheels over the man's skull. The rear of the vehicle jolted over the bump as it ground through bone.

His victory was short-lived, but it had distracted the men, giving Mesa the time she needed. The open top provided him no security whatsoever as the remaining two soldiers regrouped and took aim. They opened fire, decimating Kaizhou in a hail of bullets.

Mesa heard the gunfire—and the wailing death of her first love.

Tears clouded her vision as she ran into an abandoned, half-built stretch of a suburban subdivision. Her shuffling gait took her through the small development and into the desert beyond. Her feet moved across dry and crunchy scrub.

A small idea forming, she let the backpack fall from her shoulder. Releasing the weight was an instant gratification. She dug around in her bag, listening for the approach of the men, but heard nothing.

The stale cigarettes were buried at the bottom, beneath dirty clothes and ammo clips. She fished them out, pulling the lighter free. She took a knee, and her thumb flicked the striker. A small flash of light blossomed in the darkness— once, twice, three times. The fourth took the spark and produced a flame.

"There!" a husky voice shouted, but she didn't care.

She held the flame to the scrub, waiting for it to light. The burn was slow, and the men were fast.

"Shit," she whispered. "C'mon."

The small diamond of fire danced and skirted the dry

green firs, sending gray smoke wafting into the air. "C'mon," she urged, checking on the soldier's approach.

They rushed forward, guns at the ready and tucked close to their bodies in two-handed grips. They kept themselves turned slightly to present a smaller profile.

With a small crackle, the scrub caught fire. After that, it moved quickly and spread with a ravenous hunger, stretching to the other branches, engulfing them and seeking more fuel.

She aimed her gun just as the men were in range and ready to fire upon her. She fired twice at each man. The hot, spent shell casings fell into the scrub.

Smoke curled around her, choking her. The fire grew larger.

She turned, keeping crouched low, coughing into her arm and trying not to inhale the rising wall of smoke.

Gunshots tore through the air, and she felt their passing heat, too close. She shuffled forward, flames leaping at her back. In the still air, the smoke formed a dark shroud that she hoped was thick enough to obscure her.

The soldiers were firing blindly through the rising inferno. Geysers of sand burst into the air as bullets scoured the earth around her. As the fire spread, aided by a soft wind, its heat worsened. Its appetite expanded farther and farther, unquenched.

Her body aching, Mesa forced her feet forward. *One in front of the other,* she urged, hoping she didn't burn to death in the horror she had created.

The flames followed her, growing as they reached the green banks of the Humboldt River. Her eyes stung from the smoke, and she was gasping for air—she couldn't crouch low enough, thanks to her bleeding, shaky thigh.

She fell forward, exhausted. A lick of flame lashed out, scoring her forearm. Her leg felt warm, and she noticed, with an uncomfortable degree of distance, that the ankle of her pants had caught fire. She kicked in the scrabble and rolled, trying to put the flame out while at the same time kicking herself away from the all-consuming monster. The roar of the fire and the rushing scream of the river deafened her.

She was caught in the fire, surrounded. She coughed violently, and blood from her scored hip pooled into the waist of her pants. Her eyes refused to open, and her lungs fought to expel the burning contagion she had inhaled. Her legs were working uselessly. Her ruined hands scraped through the grass, dust, and sand, aggravating the lacerations further.

An impossible coolness kissed her fingers, and she kicked hard, letting it consume her. The chill engulfed her with a spreading wetness, pulling her under, and she couldn't breathe. Still, her lungs ached, and she fought to rise. Then her face broke through the rough surface of the river. Gasping for air, she swallowed dirty water then threw it back up, her stomach a blistering sore. Feeling punished all over, she kicked, trying to find solid land and trying not to panic. Then her swimming lessons took over. The water was unreasonably cold, and she let herself go limp, allowing herself to float. The current wasn't as strong as she had thought. Her fear had given it fuel and momentum.

In the distance, the firelight bloomed against the night, and she let herself relax for a moment. The river carried her farther away, then her arms moved with all the ease of leaden weights, forcing her toward the banks and onto land.

Mesa couldn't even begin to take account of all the aches and pains, or decide where to start. She was too tired to deal with the first-aid kit in her sodden, waterlogged bag, and she desperately needed a moment to rest.

But that dark, slithery voice wormed through her mind and demanded that she get up.

"Who are you?" Mesa asked, her voice quiet against the cool evening air. Her skin turned into gooseflesh, and she rubbed her arms with her hands, trying to salvage some warmth.

That voice was there, though, lurking. She felt her world tip and topple. She thought she was going mad, her mind dropping into an abyss.

She asked again, out loud despite the voice being locked inside her own mind, her voice raspy, "Who are you?"

*My name is Alice Xie. It's time we spoke.*

# CHAPTER ELEVEN

JADE HELD THE SMALL PORCELAIN cup, inhaling the steam and letting the heat warm her hands. She breathed deeply, enjoying the scent of the jasmine tea and cloying sweetness of agave nectar. She wished she could drink it.

The warmth felt nice against her bandaged fingers. The index and middle fingers of her left hand jutted forward. They'd been broken, reset, and splinted together. Gauze was wrapped around each fingertip, covering the tender, delicate skin that had been exposed after they'd pried off each nail with pliers.

She set the cup aside and reached for a glass of ice water beside the tea pot. She winced slightly as the rim met her swollen lips then took a careful sip. She swallowed, unable to remove the taste of copper from her gums, and kept the fluid to the undamaged side of her mouth.

"How is it?" Maxwell Schaeffer asked, nodding at the tea.

"Fine," she said, the word bulkier than it should have been. "Smells nice."

Schaeffer was a handsome man. In any other context, he would have been downright doable. He had thick, wavy brown hair and eyes that reminded her of melted fudge. The expensive mocha-colored tan played nicely with his blue pinstripe suit and crisp white shirt. The platinum cufflinks were the shape of a hollow triangle, the Greek letter delta, the symbol of Daedalus, an ancient mythological craftsman. Daedalus was also the name of the technology firm Schaeffer worked for.

The company had begun as a cutting-edge fertility treatment center before expanding into other medical avenues and winning several important government research contracts. More than a decade ago, they'd unveiled medichines and offered the nano-devices to the public as a free booster shot. This selfless act had made the company a public darling, and despite controversial maneuvers that had, at the time, allied them with the US industrial-military complex, they'd largely been given a free pass to operate without restriction. Buying politicians in bulk had certainly aided the company's executives' ambitions of expansion.

Overnight, they had altered Jade's opinion on the integrity of the company. They'd gorged on her memories and peeled her like an onion, simply because they could. By breaking her down physically, they could wear out any mental blocks she might have in place. For Schaeffer, her memories hadn't been enough. He had needed to hear her confess and make it clear that he was the one in control. All of the power in their new dynamic rested solely with him.

The experience had been unpleasant, to say the least.

"I can get you some food," he said. "A smoothie, maybe?"

"This is fine," she said, holding the glass of cold water, her jaw wired shut. The wires made speaking difficult, but given how raw her throat felt from the hours of endless agony and screaming, speaking wasn't high on her list of things to do.

She gazed out over the railing at the city below. The airship had been making a lazy route across the Western Seaboard, and the buildings and vehicles below were small and insignificant. Fortunately, the arc of clear Dura-Plastic kept the wind down but not enough to prevent a chill.

Schaeffer offered her a large smile, shining his perfectly straight pearly whites at her. She hated that smile.

"Why don't you tell me about Mesa Everitt?" he asked.

*Ah, finally, the nice approach.* They'd softened her up with hellish torment, asking the same questions over and over, cross-referencing her answers with the memories they'd pulled from her skull before plumbing deeper through the mnemonic layers.

Of course, she'd lied to her inquisitors, mostly out of fear but also to protect her friend, hoping she could call their bluff by lying. Her days as pickpocket, a thief, and a memorialist had put her on the receiving end of interrogations multiple times. Corporate, private police, the Catholic parishioners she had been entrusted to as a teen back in London—they were all the same. All she had to do was stonewall them and not give them any extra rope to hang her with. Schaeffer's methods had been different, though, and the first nervy spikes of fear punched into her heart when his guys had showed her the cold metal tools of her interrogation. That was when the pliers came out, and one by one, they tore away her resolve, asking the same questions in between each yanked nail. The pain and the promise that things would go easier on her if she told the truth brought forth a flood of honesty that made her hate herself.

Then muscled hands gripped the sides of her face while her mouth was pried open, and cold metal instruments slid against her tongue. A clamp encircled her rear right molar, and it wiggled painfully. The gurgled scream felt rough in the back of her throat. A brittle crackling noise shot her eyes wide, then a shooting lancet of pain was followed by a fresh hollow void and a coppery-iron tang trickling down the back of her mouth. She cried freely. They'd held the grisly tooth before her, allowing her a moment to study it through the fog of tears before discarding it. The dentist tore loose another molar before the questioning resumed. Schaeffer had stood beside her the entire time, leering, clearly enjoying her agony. They pried away at her mind and her body until all of her answers verified what they seemed to already know.

Once her hands and mouth were ruined, the guards had returned her to the sterile white room, dumping her inside the door in silence. She mewed like a wounded animal until exhaustion claimed her. Through it all, there had been no indications of time, no sunlight, no stars, no windows. Nothing more than sleek whiteness. When they'd collected her an hour ago and brought her outside to the airship's lido deck, she was surprised to see the sun and more surprised to find herself in flight. The ship was so quiet and smooth that discerning their travel was impossible.

"Earth to Jade," Schaeffer said, drawing her attention away from the Dura-Plast screen with the snap of his fingers.

*Condescending fuck.* She hated when men snapped their fingers at her, as if she were a pet they could summon.

"Please don't make this more difficult than it has to be. You've been through a lot already. Don't think for a single minute that you've been through the worst of it. Do you understand me?"

"Yeah." The word was hoarse and felt confessional despite its brevity. It carried the rankness of defeat.

"Ah! Good!" A large parody of a smile was plastered across his face as he clapped in good cheer. She was disappointed they'd taken away the silverware. She wanted to pluck his eye out with a butter knife.

"Now, tell me about Mesa Everitt," he said again.

All he wanted was to hear her say the words. It didn't matter that he could go right into her skull and suss out the truth. She had to speak it to him. Resigned, it took her a long time to force out the words.

"What do you want to know?"

"What does she know of her time in LA?" he asked.

She shook her head. "You'd have to ask her."

"Jade," he said, "I'm asking you. Now, before we go any further with this, with your tough-gal act, I want to remind you that we stopped with breaking two of your fingers and your jaw. OK? We took two of your teeth. We tore off all your fingernails. You know this, right? I mean, that's just where we stopped. There's all kinds of ground we could still cover.

"Now, I'm being pleasant here, yeah? Making conversation. Giving you tea. It doesn't have to be difficult anymore, unless you make it difficult. How about I quit with the monologue and you answer my fucking questions?"

It didn't even matter at all that she couldn't drink the tea. He hunched over the small art deco table, forcing her to meet his eyes. With his eyebrows raised, he seemed entirely earnest.

"I don't know what she knows of LA," Jade said. Her cheeks burning, she added a contrite "That's all I meant."

"OK. OK, see? Now we're getting somewhere."

"I don't think she remembers anything. Whatever was done to her, it fried her brain pretty good."

"Have you ever noticed her engage in odd behaviors? Say anything weird?"

"No," Jade said, thoroughly confused. This wasn't the first time they had asked that question, but no one had ever clarified what it was supposed to mean or why it was being asked.

"How much of her memory did she recover? Artificially,

I mean, like by mems."

Jade shrugged, not sure how to quantify it. "Bits and pieces. Not much. She's always looking for more."

Schaeffer sat back in the chair, chewing the inside of his cheek. It made his lips purse in a prissy way, and she averted her eyes.

"How long did you work for Alice Xie?"

Jade canted her head, thrown by the question. That was the first time Xie had been brought up. "A few years."

"As a memorialist?"

Jade nodded.

"Before that?"

"Odd jobs here and there."

"Aw, c'mon now. No need to be shy. I've been through all your mems, darling."

"Pickpocket jobs. B&Es."

"What a waste," he said.

She shrugged. "Why all the questions?"

"Baseline test," he said, without any hesitation.

She screwed up her face in confusion, at least as much as she could tolerate, but he pressed on.

"When Alice died, you received a data packet. Tell me about it."

"It went out to multiple memorialists," she said, tripping her way through the syllables.

He shrugged. "I know. Don't worry, though. You're the last one still alive. You should be honored and grateful we're having this conversation."

She rocked back in her chair, surprised at his forthrightness. She hated how he constantly had the upper hand. She hated going through all of his questions when he plainly knew the answers. *And "baseline test"? What the hell's he mean by that?* "It was a bunch of research jargon. Didn't mean anything to me."

"Unfortunately, Jade, it meant a hell of a lot to Alice

Xie. And it meant a hell of a lot to us at Daedalus. You see, Alice was passing along company secrets that she really had no right to. And when each of you received that data packet, you unfortunately all became accomplices. It's my job to clean up these kinds of messes."

"No, wait," Jade began, but she didn't know where to go from there. The words unraveled and withered away. She'd expected a greater level of brashness from Schaeffer, but instead he sat there, calmly, still.

He stared at her blankly then cracked a smile. "Huh? Had you there, right?" He pointed his index finger at her, thumb cocked in the air. He dropped the thumb and said, "Pew, pew pew." He laughed.

Then his face screwed up into seriousness. "How'd you get to know Mesa, anyway?"

Jade closed her eyes, her cheeks burning with shame. "Alice," she whispered, the name burning her raw throat. "Those were my instructions—to keep an eye on her."

"Were you supposed to do anything with the information Alice had sent you?"

"I don't know," she said glumly. "It's not as if I could ask her. She was dead, remember?"

"But still, you went to Washington. Joined the enclave there. Why?"

"What else was I supposed to do?"

"You must have been very loyal to Alice. What did she ever do to earn that?"

A pain pierced Jade. She hadn't felt it during the day previously, that stabbing, gut-deep wound. "She was a friend. She was nice to me."

Schaeffer seemed to consider the words then nodded. "And Mesa? You've very loyal to her, too. She's lucky to have you."

"I love her," Jade blurted.

"Maybe you recognize a little bit of Alice in her, huh?

What do you think?"

Jade's eyes glazed over. "No," she said, spitting the word out, hard. "They're nothing alike."

"I wouldn't say 'nothing,' but whatever."

"What's the point of all this, huh?" Jade asked. "Why all the questions? You already cleaved my mems apart. You know all the answers. What's the fucking point?"

"You talk a lot for a girl with a busted-up mouth. You know that?"

He sighed and scratched at his forehead. "Look, we're just talking here. Just trying to get a baseline."

"You said that before. Why? A baseline for what?"

Instead of answering, he took a slow sip of tea, appraising her while he drank. "How much do you know about body-shifting?"

The question knocked her off balance. She batted her eyes in confusion. She tried to speak, but he held up his hand, shushing her. He spoke for a while, and the bottom of her stomach fell open. She thought of Mesa and reflected on Schaeffer's earlier words regarding her friend and Alice Xie.

"What do you need me for?" she asked. The words came slowly and painfully. "What do you need a baseline for?"

He rocked his head side to side, equivocating on the answer. Finally, he said, "For a proof of concept."

# CHAPTER TWELVE

Cold, her back caked in river mud, Mesa tore loose a stretch of medical tape and pressed it against the gash across her belly. The shallow cut grew progressively deeper as it wended across her stomach and became a bone-deep mouth over her hip bone. Her lips pressed into a fine line as the tape pulled the skin together.

She had to get the blood loss under control. The medichines coursing through her system could only do so much, and the collective nano machines were busy dealing with the damage to her leg. That wound screamed with protestations. The little healing bots were triaging broken vessels, repairing tissue, and breaking down the bullet into atomic base components for recycling or waste. Their artificial intelligence prioritized injuries, doling out work orders. The gunshot wound was their number-one task.

The cuts across her midriff and face were low priority and presented minimal immediate danger.

Still, bleeding was bleeding. And if the medichines were coldly calculating and assessing severity, she was on her own to stop it. She tore off another strip of tape then glued it over her nose and across her cheek. The top part of the tape upset her vision like a dark ghostly image along the lower edge of her sightline, but she could deal with it.

Every part of her body ached. She lay back down, resting against the silt of the riverbank, letting the thin grassland tickle her burnt arms. The sensation was unpleasant, but she couldn't compel herself to move.

*Get up.*

And then there was that. That fucking voice in her head.

*I'm going insane,* Mesa thought.

*You're not. Now, get up. We have to go.*

*I don't need this right now. This fucking nervous breakdown. Not now.*

*That's not what this is. Trust me. You'll die if you do not move right now.*

*What are you?*

*I told you, my name is Alice Xie.*

*That's who, not what.*

*Semantics. Get up.*

*No.*

*Goddamnit, get up!*

*If I don't?*

*I told you. You will die. They're coming for you.*

Mesa laughed, a sudden insight hitting her. She had no idea if Alice was correct or not, but what the hell, right? *No,* Mesa said. *They're coming for you.*

The voice grew silent, caught off guard, maybe. Mesa smiled in spite of herself. Still, she thought Alice had a point.

*In for a penny, in for a pound, huh?*

She practically felt the curl of a smile growing in her

mind and saw it with her mind's eye. She could sense the edge of a foreign thought, which she could not quite grasp, and she probed deeper for it, knowing that she was wandering into the dark, dangerous waters of this other being.

*You're much like your father, you know,* Alice said, rocking Mesa into silence.

*Fuck yourself,* Mesa said. She worked her good leg under herself and stood clumsily. The world canted for an instant before righting itself. She took a tentative step forward, limping up the river bank. Her clothes were sodden, and she stank of polluted water. As the earth gave up the ghost of its heat and the air grew colder, she wondered if she wouldn't still die out here. Exposure, hypothermia—both were good options.

She figured her false credentials were worthless. She'd been stupid to reach out to Korgan. Protocols existed for a reason; lock-down was important for a reason. But she'd been trying to be a do-gooder. She'd compromised the only true safeguards between her and that team of killers. And Kaizhou... she forced her thoughts away from him, focusing solely on moving and putting more distance between herself and them. Kaizhou had killed himself so that she could live, and she could not let his death be in vain.

She limped away from the basin, a hand pressed against her belly to keep pressure on the still-bleeding wound. The gore and her movements conspiring to pull the tape's sticky side away from her skin, she shuffled through the grass until it gave way to the sandy claims of desert expanse.

She pulled down a sat feed and mapped it against her now-blown and useless cred. The terrain was a jagged mess, and civilization was far to the rear. Going back that way meant walking directly into the path of a couple of heavily armed men intent on murdering her. She was not entirely without options, though, and one promising target presented itself if she could move fast enough.

*An old silver mine*, Alice said, pointing out the claim marker that had caught Mesa's eye, as well. Again, she felt the curl of a smile deep within her mind.

Steadied by a goal, her spirits buoyed, she walked, dragging her injured leg behind her. It was momentarily useless but getting stronger.

With the inferno raging at their backs, Boyd and Kaften hurried back to their vehicle. The scrub was catching fast, and with the wind picking up, the fire would be spreading into the backyards of the abandoned subdivisions soon. Kaften had no desire to be there when that happened.

Crassen's body was trapped beneath the Jeep, where the driver was still slumped over the steering wheel.

Boyd looked at the body then back to Kaften, the question apparent in his eyes.

"No time," Kaften said. "We leave him to the flames."

Jogging along Last Chance Road, sodden with sweat, they navigated the alleyways and cut through empty lots. An ancient electric H6 was parked a mile away, far enough to not be directly tied to them if the authorities were called in. Before approaching the church on foot, they'd taken the time to wipe down the vehicle; if the worst should happen, it would simply be another abandoned vehicle in an empty suburb.

They circled the block cautiously, maintaining operational security and looking for anybody who may have been looking out for them. The neighborhood was silent and lifeless.

Across the dark roofs, flickers of approaching flames danced.

Kaften climbed in behind the wheel, spun the Humvee around, and put Elko in the rearview mirrors. He took

Lamoile Highway to the Pinion exit then took that road to its dead end. The tires bumped off the edge of the paving and rocked back down onto dusty shoals. Kicking up clouds of sand as the wheels bit down and gained traction, it sped north through the desert.

Boyd worked the computer, his eyes glazing over as he focused on the commands being broadcast across his retinas. Kaften drove, following the current of the river, while Boyd busied himself with the orbital deploys, recalling a cluster of drones Earth-side. In half an hour, they would see the aerials glowing brightly as the drones reentered the atmosphere over Nevada, like shooting stars barreling directly toward Elko. In the meantime, not wanting to distract himself while driving, he ordered Boyd to pull a sat feed and do a quick territorial recon.

"Last Chance follows Humboldt pretty closely. We've got some suburbs to the northwest, mostly along the river and spreading south of it. Lakspur is coming up, and we'll be hitting houses soon. Abandoned probably.

"Lots of roads, lots of land. Not much population, though. Hardly any developments at all, really. A few stabs at settlements, but other than that..." He shrugged. "All kinds of flammable stuff, though."

"The cowboys and whores will have their work cut out for them," Kaften said. He didn't care one way or the other about what happened to those shitkickers and their backwater gambling den. "Shame about the brothels, though," he added.

"Farther north, we got an open-pit silver mine."

Kaften considered it, but the open expanse of land worried him. The desert was too vast to hunt down a single person, even if she was on foot and wounded. She could have made her way to the suburbs or the settlements along the outer reaches. The fire was an issue, though, and if that didn't get under control soon, it could grow into a violent wildfire.

Mesa Everitt, and the data locked inside her skull, was too important to leave to chance. They had to find her. They had no other options. Schaeffer had been clear on that, and Kaften wasn't stupid. He knew the score.

Blind luck was better than no luck at all. He rubbed his hand across his face, trying to smooth away the tiredness. He decided to keep driving and plot out an ever-widening circle on the off chance they found her. In a half hour, the drones would be overhead and spread far and wide, hunting his prey for him.

*What the fuck are you? A virus or something?* Mesa asked.

Again, she felt that smirk coiling in the back of her mind. This presence, this *other*, was cold and deliberate. Vicious.

*I honestly hadn't thought of it that way. But I suppose it's apt enough.*

*How are you in my head?* Mesa asked. *Who are you?*

After a moment, a flood of memories scorched her brain, akin to a levy breaking. The dangerous storm-driven waves crashed through, intent on havoc. The sudden impulses were staggering, and she lost her footing and fell, outstretched palms crashing into the scrub. Dry, skeletal leaves poked and stabbed at the lacerations crisscrossing her hands.

Her brain ached. Hell, her whole body ached. But this... this sensation was unlike anything she'd experienced before. She'd tripped on DRMR plenty over the last few years, trying to recover as much data on herself as she could while experiencing the joys and horrors of others.

She'd assaulted her brain with foreign stimuli, with the chemical dumps of pain and pleasure that composed the memories of strangers. And still, none of that was similar.

Alice's personality was more akin to a foreign invasion, an army of thoughts storming Mesa's ill-defended beachhead then opening fire. The shock-and-awe assault of memories was impossible to defend against. It was mind-rape that left her immobile, and making any sense of the stimuli overloading her nerves was impossible.

She caught a glimpse of familiarity—a hand scrambling to her neck, trying to work her fingers beneath the coils of wires wrapped around her throat, choking her to death as the world turned gray and fuzzy around the edges.

*I've dreamed this*, Mesa said.

*You've* remembered *this*, Alice corrected her.

*But this never happened*, Mesa insisted, pointing to her slack form, her other self, prone on the table covered with butcher's paper.

*Not to you.*

Her brain felt blistered, and each heartbeat sent a throbbing ache shooting through her skull. The evening's stars and moon suddenly burned too brightly, and she shut her eyes against them, hoping to blot out the pain.

She reached out, her fingers scraping the earth, collected dust and sand into thick wedges beneath each nail, trying to drag herself forward. Too weak to stand, she kicked loosely with one leg. The pots and pans hammering in her skull left her nauseated. She coughed, her stomach clenching violently and shooting forth the food from hours ago. The image of Jonah choking Alice Xie to death was imprinted in her mind's eye.

Suddenly, she knew too much. But none of it was her knowledge. Instead, it was the infestation of another woman's vile perspective. *You kidnapped me. You destroyed my mind. You killed me.*

*You're still alive*, Alice said.

*But I'm not me! Don't you get that? You killed me. All so you could—what?—hitch a ride inside my corpse? Take over my mind, my body. You destroyed everything.*

Alice was silent, nothing more than a lurking presence riding out the storm of invectives, waiting for quiet. She let Mesa wear herself down.

Then, after a moment of silence, Mesa asked, *How did you do it?*

Alice smiled. Mesa's curiosity was beginning to override her need for anger, and she felt as if she'd stepped into a bear trap. Alice was cohabitating in her mind, which meant the memories were there, but Mesa was too weak to search for them. She was struggling to build walls, to partition these two halves of these selves into separate corners of her mind.

*A simple bio-fi connection and a dead-man's switch,* Alice said. *When my heart stopped beating, my DRMR unit used those precious last seconds of brain activity to send out a data packet. Your mind was already blanked, which made insertion a simple matter. You were my life raft.*

*Why now?* Mesa asked.

*You needed to heal, and I needed to rest.*

Mesa attempted to mount a protest, but a darkness, which felt keenly *Alice* stopped her before she could speak.

*Body-shifting is a delicate process,* Alice said. *I wiped your mind and chemically destroyed your memories. This wiped out all resistance, all traces of who you were. But I couldn't simply upload myself and take over. I had to repair the damage and kick-start your brain back into being able to form and retain memories. I never had that chance, thanks to your father. He interrupted the process, so my last-chance data transfer was into an empty void. You were brain dead, Mesa, but still alive. And I was nothing more than a dormant collection of ones and zeroes.*

*You had to get better,* she continued. *Your brain needed time to rebuild, to recover, to get used to shaping and storing memories. The stronger your brain got, the more my data was allowed to bleed through. In essence, we've been growing together, sharing this body, recovering ourselves.*

Mesa asked, *So you're what? A ghost in the machine?*

Alice smiled. *We're each other's ghost, dear.*

Her words sent a chill through Mesa's spine. She closed her eyes, wishing she could sleep. But that was impossible. She—*they*—needed to move, to run, to put more space between them and Elko. She needed to regroup, regather, and figure out the next steps.

But they had no time.

In the distance, a faint yellow glow broke the horizon. A horizontal shaft of light began rising above the desert floor.

Her thoughts were slow and gummy. *Is that...* she began, but the words were molasses in her brain.

*It's them*, Alice said, her voice icy.

Twenty-seven mini-drones streaked through the sky, burning brightly as they entered the Earth's atmosphere and arced toward Nevada, leaving silver contrails.

Kaften watched them fall and disappear into the high altitudes. The drones ran silently while Boyd tracked them in layers of feeds piped into his retinal displays. They broke off into a pre-programmed flight pattern, actively seeking a single girl in the desert, using an array of active motion, heat, and sonar sensors as well as high-resolution night vision.

On the ground, Kaften maneuvered the H6 through unmaintained, pot-holed streets, having followed the Humboldt River into a deserted housing development. To their rear, the wildfire was eating its way through the shadescale and spindly sagebrush, spreading in all directions. They wouldn't be going back to Elko, if there was even going to be an Elko to go back to.

Kaften had activated the night-vision display on his retinal implants, turning the world into vivid layered shades of greens and blacks. He kept his head moving, his eyes scanning all directions, meeting the rear-view and side-view mirrors, as well. He sucked at his top front teeth, an old nervous habit he'd picked up from his father, along with a host of others. Smoking cigarettes, chewing the inside of his lips until white sores formed then rubbing his tongue against them, and constantly picking and chewing at his cuticles until they bled—all were learned behaviors that lived on in him long after his old man had passed.

"Anything yet?" he asked.

"No" was all Boyd said, his voice distant, lost in concentration. "Wait, yeah, maybe. I think we got her."

"Where?"

"She's northwest of us. The river carried her farther than I'd thought, but she's tracking toward the east."

"What's there? A settlement, a town, what?"

Turning the Humvee north, Kaften sought out a break in the road, suddenly itching to go off-roading again.

"Maybe a mine. Yeah, it's an old abandoned silver mine."

"Keep the drones on her. How far out?"

"Five, ten minutes. Less if you step on it."

Silently, Kaften cursed the drones for not bearing armaments. They were strictly for surveillance and didn't carry any methods for resolution or deterrence of threats. Unlike the Kessler op, they couldn't simply bomb the bitch from orbit and leave her charred, smoking husk of a corpse among the mice and thrashers. The PRC wasn't shy about broadcasting its arsenal and using drones to carry out hostilities within their own borders; they were, after all, a functioning military presence. Daedalus, on the other hand, was corporate, and the shareholders frowned upon drone violence, especially if it opened the doors to an inquiry as to why private military were being deployed in a Free State. Messy wet work carried out by a human that couldn't be traced back to the company was another story entirely.

When Mesa Everitt died, it would be by their hands and their guns, up close and personal, and very, very human.

The horizontal shaft of light grew rapidly closer, and the wind carried the throaty growl of the H6 across the distance. Mesa's leg was wrecked. A rocky outcropping was close by but not close enough. If she could make it there, she would become a much more difficult target to run over. She wished she had more time to make it to the open-pit mine, but the thought was pointless. *Deal with what's in front of you right now*, she told herself.

She hobbled forward, the splash of light cresting across her, blinding her. She was too late. Mesa turned her head slightly, judging the distance. She had no chance of making it to the outcropping, but she refused to stand still and be ground into road kill.

She trudged forward, the H6 correcting course, staying lined up with her. The bright white lights were demonically aggressive, casting deep, stark shadows across the hardscrabble earth.

She crouched, still getting one foot in front of the other, but ready to spring. In her mind's eye, a soft countdown had begun.

*3...*

The driver was hidden behind an obsidian shield, an irresolute suggestion of a man but nothing more.

*2...*

The passenger window came down, and a gunman emerged, drawing on her. The H6 shifted slightly, popping rocks into dust beneath the heavy tire treads. Nearly right on top of her, it was only an arm's length away.

*1...*

Bullets pocked the earth, missing her entirely. She leapt

forward, pulled her legs up, close to her body, too slowly. She felt the ankle of her injured leg explode, bone crunching against metal as her knee careened off a headlight, a thousand points of pain as the glass casing ruptured, burying shards of itself into the thin layer of skin. Mesa landed clumsily, the sand scraping her face raw. The corners of her jaw clenched tight as she tried to bite back the scream.

Brakes squealed, and the backend of the Humvee fishtailed as the vehicle spun around to face her, sending up an arc of sand and grit that blinded her. Her eyes stung, and by the time she got a hand raised to protect her face, it was too late. Always too late.

Grinding her jaw hard enough to make her teeth ache, she forced herself to stand and meet her end head on. She was unsteady on her single foot, but her other leg was too ruined to take her weight.

The H6 idled in front of her, trapping her in its headlights.

The driver's side door opened, and a heavy boot crunched into the loose scrabble. The passenger repeated the movements half a second after the leader, covering her with the gun. Both were clad in black from head to toe, their faces hidden behind balaclavas. They watched her for a long, steady moment, maybe wondering what she would do.

Standing still and dying wasn't her plan. In one fluid movement, she reached to her waist, pulled the gun loose, and raised it. The smaller man fired, aiming low, but she twisted on her leg, presenting her profile to them. The bullet seared across the top of her belly. That oddly calm, cool detachment of battle glazed her, dulled her senses, and slowed the world down. While she was stepping aside, moving to the inside of the shooter's arm, she fired with a marksman's precision. A detached part of her felt the edges of Alice's influence as if the woman were a deranged puppeteer pulling her limbs and driving her focus.

The smaller man might as well have been a paper target. The bullets hammered into his face and punched out the back of his skull. He fell, his brain obliterated.

The second gunman stepped around the front of the car, his gun raised. The frag round punched through her shoulder, destroying the ball-joint and killing her left arm. She spun and fell, her face screwed up in anguish.

He stood over her prone figure. Her chest rose and fell with rapid, aching breaths. She kicked out at him and loosely connected with his hand, but the strike lacked force.

He smirked, clearly thinking that the kick was meant to be a serious effort and not a simple distraction. Mesa's hand shot up and opened before his face, flinging a fistful of grit at his eyes.

He blinked reflexively, his hand coming up too late. He took a swift step back.

Her one good leg shaky beneath her, Mesa sprung off her uninjured foot and threw herself at him. After having her shoulder blown apart, she'd lost the gun. At least she still had her knife.

Already off-balance and trying to step back, he toppled under Mesa's sudden collision, and she landed on him hard, striking him in the solar plexus with her elbow and driving all the wind out of his lungs.

After getting his arms up in front of himself, he sent a sharp palm strike to the underside of Mesa's chin. Her teeth clacked together, and her head snapped back. He kept his hand there, twisting her face up and away from him.

Her blade sliced across his throat, making a shallow cut. His hands flew to his throat in reflex, but he didn't have time to panic before she stabbed through the balaclava and punched the knife through his cheekbone.

She wrenched the blade free, jerking it slightly left to right. It had gone down hard and at an angle. He opened his mouth to cough out blood, eyes already going glassy. She stabbed down again, at his hands, then sliced through his fingers to get at the meat and gristle.

He reared up, the knife embedded in the hollow of his throat, three fingers sheared away, and jabbed those gruesome stubs into the ruined socket of her shoulder and twisted. She bellowed, her arm hanging limp and useless. She used her good hand to rip the blade out of his neck, opening a wide swath across the side of his throat.

Gore splashed against her chest and face as he fell back, his lifeblood a torrential geyser shooting forth from the neck wound. Dual waves of instant relief flashed through her as his hand fell away from her shoulder, but the pain lingered. She could nearly feel the sigh of relief from Alice, a breeze against the inside of her brain. The world around her had been reduced to a thin, foggy sliver, and her eyes grew heavy.

*No*, Alice said. *Not yet. You have more to do.*

She fell off her attacker and lay in the scrub beside him. Lazily, she reached toward his face and peeled away the ruined balaclava.

*Samuel Kaften*, Alice said.

Even though Mesa had never heard the name before, it carried an unsettling ring of familiarity.

*You know what to do*, Alice said.

She ignored the pain as she unshouldered the backpack and knelt before him. Tiny stones jabbed into her aching knee, which was already swollen. It and her ankle both strained against the fabric of her pants. She dug around in the backpack and found an antistatic bag, a bundle of chips already inside.

Despite the blood, in spite of all the fighting and death, she felt a gorge rise in her belly as she reached toward Kaften and turned his face. She found the data port behind his ear.

*I can't do this.*

*You can*, Alice said. *I can help you.*

Fingers trembling, Mesa probed at his scalp. It'd been

a few days since he'd taken a razor to the skin, and his skull was covered in rough stubble. She traced the wires running just beneath the surface of that thin layer of skin, following them north along the curvature of bone, feeling for the familiar change as the tips of her fingers stumbled across the metal cap.

She swallowed the vomit, saying again, *I can't do this.*

Alice gave no reply, but a firm mental push compelled her forward. The mental image and too-real sensation of her hand on Mesa's shoulder offered both comfort and strength.

Knife in hand, Mesa flipped the grip and drew the blade across Kaften's scalp. She cut deeper then, using the point of the blade, cut away at the muscle joining flesh and bone, peeling away a long strip of tissue.

Fused to the bone was a small metal cap. She pried it loose with the tip of her knife and reached into the core. She plucked loose the memory chip. She held the central repository of Samuel Kaften's entire life in the palm of her hand. An icy thrill ripped through her at the thought, alongside an uncomfortable sense of déjà vu. That sense of familiarity couldn't possibly belong to her, though, and she knew it was another ripple of Alice's memories invading her mind.

Mesa picked up on an unspoken thought—four simple words that Alice had not guarded from her. *Like father, like daughter.*

*What does that mean?*

Alice offered nothing more than a false smile.

Mesa was too exhausted to push her. She dropped the mem chip into the antistatic bag. Then she turned her head and threw up before she spent a few more minutes coughing up loose phlegm. She'd never felt so weak and bone-tired in her entire life. Alice gave Mesa the few minutes' rest that she desperately needed before she began needling her to move.

Unable to stand, Mesa scooted back to the Humvee,

pushing her butt across the desert with the aid of one arm. The behemoth was still idling, washing the corpses of the men who had come to kill her in a bath of brilliant white light.

Mesa smelled smoke in the air, but the flames were still some distance away. She pushed herself back, her palms and knuckles scraped raw, her behind aching. Finally, she reached the driver's-side door and realized she may as well have been at the base of Mount Everest for all the good it would have done her. To get into the Humvee meant enduring an insurmountable climb.

*Do it or die*, Alice chided her.

Mesa knew Alice was right, and that made her hate the foreign invader inside her skull with an even deeper passion. She got her good arm up onto the lower step and forced herself up, suddenly thankful for the years of endurance training, triceps dips, and squat thrusts. She was able to hook her butt up onto the edge of the foot well and bring her good leg up, then used her heel to push herself up and in.

She fell onto the seat with a shriek of agony as her ruined arm crashed sideways into the back of the seat then the center console. Panting heavily, she manhandled her crippled leg into the foot well, letting gravity bend her leg at the knee, scraping bone against bone. When her heel touched the ground, a lightning bolt of pain shot through her ankle.

Finally, she got settled in the seat, grateful that her right leg was OK and could operate the pedals. She took long, deep breaths, trying—and failing—to control the pain. Her whole body was on fire.

With her left arm, she reached across her body to uncomfortably pull the shifter into drive. The H6 lurched forward, and she spent another minute acclimating herself to the sensitivity of the pedals, as well as the sensitivity of her own limbs, which didn't seem capable of enduring much more.

Alice was behind her, though, sending encouraging thoughts, pushing her forward, pulling her strings, and manipulating her limbs. She refused to give up on her, even when Mesa was well and truly beyond wanting to give up. She wanted—and needed—sleep. But Alice refused to let her eyes close.

*We'll rest soon,* she promised. *But we need to put distance between us, these bodies, and that fire. You can do this. You have to do this.*

Again, Mesa hated how right that bitch was. *OK, fine. Let's do this.*

She pressed down on the gas, more smoothly this time, the massive vehicle more firmly under her control. Slowly, she built up speed, and moments later, Samuel Kaften was finally behind her.

After a while, Alice began to slip away. The night grew darker, and the world shrank and shrank. Then that, too, fell away.

172  MICHAEL PATRICK HICKS

# CHAPTER THIRTEEN

SCHAEFFER'S FINGERS CURLED AROUND THE cold tumbler. He shot back the whiskey, trying to soothe ragged nerves. Booze wasn't helping.

He rolled his head from shoulder to shoulder, stretching out the trapezius muscles where all the stress and tension were knotting together.

When that, too, failed, he tried to look at the bright side. *At least we don't have to invest any more money in Korgan, that psychotic little cunt.* Her loyalties had been too easily bought, but at least that situation had remedied itself.

Given his climb up the ladder at Daedalus, Schaeffer knew not to trust those who straddled both sides of the fence. He'd played that game himself in his younger years, and he knew ambition was a thirst that could never be slaked.

Losing three operators, though... that was a blow. The girl would disappear. She was smart. Most of that intelligence, he had no doubt, was because of Alice Xie.

*Another psychotic bitch.*

He poured off another two fingers of whiskey. *Why me?*

No matter. That was the job.

He gazed out the clear Dura-Plast window of his ship, *Alabaster,* at the city lights below, watching the trails of movement. White headlights came, and red taillights went. Bright office windows filled the spaces between darkened panes, like broken teeth in a gaping mouth.

He slung back the drink then pushed away from his desk. The heels of his loafers click-clacked across the marble floor to the entrance.

*Alabaster* was his pride and joy, the culmination of his success. When he'd bought the ancient sky freighter and had it restored, he'd known that he had truly made his mark. He conducted all of his business from what had once been the captain's quarters. Obviously, he'd had it gutted and expanded, but it was still thematically sound. It only made sense that a captain of industry would operate from the captain's quarters.

He boarded the lift, straightening his tie, and rode the small metal platform into the bowels of the ship. He was grateful that a large complement of crew was not necessary to the daily functions of *Alabaster,* and he rarely saw the twenty people he had hired to pilot and maintain the vessel. He did not generally enjoy dealing with people, unless it was to grind them beneath his heels. Once, purely by accident, he'd stumbled across the engine master, who was covered in black grime, but after switching him to the midnight shift, Schaeffer had not seen him again.

The panels and wall coverings had been removed to expose the maze of pipes, wires, and circuits. Schaeffer appreciated its old-world appearance and the sense of industry. Such an aesthetic was rare in the modern age.

At the end of the corridor, he ran his index finger across the security pad, making a complex squiggle and a wave of zig-zags. Recognizing the authorization code, the door popped open with a slight *whoompf* as air escaped.

Inside the white room, an old woman lay prone beneath the white blankets of a hospital service bed. A thick data cable ran from the port behind her ear and split off to a series of machines engulfing her body. Because the bedframe was slightly arched upward, she was able to follow Schaeffer with her eyes, but she said nothing.

Even if she did have something to say, speaking was impossible. A breathing tube was shoved down her throat, her respiration conducted by machine. When Schaeffer questioned her, the woman's answers were supplied via the cable to a thought-to-speech processor and a small bookshelf speaker.

Jade was next to her, holding the woman's hand. Schaeffer sat down in his usual chair, across from the women.

"Hello, Jade."

"You're a fucking monster," she said, staring at him.

Schaeffer clucked his tongue at her. "Tsk-tsk, now."

Jade rolled her eyes at him. Not for the first time, he recognized how happy he would be once they were finished with her. He was more than eager to begin human trials.

He ignored the insubordination and turned his attention to the old woman.

"Hello, Alice."

Jade held the old woman's limp hand in her own. Her skin was soft and thin, like crinkled tissue paper. She knew nothing of the shell that housed the mind of her old friend and mentor, Alice Xie, but the ramifications chilled her. Fear, sorrow, and anger all combated for superiority, exhausting her. She stared across the bed at Schaeffer.

"What did you do to her?" Jade asked.

"Nothing she wasn't already intent on doing to herself. Although, it did take some time to convince the higher-ups to proceed. Then, all we needed to do was simply find a suitable donor."

"She's supposed to be dead."

"And yet she's not. The miracles of modern science."

"I don't understand any of this," Jade said, her voice taking on a high-pitched whine of flustered annoyance.

"There's no need for you to."

"You brought me here!"

Schaeffer nodded, his hands folded in his lap. He leaned back in the chair, his eyes sliding over Alice's decrepit form. "Yes, to say goodbye."

Again, Jade glared at him, feeling lost in the woods.

"You see, Alice," he said, turning his attention to the old woman.

A surprising amount of strength and clarity dwelled in her eyes, and she locked onto his with no trouble.

"Your intel has been very valuable. We were able to find your friend here." He nodded toward Jade. "More importantly, we were able to find Mesa Everitt, which allowed us to learn some very unique things.

"The body-shifting protocols you stole, that you released into the wild—they work. And they work wonderfully. Unfortunately, it appears you've also made yourself a bit redundant. Daedalus has no need for two Alice Xies. Sadly for you, there's a younger, sexier model running about, and we're planning on trading up."

He flashed Jade a sly grin. "And that, my dear, is where you come in."

"I'm not bringing Mesa to you," she said, appalled.

He laughed. "No, no, I wouldn't expect you to. But that

perky little body of yours? Yeah, I think that'll get us close enough to her to take care of the rest."

"What are you talking about?"

He sat back, a cunning gleam in his eyes. She felt trapped by his predatory fox-like gaze.

"Alice here,"—he squeezed the old woman's breast roughly—"stole a bit of old tech from us and set about trying to replicate it. It didn't quite work out for her, or at least not as she'd hoped. Before Alice died, she sent out packets of information to several memorialists and a last bit of marching orders."

A faint glimmer of recognition hit Jade.

"You, of course, were told to find Mesa Everitt, if you could. And thankfully you did! Our med-sci division was responsible for helping Mesa's damaged brain regroup and move forward. We knew, thanks to Alice here, that a remnant of the original Alice Xie was hiding somewhere in that young girl's mind. We weren't able to repair the damage, but we at least were able to help her get back on her feet and take steps toward living a normal life. We were also able to put some small implements in her, simply for tracking and observational purposes."

Schaeffer regarded the old woman lying helplessly on the bed. "We were very eager to learn more about what had happened, but even with Mesa's brain fried, we had one avenue left. We mined the DRMR unit on the corpse of Alice Xie and plumbed her for information. When we learned that she had attempted body-shifting, we reopened old research files.

"The war in LA disrupted a lot of our work, knocked us back twenty years in R&D projects, cost us a shitload of money. There was a lot of administrative changeover, and a lot of people got sacked while Daedalus was sinking. We needed to rescue the ship, you see. It was a very tumultuous time for us, but science and warfare are nothing if not mutually compatible. Body-shifting was a high-concept idea that we'd tabled once the PRC invaded.

"Again, thanks to Alice, we recognized the potential in this pursuit once again. She'd gotten very, very close to actually doing it, all based on our own theoretical frameworks. So we reopened our work, and decided to go whole hog. And thankfully, we had what was arguably a very willing test subject."

"You threw Alice Xie into this old woman's body, just to see if you could?"

Schaeffer smiled. "Basically. Yeah."

He stood and stretched his legs. "It took multiple trials to perfect and observe. We didn't start off immediately with this crone. There were other practicalities to consider."

"Such as?" Jade's mouth had run dry, and the aches of her earlier tortures heated her face.

"Being plunked down into an unfamiliar body takes a traumatic toll on a human mind. We ran into several... complications, let's say."

A shiver went up Jade's arm, sending goose pimples along her skin. Slowly, she said, "What kind of complications?"

"The first subject ripped her own throat out with her bare hands and bled to death."

"The first? How many were there?"

"Twenty-seven. This Alice is number twenty-eight. This shell she is in, the previous owner suffered a severe stroke and became catatonic. Wiping her mind was child's play, and we plugged Alice in. Because she can't use her limbs and this body is kept alive by machines, transferal was much simpler. The psychological trauma is still present, mostly, but with a steady stream of injections and therapy, we seem to be making some remarkable breakthroughs."

"This is your idea of success?" Jade asked, making her disgust apparent.

"No, actually. Now, your friend Mesa, she's a win for

sure."

"And you've been monitoring her for three years?"

Schaeffer nodded. "Her and several other memorialists."

"Alice's distress packet," Jade said, piecing it together. "That's why those other memorialists were killed."

Schaeffer nodded, smiling slightly. "We began noticing a revivification of secondary brain activity, a secondary stream of consciousness, in your friend Mesa. After downloading the scans, it became apparent we had a match. Alice is still alive, or at least a part of her is, inside your friend's skull."

"And you thought she might have gotten into other people's heads, too. So you decided to start killing everybody."

"Oh, come now. You make it sound terribly crude. We couldn't risk this technology going mainstream. Yes, we tracked down the carriers of Alice's data packets and began eliminating them. Unfortunately, other memorialists began picking up their mems, and we were forced to expand our efforts at containment."

"You brutally murdered dozens of people."

"They were complicit, regardless of their cognizance or lack thereof. They were infringing on corporate technology and the theft of proprietary information. Alice gave them the keys to body-shifting. There is no way we could risk that information getting loose. What if it went rogue? Do you know what kind of disaster this would be? Our hands were tied."

"All because Daedalus would look bad if word got out."

Schaeffer shrugged. "It would be a PR nightmare."

"I'm not getting out of here alive, am I?" Jade asked.

"You're very astute," Schaeffer said.

Jade slumped in her chair. Her earlier conversation with the suit made more sense. These conversations, the torture, establishing a baseline—they'd been reading her chemical reactions, creating statistical analysis of behavior and emotion. The baseline was for something Schaeffer had called a proof of concept.

Observing the frail old woman, she began to get an inkling of what that concept was. "That's how you're going to get Mesa, isn't it?" she asked. "By doing to me what you did to her. You're going to destroy my mind and put somebody else in charge of my body."

"As I said, Jade, you're very astute."

Standing, Schaeffer stared down at the two women. "I'll leave you two for now. Alice, if you want, you can say your goodbyes now."

# CHAPTER FOURTEEN

The interior of the H6 was an oven. When Mesa pried open her gummy eyelids, she was sweating profusely, and her mouth was completely parched. She put one hand on the too-hot steering wheel to help peel herself away from the seatback. She'd sweated through her blood-stained pants, and her legs were glued to the seat. Her whole body was a catalogue of bruises, pain, and suffering.

After twenty minutes of idling, the vehicle's battery-saving measures had kicked in and turned off the car. She'd been too exhausted to notice and was lucky she hadn't baked to death. She rebooted the Humvee, grateful for the battery's charge and the one minor miracle in recent days. The AC belched out a blast of hot air, but in a few minutes, it would start running cool.

She opened the door—the desert heat was a pleasant

chill in comparison to the sweat box—and stood. Her knee and shoulder were still severely damaged. Her arm was immobile, and the knee couldn't take her weight. She needed protein, something to help kickstart the medichines and give them the necessary oomph to work harder. Beyond that, she desperately needed food and water. She'd tossed up the previous night's dinner, and she was severely dehydrated from vomiting, blood loss, and having sweated out her body's liquid reserves.

She pressed a hand to the side of the Humvee, using the behemoth for support as she limped toward the back hatch.

When the hatch lifted, she was caught with another blast of hot air. Turning, she rested her butt on the edge of the hatch then scooted inside.

For the cargo of a paramilitary hit squad, it was about what she'd expected and, in some respects, hoped for. She shoved herself toward a communications bank and rested against the console before hauling herself into the chair. The old-fashioned piece was redundant to the standard comm packs she was sure the soldiers had been installed with, particularly since the comm packs were a common enough commercial unit and a basic DRMR app. A physical comm unit, though, would tie them down to a particular place at a particular time and risk generating a feedback trace. Using that tech was risky, maybe, but it also made the evidence easy to walk away from and provided a level of disconnect between hardware and operator. In the end, she decided it was pretty smart.

She found guns, of course—all sorts of guns. She recognized the Glock sidearms, the H&K automatics, the Mossberg shotguns, all safety-clipped and secured to the wall, all unloaded. *Good precaution. Wouldn't want to hit a bump and accidently blow off the back of your skull.* Beneath the weapons racks was ammunition for each weapon.

Opposite the artillery were the provisions she'd been

hoping for. One bin held bottles of water, and another held brown envelopes she identified as MREs. She peeled open the zein packets, fished out the heater envelope, and filled that to the marked line with the bottle of water. She was pleasantly surprised to see that the entrée she had grabbed was pork rib. She dropped the entrée envelope into the flameless ration heater. The chemical pack was already turning the water warm, and she propped it up against the comm relays.

She'd never had an MRE before, but after the first bite, she learned why the pre-packaged food had earned its nicknames. Some called them "Meals Rejected by Ethiopians" or "Meals, Rarely Edible."

Her rumbling stomach reminded her she was in no position to be choosy and that the packets of food were a veritable banquet. She ate the pork then moved on to the crackers and peanut butter. She washed those down with water, finishing the bottle. She cracked open another bottle and mixed in the instant coffee. Stomach still growling, she finished the HOOAH! Bar in several large bites.

The twelve-hundred-calorie meal would help boost the medichines. In another day or two, she would be able to walk normally. The shoulder, though... that was going to take some time.

She took a deep breath, trying to steady her nerves for what came next. At waist level, flush with the comm area, was a drawer with a Red Cross logo on it. She fished out the combat tactical first-aid pack and rested it before her. A small mirror was built into the interior of the lid, and she had to play with the angle until it was just right.

Very slowly, she peeled back her ruined shirtsleeve. The fabric was shredded, pressed into the pulpy flesh below, and scabbed over. She whined to herself as she pulled, working the shirt loose and pulling it over her head then down and away from all the damage.

A chunk of shoulder was completely gone. The collarbone and the flesh above her breast were brutal affairs. The skin was raw ground meat, and she could see flecks of bone amid the globs of yellow subcutaneous fat. Light glinted off slivers and chunks of metal buried in the oozing wound.

The medichines would take a long time to break down the metals. She needed to heal sooner rather than later and get her arm back together.

The kit included a small needle and a jar of Novocain. She filled the syringe, clamped the plastic MRE spoon between her teeth, and bit down. Through her nose, she took a long pull of air, held it—then stabbed the needle into her ruined shoulder. She screamed around the spoon, and her eyes squeezed shut of their own accord. She pushed the plunger down, sending an icy crawl creeping slowly into the skin. She withdrew the needle. Her hand was shaking hard, and she dropped the syringe.

She'd bitten the spoon in half, and she spit both ends of the utensil onto the table. She extracted the Kelly forceps and unwrapped them from the sterile packaging. Tears ran freely down her face and mixed with rivulets of sweat.

She adjusted the mirror again, angling it to make it easier to spot the metal shards. Between the metal prongs of the forceps, she gripped the splintery shards and pulled. The metal was barbed on both sides, similar to a bee's stinger, and it tore open the pulverized flesh. The Novocain reduced the pain down to a very unpleasant plucking sensation, and she moved on.

Slowly, methodically, she extracted six more fragments then used a wad of gauze to blot away the fresh streaks of blood, wincing beneath each dab. She lifted the box, held it open, and used the mirror to explore the wound. The back of her shoulder was even worse—the rounds had expanded under the force of propulsion, and the shards that had traveled through her body had created larger exit wounds. All in all, the wound was nasty, and she was lucky to be alive and that her arm hadn't been blown off entirely.

She saw the tails of more metal shards in her breastbone and the area below her collarbone. Kaften's shot had hit her high, sparing her life by inches. She could have lost her head as easily as the arm. The pain and shock had been so terrible, she was only just noticing the barbs caught in the side of her neck. They were painful little pricks, but they'd merely dug shallow trenches.

After unscrewing the bottle of hydrogen peroxide, she dumped the cold liquid across the ground-up meat, down her scraped arm, and over her neck, letting it wash down her bare chest and across her belly, not caring about the waste. There were other kits, which she hoped she wouldn't need.

She realized that, at some point, the car had entered power-saving mode and turned itself off again. That little bit of air conditioning she'd felt had been a welcome reprieve, but she knew she had to be conscientious about saving the vehicle's battery life.

Exhausted and nauseated, she riffled through the storage bins surrounding her. She was good on water and MREs for at least two weeks. By the third row of bins, she hit the jackpot and found black cargo pants and a black tee. Both were too big for her, but a utility belt cinched the waist of the pants enough to loosely hang on her hips.

She sat down for a second meal, paying more attention to the selections than she had last time. After spending a minute digging around, her stomach making crazy loops and spasms for attention, she felt brave enough to try the pork sausage and gravy.

Satiated and searing with agony as the Novocain wore off, Mesa felt ready to get down to business.

*You knew that man. Kaften,* Mesa said.

*I did.* Alice's response came without delay, and Mesa had recognized her ethereal presence clouding her mind all the while.

*How?*

*It's a very long story.*

*Well, you seem to be very stuck in my skull, and I think we have time. So, spill.*

Mesa caught the ghost of a sigh as Alice prepared to speak.

*He's a private military contractor. Most of his work is for Daedalus. After the PRC invaded California, Daedalus was among the first corporations to extend an olive branch and work to ease relations. They were not shy about profiteering the region and getting in on the ground floor of the reconstruction efforts. Not all were in favor, and among some, any peace offerings toward the PRC were considered an affront.*

*They contacted me,* Alice continued, *using Kaften as a go-between. He was charged with eliminating what little remained of American hostilities in the Los Angeles region, and I provided him with weapons and access.*

*How do they know about you?* Mesa asked. *About us, I mean. Or, whatever this is. Why are they after me?*

*I don't know.*

*You sure about that?*

*What I mean is, there could be any number of reasons, really. I have theories.*

*OK, and? Let's hear it.*

Mesa could practically feel the rushing breath of another one of Alice's sighs inside her brain.

*How long have you been operating REMIND?*

The question caught Mesa off-guard, zipping at her

from left field. *What does that have to do with anything?*

*REMIND is a DARPA project, but much of the research was conducted through university research and project grants. Daedalus has extensive governmental contracts and is among the top-ranked funding agencies for university research programs. In a round-about way, Daedalus is as responsible for REMIND as DARPA is.*

*What are you saying? They're spying on me through a psychiatric app?*

*More or less, yes. You freely update it with your brain impressions and meet regularly with a virtual counselor, don't you? Where do you think all that information goes? Everything you do is watched, monitored, recorded. You're a memorialist—you know this. You cannot possibly be that surprised that you're being watched. You live under a constant state of surveillance. This is what you have embraced with your life, and you make it so goddamn simple for them.*

Mesa felt a swell of indignation rising inside herself. *If it upsets you that much, you're free to leave.*

Alice was contritely silent for a long moment while Mesa stewed.

*It's as much my fault as it is yours,* Alice said. *In the end, it's my own hubris that has led to this.*

*What do we do about all this, then?* Mesa asked, hardly believing that she was seeking the psychotic's input. But, really, she didn't see any other choice.

She unzipped the backpack, balancing the bag in her lap. She pulled out the contents one by one, taking inventory. The clothes all went into a pile, to be abandoned. The gun, ammo, and a pack of stale cigarettes, she lined up on ledge of the comm center.

*You wanted to go on the offensive earlier. That's what you told Kaizhou.*

Hearing his name come from Xie's lips was a brutal gut punch. She'd been focused on avoiding thoughts of him, of accepting his death even after having witnessed his harsh death.

*You don't get to say his name,* Mesa said.

*Do you want to avenge him, Mesa? Do you want to go after the people who have set all this in motion?*

"*You* did this! You set all this in motion." Mesa railed against the intruder in her mind, screaming out loud in the back of the Humvee. She upended the bag, scattering its contents across the comm terminal. She violently swept her arm through the clutter, flinging ammo clips and currency.

*You fucking did this to me! You killed my father! You killed Kaizhou! And Sri, and Ashita. Do you hear me? You did all of this. You fucking killed me!* Mesa let her anger crash over Alice Xie, unsure whether she was shouting at the woman solely in her head or out loud.

*You ruined my life. Do you understand that at all? You destroyed my mind, and then you fucking show up out of nowhere like this is all OK? Like you have any right to me at all? You don't know what the fuck you're doing.* She fell back against the padded chair, exhausted. Beyond exhausted.

After a long, quiet moment, she asked, *What did you do to me?*

She thought Alice was going to ignore the question, but then a crippling flood of memories washed over her hippocampus, breaking through the mental dam that divided her from Alice and splintering her mind.

Alice showed her everything, all of her memories, giving shape and form to Mesa's nightmares.

*I couldn't have done it without your father's help, Mesa. Jonah made all this possible.*

Mesa's stomached heaved, as if the entire organ wanted to rip free and escape the escalating madness. But she saw the essential truth behind Alice's thoughts: Jonah had killed for Alice and provided her with the memories of a dead man, who made the horrors of body-shifting possible.

*And then he killed me,* Alice said.

*Good,* Mesa replied, but the fight had been sapped from her.

Her fingers curled tightly around the fabric of the bag, and she twisted in the seat, turning away from the first-aid mirror. All she saw was an upturned and broken reflection that meant nothing anymore.

Then she saw the small black storage drive. She drove it into the port behind her ear. The kill stick initialized, and the menu prompts displayed across her retina display.

DO YOU WISH TO PROCEED? YES or NO.

Mesa considered Alice one last time and thought of Jonah choking her to death. Mesa was oddly proud of the man, even if she'd never truly known him. She said to Alice, *Now it's my turn, you sonofabitch.*

She gave a mental push.

YES.

# CHAPTER FIFTEEN

JADE'S FINGERS CURLED AROUND THE old woman's hands. She studied the faint streaks of purple bruising on either side of Alice's face. Much darker, nearly black bruising splotched the backs of her hands and crooks of her elbows. Jade wondered how many injections they were giving her and what kind of cocktails they were jamming into her when they rotated the needles across her body to avoid collapsing a vein.

The marks on her face were not from needles, though. Among the freshest scoring, she could make out the ghost of an open hand.

Curious, she pulled the blanket away from the old woman, her breath hitching in her throat.

One of Alice's legs was missing, amputated just above the knee. Three toes had been removed from her remaining foot, the injuries recent and inflamed with infection. Her shin was badly bruised, the knee a swollen black ball.

Jade lifted the hem of Alice's gown. The electronic translator made an odd warble that prompted Jade to glance up in time to see a trail of tears run down the craggy valley of the old woman's face. The rough thought-to-voice module was telling her "no." But Jade had already gotten a glimpse of deep purple finger marks on the older woman's thighs, and she pressed on despite the tears, protests, and embarrassment.

Alice's chest was a warzone of scars and swollen, discolored tissue. Her stomach, distended and battered, resembled a cut of raw beef. A long, thick stretch of deep blue was haloed by a greenish ring that faded to yellow at its margins. Her chest rose with a hitch as she took each stuttered breath, and Jade concluded that the woman had multiple broken ribs.

Upon being brought to the room, Jade had clung to the delusion that she was to say goodbye to her old mentor because, it seemed, Alice was plainly near death. But, as she learned more about Schaeffer, she knew she was merely another instrument of torment, the hours of Alice's life, as she had known it, fleeting and nearing their end.

"Why are they doing this you?" Her voice was still husky from her own torture, but even those memories were fleeting.

"Because they can," Alice said through the voice synthesizer's rough and edgy approximation of human vocals. "To punish me. To glean every last drop of information. To humiliate me, degrade me. To destroy me."

"But why? What did you do?"

"I stole from them."

"That's all?"

"That's enough."

Jade simply nodded. For most of her life, she'd known

only poverty, and she knew, too well, how much her financially sound betters looked down upon her. Much of Jade's education had come from the streets, and she had no formal documentation of such higher learning. She could raid a rival with all the proficiency of her corporate equivalents, steal all their money, and utterly destroy them. Because she didn't wear a suit or have an MBA, it was an unsanctioned criminal act. She could slick back her hair, buy a sharp blazer and a team of lawyers, and suddenly become untouchable. She could ruin lives with impunity, all in the name of business and shareholdings.

Life in her native London had been a hand-me-down existence. After hacking out a false ident and back-stopped credentials as a student with top marks, she was granted a visa to attend school in LA. A few worms in some random bank accounts netted her the cash to fly and disappear.

Never lucky, she'd arrived barely a month before the PRC attack. She hacked modestly, never taking too much from any single account, and rarely returned to the well more than once. Ashita had said she had mad skills, but both were high on posh at the time. Once the guns had started firing and the bombs had begun dropping, though, she was back to square one. The old, rich white people were among the first out of LA, under armed protection from the National Guard or with Air Force escorts for their private jets and helicopters.

Street connections kept her alive, and her educational opportunities grew under Alice Xie's tutelage. She became a memorialist, something she had already dabbled in back in the UK. Organized crime had helped her hone her natural gifts, and before long, she'd started raiding more than private stock accounts and the savings of housewives.

Every time she stepped outside her door—in LA or London, it didn't matter; everywhere was the same—she got that look, as if people knew she was somehow their lesser.

Her hair, the way she dressed, and her attitude all practically screamed poor. From a very young age, she had learned that the worst offense in the world was being poor. Poverty was an albatross, and no matter what she did to work her way out of it, that pressure squeezed tighter and tighter. If she asked for a handout, she was greedy. If she worked hard at some low-wage trashy joint, people would tell her all about how she had options and ask why she didn't just get a better job, as if finding any kind of work that paid serious credits was easy to come by.

Maybe that was why she had such a strong desire to cut out Schaeffer's eyes. He carried that look every time his gaze fell upon her, as if he knew she was gutter trash. If she cut out his eyes, though, suddenly she would be his better. She would have the power. Her jaw ached.

"What do we do?" she asked Alice.

The old woman gazed blankly at the ceiling. The one person of class who had ever looked at Jade with fondness, Alice was no better than she was. She, too, had clawed her way up, fought tooth and nail to reach the top. Jade respected Alice for that, a lot. But Alice couldn't even look at her. They'd destroyed everything about her, leaving nothing but a broken, weak shell.

"I will miss you, Jade."

Alice tried to squeeze her hand around the fingers pressed to her palm, but the effort was completely devoid of strength.

"The data packet you sent me. There has to be a back door to all this, right? Some kind of escape hatch."

"No. I'm sorry, but no. I was a fool to involve you."

"I could recognize bits of you in Mesa, you know. There were signs."

If anything, Jade thought, those glimmers of Alice that shone through Mesa were far closer to the real deal than the version lying in that bed, broken and too full of self-pity.

Schaeffer had turned Alice Xie into a frightened lab rat, and the scars and traumas of abuse ran so very deep. Though Jade had once admired Alice, she only felt pity anymore.

"Perhaps I will have the luxury of dying twice, then," Alice said.

"I'm just saying, there's got to be a way for me, too, right? Isn't there?"

Alice closed her eyes and gave a small, tremulous shake of her head. She withdrew her hand from Jade's and lifted her quaking arm to Jade's head. "All that you were," she said, her fingers a whisper upon Jade's forehead, "will be destroyed. You will only be a memory."

Her hand fell away, and, for a time, Jade watched her sleep. Schaeffer returned after an hour, accompanied by his two muscle-bound stooges.

"Jade?" he asked.

She appraised the three men and recognized that Alice was not the only one who had been turned into a ruined shell. She had no fight left in her. Only a dull resignation remained.

"You don't need these gorillas," she said. "I'm ready to go."

While Schaeffer seemed surprised, his companions wore their disappointment clearly across their faces.

"I promise you, the procedure will be painless. It may take some time, and you may feel disoriented, but there will not be any physical harm."

"Blow it out your ass, Schaef."

He laughed at her blithe profanity. He turned to lead the trio out of the room and, glancing back over his shoulder, he said, "It's almost a shame, really. But at least you'll be special now."

# CHAPTER SIXTEEN

AFTER THE KILL STICK FAILED to initialize, Mesa hit YES again.

YES.

YES.

YES.

Nothing.

She pulled the kill stick loose and whipped it into the hatch door. She was rewarded with the sharp cracking noise of plastic splintering, followed by the gentle thud of the stick dropping to the floor, broken and even more useless. "God damn it!"

*How?* Mesa said.

*I was careful to ensure my safety before allowing you to grow aware of my presence.*

Still reeling from dehydration, Mesa popped open a

new bottle and sipped slowly. Her heart was racing, her body flushed with fear, anger, agony—and, perhaps, a small measure of defeat.

*What do we do now?* Mesa asked.

Mesa's first order of business was figuring out where she was. A soft ping off a hacker sat gave her the GPS coordinates. She wasn't too far from where Kaften and Boyd lay dead. Real-time imaging showed that the fire had spread toward the outer reaches of Elko, but it had mostly died out as it stretched into the desert, where fuel was scarce.

Her second order of business was putting more distance between herself, the corpses, the fire, and the small city of Elko, Nevada. Studying the local terrain, she found a marker to the east for a town called Ely and set up a quick route. The Humvee fired up without complaint, but a small message appeared on the windshield display, alerting her to a software update. She ignored it and drove.

Soon enough, she passed Elko Mountain and made her way back onto I-80. Crossing the border at the instate checkpoint carried too much risk, so she took the exit for Alt 93 and headed south to Ely, where she could take on the third order of business: rest and recovery.

Ely was a tiny blue-collar town squatting in the crotch of a few hills. Riddled with cheap motels and a few casinos, it reminded her of an even more impoverished Elko. Unlike Elko's dead polar bear, Ely's main claim to fame was a historic railroad, a couple dozen ghost towns, and McGill Drugstore, a time capsule from the 1950s that still featured soda jerks.

The Main Motel was in a scrappy neighborhood on its last legs, and the main office looked about how Mesa felt— brutally beaten and falling apart. Still, the rates were dirt cheap and the desk clerk asked her no questions and offered her no advice. He exchanged the cash for a key with barely a hello. If the exterior was any indication, the clerk probably saw women like Mesa all the time and figured she was yet another beat-up housewife.

She limped through the weed-riddled gravel drive, down to Unit Three. The red paint on the door was sun-faded and cracked, and the white frame around it was chipped. The screen door was a tattered suggestion more than anything else. Inside, the room was practically a clone of her room in Elko. Mesa locked the screen door, closed and locked the red door, then tossed the key onto the dresser. She dropped the bag onto the floor and collapsed onto the bed.

She utilized a hard-secure hack and pulled up the commNet. Rameez was online, as always, using his cloner ID.

"You look like shit, Mesa."

"Thanks. You're a doll."

He blushed. "I'm sorry. I didn't think..."

"It's OK. Things are bad. The idents you worked up for me are blown."

"What happened?"

Mesa let out a long exhale before answering. How to even answer that was a big question all by itself.

"Short answer—I blew it. I made contact on Somnambulist with an LA survivor, but she was a plant, and our meet-up was a trap."

Rameez shot her a disappointed look, the kind Jonah had given her when she'd screwed up. "I'll work up something fresh, but it'll take time."

"I think I'll be OK where I am now. I'll be here for a few days, probably."

Rameez glanced around at his own surroundings. He'd made it to the seasteaders; she could make out the clear blue sky around him, and the wind ruffled his hair. Softly he said,

"I, uh... I think I've been blown, too."

"What?" She shot up in panic.

"I am not one hundred percent sure, but I think I am being followed. There were some guys I started noticing after I got here. I think they came in after I arrived."

"You stay away from them. Hole up in your room and do not go anywhere. Do not open your door for anything. Do you understand me?"

"I can't stay there indefinitely. And what if they break in? I mean, this is big, right?"

"Calm down, first of all. Cool it. And you won't be in there indefinitely. I'm coming to get you."

"No, Mesa. You can't."

"I will. You get me a new ident, and I'll be there. It's not even a question."

For all of his technical proficiency, Rameez was not a fighter, and she didn't believe that he would be able to evade the men tracking him forever. And if others were following him, people he had not noticed, it would only be more difficult for him to remain elusive.

She needed him—and his help. More importantly, she could not stand by while another one of her friends stood firmly in the crosshairs. Although she was safer on her own, she knew leaving Rameez to fend for himself would mean certain death for him.

Rameez thanked her, and they watched one another across the distance. He surveyed the damage to her face, but seemed ashamed at his open curiosity.

"I appreciate it," he said.

She nodded. After a pause, she confessed, "You're all I have left, I think."

His eyes cast downward as he spoke. "What about Kaizhou?"

She palmed away a tear. "He didn't make it. And I think he's a large part of why I'm still alive right now."

"What are we going to do?"

She waited for him to raise his eyes, to meet her gaze directly. "We're going to stop this," she said with steely conviction. "But I need you. You keep your ass safe. You got that?"

He grinned, but his eyes were plainly distressed. "I'm heading to my room now." He snapped off a smart salute and disconnected.

*We don't need him*, Alice said.

*Yes, we do. I need him.*

*He'll die, you know. Same as the others.*

Mesa balled her fists in her lap and squeezed her eyes shut. She wasn't in the mood to argue or to listen to Alice's unwelcome input. *I need to sleep. I'm exhausted.*

*You need to face reality.*

*What the fuck do you want me to do, huh? We can't do this alone.* Her hands were clenched so tight that her knuckles were white.

*Your connections are a weakness, Mesa. Daedalus will exploit those people to their fullest, simply to get to you. That's probably why Rameez is still alive right now. He's bait.*

*If we're walking into a trap, then at least we'll be prepared for it. Having Rameez with us may be the only way we can be sure we're not walking into a lion's den later.*

A ripple of aggravation washed over her, and Alice turned sullen and quiet, back to ignoring her. Mesa pushed her good arm under the pillow, propping her head up. She closed her eyes and slept, but the rest was unsound, and too many horrors lurked in the dark recesses, waiting for her to submerge fully and pounce.

The day's last light fell in thin slats across the bed. When Mesa woke, she was starving and still in pain. And still far too tired. She dismissed the idea of trying to make her way to the grocery store kitty-corner to the motel and settled on forcing her way through another awful MRE. The meals never tasted anything close to what they advertised, but the high-calorie content helped to stitch her body back together and left her full, if not satisfied.

Once she was done eating, she fished out the antistatic bag containing a stained chip. Kaften's memories. She slotted the chip into an external reader, plugged that into the port behind her ear, and prepared herself to hit Play.

Diving into Kaften's memories was harrowing, and she felt as if she'd stepped through a spider web. The experience was unsettling. A constant shiver ran the length of her spine. She'd tripped on some seriously scary mems in the past, but his were different. Darker.

The superficiality of his personality was clear, even before she accessed any of the content. He was a company man, through-and-through, who relied on violence whenever necessary and enjoyed the adrenaline rush of combat. If he hadn't found a place in private military, he might have simply been another run-of-the-mill sociopath. Instead, he was given a mission and a way to focus his peculiar brand of craziness.

She arranged the mems in a standard cascade. Most individuals placed themselves at the top of their own personal hierarchy, which wasn't a surprise. Ninety percent of the population organized themselves as the top tier.

People with military-shaped minds often viewed themselves as secondary, if not lower, depending on their service ranks. Above them were varying levels of superior officers and institutional figureheads, who were sometimes nothing more than vague associations rather than memories of direct experience.

Kaften was not particularly unique in these regards, even as a privately commissioned industrial-military man.

He filled the second tier in his current self-configuration. Below him were Boyd and Crassen. Above him was a man named Maxwell Schaeffer.

*What do you know about him?* Mesa asked.

*Big name in the press,* Alice said. *Beyond that, I don't know much.*

Mesa couldn't help but feel that Alice was being illusive, and the way Alice shrugged off her question was frustrating. *I thought you helped Daedalus? Isn't that what you said?*

*I did but always through a cut-out. I dealt with Kaften directly. As you can see, he practically defines "middle-man."*

Mesa filtered the mems in chronological order, most recent first, and let the cascade play out simultaneously while she scanned through them. Rather than doing a direct mem tap, she let them run in display windows across her retina display.

Some she recognized with dreadful clarity. She saw Sri and Ashita sharing their bed, forced to watch the other die. And in a more recent recog, Kaizhou was slaughtered in a hail of bullets. Sparks pinged off the Jeep as semi-automatic weapons fire tore into the engine, spiderwebbed the Dura-Plast windshield, then bit into his flesh. His body jerked under the rapid assault. Mesa flicked past the memory quickly, avoiding its absorption as much as possible. Her own memories of his death were sufficient for too many nightmares without the added layers of Kaften's psyche.

Others, she did not recognize, but she knew, simply because Kaften knew, that those were the murders of her LA counterparts. Kaften had led the assault on a hidden Tong compound and the slaughter of memorialists in the basement of their restaurant hideaway.

Alice's anger burned, long and steady. The emotion was vivid enough to make Mesa's skin flush and kick her heart rate up a notch. She thirsted for a deeper vengeance—that chemical reaction worked its way into Mesa's thinking, making her hungry for revenge. The loss of self was shocking, a deadly reminder of what Alice's continued presence in her mind meant, and sent her reeling. Mesa suddenly recognized that she was even more lost than she had realized. As long as Alice was a part of her, Mesa could never truly know who she had been—who she was. That put everything in doubt. She wondered how much of the last three years had been a recovery versus a hostile takeover.

She thought back to the casual violence she had employed against the scavengers in Des Moines. Killing them had been simple—far simpler than it should have been. Had that been her, or Alice? What she'd assumed had been muscle memory exerting itself, using the neuronal pathways forever carved into her brain thanks to years of training and developed by memories and experiences she no longer remembered might have been entirely Alice.

Mesa thought she had developed a basic understanding of herself, even despite the trauma that Alice Xie had inflicted upon her. But that was all in doubt.

*You need to focus*, Alice said.

Mesa's head was spinning, but she knew Alice was right. She tried to button down the thoughts raging through her… if she even was herself. She swam in confusion, reeling from a devastating sense of loss. All her assuredness had been swept away.

*Mesa. Look.*

She followed the voice to the screen Alice had been watching throughout her sudden existential crisis. She tracked the words to the mem and gasped, her heart hammering while her stomach lurched heavily into her throat.

Jade. Wearing fishnet stockings and a too-short skirt, she marched up Occidental, her hair mussed up into a faux hawk. Mesa couldn't help but smile at the sight of her friend's typical "don't screw with me" look. Then her face contorted into writhing agony as a shock stick was jammed into the base of her spine. Then she was pushed into a van while Kaften watched through the vehicle's mirrors before he turned his full attention to the road before him, happy with the cleanliness of the abduction.

*They took her.*

*Yes,* Alice said.

*They didn't kill her, I mean. They killed everyone else. But not her.*

*I saw.*

*Well, why? What's that mean?*

Alice tried to hide it, but Mesa could feel the shuffling of memories. They were too closely a part of one another; Mesa knew that was a hiccup in Alice's plan. Kaften was a foot soldier, operating only on the orders he'd been given. His understanding of the full importance of Jade's abduction had not been necessary. Alice, though, knew more than she was letting on. Mesa pressed forward, seizing the strands of thought that her other tried to keep hidden.

*Jade worked for you?* Mesa's entire world shifted and writhed, forcing her to wonder what, exactly, was real. The loss of absolutes pounded into her like rapid-fire body shots and an elbow jab to the face. It ached.

*She was a memorialist. Before I died, I sent out multiple data packets and instructions.*

Mesa narrowed her eyes, pinching her lips together.

*Jade was to find you and befriend you then wait for me,* Alice continued.

*She was spying on me?*

*She was your friend. She was my friend.*

*And these data packets were... what? What were they?* Mesa fought off a wave of vertigo as the small hotel room spun around her, upsetting her stomach.

*Fragmentary personality.*

*They were you?*

*Yes.*

*You divvied yourself up and sent them off?* She fought down the rising stream of bile that burned her throat.

*Crude but essentially correct.*

*Jade had a data packet?*

*No. She merely had an objective. The data packets were sent to multiple individuals with instructions to wait. Once the various aspects of myself emerged, we were to unite and offload the data. Once that was completed, the personality construct could reassemble and merge.*

*Why divide yourself up?* Mesa asked. She felt as if she were about to throw up, and sweat blossomed across her forehead from the heated anger boiling inside her.

*Insurance, primarily. But I also had to weigh the repercussions of sending a single data packet to an individual or multiple individuals. File size, transfer time, those were all factors. But inducing an entire personality whole-cloth into a brain already firmly lodged with another personality could be disastrous.*

*You're talking about body-shifting.*

*I am,* Alice said.

*That's what you tried to do to me?*

*It is. Your mind had to be destroyed so that I could implant myself into your body without further complications.*

*And by complications, you mean... this. All this. You and me, here, together.* She waved her arms at the motel room walls, as if Alice were a physical being sharing more than headspace.

*The risk would have been exorbitant, to both of us. You are having trouble processing all of this, I know, but I assure you—this is nothing.*

*It's nothing to you,* Mesa said, her anger fully bleeding through her thoughts.

*I understand you're distressed, but—*

*Distressed? Seriously? That's what you call this? Fucking*

*distress?* She wanted to scream. She settled for grabbing her bottle of water and throwing it across the room, seething. Her heart was pounding, her lips furling in hatred. She wished Alice were a physical creature simply so she could have the satisfaction of beating her ass and bloodying her face with her fists.

Alice went silent again, waiting for Mesa to calm.

*What was the big plan, then? You sent out all these packets, waiting for emergence, and then what? Where were you going to put all these files?* Her thoughts raged, buffeting Alice's presence with a wall of fury.

Again, Alice stayed silent, letting Mesa put the pieces together herself. After a moment, it hit.

*Oh.*

Mesa saw the plan unfold. The multiple data carriers were each a potential host or a puppet that could be seized and used to find another suitable body. Using the carriers, Alice could resurrect herself and body-shift in full into a new host. She could cheat death.

Kaften's memories made the dent in her plan rather clear, though. All of the other carriers were dead. Their memories might have been transmitted and disseminated. The data packets had likely multiplied and been replicated far beyond the original scope. Instead of isolating the data, it could have been disseminated and spread far and wide.

The LA memorialists had picked up much of the labor load. Smaller groups in Denver and Traverse City and one small batch in the Philippines had all been dispatched, quietly, effortlessly, with barely a blip. The kills had been covert, more precise, less hostile.

*They're starting to panic,* Mesa realized. *Daedalus doesn't know how far things have spread. They're trying to scare off the memorialists.*

*Scare them or kill them, whatever works best—it doesn't matter.*

*How did Daedalus know about the data packets?*

*I told them,* Alice said.

That simple admission made Mesa reel, and she spent a moment recovering. *What?*

*Kaften was there when I died,* Alice said. *It is a safe guess that my body was transferred to Daedalus custody, where, I'm sure, they invested plenty of man-hours gleaning as much data off my mem chip as they could. Then it was simply a matter of enacting containment and termination protocols.*

*Do you realize what you've done?* Mesa asked. *You made yourself viral.*

*I wouldn't worry, sweetie. I'm sure that while Daedalus has been busy killing people, they have also been working on security patches. You'll soon be getting a software update fixing known bugs and other issues. It will be a security patch that will inoculate against me. It will prevent the spread and will likely also include a surveillance worm. Daedalus will contain this.*

*And how many lives will you have cost in the process?*

*Too many,* Alice said with surprising frankness. The weight of burden was clear in her tone. *The real question now is, do you want to live more than you want to kill me?*

Mesa shut her eyes, clearing away the mem display and thumbing off the power node. She disconnected the DRMR and set it aside.

She pinged Rameez on the commNet again, relieved by the distraction his face provided. "You holed up yet?"

"I'm in my room."

"Good. While you're lying low, I need you find out whatever you can on Maxwell Schaeffer. Be discreet."

# CHAPTER SEVENTEEN

THE NEXT THREE DAYS PASSED with little incidence. Mesa had kept the "do not disturb" icon lit on the door, but she had still seen the manager trying to peek through the window shades, probably making sure she hadn't OD'd and died. She'd paid for the room for a week, and beyond that single instance, there had been few signs of life beyond the motel room. A car groaned past on occasion, but even noises such as that were rare.

By the morning of the fourth day, and after a steady diet of MREs, she was starting to feel vaguely human and less broken. She began putting weight on her injured leg without incident, and she'd changed the shoulder dressing daily, noting its progress.

She flicked on the bathroom light and peeled back the gauze. The gunshot wound was barely discernible, but the scarring was significant, leaving the rebuilt pink flesh ropey and tender. She pressed her fingers along the stretch of collar bone, wincing slightly. The musculature was weak, and she worked on rotating the arm. The pain was excruciating. The limb, stiff and heavy, couldn't even make one full rotation, and she couldn't stretch or lift the arm above the bottom of her ribcage. Still, the progress was remarkable, and the wound had stopped seeping the previous day, leaving scabs bridging the gap.

*It's much better,* Alice said. She'd been radio-silent for most of the last few days, and her attempt at encouragement felt disingenuous at best.

Mesa rolled her eyes at the mirror and taped a fresh sterile pad across her shoulder.

*We should get moving if you plan on saving your friend.*

She nodded. Though she wasn't up for more traveling, she had no other choice. Move or die, those were the options.

After disconnecting with Rameez, Mesa had spent much of the night cataloguing her losses and crying over the murders of her father, her boyfriend, and her friends.

A year ago, Kaizhou had proposed to her. Somewhat, at least. They'd gotten dinner and gone to a movie, and as they stepped out of the theater, Mesa stared skyward to take in the stars and moon. They leaned against the wall, and she felt him watching her. She turned and smiled. He pulled her close, his body warming her as their tongues circled each other's. They'd confessed their love to one another three months prior, and it had felt like an awakening.

Holding her hands, he asked, "Would you marry me?"

A smile exploded across her face. She looped her arms around his neck, whispering, "Yes."

Tears welled in his eyes as he pulled away. "I don't have a ring. I'll have to ask you again later, when I get one." He shrugged. "I wanted to know, though. You know?"

She laughed, and after a moment, he did, too.

They didn't speak of it again, but she'd idly wondered if the day would ever come. She knew it never would. She'd never told Jonah of it, nor had Kaizhou. Their engagement had been a secret between two young lovers. Neither had any need to rush—their entire lives were ahead of them.

Thinking back on it, in a dirty, run-down bathroom, she wiped away the tears and blinked until her vision cleared. She finished wrapping her shoulder then pulled on a too-large black long-sleeved summer shirt.

Ely was small and sparsely inhabited, but it did have a small county-run airstrip that offered private jet travel. Rameez had come through with fresh fake creds for her two days before, and she still had a bundle of u-cash to cover the fare.

In the lot, she pulled herself up into the back compartment of the Humvee and unzipped the backpack. She'd gotten rid of her other clothes and replaced them with a fresh pair of pants, boxers, and shirts, all too big but adequate. She found a black army hat and pulled that on, too.

She pulled two pistols off the wall mounts, inspected them, then broke them down for a quick cleaning. Reassembled, loaded with one in the chamber and the safety on, they were buried in the bag beneath the clothes and wrapped in a large shirt along with plenty of spare ammunition. She tossed a sheathed Ka-bar knife into the bag for good measure. Opening up the front pockets, she stuffed in more MREs and bottles of water.

*You're walking into a trap, Mesa. You know that, right? Daedalus will not stop hunting us just because you killed a few of their men. They have Rameez under surveillance, hoping to lure you out. He is bait, nothing more.*

*I know,* Mesa said. *But I still have to try.*

Along with the fake credentials, Rameez had sent along his mems so she could study the men following him and be prepared to spot them. She found two candidates, and Alice had discovered a potential third. All three were nondescript. A casual observer wouldn't have noticed any of them, but fortunately, Rameez had been paranoid enough to notice.

Given the nature of the seastead, moving a full team into place and keeping a running surveillance operating for a long period of time would have been difficult. Faces were bound to become familiar, even if players were rotated in and out. On the other hand, Mesa had to be mindful that there could be many more operators in play. Rameez had simply chanced upon these three.

Jade watched with detachment, an almost clinical cool, as the needle slid into a branch off the dorsal venous network on the back of her hand. Clear liquid slowly pushed into the vein, sending a cool flush through her, and a few moments later, she felt as if she were floating. The nurse was a stranger. The antiseptic white room was a foreign cube.

The nurse slowly withdrew the needle and replaced it with a small puff of cotton. She affixed a small stretch of tape across it, offering Jade a small, tight-lipped smile.

"See, it's OK."

"OK," Jade said. She closed her eyes to block out the nauseating spinning sensation but reopened them at the sound of shuffling cloth. Focusing was supremely challenging, but she made out the impression of a tall man standing over her, his arms crossed over his chest. He wore a dark business suit, his hair freshly trimmed and neatly combed. His smile was beautiful and carried the faintest pang of recognition, even though she couldn't quite place the why or how of it all.

"Jade, I'm Maxwell Schaeffer. Do you remember meeting me?"

She was puzzled, her head still swimming. She squinted, trying to discern the details of his face. He did seem familiar, but she wasn't sure why.

"I don't," she admitted. "No, I'm sorry."

"No, no, there's no need to be sorry about anything. It's fine." He smiled, his teeth competing with the room for bright whiteness.

She'd never seen such perfectly straight teeth. And what a strange thought that was.

"How are you feeling?"

"Dizzy," she said.

"Upset tummy?"

She nodded weakly. "A bit. I feel…"

He arched an eyebrow at her, taking her hand. He settled into a stool beside her bed and leaned over her, placing a bare wrist against her forehead.

She felt neither hot nor cold.

"What is it, sweetie? What do you feel?"

"I… I don't know," she said. "I don't remember what I was going to say." She laughed quietly to herself, devoid of humor.

"It's going to be all right. We're going to have you right as rain in no time."

"Are you my doctor?"

"No, I'm not. I'm very interested in your case. That's all."

"Why are you interested in me?" She stared at his white teeth, beatific smile, and coiffed hair. A part of her felt flattered. Another part of her, though, something inexplicable and primal, recoiled from his attention, sensing the threat beneath his gaze. But it was short lived. There and then gone.

"Well," he said, "I guess I'm a humanitarian, now aren't I?"

She smiled uncomfortably. A dark cloud formed in her mind and left her unsettled. Her limbs were lead weights, and a wave of exhaustion swept over her, threatening to drown her. Her eyelids felt impossibly heavy.

"You go ahead and sleep now, darling," Schaeffer said.

Schaeffer supervised as the nurse installed an intravenous drip into Jade's data port, where the inhibitor device had been removed and replaced with an adapter port. Rather than a saline solution, the bag on the IV stand infused a PKMZeta inhibitor named ZIP directly into Jade's hippocampus. The ZIP solution was rapidly destroying Jade's short-term memory and slowly eradicating her long-term memories.

In an hour, she would forget that their conversation had ever happened, and Schaeffer would once again be a stranger. The process of removing himself from her memories had taken two days, since many of her memories involving him were closely tied to fear.

Fear tended to leave very strong mnemonic imprints, particularly in youthful individuals. The rigorous torture sessions that had greeted her on *Alabaster* had woven very strong bonds of terror into her brain's neural pathways. Still, after a few more sessions, all of that would be erased. By the end of the week, if past research was sound and effective, Jade would be gone entirely.

Soon, she would be nothing more than a vacant shell lying prone in bed, her fully functional brain merely an empty vessel.

Once the ZIP wiped the slate clean, the body would be weaned off it and restarted on a regimen of PKMZeta builders, to help restart the brain's ability for memory retention and storage. By the time they got to that stage, Schaeffer planned to be finished weeding through the volunteers to find a suitable candidate for transference.

Although Alice Xie had already experimented with

much of the process in Los Angeles, Xie was hardly a suitable test subject. She was, in fact, a rogue element and a thief. Still, she had shown the viability of the research. Jade, however, was a much more suitable test subject, like the volunteer Schaeffer would eventually settle on. The entire endeavor was being carried out under Daedalus supervision and control, with nothing left to chance. No rogue elements. No PRC. No Alice Xie, in as much as that could be controlled.

Losing Kaften had been a serious blow, and Mesa was in the wind, yet again. He was beginning to admire her craftiness, and not merely because she had tried to lay waste to an entire backwater gambling town with a wildfire. That had been good for a few laughs, and he had learned not to underestimate her. She was clearly far more volatile than they had been led to expect—he would have a few words with Alice Xie about that.

*Volatile but not uncontrollable, and certainly not untouchable.*

Mesa had two people left in the world. Rameez and Jade. And Schaeffer had eyes on both of them. If Mesa made it to Jade, Schaeffer would certainly know about it. Rameez was another issue entirely, and the team surveilling him had been warned to take the appropriate measures of caution.

Waiting for Jade to open her eyes, he reviewed the volunteers' profiles. He enjoyed seeing the hard results of their cerebral formatting efforts. He also enjoyed being the first thing Jade saw upon waking. That momentary confusion was priceless.

Slowly, she worked her way up from the delirium, blinking languidly at him. "Who are you?"

He smiled at her and took her hand in his.

MESA LOST HERSELF IN THE expanse of the Pacific. The water stretched out beneath her on either side of the small private jet as far as she could see. Subtle shades of blue separated clear sky from ocean. She felt humbled and insignificant in the seemingly infinite stretch of nothing.

The flight from Ely was a non-event. The county–run airport seemed to be on its last legs, and the desk jockey was unconcerned with the minutiae of paperwork. Money was far more important, and Mesa had it. He handed her a stack of papers to sign, gave her initials and signatures a cursory glance before tossing them onto a different stack of papers, and printed her ticket. More concerned with the wad of chew that ballooned his right cheek, he'd hardly examined her identification.

The desk jockey ended up being the stick jockey, too.

After working his way loose from the desk, he led her outside to the small single-engine quantum jet and spat in the dirt. Then he went up a small ladder, opened the door, stepped inside, and waved her up—all without saying a word.

Two hours later, she lost sight of land and began to relax, slightly.

A half hour later, she caught the first edge of humanity's touch. She stared hard at it, waiting for the details to resolve.

Passing over the enormous floating breaker walls that protected the city from large waves, Mesa caught sight of the giant polyhedral aquaculture farms. Beneath the clear Dura-Plast were the most vivid, freshest greens she had ever seen. Ocean algae was grown for food and energy and helped keep the startup cities that shaped the growing and evolving seasteading movement operational and independent. Domes were dedicated to farming brown microalgae to produce bioethanol. All of the city's fuel needs were met by what they produced in the massive greenhouse domes and by capturing the ocean's thermal energy and converting it to sustainable power.

As the jet descended toward the landing area, she could make out the men and women working the fisheries and hauling in oysters, clams, and mussels. The marina was a vibrant hub of activity as ships maneuvered the channels and boat crews rushed along the gangways and decks.

Mesa followed the main artery of the docking ring north, to a multi-storied residential square lush with greenery. Men and women jogged through the neighborhoods, where sunlight glinted off the enormous stretches of Dura-Plast.

Helicopters navigated the sky, where the air traffic was surprisingly busy. Sea taxis maneuvered through the canals, passing under the bridges that connected the cities together in a ring formation and joined them to the marina along the outer stretches. There were six distinct cities, each defined by the effusion of multiculturalism that generations of seasteaders had embraced.

In the center of the six city-states was a tall winding spire that rose in steppe-formation, the tallest structure among the collective. Part of its height was achieved by a collection of data arrays and antennas. Housed inside was the central seat of government that united the city-states, while the exterior twisting arms collected rainwater and extracted moisture from the air for freshwater production. The surface of the building was a solar capture array, making it one the largest natural energy producers within the community.

The quantum jet settled on the landing pad with a slight jostle. Outside, a service crew pushed a ladder toward the jet. A moment later, the captain was striding down the aisle toward her to open the door.

"Hope you had a nice flight," he said.

She thanked him and gave him a slight bow then turned to set foot on solid ground. She took a deep breath, enjoying the saltiness of the air and the warmth of the sun on her skin as she tilted her face skyward.

The city's calm quiet certitude and sense of security was infectious. For a moment, she actually felt safe, before reminding herself of why she was there. The seasteaders had worked hard at building an idyllic haven that nearly resembled a perpetual ocean-side vacation, but Alice was subtly reminding Mesa not to let her guard down.

Rameez was quartered in a hotel on New Venice, three rings away from the landing promenade. Mesa studied the map and decided to walk, the bag heavy on her shoulders. One strap bit painfully into the fresh, tender skin of her recovering shoulder, which protested the weight.

White winding stairs led down to the central thoroughfare, and she melted into the crowd of walkers occupying their own lane alongside the bike path.

After a few minutes, Mesa already felt out of place. Her black militaristic garb stood out against the airy beachwear most of the natives wore. Shorts paired with silk shirts with flower prints, if any shirt at all, appeared to be the standard attire for the men, while most of the women were clad in loose blouses or T-shirts with shorts, skorts, skirts, or bikinis. She felt as if she were walking along the Santa Monica pier before realizing Alice was recalling the comparison. A chill ran across her arms as a teenager on skates whipped past, a corgi chasing after her. The only people wearing more clothing than Mesa were three Muslim women in black burqas, sitting primly on a stone bench and talking to one another, their eyes hidden by black mesh screens.

As she walked, she casually studied the faces and scenery around her. She randomly altered her pace but never went too fast or too slow. A few blocks deep, she turned down a path that ran through the commercial district and passed the storefronts. Window-shopping gave her a good excuse to stop, and the Dura-Plast provided a convenient reflective surface where she could watch people come and go, wondering if any would stop with her and linger nearby. Slowly, she moved on, smiling at the store clerks, occasionally stopping to touch the clothes on the sidewalk displays.

Casually cataloguing the faces on the street, she decided to enter a women's clothing shop. The small boutique had caught her eye, particularly the emerald dress on display behind the window. She found the rack, searched through the dresses for her size, then went to the dressing room.

She took off the hat and shook her hair loose, letting the long tresses of one side hang loose over her face, half-punk, half-1950s LA starlet. She worked her way out of the boots and clothes then slipped the dress over her head. The fit was both sexy and fashionable, and she admired the way the fabric accentuated her curves. She turned in the mirror to study the angles, a smile curling onto her lips. The dress was the nicest thing she'd worn in what seemed like forever, and it made her feel remarkably good—not at all like a woman on the run, with death chasing her. The dress was a fantasy, but she felt the need to indulge it. And besides, it would help her blend in with the community. The material was light, virtually weightless, unlike the heavy cargo pants and sweaty black tee.

She picked up her clothes, stuffed them into the bag, struggled to get the zipper closed, and went out to tell the clerk she was going to wear the dress. She paid, taking note of her dwindling supply of u-cash, then realized she needed shoes to match the dress.

*May as well go all out.*

*You shouldn't be wasting money so frivolously*, Alice chided her.

*Think of it as an operational necessity*, Mesa said. *I need to blend in.*

A nice pair of flats, a few pairs of underwear, and a new bra later, she was finished shopping. She left carrying the undergarments in a recycled paper bag, the backpack hooked over her shoulders once more.

Stepping back into the bright sunlight, she let her eyes readjust then scanned over the faces. She saw nobody familiar, and no one sprang into action. She checked both ways before joining the slow-moving crowd then worked her way north, through the commercial district, maintaining her nonchalant browsing.

As the stores grew closer to the docks, they took on a more obvious nautical theme. Storefront logos became variations on old-world wooden steering wheels, and she spotted more than one wooden pirate with a peg leg and a bright red-and-green parrot atop his shoulder. The fashions catered toward an old-school yachting clientele, with masculine mannequins wearing white khaki shorts, pastel polo tops, and white sweaters tied around the neck. She passed a few garments for women and was practically electrocuted by sticker shock. The cheapest blouse she saw cost five hundred credits.

*It's become a fucking yuppie-fest*, she thought. A certain amount of willpower was required to not utterly condemn the entirety of seasteaders on this small cult of *nouveau riche* debauchery.

She followed the promenade around the outer ring of the city to the bridge connecting one island to the next, stopping to admire the view. The community was truly a beautiful sight. While it had been deeply impressive from the air, the enormousness of her new surroundings struck her hard as she stood among the buildings.

There was much to be said for the perverse will of mankind to make a home of even the most uninhabitable. Some would have called the initial builders madmen and their financial backers crazy, but the results were undeniably amazing. The founders had broken free of their nations and established a new place to live and a new way of living—one that was respectful and entirely at the behest of the sea.

With the land overcrowded, polluted, and stricken with violence and warfare, the planet's oceans were truly the last frontier for mankind. While plenty had gone off-world to build new lives for themselves, a few had sought such harmony and kinship with their home planet on the ocean.

The community planners had turned to the oceans for support, enrichment, growth, and sustainability, turning their backs on the politicians and armies who fought for dirt and oil. The seasteaders had their eyes toward the future, and they had built it themselves. Their creation was a beautiful sterling testament to mankind's tenacity and will to succeed. Six cities with the promise of expansion, the seastead was home to more than two hundred thousand souls.

Standing on that bridge, watching over the seataxis ferrying their passengers to and from the neighboring island states, Mesa realized that she could live here. She could turn away from Daedalus and lose herself in New Venice or one of the other habitats.

*You think they would just forget about you? That you could disappear and never worry about them again?* Alice pulled Mesa back to reality and the threat of the present.

Of course she was being stupid. She had business to attend to, matters to resolve.

*Maybe after all that's done*, though, she thought. *Maybe after that.*

Like the original city that was its inspiration, New Venice was navigable by narrow channels cutting paths through the city. Slow-moving smart-boats utilized the waterways, their passengers taking in the sights around them and enjoying one another's company, unable to escape the romance of the experience.

Storefronts and habitats along the branching channels attempted to mimic an old-world ambiance of Venice and capture the Mediterranean influences and Gothic architecture. Balconies overlooking the water were adorned with Gothic arches and traceries, and boat moorings resembled ancient barbershop poles with their red-and-white candy-cane striping.

While the design aesthetic of New Venice was a far cry from the modern constructs of the surrounding cities, the architects had gone to great lengths to incorporate new-world tech into the old-world appearances. The solar panels were an obvious departure from the ancient Venetian influences; more subtle, however, were the carbon-capture nodes, desulfurization systems, and hyper-filter arrays used to draw in harmful gases. Many of the boats and transit systems employed in the community relied on solar or blue energies, but the occasional old-fashioned gas-powered or oil-driven machine, particularly ancient freighters that much of the third world had bought from shipping agencies undergoing upgrades, visited the seastead. The seasteaders employed anti-pollution measures as a natural artifice to their buildings and design schemes to absorb the hazardous waste produced by those ships reliant on the scant remnants of fossil fuels. The hyper filters absorbed the waste and converted it into clean oxygen. On the underside of the structures, multiple layers of baleen filters drew in water waste, such as gas and oil residues left behind in the wake of the freighters, then clarified and purified the seawater before discharging it back into the ocean.

Mesa kept her head on a near-constant swivel, appreciating the clusters of people flowing around her as much as the architecture. An active scan protocol was running in the background, filtering each individual she saw against a facial recog program. If the men trailing Rameez were in the vicinity, the scan and capture software should pick them up. Despite the thick crowd and sea of faces, Mesa barely took notice of those around her. The cybernetics absorbed it all for her, storing the visual stimulation for later recall or using it for the active data comparison she was currently relying on it to carry out.

She stopped at a small café and took a seat on the patio. She dumped the backpack and shopping bag in the empty chair opposite. Her eyes roamed over the passing figures as she readjusted the spaghetti straps on her shoulders and smoothed the fabric of the dress.

A waitress approached, and Mesa ordered café mocha, no whip.

*You should have tea,* Alice advised. *It is a smoother balm for your soul.*

*Too bland,* Mesa said.

*You need to work on your patience, learn to savor the delicate things in life.*

*And switching to tea would help with that, huh?*

*It's calming, nourishing.*

*You sound like it's a spiritual thing.*

*In some ways, it is. Coffee is acidic and potent. It frays your nerves, eats away at you. Tea soothes. It's pleasant, relaxing.*

*Whatever. Maybe later.*

The waitress set the mocha on the table and smiled softly. Mesa inhaled the sweet aroma, enjoying the intermingling of coffee and chocolate notes on the back of her tongue. This, she could savor. She didn't know what the hell Alice was talking about.

*How long did my father work for you?* Mesa asked.

*A few years. Life in California… it was not easy, Mesa. I'm not sure you would understand.*

*Because my life has been such a fucking walk in the park, huh?*

*Comparisons are relative. I will concede that the last few days have been unusual.*

Mesa gripped the hot cup in both hands, trying to force herself to relax. *Oh, you'll concede, will you? These last few days wouldn't have been so fucking unusual if it weren't for your insane, megalomaniacal plans.*

*We will make this right, Mesa.*

*You know what? I don't think we can. What you did? What you did to me—I don't think the genie goes back in the bottle. Making this right means you getting the fuck out of my head. Do you understand that?*

*I do. And in order to do that, we need particular resources.*

Daedalus. Schaeffer. Mesa knew all that already.

*And what exactly are you going to do?* she asked. *Neither of us is exactly whole. And if I understand the score correctly, you're only one-fifth of the woman you used to be.*

Because Alice had divided up her mems into separate data packets, which she disbursed to multiple individuals rather than a single source, large parts of her personality, mind, and memories were missing. And with her data carriers gone, she could never return to her complete original personality.

*Perhaps we are more equal than you care to admit,* Alice said.

The barb took Mesa off-guard, but she had to admit that Alice was right. Neither of them was whole, and neither could ever be made cohesive. Both had suffered too much damage, loss, and destruction to fully recover from any of it.

After finishing the mocha, Mesa set off for the hotel. She approached Cavour without slowing and walked past, down to the next block. She kept her speed consistent, using the reflections of the Dura-Plast to check for people either following her or taking an obvious notice of her. She headed east, putting more distance between herself and Cavour. Then she looped back around the block for her approach. Feeling safe, she moved toward the door, which slid open smoothly upon sensing her.

Cavour's interior was a study in elegance. She admired the marble floors and the brilliant white columns. Plush black chairs decorated the lobby, and stained cherrywood tables and spacious sofas formed a sitting area where guests could take their drinks and reading material or enjoy conversations.

Moving past a massive winding staircase to the check-in desk, Mesa pressed her thumb to the touchscreen and clicked the Arriving Guest button. The biometric sensors captured her fingerprint, recognizing her as Juliet Landreau. The fake ident was courtesy of Rameez's fresh set of credentials, and she was grateful for his expertise. The check-in process was fast, and a moment later, a room key was dispensed from the console.

She took the elevator to the fifth floor and found her room. The accommodations were as luxurious as the lobby had promised. The door separating the adjoining rooms was already open, and she was delighted to see Rameez sitting on the edge of the bed.

The gun in his hand, however, was a complete surprise.

# CHAPTER NINETEEN

"You scared the shit out of me," Mesa said. "Fuck's sake, Rameez."

He blushed, apologizing profusely while she turned to lock the deadbolts and slide the chain into place.

"I've been on edge," he said. "I'm sure you can understand."

She pulled him into a bear hug, threatening to squeeze the life out of his chubby body. "God, it's good to see you."

"I didn't mean to scare you."

"It's fine," she said, smiling at him. She was surprised at how happy she really was to see him. "I get it. Things have been good and truly fucked up."

She dragged a chair away from the desk, piled her bags atop the dresser, and sat across from her friend, while he sat on the edge of the bed.

"I'm sorry about..." As his voice thinned out, Mesa knew Rameez wasn't referring to the gun.

Kaizhou.

She felt the burn in her eyes and shut them to stem the tide of tears. She'd spent days grieving in the motel, and she had no more time for that. Not right now.

She squeezed his hand and mouthed a thank you, her throat suddenly dry. "What did you find out about Schaeffer?"

Rameez laid out the basics for her, and she found herself relaxing a bit under his melodic accent as she absorbed the information.

"His credentials are very impressive," Rameez said. "Before he had turned forty, Schaeffer was in charge of Daedalus's Emergent Tech and Development division. He was a bit of a child prodigy and had earned his PhD at a young age, then joined Daedalus as a researcher."

Mesa asked, "What his research in?"

"He focused on neuronal engineering, with a keen eye on bioware programming. Prior to working for Daedalus, his postdoc research was with a joint DARPA-TARDEC project and earned him him more than a dozen new patents in what was then an emerging field in Databiologic Receiver of Mnemonic Response. Schaeffer worked closely with scientists from the Department of Defense as they began engineering DRMR for military use.

"His work there caught the eye of the higher-ups at Daedalus. With some slight tweaks, Schaeffer began modifying the DRMR platform for public consumption. DARPA, at the time, had been working very closely with medical research schools, and Schaeffer helped bridge the gap to deliver the platform to industry." Rameez sipped from a glass of water.

Mesa waited patiently for him to continue, reviewing the information he had collected on the tablet.

"He made a big splash, and within a decade, he was running the show in Emergent Tech based solely on notoriety. By capitalizing on his contacts across DARPA and within industry and research, he very nearly single-handedly changed the scope of the human experience and made cybernetics a household norm."

"Kind of a big deal," Mesa said, a chill running down her spine. Rameez had collected statistics that made it clear just how much Schaeffer had personally sculpted the world. Current estimates pegged twenty percent of the world as non-enhanced, mostly in undeveloped countries. The explosion of the DRMR platform into people's daily lives had made Schaeffer a *TIME* Person of the Year fifteen years prior.

A recent article stated he was fifty-three years old, but in the accompanying photo, he looked to be perpetually stuck in his thirties. Not a single image, not even the cheap paparazzi shots, showed anything but a neatly styled coif and bright smile. Always sharply dressed, the man was clearly vain about his appearance and never appeared mussed. He was the epitome of old-American business success.

"The wonders of medichines," Mesa said.

Rameez nodded. "His professional track record reads like a best-case scenario for executives-to-be, but his personal affairs are a disaster."

Rameez took the tablet back and scrolled through to a new data packet regarding Schaeffer's personal details. Mesa eyed the collection of news clips and magazine images.

"He's been married twice, and his first wife died under mysterious circumstances. I tried to find out more, but the official investigation records were slim to nonexistent. The police chalked her disappearance up to a boating accident."

"And Wife Number Two?" Mesa asked.

"She initiated divorce, citing irreconcilable differences. Some websites hosted paparazzi images of her sporting bruises on her face, and at least four gossip rags claimed to have official medical records indicating she had suffered long-term abuse. All were sued, opted to settle out of court and pay Schaeffer millions of credits, and removed the stories and images from their sites."

"Luckily," Mesa said, "nothing ever truly dies on the Internet." Regardless of the lawsuits, cached rumors constantly repopulated on alternate sites. Time was the only thing that kept them buried beneath more current rumors about more popular subjects.

"A few years ago, he was found guilty of aggravated assault against a photographer and fined three hundred thousand credits, which he paid immediately." Rameez scratched at the corner of his eyes then continued. "The publicity was kept to a minimum, the result of Daedalus' PR spin machines and public goodwill."

Mesa thumbed her way through the data, landing on an image of a pretty woman. The metadata indicated she was older than she looked. "Who is this?"

Rameez studied the image. "Oh, yeah. Some of the rumor sites said Schaeffer began dating a superior in Emergent Tech, prior to his ascent to more official degrees of power, while still married to Wife Number Two. This lady, too, disappeared under mysterious circumstances. Nobody ever found out what happened to her."

"And with her gone, Schaeffer was next in line for promotion," Mesa said, filling in the blanks.

*He contributed rather handily to their bottom line,* Alice added. Mesa nodded.

"He has a private airship," Rameez said. "*Alabaster.*" He tossed the images onto the air-display before them.

The white vertical sky-ship hovered before them. Solar

wind sails stretched out on either side of the oblong vessel. The freighter had once been a sleek pleasure ship for tourists, hugging the skies above major American metropolises such as New York and Los Angeles, before both fell under the weight of war. The liner companies fell, as well, and Schaeffer had secured *Alabaster* in a private auction.

"The ship is largely green," Rameez said. "Wind and solar keep its turbines turning. Other than food stocks, *Alabaster* is pretty self-sufficient. There's a rare need for him to dock it, other than restocking and the occasional maintenance check."

"Please tell me he's docking soon."

"He's not. I checked."

"How the fuck do we get to him?"

Rameez studied the space between his feet.

Mesa stood and paced.

Alice said, *We force him to dock.*

*How?* Mesa asked.

Alice explained, and Mesa relayed it to Rameez.

"What about falsifying an emergency?" she asked. The idea was pure Alice, but Mesa was, for the moment, reluctant to share that information with Rameez. "Insert a software update that requires docking, maybe some kind of patch that demands immediate attention?"

Rameez mulled it over for a few minutes, his head cocking back and forth from shoulder to shoulder as he thought. "That could work," he decided. "How to get aboard then?"

*We don't have enough surveillance data for this to work,* Alice said.

*It was your fucking idea,* Mesa reminded her. "Any idea what his behavior patterns are when the ship docks? What does he do? Does he leave the ship? Does he stay aboard? What?"

"I should be able to review past maintenance records

and check out the city cams or securiwebs, figure out what he does."

"That's good. Let's start with that."

"What are you going to do?"

Mesa shrugged. "We need to find the men following you. They may not know I'm here yet."

"I've been playing hide-and-seek," Rameez said then explained himself.

He had four rooms rented in Cavour, each under a false burner ID. The security systems were soft and hadn't correlated the facial recognitions against the multiple identities. The flaw was a giant gap in the hotel security that went willfully unrecognized in a vast array of systems. Most private security firms didn't pay much attention to that exploitation because the presence of security was largely to appease the masses. Many security systems were in place simply to give the illusion of security and apply a psychological balm on its customers. If somebody exploited that gap to rent multiple rooms, no one really cared. The man-hours required to patch that gap with more vigorous security metrics were expensive, especially for a security protocol that was largely superficial. That gap might have mattered in an airliner security system, where the threat was far more significant and could be leveraged into an attack with the potential to kill hundreds of people. But the hotel was a significantly weaker target.

Although he wasn't able to change his fingerprints, at least not easily, he could falsify the digital fingerprints the lobby scanners read, providing a false positive reference. The scanner would read the genetic whorls, but his algorithms would fool the authentication process. By installing a worm in the algorithm reader, Rameez could use more than one identity with a single image and set of fingerprints. He had secured four rooms, which hotel security thought were occupied by four distinct identities, rather than one individual using multiple false idents.

"If they made it far enough into the security system," Rameez said, referring to the men who had been following him, "they should know I'm here but not exactly where. I've got multiple rooms on multiple floors."

"And if they set up active security protocols to find you?"

Rameez smiled. "That's the beautiful part, right? You're here, and they may not know it. They can scan those four rooms, while I'm sitting right here in this fifth room with Juliet Landreau."

Mesa couldn't help but smile. She even detected Alice's grudging admiration toward the man, which made her smile wider.

"Plug their images into hotel security and get a worm going. Let's put the facial recog to work for us and see if we can't suss them out."

"I'll get on that now," Rameez said, his gaze softening as he patched into the security system's back door, focusing on the work.

"And get me a line of credit while you're at it. I'm out of cash."

"Yes, Ms. Landreau."

They smiled at one another, and Mesa left him to work.

*You asked about your father earlier. Was there more you wanted to know?*

Mesa thought about it, holding a loose grip around the rails that encircled the park's edge overlooking the water. A slight breeze sent a salty mist across her, while the brilliant sunlight warmed her skin.

*There's a thousand questions. Maybe more. But I don't think you're the one to turn to for answers.*

*Fair enough*, Alice said, surprising her.

*Really?* Mesa wasn't able to hide the derision.

Alice took it in stride, a ghostly smile passing through their shared thoughts. *We had a complicated relationship.*

*You used him to kill people, kidnapped me, destroyed my mind, buried one-fifth of a backup mem in my dead brain, and then he killed you. To you, that's "complicated"?*

*Is it not?*

*You're something else, lady.*

*It's strange, isn't it? I can't help but feel a certain simpatico.*

*Well, you have seen me naked,* Mesa said.

*Do you not feel it, too?*

Mesa shut her eyes against the breeze, wishing she could avoid the answer. The truth was, an uncomfortable degree of familiarity was settling between them. Mesa wanted to hate her, but she had also been run far beyond ragged. She felt beaten down, both emotionally and physically, and she simply didn't have the energy to hate the creeping voice in the back of her mind. She'd worried she was going crazy, but the reality was too ridiculous for such an answer as simple as insanity. And at the core: Alice Xie, like it or not, was a part of her.

*What was he like?* she asked, against her better judgment.

*Jonah? He was strong. In my business, weakness can easily be a death sentence. But I felt a certain degree of familiarity with him, as I do for you, a sort of kinship. I always felt safe in his presence.*

*Even when he was killing you?*

*That was purely business, my dear.*

*I remember it, you know. What you remember of it, I mean. Those final moments, of being choked to death.*

*I've tried to keep our memories separate, but perhaps I was too late.*

*There's too much seepage for you to even try,* Mesa said. *Two minds, one brain. The math doesn't work out very well.*

That was why she did not want to know her father by proxy of Alice Xie. She wanted to remember the man who had introduced her to warm delights of mac and cheese at Beechers on a rainy day, huddling around a thin wooden counter as the growing crowd pressed against them. She wanted to remember him holding her, the smell of sandalwood on his skin, the pier redolent with freshly caught fish, hand-crafted leather goods, and Starbucks coffee. Strong and brusque but always quick to smile when he caught sight of her, Jonah was always the first to cheer when she took down an opponent on the mat during her self-defense sessions. He taught her how to be confident around guns and helped her aim, squeezing his finger around hers as they shot paper targets together. She wanted to think of him as the artist who drew quick sketches of her and shared the old drawings he had made of her and her mother, Selene. Wrinkled, perpetually curling, and water damaged, the drawings were among the few possessions besides guns, ammunition, and mem chips that he'd been able to take with him during their exodus from Los Angeles. That was the man that she loved, the father she wanted to remember. Those were the memories of Jonah Everitt that she desperately needed to preserve and to protect.

*I can help you recover what you were. Your memories,* Alice said.

*You made a backup,* Mesa said, knowing it was true, because Alice knew. Seepage. The location of the backup was a mystery, though. And she sensed that not even Alice had an answer to that one.

*Daedalus has a complete mem composite of me. Schaeffer is using it to hunt down and kill memorialists, to kill you, and to eliminate me. If we can secure that data, we can recover your history and restore you.*

*In exchange for the complete set of mems of Alice Xie,* Mesa said, finishing Alice's thoughts. She dug in her bag for the pack of stale cigarettes and the lighter. A moment later, she blew a cloud of smoke over the park railing and across the Pacific Ocean, watching it expand and dissolve into the blue.

*Once Rameez figures out how we get to Schaeffer, we get you your mems, and you get me mine.*

*Deal,* Alice said. Once again, a flush of happiness tripped through Mesa's hippocampus, and the ghost of a smile lighted its way through her mind.

And, briefly, she felt the constricting press of wire around her throat. She coughed out the smoke burning her lungs, the unease passing. She spit out a flake of tobacco stuck to her tongue and finished the smoke. Alice retreated into the recesses of their shared mind once again.

She tossed the stub into a recycler, casually surveying the crowd. Attractive men were milling around, and a few bikini-clad women were tossing a Frisbee. She heard a minor commotion and turned to a couple's volleyball game, but their tiff quickly turned to good-natured laughter as they resumed. Watching them play was a nice break for her eyes. It gave her a reason to pretend that she hadn't noticed the man in a white polo and shorts eating a chocolate ice cream cone farther down the pier, surreptitiously turning his attention to her.

The facial recog software had sent out an alert two minutes ago, and she'd been waiting to see what he would do. Thus far, he'd only sat and ate. She never would have noticed his glances toward her if she hadn't been watching for them. He blended in and was casual as he kept a loose tail on her.

She adjusted the bag on her shoulder and walked slowly down the pier, letting her fingers dance sprightly across the rail as she went. When she turned to check across the street, she caught the man's reflection in the Dura-Plast window. Following her, he'd abandoned his ice cream. His intent was clear.

240  MICHAEL PATRICK HICKS

# CHAPTER TWENTY

Mesa walked through the piazza, noting the men following her. After the ice cream guy had started his tail, two others had peeled away from the crowds and spread out. One man was ahead of her, while the other two hung back—one directly behind her, the other following on the opposite side of the street. She stopped suddenly outside a fashion boutique and pretended to check the price tags on a few articles of clothing, watching the men's reflections on the windows and in a smartly placed mirror inside the shop. The two men reacted smoothly, nearly mimicking her as they found their surroundings suddenly interesting, setting themselves up outside the shops where they could observe her movements.

*Nicely done*, Alice said.

The piazza was a natural dead end, but rather than

looping around to the opposite side of the wide U-shaped street, she entered a grandiose market square. Passing through massive arches, she encountered fruit stands, meat markets, artisans, shoemakers and haberdasheries, custom clothing sellers, and tattoo artists. It reminded her of the public market center at Pike Place in Seattle.

She wended through the noisy crowd, gently jostling past those vying for the attention of the butchers, salesclerks, and cheese makers. The market was a crush of people, neon, freshly cut meat, coffee, chocolate, smoke, soups, and dairy—all of it bordering on madness in its sheer excess.

Behind her, the two men had followed her in. The third had entered before her. He had either anticipated her entry into the market or had planned to stop and wait on word from his companions that she had passed by.

The ground floor was the main center of attraction and held the most prime real estate, hence the pulsing crowds. Mesa worked her way to the back of the market square, where stairs descended to the next floor, which was still crowded but less so. She continued her way down, and down farther still.

On the fourth subfloor, deep below the ocean, she found a smattering of people enjoying the aquatic sights. The group consisted mostly of parents out with their children. The kids had no doubt been coerced with the promise of catching a glimpse of a shark. The families huddled around the thick, heavily reinforced Dura-Plast, watching the uninterrupted displays of sea life around them.

Mesa followed the annex to the opposite end, where another set of stairs wound down to the fifth and final sublevel, which was entirely deserted.

Whatever stores had once occupied the zone were defunct, their spaces shuttered, without even a Vacancy or For Rent sign to coax would-be businesses into setting up shop. Old posters hung on the walls beside empty trash bins, and the advertisements posted around the square were long since expired.

Mesa moved to the center of the square, thinking of it more as an arena, and let her shoulder slump. The bag fell and hooked in the crook of her elbow. She lowered it the rest of way and waited, counting the seconds in her head.

*Three against one,* Alice said. *You really think you can do this?*

*I've got you, right? That's two on three.*

*And this is your whole plan? Stand here and wait?*

Mesa figured the trio would split up and come at her from both sides, but it would be an uneven split. Two would come down the staircase she was facing, and the third from the stairs behind her. She was standing roughly in the center of the floor.

Handguns wouldn't be an option, not underwater, where the risk of an errant gunshot could do who knew what, despite all the impediments between solids and liquids. Unless the guns were silenced, the shots would be loud. Somebody would notice, particularly on the sparsely populated floor above, where the constant strum of noises, overlapping voices, and sound waves would not mask it. People would hear it, and they would certainly notice the three men rushing up the stairs to get back outside.

That left the plan of attack down to fists, knives, or another kind of melee weapon, maybe a shock stick or billy club. She wasn't planning on giving them enough time to intimidate her or coordinate an attack. Her plan boiled down to a simple concept—strike first.

Her silent count hit ten. Then twenty. When she hit thirty, she wondered if she'd been wrong. Maybe she'd been overly paranoid. Maybe the recog system had been incorrect. Or maybe she'd only been looking for what she had wanted to find. By fifty, she chided herself for being stupid but gave herself another ten-count.

She hit sixty, wondering if she should wait it out another few seconds. At seventy, she was ready to pick up her bag, telling herself to stop being foolish. Then she heard soft steps winding down the stairs.

She straightened, keeping her limbs loose but ready to strike.

A bark of laughter echoed down the stairwell, and a small cleaning crew stepped into view. They gave Mesa a cursory glance and moved on, resuming their conversation and laughter.

*Idiot*, she thought.

She scooped up her bag and climbed the stairs back to the central pavilion, rejoining the cramped confines of the marketplace. She looked around for the men, but they were nowhere in sight, even with the background layers of facial recog scanning for them. They were gone.

She pinged Rameez, and when he answered, she said, "Get your stuff and go to the lobby. Stick to areas where there are people. I'll meet you soon. We're leaving now."

The doors of the Cavour Hotel slid open, and Mesa stepped into a wonderfully cool lobby, leaving the warmth of the Pacific behind her.

The lobby hummed with conversations, music, and the sounds of the interactive concierge displays and check-in AIs. A train of suits marched past, heading to a glass-encased conference room.

She moved through the seating areas and the cloying smells of perfume and natural flowers. When she picked up the scent of coffee, her stomach quivered in need. A PetHuman robot was expertly playing the piano, and a few stylishly dressed women were gathered around it, talking animatedly. Past the waterfall display, Rameez sat at the bar.

Another PetHuman serving drinks was in the process of setting down a glass of rye on the rocks.

Rameez caught sight of Mesa and tilted the glass in her direction. The ice clinked against the tumbler.

"How much have you had to drink?" she asked. It hadn't been that long since they'd spoken, and it seemed unlikely that he could have gotten plastered in such a short amount of time.

"My second," he said.

"You feeling it?"

"I feel good."

"Okay. We gotta go. You have all your stuff?"

"What's happening?"

"The same shit that's been happening. Now come on." She hooked a hand around his biceps and pulled him to his feet.

He stumbled, spilling his drink across the bar, but recovered quickly.

"Mesa," he began then shut his mouth.

She followed his line of sight in time to hear the first shocked gasp, a scream, then a cry for help. Somebody yelled, "Gun!" That was enough to quicken the panic.

Although her dress was billowy, it also clung to her curves. Hiding a gun on her body had been out of the question. She pushed Rameez against the wall, told him to get down, then hunkered next to him, unzipping her bag in the process. She dug through her clothes then her fingers found the cool grip of her pistol.

"You stay close to me," she said.

He nodded numbly, eyes wide under the pulsing noise of semiautomatic gunfire and wretched screams.

She slid against the wall as she worked her way back to the lobby. She risked a quick glance back and saw Rameez close by, mimicking her movements.

Five gunmen were spread across the lobby, clad in black,

faces masked. She assumed three of them were the men she'd seen earlier. And she wondered whether the other two had been holed up somewhere or if she'd missed them. *Could there be more?*

Sparks flew as a hail of bullets punched through the PetHuman, shattering the white Dura-Plast casing of its torso and skull. The synthetic crashed against the piano keys, sending up a jarring shriek of notes before it crashed to the floor. The women who had been gathered around the instrument were caught in the crossfire, bullets stitching across their chests and bellies. Martini glasses fell from lifeless hands and shattered against the marble floor. The shards twinkled brightly in the blood seeping from their bodies.

Mesa moved quickly, keeping herself hunched low. She waved at Rameez, hoping he understood that he needed to stay put while she darted behind the cover of a thickly padded leather chair.

She got a bead on one of the soldiers and took the headshot, immensely gratified that her aim was true. Before the others could react, she swiveled her aim to another and fired, catching him in the throat.

Mesa ducked quickly as the three gunmen returned fire. The chair exploded in puffs of cotton, leather, and bits of wood as the rounds ate through it. She sprang forward, leaping behind the couch, the trail of ammunition following. She fired blindly over the side, hoping it would scatter the three men and hoping she didn't hit some unlucky soul. She hustled to the opposite end of the couch, risked a peek over the corner of the arm, and opened fire again.

She had their full attention, but none were the worse for wear. At least a dozen guests were dead, the lobby was ruined, and the stink of cordite hung in the air.

Despite the shock of the assault and the ringing in her ears, she heard the soft *thump* of an object landing nearby.

She didn't even look. She broke out into a straight run, moving quickly, keeping her head low and tucked between raised arms. Gunfire shattered the floor around her as she moved, and a painful sear tore across her back, followed by an uncomfortable stickiness that pasted the dress to her skin.

An explosion sent her off her feet, and hot shards of pottery and furniture were blasted around her. She rolled, ungainly, across the floor then leapt over the unmanned check-in counter. Bullets chunked into the thick facing, but none punched through it.

Mesa hurried to the opposite end of the desk, still low, and put as much distance as she could between herself and where she'd landed. The last thing she needed was another grenade landing on top of her.

The men were careful not to empty their magazines simultaneously, opting to fire in rotating spurts instead. If one ran out of ammo, two others still had rounds in their magazines.

She reached for her bag, grabbing air. *Shit!* The bullet that had screamed across her back must have cut through the bag's straps. *Not good.*

Bullets struck the wall above, sending plaster into the air and forcing her to think twice about standing to open fire on her assailants again.

A scurrying sound cut through the moment's quiet, followed by the blast of a single shot. She heard the wet splash against the automatic doors, the quiet hydraulic *shush* of their sliding open, then the meaty smack of a lifeless body crashing into the Dura-Plast.

The check-in desk was a long slab that ended in a curve on either side. Tucked into this corner, Mesa weighed her options. If she moved quickly enough, she could leap the counter and proceed down the lighted arch of the Cavour's restaurant. But she would have to be fast.

*Too risky,* Alice said.

Before Mesa could argue her plan any further, a man's panicked scream preceded a brilliant spark of light and a rush of heat. Gun forward, she stood, homing in on the direction of the shout. What she saw surprised the hell out of her.

The man was on fire, his limbs flailing beneath massive flames, smoke curling off his black clothing. His feet crunched against the shards of broken glass, and he tried to drop and roll. His hip bumped into the counter, and Mesa shot him in the face point-blank, silencing him.

On the far side of the lobby, Rameez readied another Molotov cocktail. A dishrag was stuffed into the open mouth of a whisky bottle, fire dancing its way up the fuse. He took aim at one of the soldiers and threw it hard, even while the man raised his weapon and opened fire. Rameez ducked quickly behind the lip of the doorway, and the gunfire shattered the small collection of bottles he'd assembled.

While Gunman One was distracted, Mesa turned her attention to the second man. They had their sights aimed on each other and fired at nearly the same time. Mesa had the good fortune of being a hair quicker, and her aim was true. His bullets missed her by a whisper.

She jumped, rolled over the counter, and landed in a dead run. She didn't care how loudly her shoes slapped against the marble floor. The noise was enough to draw the attention of the figure she had dubbed Gunman One, and that was all she needed.

Out of ammo but not out of options, she rushed him and raised the gun. She hammered it down against his skull as he turned toward her. She pushed his gun arm away and clubbed him again. He sagged, and the third time was the charm. Mesa felt his temple crack beneath the weight of her gun, and the life blinked out of his eyes. She hit him once more for good measure, then again, briefly reveling in the crunch of bone as she ruined his face beneath the black mask. The wail of approaching sirens drew her away from her own fury.

Rameez was tentatively staring past the edge of the bar's entry.

"Grab my bag," she said, motioning him toward the black lump of fabric and the splayed straps.

Darting toward the pack, he nearly slipped on the gory marble. His arms pinwheeled as he tried to rebalance himself. He caught the top loop of the bag while on the run and followed Mesa down the corridor, beyond the elevators, and down a hallway that hid the bathroom and emergency exit.

She didn't even slow as she barreled through the door and into an alleyway. The sirens were getting closer, sending waves of sound off the surrounding buildings.

Rameez hugged Mesa's bag to his belly.

They followed the alley away from the hotel and, not wanting to appear out of place, slowed to a more normal pace as the path bled into the heart of the commercial district.

"My God, Mesa, your back. You're bleeding."

"Shit!" She ducked back into the alley before she got too far out. Adrenaline had numbed the pain, and she'd forgotten about the injury. Nobody seemed to pay her much attention, and she stared down toward the opposite end of the alley. On the other side of the block, the sirens were still loud, but most of the people around her seemed unaffected. She took one of the oversized shirts from the bag and pulled it on. The fabric immediately turning sticky and bunched against the dress. The feeling was awful but better than pointing and gaping people yelling for the police or trying to help.

She stuffed the empty gun back into the bag, zipped it shut, and left him holding it. "C'mon."

She hooked her arm through his, trying to make them

appear as innocuous as possible. She could tell he was a nervous wreck, and she wasn't faring much better, especially since she had no idea how many more of Daedalus's agents were hunting them.

"You never took notice of anyone aside from those three?" she asked.

"I didn't even notice all three until you pointed them out to me."

She steered Rameez toward the edge of the floating island and took the stairs down to the docking level. As they moved to the far end of the marina, Mesa and Rameez returned the polite nods and smiles of the passing boaters.

"Have you got credits or u-currency on hand?" she asked.

Rameez was sweating profusely. He nodded curtly, constantly looking around and over his shoulders.

"Stop it. You're way too nervous. Give me the money."

With one hand, he dug out a fistful of chunky bronze coins and handed them over. She stepped over the seataxi's gunwale, took the bag, then helped Rameez aboard. She gave him the bag and told him to sit, while she fed the coins into the start-up scanner and followed the voice prompts.

"Central port," she told the boat's AI when it asked for their destination.

The vinyl seat squeaked as she sat, and a moment later, the little yellow boat motored away from New Venice. The cruise was slow, but it gave Mesa time to study the passing boats and their occupants. For his part, Rameez seemed to be calming down a bit, even though he was still hugging the bag with a death grip.

Mesa managed to free the backpack from his arms and opened it. Keeping the gun inside and out of sight, she ejected the empty magazine and exchanged it for a full one, racking the slide to put a round in the chamber. Then she fished around for a bottle of water and took a long pull before offering Rameez a drink. He nodded and took the bottle in shaking hands.

She stretched, her back tight but pain-free. Probably used to the regular maintenance of late, the medichines had sealed up the shallow groove of the gunshot wound. Those little nano devices had been put through the wringer over the last several days.

The taxi jumped a bit on the choppy waves caused by passing boats, but it ran quietly, and the ocean spray felt good. The last time she had been on a boat, she was with Jonah. A friend had died, and they had buried him at sea, wrapped in bedsheets and chains to weigh down his corpse.

The memory was jarring, least of all because it was not her own but Alice's. She didn't have time for another existential crisis or to weigh and examine each memory's origin and integrity.

Still, worry gnawed at her, leaving her shaken and unsettled. Mesa didn't even notice the small, fast-moving boat gaining on them until it crashed against the side of their seataxi. Fiberglass hulls screamed in protest as the boats slid against one another.

A quick flash of insight told her the baddies must have had the marina under surveillance. Probably, they'd been patched into the securiweb network and had watched her and Rameez marching down the steps, arm in arm, fake smiles plastered onto their faces, unable to hide the worry in their eyes.

She counted three men: two on deck, assault rifles bearing down on her and Rameez; the third stood at the helm. Their twenty-foot-long cuddy cabin seataxi was no match for the sleek, triangular high-performance speedboat the shooters were in.

Mesa grabbed Rameez's arm and threw him forward, pinning him to the ground against the high-walled gunwale, blind-firing as she dove for cover.

The taxi skidded over a wave, and she felt a momentary weightlessness as the craft rose. The shooters had veered sharply toward them, using the angular momentum in their favor to slam the thirty-footer into the taxi's portside hull once more. The boat's AI had registered the damage, and its blue emergency beacons were flashing.

Over the gunwale, Mesa saw the flash of curved silver as the speedboat clocked them again. Gunfire rang out, destroying the bow's solar panel array. The taxi jumped another wave then crashed into the breaking surface of the Pacific, spilling water over the gunwale.

Helpless, Mesa watched as semiautomatic gunfire obliterated the nonskid flooring and punching through the fiberglass of the stern. She rose and fired, catching one of the shooters off-guard but missing, nonetheless. The chop threw off her aim, and she hoped the other shooters were having the same difficulties compensating for the rough water.

The speedboat's pilot glanced her way, judging the distance, and spun the wheel, putting them on track for another collision. She knew she needed to time her actions exactly, while a part of her mind railed against her for being reckless.

She fired again at the shooters as the speedboat drew closer, readying herself to take the leap. As her opponents neared, she took a quick step up onto the gunwale then leapt forward, just as both boats cut through another rough wave.

The speedboat was longer and faster, and it shot up into the air with ease. The path the smaller, slower seataxi took was not nearly as angular. When Mesa leapt, she barely caught hold of the speedboat's metal cleat. Her shoulder howled in protest as her weight jarred the still-healing ligaments and fresh muscle before she smashed into the boat's hull. Her feet briefly touched down on the seataxi's gunwale as the speedboat crested the wave. Then it settled back into its natural buoyancy.

Scrambling for purchase, her flat-soled shoes slid across the slick hull. She raised her other arm to the next cleat, thinking of all the pull-ups she'd done for fun and exercise over the last few years. The haul would have been much, much easier if she hadn't nearly lost one arm a few days ago, and she gritted her teeth against the strain, forcing herself to work through the pain.

*C'mon, goddamn it,* she screamed at herself, her biceps bunching and shoulders aching as she edged up over the gunwale. The shooters were on track to smash into the taxi once more. Her options were either get up, over, and into the speedboat or be pulverized between the boats.

A gunman hurried to the gunwale, looking down at her. A wicked smile crossed his face, owning her dead to rights. Then he glanced up, startled.

Rameez was running across the stern of the seataxi, ducking behind the backpack as if it were some kind of shield. He built up speed then jumped between the two boats and landed clumsily on the stern of the speedboat. He slipped and barely had time to hook his fingers onto the back of the bench seating to save his life.

That stupid distraction saved Mesa's life. She raised her gun, fired a round under the gunman's chin, then put a second one through his Adam's apple. As Mesa hoisted herself up and over the gunwale, the second gunman took aim at Rameez. She dropped to a knee, bringing her gun up, and fired.

A line of bullets chewed through the stern before the assault rifle jerked up. A surprised yelp cried out over the gunfire. Two more pulls of her trigger silenced him for good.

Mesa rushed to the stern. Tackling the bench seat, she pulled Rameez toward her.

"Behind you!"

She barely dodged the butt of a machine gun intended

for the back of her skull. The speedboat's captain took another swing at her, and she jumped back, just barely out of the gun's arc. As the momentum of the wild swing pulled the man's torso away from her, Mesa stepped into the opening and clobbered him with her own gun, as he had intended to do to her. He stumbled back, in a daze. She stepped to his side, sending a quick kick into his knee. She heard a satisfying crunch of the meniscus and articular cartilage being destroyed under her blow. He collapsed to the ground, in too much shock to scream, and she wrapped one hand around the underside of his jaw. After clamping the other hand on the opposite side of his skull, she twisted, fast and with no remorse. She heard, as much as she felt, the vertebrae being torn apart as his neck snapped.

He dropped to the floor, paralyzed, but not dead. Not yet. She had severed the spinal cord between the fourth and fifth of the seven vertebrae in his neck, paralyzing the nerves that controlled the man's diaphragm, which controlled his breathing.

She moved away from the soon-to-be corpse and pulled Rameez to safety. Somehow, he'd managed to hold onto the bag, which she was grateful for. She tugged him into a firm hug.

"That's the second time you saved my life today," she said.

He blushed and turned his attention to the bodies scattered across the stern of the boat.

"How did you do all this?"

"I guess you could say I've picked up a few things here and there. That's for later, though. First, we need to get scarce before we put any more people at risk."

"Is that all of them, do you think?"

"I have no idea," she said, gutted at the prospect of more corporate goons chasing after them.

She took to the wheelhouse and steered toward an open

dock of the closest island. She wasn't even sure where they were. *Fuck it. Any port in a storm*, she thought.

Sirens wailed across the silent channel.

"We'll be keeping the police busy today," she said.

Rameez didn't seem to see the humor, but that was fine.

She nudged the boat against the dock then disembarked sprightly without bothering to tie it off. She helped her friend up and onto solid land once again.

They hauled tail back to the closest city square, where they were able to melt into the pedestrian crowds. Word of the assaults was buzzing through the collectives, and the individual states were ramping up security. Police presence had grown very visible surprisingly quickly, and the men and women of the security units seemed quite vigilant.

Mesa was grateful that her dress and shirt had dried quickly beneath the bright afternoon sun. She was still a mess, her hair wind whipped and salty, but plenty of women had similar fashion staples. By luck, they had wound up near a waterpark.

Mesa took the backpack from Rameez and went into a private changing stall. The bag was ruined: the straps had been shot clean through, and a long tear crossed the back. She rummaged through it, dumping out the MREs and bottles of water into a nearby garbage can. Having guns and ammunition on her was too risky, particularly with harbor security on high alert. All of it went into the garbage. She kept a few mem chips, false IDs, and a few tiny scraps of universal currency.

She gathered the chips into her palm and contemplated them for a few long seconds. They were her last ties to her father, the last vivid memories of Jonah and her time with him. A few were his mems, recollections of her as a child in

Los Angeles. The small fragments of data were all she had of a life she had no direct memory of and no other connection to. With a sigh, she snapped the chips in half, one by one, then released them into the recycler, burying them beneath the ruined bag and the detritus of previous visitors.

Back outside, she gave the paper money to Rameez to pocket, along with the fake ident chips. He stuffed them in his pants without a word.

Rameez took a long time getting his shakes under control and figuring out how to walk straight. He looked dazed, drugged. She spotted an open seat at a patio-side coffee shop and led him to a chair. She brought him water and hot tea, remembering Alice's words about the beverage being soothing.

She carried her coffee and sat. He sipped the tea, shutting his eyes against the steam, and for the first time in a while, he seemed to be at peace.

"Thank you," he said.

She reached across the table to squeeze his hand. They sat for a while, saying nothing, sipping their hot drinks. After twenty minutes, he seemed to be getting himself together and no longer visibly started at the sight of the roving foot patrols. A trio of police passed nearby, and Mesa nodded at them. They nodded back and continued on.

"Nothing to worry about," she told Rameez, worried that his pale complexion and intense interest in the tabletop would draw undue attention.

"What are we going to do?" he asked.

She'd been thinking about that, but she was at a loss and admitted as such. "Obviously, we can't stay here," she added. "We'll head over to the central harbor and catch a ride back to the mainland. After that, I don't know. I'm done running, though."

He nodded silently. A small measure of color seemed to be returning to his face as he finished the tea.

They took their time walking to the central harbor, passing over the bridges joining the cluster of city-states that encircled the port city's outer edges. "Central harbor" was a bit of a misnomer, as it wasn't actually the center of anything. It was, however, the main port for embarkation and debarkation of passenger liners heading to and from the seastead.

The lines to purchase tickets and for boarding were long. After another half hour of moving through a circuitous path to the automated teller, Mesa secured passes under the names Juliet Landreau and Abdulrahman Sufi.

While the line moved slowly, Mesa passed the time by reviewing Rameez's data on Schaeffer. She'd been over it half a dozen times, debating a course of action. Eventually, she settled on a plan, and after finding Schaeffer's secure contact information, she cobbled together a delivery packet.

Rameez spent most of his time in the line shuffling forward, thinking to himself, and it was rather late when he realized their destination.

"LA?"

"That's right," Mesa said. "We have some unfinished business to attend to there."

"We do, do we?" He arched an eyebrow at her. He'd never even been to LA before.

"I'll explain when we're on board. Be cool. Don't bug out, OK?"

He grumbled, but his face softened, and the perpetual worry lines of his brow smoothed a bit.

She hooked her arm through his and rested her head against his shoulder. "I'm sorry, Rameez."

"For what?"

"All of this," she said, her voice low. "This is all my fault."

"It's not," he said. "This whole thing is fucked, yeah, and you're caught up in the middle, OK. But, it's not your fault. You didn't cause any of this."

She gave his shoulder a soft kiss, grateful for his friendship and kindness. He'd always been a shoulder to lean on, literally or otherwise. Despite that, she could not convince herself that he was right or that he was saying anything other than kind, undeserved platitudes.

They navigated the rest of the winding line quietly. Then the tickets and biohacks gained them passage to the boarding ramp. A short time later, they found their cabin.

"Why LA?" he asked, after they'd spent a few moments getting settled.

"While we were in line for tickets, I skimmed through your info on Schaeffer. I hacked into his comm line and delivered him a message."

"You what?" he shouted.

# CHAPTER TWENTY-ONE

SCHAEFFER WATCHED THE DATA SCROLL in, cursing himself. Eight dead. But that was why they were the B team. He set the pad aside and stared at the decrepit form of Alice Xie, lasering her with a look of pure scorn. He should have known better than to give them the go-ahead to initiate. He'd let his eagerness get in the way.

In the long run, the consequences were minor. Each man's death would have signaled the nanos jetting through his bloodstream to begin rapid cellular decay. Medichines were powerful tools for healing, but with a bit of reverse engineering, they could be used to wreak severe trauma. The machines would begin by destroying fingerprints, facial features, teeth, and retinas.

The process was surprisingly quick, and by the time authorities responded, little information would be left to glean, and linking the corpses directly to Daedalus would be impossible. The violence at the hotel would create confusion and chaos, and authorities would chalk it up to a terrorist attack. With a few words in the right ears, it wouldn't take much cast suspicion on organization like the Earth Liberation Front or Al Qaeda, which had carried out similar attacks. If Daedalus was ever mentioned in the same sentence as the assault on the hotel or the chaotic shootings in the channels of New Venice, the discussion would quickly devolve into nonsensical conspiracy theories. So the company was safe in that regard.

Still, the loss of eight more troops stung, and his professional pride was deeply bruised. He salved his conscious with a glass of scotch, reminding himself of the pointlessness of self-recrimination. He had other matters to attend to.

He put his feet up, resting his heels against the edge of the thin mattress, near the woman's frail legs.

"You'll be glad to know your security protocols are functioning."

Alice's eyes flicked toward him, but she said nothing. The susurration of the assisted breathing machines pulsed.

"I had no idea you were that adept," he told her. "You really should have told me."

"She's still alive?" the speech modulator croaked.

"Oh, yes. Very much so."

The old woman's eyes closed, but he detected a subtle uptick to her lips. The hag was smiling at his failures.

He moved quickly, snatching her hand in his. Although a stroke had left Alice's entire body paralyzed, two fingers still managed to function properly. He grabbed her index and middle finger and savagely yanked the digits back. The scrape of bone and the snap of tendons stretched far beyond their natural elasticity was pleasing to his ears. Her eyes scrunched closed, but her eyelids were unable to stem the tide of tears. Rather than releasing her hand, he twisted the two broken fingers, applying a downward pressure to grind the bones of the proximal phalanges against the metacarpals, rolling her knuckles beneath his meaty fingers.

The corners of her jaws flexed, her mouth tightening against the respirator, her face screwed up in a horrendous grimace while she whimpered and cried. He dropped her hand then swiftly backhanded her face.

He tried to collect himself, but the anger was overwhelming. She was laughing at him, in spite of the pain he'd inflicted upon her. He straightened but thought of how easily he could wrap his hands around that frail neck and squeeze. He could rip that tube right out of her face, taking her throat with it, then choke her. He imagined her face empurpling, her mouth gasping for air, her eyes wide, while he squeezed and squeezed and squeezed.

*This fucking bitch.*

He sent a quick jab into her face, crumpling her nose beneath the large knuckles of his hand. Blood and snot flew from the pulped flesh. The bulbous cartilage of her already-deformed bridge had not quite healed from the last time he had broken it. The bruises circling her eyes were fading, but they would soon re-bloom with brilliantly dark shades of black, blue, and purple.

"Why do you always have to make things difficult for me, Alice?" he asked.

Of all the iterations of Alice Xie, the woman before him had been the most stable. She was temperamental, though, and prone to fits of uncooperativeness. For the most part, he had broken her. She was also proof that body-shifting could work, if applied with the right measures, under the right circumstances, with a specific protocol.

They had tested the procedure under various circumstances, with different variables, different drugs, and different degrees of mnemonic imprinting on brains of varying degrees of erasure. A complete template of Alice Xie had been implanted on a test subject who had not undergone a full-scale brain wipe, but the results had proven disastrous. The individual could not cope with multiple, fully cognizant personalities inhabiting a single, shared brain. In a fit of psychopathy, she had ripped out her own throat with her bare hands.

After that, Schaeffer and his team experimented with ZIP solutions, but in the end, it became clear that only a blank slate could handle the imprinting process.

And the old beaten hag was their greatest success. For all intents and purposes, she was an exact replica of Alice Xie. Mentally, at least.

Daedalus had attempted to replicate a more mobile and youthful Alice Xie, but those had all been mistakes. Schaeffer still bore the scars along his abdomen as a reminder. He was slightly proud of them, in fact. That Alice had tried to gut him with two shards of broken glass. Kaften had shot her twice, point-blank in the skull, despite Schaeffer's protests. That had been their earliest success at revivification and their largest failure. That was not to say, however, that the experiment had been a disappointment. Rather, it had been a teaching moment.

"You could have been much more than this," he said to her. He watched as her tears, blood, and snot dribbled down the crags of her ancient face, pooling between the strands of the crow's nest that was her hair and stain the white fabric of the pillowcase.

He couldn't help but feel that the wrecked woman they had transformed into Alice Xie had, in fact, been his largest failure. All her cunning and intelligence was wasted inside the frail body. Before the Daedalus experiments, the woman had been clinically brain dead, but they'd sparked a fresh life into a dead soul clinging miserably to a pointless existence. The shell was unfitting, too unbecoming, for a mind like

Alice Xie's.

Mesa Everitt, on the other hand... the poor girl probably did not even understand what was happening to her. It was certainly unlikely that Alice would have shared everything, openly and fully. That was hardly her style. But the Alice inside Mesa was merely a shard.

Mesa, though, was beautiful, agile, and graceful—certainly a far more worthy host than the dried-up husk before him.

"Jonah," the modulator croaked. The translation came with a noticeable hitch as the software stumbled over the mental and physical anguish of the old crone's thoughts.

"He's dead," Schaeffer told her.

And again, the hag laughed at him. The electronic warble was like nails on a chalkboard, zipping an uncomfortable shiver up the length of his spine, bunching the muscles in his neck and shoulders. Her lips pursed around that damnable breathing tube, forming as close to a smile as she would ever get. The enjoyment was clear in her eyes, though, beneath the pool of tears.

"She'll kill you," she said.

Schaeffer wondered which "she" Alice was referring to—Mesa or the data packet that recognized itself as a small measure of Alice Xie.

It made no difference, he decided. He stood, feeling more drained than usual but no longer angry. She had sapped him of that raw emotion, and he'd inflicted the pain he had so very much craved. He smoothed out the tangles of hair across the top of her skull and kissed her forehead, feeling the balance of power shifting between them. He'd broken her nose and two of her fingers, but he still felt as if she had somehow gotten the better of him. He could punish her further, but he knew it would accomplish nothing. This Alice Xie was waiting for her death to arrive, and he refused to be complicit in that. She wanted to goad him, to push him over the edge. Instead, he stood and left the room. Another Alice Xie was out there—one who wanted desperately to live. Killing her would be reward enough.

He thought to check in on Jade, but he doubted their meeting would be productive. He'd visited her earlier in the day, and the ZIP solution was progressing nicely. She was fully regressed and nearly vegetative. They would be able to imprint her body in the morning, and Schaeffer had twelve hours to settle on a candidate.

He returned to his room and was about to undress when his data pad pinged. *Strange.* He tapped the controls and found a file waiting for him, although he had not downloaded anything. A host of antivirals deemed it clean, and curiosity got the better of him. Indecision had never been one of his traits, and he opened it, a smile crossing his face.

*Speak of the devil, he thought, and the devil appears.*

The face of an attractive twenty-something was projected into the air before him. One side of her scalp was buzzed to little more than peach fuzz, while the other side was long and hung loosely over her face. He saw the hint of Japanese ancestry in her dark, almond-shaped eyes.

"I'm done playing these fucking games," Mesa said. "We meet, and we end this."

He couldn't help but wonder which woman was relaying this message. It made no difference. He closed the file, feeling oddly content.

He opened a commNet line to his pilot. "Take me to LA."

As he drifted to sleep, he felt a calm measure of assurance, as if the balance of power had begun to slide back into his favor once again.

# CHAPTER TWENTY-TWO

**"Y**OU WHAT?" RAMEEZ SHOUTED.

"I sent him a message. We're meeting him."

Rameez looked too shaken to even know how to respond. His arms flailed as he sputtered, obviously trying to strum up an objection that would vindicate his frustration.

Sitting across from her, seething and red-faced, he said, "You can't do this."

"Why not?" she asked.

"He'll kill you!"

"I'm really kinda hoping it goes the other way."

They went back and forth for a while, then each gave up on the other and retreated to opposite corners of the cabin. Even with some distance between them, Mesa could still feel the aggravation boiling off him.

"You don't have a better plan," she told him.

His mouth dropped open. Shut, open, shut. He was utterly without a plan. After a long moment of silence, he asked, "So, what's your plan?"

"We put the shoe on the other foot. I gave Schaeffer the when and the where. I'll be able to get him to a fixed location. All I need to do is get there before him and observe. I doubt he'll come alone, so it'll be a matter of neutralizing the opposition and then dealing with him."

"What makes you think he'll show?"

Mesa nodded in concession. The question was valid, but the answer wouldn't make Rameez any more comfortable.

"He wants me. And, maybe more importantly, he wants what is in my head."

Rameez scrunched his eyes, balling one hand into a fist in his lap. "Which is what?"

"Alice Xie."

His mouth fell open.

"Or at least a part of her anyway."

"Alice Xie is dead."

"Four-fifths of her is dead," Mesa said. "She sent out fragments of her memory, data packets that were composite slices of her personality. They were essentially portions of backup files. That's why Daedalus has been killing memorialists. They're trying to wipe her out."

"And somehow, you have one of those packets?"

"She abducted me three years ago and wiped my memory. I have a part of her in my head."

"Was this all her idea or something? Going to LA and doing the meeting?"

"We talked it over."

"This unfinished business then. You said 'we' had unfinished business in Los Angeles. That was you and Alice then?"

"Correct."

"Let me see if I've got this right. Schaeffer wants Alice,

who you're sharing headspace with. You set up a meet, and the plan is to kill him first?"

"Basically."

"That's thin," he said. "That's really fucking thin."

"Why complicate it?"

"I don't think you've thought this through."

"I have, Rameez. More than you can possibly realize. It's all I've been thinking about."

He sighed. "I didn't mean..."

"I know. It's OK. But you need to trust me. I have thought this through. *We* have thought this through. And I think we have a handle on it."

"What about Jade?" he asked.

"That's what I need you to work on," Mesa said. "While I deal with Schaeffer, you figure out a way to get us aboard his ship. I need schematics, crew rosters. Figure out how many people are aboard, keep an eye out for who comes and goes, how tight the security is. Find out where Jade is. I'll deal with the rest."

"This is insane."

"Playing it safe hasn't made things any better. There's no reasoning our way out of this. Schaeffer won't stop until I'm dead. Or until I stop him. That's the bottom line. That's what I'm going to do."

"You really think it will work?"

She shrugged. "As I said, there's two ways through this. It'll work."

Rameez turned in his chair to watch the waves beyond the porthole. The ship had caught the attention of a pod of dolphins, and he watched as they swam along the starboard side, occasionally breaching and diving back down.

Mesa stood beside him, watching the beauty and grace of the animals. Ancient Greeks had considered dolphins to be a good omen, and she hoped they had not been wrong. She found a simplistic joy to their playful display. She squeezed Rameez's shoulder and told him to get some rest.

"What are you going to do?" he asked.

"I'm too amped up. I need to go for a walk or something, burn off some energy." And, she thought, probably try to find yet another pair of clothes to replace her dress and salty T-shirt.

She roamed the ship, working her way up to the lido deck. She felt an urgent need to get drunk on hard liquor. The barman put down a tumbler with two fingers of whisky, and she shot it back, letting the burn flood through her chest and belly. She put the cool glass to her forehead then knocked it toward the bartender.

"One more," she said. He nodded and refilled it. She took her time on the second drink.

*It's almost over*, Alice assured her. But really, Mesa wasn't sure whether Alice had spoken or if she'd heard herself trying to be positive. Alice had said she'd put up walls between them, but they were tumbling quickly, the foundations weak, the mortar cracked and brittle. Nothing divided them, and the more Mesa probed, the more she realized Alice was fully enmeshed in her mind. Distinguishing her own thoughts from Alice's was increasingly difficult.

She realized they were more united than separated. The ease with which Mesa killed, even going back to the men she'd murdered in Des Moines—that wasn't her, and yet it was fully her. When she tried to figure out if that part of her was more Mesa or more Alice, she couldn't distinguish the two.

*Or maybe we're not all that different, you and I*, Alice said.

*You said I was a lot like my father.*

*He killed to survive, same as you. Same as me. You have his toughness. His tenacity.*

*But is that mine, or is it yours?*

*You possess it. That is the important part.*

*I want this to be over,* Mesa said.

*Soon, it will be.*

*I don't even know who I am,* she said. *I thought I was putting the pieces together, but now... I'm more lost than ever. I don't know anything anymore. This isn't me. Do you get that? Killing people, running, being a fugitive—that isn't me. That's you. That's all fucking you.* She spun the tumbler between both hands then drew slowly from the cool glass.

*Do you think life ever gives you what you ask for, Mesa? Because it doesn't. Not ever. You have to fight just to scrape by. You do not ever get what you want simply because you think you've earned it. This is almost finished, though. We will finish this, together.*

*And then what? We go our separate ways? How does that work? How do I get you out of my head? I don't think I can. I think you're stuck inside me, a part of me. You're a fucking infection.*

*There are ways, child, but I doubt you'd appreciate the answer.*

*Is there even a backup of me, or was that a lie, too?*

*It was the truth.*

She knew that Alice was being honest, as much as she knew that the kernel of data held no answer as to the whereabouts of that backup. The answer to that was on *Alabaster,* in the full dataset of an Alice Xie that had died three years ago. She hadn't told Rameez that part of it, though. He was better off believing that Jade was the only reason she wanted aboard that airship.

Mesa finished the final sip of whiskey, savoring the last swallow. She shut her eyes against the voices in her head, and when she caught the bartender's questioning eyes, she nodded.

"One more," she said.

# CHAPTER TWENTY-THREE

As the transit ship approached, Mesa stood at the bow railing and marveled at the collection of vessels: cruise ships with foreign names and flying international flags, cargo ships with massive containers, and pleasure yachts and sailors.

While border relations were far from normal, the Pacific Rim Coalition was easing restrictions on tourist travel to and from California. Though the flow of information was still strictly monitored and controlled, the PRC's leaders and their advisors were not blind to the benefits of tourism and trade.

Following their occupation, the PRC had placed a heavy emphasis on reestablishing the port authority and expanding the Los Angeles Harbor.

"Check out the tall ships," Rameez said, pointing.

She followed his gaze to the *Kaiwo Maru*, a four-masted barque more than ninety feet long. They passed more full-rigged ships, schooners from Germany and Portugal, a brig from the UK, and a full-rigged ship from Italy.

"They're beautiful," Mesa said. The vessels held an elegant, old-world charm that beckoned to the period of colonial expansion and the majesty of the sea.

The harbor occupied more than eighty acres of seafront, and their ship navigated past the cargo terminals to one of the thirty passenger terminals. She and Rameez watched the flurry of activity around them, the squawking gulls as they dove through the air, and the slow-moving march of passengers unloading from the ships around them.

Other than the clothes they wore, Mesa and Rameez had no belongings to speak of and no reason to return to their room. Mesa had visited the gift shop and bought a fresh pair of jeans, new sneakers, and a T-shirt bearing the ship's logo. She'd also bought a cheap pair of dark sunglasses, which rested atop her head.

After letting the crowd have a solid head start off the boat, Mesa and Rameez disembarked, taking in the sights around them.

The port was a glamorous construct of multi-storied glass, the ferry terminal building a fusion of high-end Asian couture and art deco. Metal red lanterns lit the way to customs, and they passed sporadically placed terracotta warrior statues, pairs of lions, and a profusion of Buddhas. From customs, they took a taxi into the heart of the city.

"Destination?" a tinny, disembodied voice inquired.

"Corner of *Dai Hok Gai* and *Lei Min*," Mesa said. Alice had provided the address of her restaurant in Chinatown, and after both Mesa and Rameez were buckled in and traffic had cleared, the cab merged and followed an automated route toward downtown.

The driverless vehicle provided them a small respite

from the noise and chatter of the vibrant city. Mesa couldn't get over how much things had changed since the last time she'd been there.

*No,* she corrected herself. The last time *Alice* had been here.

The city's nightlife was active, and while she found plenty of reason for concern in the heavy, obvious presence of armed soldiers walking the streets, most of the civilians seemed untroubled by the active security.

Terrorism and threats of random violence were as prevalent as they had ever been. After the US lost California to the PRC, multiple other states seceded from the Union to go it alone, create their own coalitions, or join Canada, as several northern states had. Then Liberty's Children struck out against Pacific Rim Coalition forces.

There was little actionable intelligence on the group, and most presumed they were ex-US military who had stayed behind enemy lines following the dissolution of their government. Occasionally, they released statements, but their patriotic vitriol was hidden behind self-indulgence and a wayward, embittered sense of entitlement. They claimed to be the last bastion of American freedom fighters, but in reality, they were nothing more than zealots and child killers.

Mesa watched the scenery pass as more of Alice's memories bled through. What she saw nearly defied comprehension.

Before, much of downtown had been reduced to rubble. Demolished skyscrapers had been nothing more than jagged, broken reminders of a richer past among streets littered with corpses, burned-out husks that vaguely resembled twisted automobiles, and shards of glass.

That atmosphere had given way to jazz clubs, sushi bars, a whiskey bar called the Highlander, and street vendors. Even though the cab's windows were rolled up, Mesa could smell garlic and onion frying in fat, and the air was redolent with aromas of chicken and pork hitting hot oil. Lines of good-humored smiling people formed around fusion-themed food trucks. Bright neon lights flashed and vied for attention, reflecting off the windows and rain-slicked streets.

"What the hell?" Rameez said, laughing.

She turned to look out his window. A small Chinese man dressed as Conan the Barbarian was tussling with Spider-Man for a chance to win a kiss from a Korean woman wearing a large platinum-blond wig. She wore a lovely white dress and was standing over an automated steam grate that, at regular intervals, blew air at her, sending her skirt up in the air.

*Marilyn Monroe*, Alice said, filling in the blanks for Mesa. The name meant nothing to her.

People applauded the street-side performance as they ate noodles from disposable cups. A few tossed coins into a nearby tip jar.

A network of spires rose and twisted above the highway, curling into an antiprism. A manicured greenscape was built into the snaking construct, like vines wrapping around, between, and through the mind-boggling building. The structure contorted in defiance of basic geometry as well as the laws of space itself, as if it weaved through multiple dimensions simultaneously. Neither Alice nor Mesa had ever seen anything like it before.

Alice's confusion pushed Mesa into sensory overload. She felt an irreconcilable conflict between the familiarity and strangeness of her surroundings. Nothing was familiar, yet it was also home. Both had lived and walked these streets many times, but each woman was equally lost in her own separate way. Whatever had once been there for either of them was irrevocably lost to the past. Progress had stepped in while they were away and turned over everything, from stem to stern. Everything was different, and there was an uncomfortable quietude in that.

A headache blossomed deep inside Mesa's cerebral cortex, and she wasn't sure if she wanted to scream, cry, laugh, or dig her nails deep into her wrists, tear out her veins, and paint the inside of the cab with her own blood. Then she had her face in her hands, trying to breathe, to get control, but her chest felt tight. The cab was small, too small, and she was lost. A horrifying squeezing sensation pulled taught across her neck, and she tried to work her fingers beneath the cords, her nails scraping across skin. Rameez grabbed her hands, pulling them away, and Jonah was standing over her and behind her, his face taught and his lips thinned with strain and—

Mesa snapped forward, dazed, blinking rapidly. Rameez stared at her, his breathing ragged—as ragged as hers.

"Rameez?" she asked, confused. She glanced around. The cab slowly resolved before her eyes. It took her a long moment to reorient herself and realize where she was. *I'm still in the cab*, she thought. *Still in the cab.* Beyond the windows were unfamiliar terrain, smiling people, and foreign buildings where Asian adornments challenged the generic facades of McDonald's, Gucci, and Victoria's Secret.

"I'm sorry," she said, curling up into the corner of the seat. Although she had pulled her hands away from his, Rameez's hands still hung in the air before him, palms up. She had never realized how pale his palms were, and after a moment, he took them back. She wrapped her arms around her legs, pressing the side of her head against the cool window.

"Are you OK?" he asked, the words drawn and measured.

"I don't know," she said, equally slowly. "I don't know what happened." She took several deep breaths, her lungs aching. Her heart was racing, her palms sweaty. She shut her eyes and fought to calm herself.

"How much do you remember?" he asked. "You know

where you are, right?"

"Yeah, dummy. I'm in the back of a fucking cab."

"Okay."

She stared out the window, where everything was still uncomfortably unfamiliar. "Fucking California," she said.

"Well, you know that much, at least," he said. "What happened?"

She bit her lower lip, slowly shaking her head, at a loss for words. "I don't even know how to explain it. It was like... Alice, you know? She freaked, I think. She freaked, and it made me freak. We freaked out, I guess. It was weird."

"You are still, um, you? Right?"

Too tired to laugh, she let out a dry snort. "Yeah," she said. "Yeah, I'm still me. Far as I know anyway."

"Do you remember anything?" he asked again.

"What is that, a trick question?"

"Huh?"

"Ask the girl who doesn't remember anything at all what she remembers?" She tapped her head. "Whole life. Gone. I remember that much."

"Oh. Right."

"Alice said she had put up walls between us. I don't think that worked out too well."

Rameez's shoulders slumped, and he clasped his hands together. He was lost in deep waters. "Did she try to kill you?"

"No, I don't think so."

"How do you know?"

She tossed him a sour expression. "I don't know. I just know. You know?"

"Oh. OK."

"Christ, my head hurts," she said, massaging her temples with the index and middle fingers of both hands. She ground out wide circles on either side of her head, hoping to loosen the tension.

*You still in there?* she asked, not sure if a reply was a good sign or not.

*I'm here,* Alice said.

Mesa let out a deep breath. *What was that?*

*Bleedthrough.*

*Yeah, I got that much. That was epic.*

*I'm not sure what you want to hear,* Alice admitted. *This is all very new for me.*

*I guess that seals the deal then, huh? We find your other you onboard Alabaster and get you transferred the fuck out of my skull.*

*Were there really any other options?*

*Nope.*

"We're here," Rameez said. He nodded out Mesa's window, toward the bright lights of Alice's restaurant.

Mesa hadn't even noticed the taxi had stopped. She popped the door open and stood on wobbly legs, grabbing onto Rameez for support. He helped her over to a statue of a lion. Its large front paw rested atop a small sphere, where she leaned and waited to get her bearings.

"OK," she said after a long moment.

He helped her navigate around the side of the restaurant to an alley-side entrance. The solid black door was flush with its frame and had no window or doorknob. It did have, however, a coded touchscreen panel.

Mesa approached and, using Alice's mnemonic input, entered the sequence. The entry code was sixteen digits long, followed by a complex trace pattern that required her to run her index finger in a confusing jumble of lines, dashes, and swirls. There was no indication that she had gotten the data entered correctly, then a heartbeat later, the black door released with a pneumatic hiss.

She stepped through, taking hold of the guide built into the wall, and descended the stairs. Another touchpad just inside required another complex sequence of gestures and alphanumeric entries.

The door released, and the automatic lights sensed her movements, bathing the room in a cool-white glow.

Blood was smeared across the walls. Bullet holes pockmarked the work areas and stained desktops. The room had a distinctly metallic stink, and she could very nearly taste the copper on the back of her tongue.

Despite the apparent violence, a part of her—a part that was distinctly Alice—felt perversely at home. The room felt empty in the absence of their fellow memorialists.

# CHAPTER TWENTY-FOUR

MESA SET THE ALERT FUNCTION on the DRMR dash to lull her out of sleep after three hours. She couldn't afford to sleep longer, or more deeply, than that.

The software protocols slowly dragged her consciousness back to the surface, and she opened her eyelids. For a moment, she was lost, until her memory caught up and told her where she was.

Sleep had been a bad idea. Mesa awoke more exhausted than she had been before drifting off, and her body was stiff and achy. Lying on the floor had been uncomfortable, and her back felt painfully torqued. She sat up, stretching her arms up high over her head, eliciting a gentle protest from her still-healing shoulder. She wondered briefly if she might turn into one of those old fuddy-duddies she often heard complaining of aching joints, using their swollen arthritis to predict changes in weather.

Rameez snored softly beside her, and she moved quietly but swiftly. Alice had planned smartly, and Mesa and Rameez had found sleeping bags tucked away in a compartment in the corner of the room. Rameeze seemed to be having an easier rest than Mesa had, at least.

Crawling out of the bag, she went to a nearby false panel set into the flooring and removed a piece of three-by-six slate. The crevice revealed a score of old, palm-sized Exabyte drives, credit chips, and loose paper currency for both the PRC yen and u-cash. More importantly, though, were the guns.

She drew out three Heckler & Koch P30Ls with lightweight trigger pulls. The serial numbers had been removed, and the rubber grips were worn. The guns felt comfortable in her hands, and she lined them up on the opposite side of the hidey-hole, ejecting the clips for each and racking the slides to clear the chambers. A dozen magazines were stacked alongside the guns, each full of standard ammunition stocks. There were no fancy fragmentation rounds or smart bullets with muscle-wire guidance and heat sensors for precision aiming. She had multiple clips, each filled with fifteen rounds of nine-millimeter ammo, and luminous contrast points for aiming on each gun barrel. She also had a single silencer, which rested beside the guns and magazines.

*Good enough*, she thought.

After breaking down and cleaning each gun, she reassembled them and tucked one into her waistband. She pulled her loose T-shirt over it, hiding the gun.

She took a black shoulder tote from the hole and filled it with the other two guns and spare magazines, along with the currency and credit chips. The Exabyte drives were of no use to her; she left them where they were and slid the slate panel back into place.

Rameez was coming to.

"Sorry," she said, brushing her hair back behind her ear.

He smiled. "It's fine."

She smiled back, fingering a long, errant lock of hair that had fallen in front of her cheek. Standing, she slung the bag over her shoulder. "You good?" she asked.

"I've got the easy part," he said.

She'd gone over the game plan with him the night before. She was going to be in place early and wait on Schaeffer to arrive. Rameez was to stay hidden in the enclave den, where he could work on gaining her access to *Alabaster* and try to find Jade's location aboard the ship.

The alley was lined with a tight network of securiweb nanos, and he'd hacked into the security feeds. If anyone approached the restaurant, Rameez would know about it immediately. More guns were secreted around the room, and Mesa had cleaned another pistol for him so that he wouldn't be completely defenseless. If worse came to worst, though, he could flee through the network of escape tunnels. Mesa didn't expect that he would need to use them, but Alice reminded her that they had proved useful in the past and were there for a reason.

"Okay, then," she said. She knelt beside him and gave him a chaste kiss on the forehead. "You be careful. Keep an eye on those webs."

"I will," he promised. "I'm more worried about you, though."

She smiled but said nothing.

Alice had been unusually withdrawn—Mesa wondered whether the woman was still a part of her or if she had somehow been flushed away. Then, in a deep recess of her mind, she felt the other woman silently making her presence felt. If Mesa wasn't careful, she could easily forget that Alice's subtle and hidden presence was still there. The change in Alice's behavior made Mesa more guarded and left her more uncomfortable and wary of the secondary personality. She felt as if she were watching a snake readying to strike, but at even that thought, Alice was quiet. Mesa sensed Alice at the corners of her peripheral awareness more than she actually heard the other woman.

*Is this how madness feels?* Mesa asked.

Alice refused to take the bait and buried herself deeper. If Mesa had not known better, she might have thought the woman was coping with panic or a madness of her own.

Closing the door behind her, Mesa was careful to lock it and reengage the security grids. She gave silent thanks again to Rameez, hoping for his safety. She couldn't help but wonder if she would ever see him again, but rather than being damned by the raw emotion, she felt peace and acceptance.

She was prepared.

Mesa swore softly to herself, staring down at the city streets seven stories below. Traffic was at a standstill, halted by a random PRC vehicle checkpoint. Four soldiers went down each lane, stopping at driver's-side windows, asking questions, and studying vehicle interiors. A slightly visible mobile securicloud hovered through the air, moving around and beneath the cars, sniffing for bombs.

On one hand, the checkpoint was stupid, bad luck. On the other hand, she was three hours ahead of the scheduled meet time—that gave the soldiers plenty of time to deem the area safe and move on. None of the PRC troops seemed interested in the street-side coffee shop where she and Schaeffer had planned to meet; however, she couldn't help but feel a little paranoid.

She sat on the roof of a parking garage, which was nearly deserted. The neighborhood was struggling to rebuild, and open storefronts were scarce. The most the neighborhood had going for it was the coffee shop, which actually seemed to be doing decent business based on the smattering of people sipping drinks on the patio and acting oblivious to the PRC shouting at drivers nearby. Vehicles were parked along the curb, and Mesa could count the number of cars inside the garage on one hand.

*Nothing much to do but wait,* she thought.

She was counting on Schaeffer and his team to get into place early and set up a watch for her own arrival. She was also counting on being in place before that and having a chance to observe the Daedalus forces she would be going up against.

Three hours had seemed a reasonable amount of time to ensure beating them to the meeting spot. The garage roof gave her the elevation she needed to watch for them. She figured they would want at least an hour of lead time on her.

The PRC were a sticking point, though. If they were still around in three hours, they could inhibit whatever Daedalus was planning—and that was fine. But the problem remained on her side of the equation. Did she dare to risk striking out against the opposition with armed military so close? Or what if Schaeffer was using them to get to her?

*Just wait and see,* Alice said, her echo slowly bubbling to the surface. *Be patient and observe.*

*Yeah, yeah, yeah. I know.*

After an uneventful hour passed, the PRC packed themselves back into their armored carrier, and traffic resumed its normal flow. Not long after that, Schaeffer appeared, rounding the corner of the block on foot. He strode confidently to the open-seating area outside the coffee shop and picked a seat that afforded him a wide view of the street before him.

He appeared to be alone. Mesa hadn't taken note of any unusual behaviors from others in the area. No other new arrivals had immediately preceded his arrival or followed directly in his wake.

Mesa watched as a waitress took his order. Alone again, he slowly scanned the area, taking a very long time to track right to left.

She let him get comfortable then pinged him with an audio file she had uploaded to a secure drop box. "Make sure you leave her a good tip. Meet me at Descanso Gardens in an hour. Alone."

He discreetly checked out his surroundings but made no other movements. When the waitress arrived, he asked for a to-go cup and passed her a large bill in payment. His eyes studied the people nearby but took no apparent interest in anyone in particular. Waiting for the waitress again, he resettled in his seat.

Again, Mesa did not notice any changes in anyone else's behavior. Nobody broke away in a hurry, no speeding cars peeled around the corners—she saw no obvious indications that Schaeffer had brought anyone with him.

She worked her way down the stairs and exited through the rear entry well, to the street facing the opposite side of the block, where she was out of Schaeffer's sightlines. Then she boarded a bus and spent the next twenty minutes debating whether or not he would wait the full hour to show.

Opening the commNet, she pinged Rameez. In addition to her street-level surveillance, Rameez was hacked into the city's securiweb and monitoring the street cams.

Mentally, she asked him, "What's happening?"

"You were right," he said. "Schaeffer is not alone."

"Can you take care of it?"

After a few seconds of silence, he patched the city cams into her retinal heads-up display. "You can see the feeds?"

"I can," she said.

"One team is in the black sedan," Rameez said.

Mesa watched the car approach a traffic light at a four-way intersection, which turned from red to green on all sides. The result was pure calamity, and a smaller economy-class vehicle collided with the sedan. Confusion and chaos took over as drivers swerved, braked, and crashed into one another. The sedan was completely blocked in.

Quickly, she set up another audio file and pinged Schaeffer with it. "I told you to be alone. I took care of your backup. No more games."

Turning her attention back to Rameez, she said, "Keep connected with me, just in case. And watch out for any others. Can you do that?"

She worried about overloading him with too much multitasking in addition to trying to find Jade.

He shrugged. "It's not a problem."

"Good. This next stop is mine," she said.

Established in the mid-twentieth century, Descanso Gardens was an urban retreat consisting of one hundred sixty acres of gardens and woodland. She passed through Magnolia Lawn, where a flurry of children chased one another across the bridge then took off down the trail, disappearing from sight. On the Main Lawn, vendors sold bento box lunches and cocktails, and the reverberations of taiko drums drowned out the raucous cries of unseen children.

After crossing a stone bridge, Mesa moved across the lawn to an empty bench beneath a newly blossomed cherry tree. Using the shoulder tote to hide her movements, she sat with the H&K in her lap, hidden beneath the bag.

Masked by the lush grounds to her rear and obscured from the sides by the profusion of cherry blossoms, she felt safe enough. Plenty of people were taking in the fresh air and the beauty of the garden, and she decided Schaeffer would be unlikely to launch a direct attack there, not while he was present and right in the middle of the action.

She reached into the bag and withdrew the silencer

then screwed it into place beneath the tote. She felt surprisingly nervous. While she was certainly no stranger to killing—thanks to the tumultuous week, Daedalus's goons, and, probably, Alice's moral subroutines—her plans for Schaeffer were clouded with an uncomfortable degree of premeditation. She struggled with the morality of deliberately planning a man's execution, and in public, no less. In a park, where children's laughter and shouting filling the same air, she was planning to pollute that air with the whisper of a gunshot and her prey's final gasp.

*This isn't who I am*, she thought with sudden clarity.

*Isn't it?* Alice replied with a churlish tone, mocking her.

*This is you*, Mesa insisted, but even in her own head, the words lacked weight.

*You can't even convince yourself*, Alice said.

Mesa watched Schaeffer approach, one hand at his side, the other carrying a cardboard coffee cup.

*This is who we are*, Alice said.

Her finger tightened on the trigger, but Mesa willed herself to relax. Alice's desire to kill was keen and primal.

*Not yet*, Mesa said. *We need answers.*

"May I sit?" Schaeffer asked then waited for Mesa's acquiescence. "This was smart," he said. "It's a beautiful day. And this tree... you picked a good spot."

"Wasn't really my plan to talk horticulture," she said.

He flashed a good-humored grin. "That's good. I think I used up all my knowledge on vegetation."

"Okay. Let's cut to the chase then."

He nodded, waving for her to continue.

"I gotta say, I'm not too thrilled about the way you've been conducting business."

"Daedalus is very protective of its intellectual properties. You're violating a shitload of patent rights, kid. And you're in possession of stolen information, which is a little thing known as industrial espionage."

"Uh huh," she said. "So, like I said, let's cut the shit and deal."

"A deal?" He sounded surprised.

Her heart hammering, she said, "I'm saying, you're a business man, right? Your little shock troops have killed my family, my friends, and you've run me out of Dodge six ways to Sunday. And yet, I still have everything you're after, which means your plan has gone the entire straight fucking way to hell.

"So, yeah, let's deal. Your way isn't working too swiftly, which you must have realized by now and which is why you're sitting in a fucking park with me. I've got what you want, and you've got what I want."

"And what is it you want?" he asked.

"I want my friend Jade back," she said, her mouth dry. "And I'll give you Alice Xie for her."

"Hmmm. See, now, that's where the rub is at, isn't it?" Schaeffer held her gaze, his eyes hard and cold. "Because I already have an Alice Xie. Which is how I know you have an Alice Xie. And since you have her, you know some company secrets that we are not quite yet ready to go wide with. Now, before you think that I've been a bit fussy about all this, I can promise you, if our marketing gurus got wind of you stealing our thunder before we go to market—well, sweetheart, you ain't seen nothing yet. You think you've got nothing left to lose, and I've seen people in your same position before with a similar attitude. Let me tell you straight up—there is always something more for you to lose. I can promise you that."

Mesa nodded, weighing his words. She looked out across the stretch of green grass, seeking any movements through the tree line and finding none. "I give you Alice, and you do whatever you need to do to get my head back on straight and make sure I'm free of your little industrial-espionage bullshit. You give me Jade."

"Those are some remarkable lengths you're willing to go to for a girl you don't know that well."

"She's my friend."

Schaeffer took a long pull from his coffee cup as she spoke. "Mmmm, see, that's interesting. Is she your friend, or is she Alice's friend?" He wiped a small dot of foam from his upper lip with the back of his hand.

"What?" Mesa asked, caught off guard.

"Huh. I guess that means Alice didn't tell you."

"Tell me what?"

Her finger curled around the trigger of the gun still hidden by her tote bag. A tight voice insisted that she pull it. She fought to stay herself from shooting him, despite the powerful urge.

Schaeffer gave her a small smile full of mock pity. "Seems your sweet, dear, good friend Jade is actually in cahoots with Alice. In fact, seems she was sent to spy on you and make sure Alice started poking through. She was supposed to help round up the other data carriers, get our old girl reunited with her bad self and made whole. It's kind of funny you call her a friend, because she is *really* not your friend."

"You don't know anything about us."

"You mean like how you and her got... oh, let's say... *familiar* with one another."

Mesa's cheeks burned.

"But then you traded up to Kaizhou. Hey, how's he doing, by the way?"

Her eyes stung, and the blush deepened until her whole face felt aflame. Her heart knocked against her breastbone in violent spasms, missing entire beats. The gun felt weightless, and she spun as the world canted sideways and her finger tightened on the trigger.

A small boy ran by, chased by a young girl with long black pigtails. Their shrieks snapped Mesa back, but seeing Schaeffer's smiling face sent a shiver through her.

"Ah, that's right," he said, sounding not the least bit remorseful. He pulled the coffee to his lips and took another long, appreciative sip, his eyes never leaving Mesa's.

"You know, I think maybe we could have come to an arrangement on this," he said, "if we weren't so far down this path already. I've cost you, and you've cost me. I can't help but think there may be some bad blood between us, mostly on your side, of course. I know you're young and you don't understand the economics of all this. You're all wrapped up in the emotions of it all. I get that—I do.

"I'm just not sure that, one," he said, ticking the points off on his fingers as he spoke, "you would be a very reliable business partner. And, two, the expense of all this has been very taxing. I can't simply roll over and cut you a deal. It wouldn't be a very shrewd investment, you see? You are the living embodiment of what we call a volatile market. One day, you're high; the next day, you're low. We don't know how you'll perform in the long run. So, no. I don't think I can take you up on your offer."

"I understand," she said, gathering all the composure she was capable of. "I suppose it's on to plan B."

He watched her with an expression of mild amusement, then his hand went to his stomach. A scarlet circle blossomed above his hip, covering his fingers with red. He seemed genuinely surprised that he had been shot.

The children and tourists had moved on, and Mesa found herself alone with Schaeffer in the garden, beneath the cherry tree. She stood, using her body to block the view of the gun in case any passersby came near. She leaned over Schaeffer, pretending she were about to kiss him.

He tried to speak, but his lips curled around gasping noises. Blood bubbled in the corners of his mouth. She thought about the angle of his wound and the closeness— the bullet was probably lodged in his spine.

Bent over the man, she fired twice more, directly into

his chest. She felt his last breath against her neck and face, carried on a gentle breeze that ruffled the white petals of the tree's blossoms.

Mesa dumped the gun back in the tote then turned heel, quickly surveying the garden. She was the only soul in sight, and she headed back toward the trail, quickly forgetting the unease she had felt over murdering the man minutes before.

Alice's words still hung over her, though, damning her.

*This is who we are.*

# CHAPTER TWENTY-FIVE

RAMEEZ BROKE CODE, REBUILDING IT with algorithms of his own design, ghosting the system full on. Racing through tangents of ones and zeros, data hounding them, he felt completely at ease and in his element for the first time in a long while. Hacking was what he was good at.

Mesa, it seemed, had found her own unique capabilities, and he trusted her enough to not be totally disturbed by her new skill set. *Or Alice's old skill set, maybe. Whatever.* She'd pulled his fat out of the fire, literally, and he was grateful. Compartmentalization was another of his skills he was proud of.

He weaved his own web deep within the securiweb of Los Angeles, tracking Schaeffer and keeping a very close eye on Mesa. He kept her off the grid, making her invisible. She was free to go wherever and do whatever she needed. Including, apparently, shooting a powerful business executive multiple times in a public park.

"Fuck," he groaned, wiping out all the traces of his friend that he could reach—drones, nanosurvelliance, discreet visual actuators, business security, traffic cameras, DRMR captures, bio-fi resonances, and active retinal recorders. He piggybacked her ident and made her the equivalent of a black hole. The absence or omission of a presence could tip off a careful observer, the way astronomers could infer the existence of celestial bodies without laying eyes on an actual planet. However, Rameez doubted anyone would be as diligent as he was, but to obfuscate matters, he inserted code that digitally squeezed the image ever so slightly, just enough to make Mesa's erasure from the records less apparent.

"You'd have really gone with him?" he asked across the secure commNet while he worked.

"If he'd have bitten, then yeah."

"I'm working on getting you access to *Alabaster*. The ship is docked at a private sky park at Quail Lake. Getting to it is easy enough. Some simple biometric hacks, and you're through the gate automatons. Ship security is quite a bit tighter."

"I'm on my way back downtown now. I need everything in place by the time I get there."

"I'll be ready," he promised. "I'm setting up a car rental now for you. You've got about an hour's drive to the sky park."

"Thanks, Rameez," she said.

"What he said about Jade, though... are you sure this is worth it?"

"She's our friend, Rameez. I need to know what they've done to her."

After a long moment's pause, he said, "I'll ping you when everything's ready."

Mesa rested her head against the window, watching the traffic pass by in a blur. The bus was empty, save for an elderly man in a wheelchair. He was encased in a cloudy plastic tent adorned with PRC flags and bumper stickers with the kind of trite slogans fools mistook for wisdom. Things like Shit Happens or Who Would Jesus Bomb?

She read over the collection of stickers, using the distraction as an excuse to keep her mind off greater issues. Although she couldn't see the man inside, he made all kinds of noises. He wheezed, gasped, groaned, swore, muttered, and occasionally shouted. At one point, the tent shook violently then settled, and the swearing renewed.

*What was Jade's mission?* she asked Alice.

She didn't bother to doubt Schaeffer's words or question her friend's apparent duplicity. Alice didn't bother to object or cajole her into believing otherwise. Soon enough, the memories opened to her as their shared connection deepened and Alice invaded another portion of her mind.

*Her short-term goals were simply to observe. In time, our data packet, and those of the other memorialists, would have self-initiated an offload to a secure server for recompilation.*

*We were archive hosts then,* Mesa said.

*Yes,* Alice said. *My escape hatch wasn't perfect, but it would have worked if not for Schaeffer.*

*In some ways, it's hard to blame him for all of it. You turned yourself into a virus. The implications of that alone are staggering.*

*He tried to kill me.*

Mesa felt the burn rise in her cheeks. She forced herself to calm, folding her hands together in her lap, atop the tote bag. *Whereas, you actually did kill me. And it still wasn't* enough for you. *You don't even realize what a monster you are, do you?*

*Monsters never do, sweetie. That's what makes them interesting.*

*This isn't a joke,* Mesa said.

*My motivations are selfish but hardly as nefarious as you presume. And you give Schaeffer too much credit. Do you really believe he was eliminating all of my archive remnants out of nobility or simple altruism? Don't be such a pathetic, naïve little child.*

Mesa eyed herself in the reflection in the window, wondering if she could make out any signs of Alice in her own eyes.

*Your ambitions opened a Pandora's box, Alice. What you've done—that wasn't selfish. It was the realization that humanity can make the world even worse off than ever before. I understand that Schaeffer didn't have any grand nobility in stopping you. He was interested in profit, because you showed him the way to get rich. This isn't about you or me. Not anymore. This body-shifting crap, it's hardly as banal as your selfish whims to escape your old life and go into hiding. It's a weapon. Tell me you see that much, at least.*

Alice's churlish smiled lit up Mesa's hippocampus. The silky, ghostly voice inside her head said, *I'm glad to see you demonstrating that you are not quite so stupid after all.*

*Don't try to goad me, bitch,* Mesa said. *The bottom line is, this is all on you. This is your fault. Your selfishness is an inspiration to all the asshats of the world, dipshits like Schaeffer and the other goons as Daedalus. Have you even stopped to think about what they can do with this?*

Alice smiled wider, an ugly tear in the back corner of Mesa's mind. *Perhaps they can use it to treat coma patients and give them a second chance at a better life.*

*Now who's being naïve?*

*You used to appreciate the sanctity of memory*, Alice said, forcing Mesa to recall the better days spent with her enclave. *Do you realize how long mankind has sought to capture those fleeting moments in life and to make them permanent? Paintings, statues, art, DRMR. Death can be merely an option now.*

*To what end? And for who? You call me naïve, but you wrap your own selfish goals in ridiculous justifications and try to sound smart. This isn't about philosophy or immortality. It's about dividing and conquering. Schaeffer has already proved that. That's your sanctimonious legacy.*

*All raze and ruin then, is that it?* Alice said.

Mesa's self-control was slipping, and her fingers tightened against one another. *Oh, get off it. Having the ability to do something doesn't give you the right to do it, or even mean that you should. Sometimes you need to know a little bit fucking better and look beyond yourself.*

*Maybe you should put that on a bumper sticker. Slap it on the old man's tent over there.*

*And you want to call me a pathetic little child, huh?* Mesa said.

Alice's scoff was an unpleasant, electric tingle in the core of Mesa's brain. Finished arguing, the woman receded and left Mesa alone to stew in her own anger.

*Fucking bitch*, Mesa shouted, railing at the retreating presence.

She pressed her head against the bus window, took several long, slow calming breaths, and fought to align her chaotic thoughts.

"Mesa, I think we're through." Rameez's voice rattled through the inside of Mesa's skull, surprising her after the prolonged silence. He broadcast the *Alabaster's* schematics to her. The ship's entry points were highlighted in green.

"Thanks, Rameez," she said, standing at a counter, waiting on the PetHuman to complete her authorizations for the rental car. "I've got one more thing. Something I've been thinking about."

"Shoot," he said.

"Whatever Schaeffer was working on—we need to throw a big old monkey wrench into it. This body-shifting crap—we can't let it go wide. We need to stop it, right here, right now."

"I'll code up some virals and have them ready."

"You're the best," she said.

"I'm sending you ship schematics and crew complement."

"I see it. I'll be heading to the hangar soon." She disconnected the commNet and nursed a hot coffee while Rameez uploaded his files to her.

The information was straightforward, and she spent the most time studying the layout of the aircraft. *Alabaster* was staffed by nineteen crewmembers as well as a handful of stewards and medical technicians. In fact, the number of medical staff was surprisingly high, at eight souls, and she wondered why the ship needed so many.

*Researchers?* Alice suggested.

Mesa gave her a mental shrug. They could be a part of Schaeffer's R&D team, and she worried over the implication of what their presence meant for Jade's welfare. She blew against the rising steam and took a long pull of coffee. The caffeine sent delightful spikes through her endorphins, punching all the right pleasure centers between her taste buds and sensory inputs. She wished she had more time to savor the drink, but she was also afraid of wasting time. She wondered how long she had before the company and crew aboard *Alabaster* got word of Schaeffer's death. Rameez would do everything he could to foul up their communications protocols and keep the news under wraps, but if she didn't hurry, his interference would eventually become obvious and further complicate the threat response.

She couldn't dally. Unfortunately, the small human staff of the rental agency was trying hard to impress her and present a united front of professionalism, which made her wonder how much business was suffering and what kind of credentials Rameez had set her up with.

After the car was cleaned, inspected, and signed for, she settled in behind the wheel, punched in the destination, and engaged the driverless steering functions. She slowly sipped on the refilled coffee and used the drive time to Quail Lake to study and memorize schematics. The drive would take a little more than an hour, which gave her plenty of time to prepare.

Although the H&K still had a number of rounds left, she ejected the magazine clip and replaced it with a fresh one, chambered a round, and freed the safety.

Among Rameez's notes were possible locations where Jade was being held. The ship's logs showed that she'd been given a private room with limited access by ship staff, and she had been scheduled for several rounds of medical testing.

Schaeffer had clearly begun the body-shifting process. An echo of déjà vu from Alice bounced uncomfortably through her mind, while a dark, burning void bloomed in her belly. She felt sick as the implications reeling her.

*Please let Jade still be Jade*, she thought. She was afraid of what she would find aboard *Alabaster*, and Mesa wondered at the sort of emotions Jonah had experienced during his hunt to rescue her from Alice. She fought not to buckle beneath the enormous, horrifying weight of that thought.

As the hour ticked by, the smart car left behind the vibrant, traffic-clogged city for the rolling hills and scrub of Castaic and the desert surrounding Quail Lake. The car followed a dirt road off Lancaster and parked outside a large white hangar.

Mesa powered down the car and got out. There didn't seem to be much in the way of life. A small red turbo prop sat nearby, its disuse apparent.

Daedalus owned the sky park, but they obviously didn't put any effort into its maintenance. The area was merely a divestment of their property portfolio and nothing more.

*Alabaster*, however, was rather easy to find.

The vertical sky ship stood near the far end of the runway on a thick tri-legged assembly that surrounded the massive magnetometer lifts. The aircraft was a shark's fin with engines, a sleek, almost-triangular construct that, while in flight, dominated the skyline with an art-deco flair that fell somewhere between a 1930s Philips chapel radio and the topmost segment of the Chrysler Building spire.

She was impressed. The ship was beautiful, curvy, and elegant.

Climbing the stairs to the entry bay, she hoped Rameez's biohacks would do the trick. She didn't truly doubt him, but her nerves made her antsy. Relief flooded through her when the door slid open after the security panel recognized her thumbprint.

Inside, the ship was cool, frosty almost, in comparison to the desert heat behind her. The geometric art pattern on the outside carried over into the ship's interior, where the walls and archways displayed a clean-cut pattern of squares and rectangles and the lighting was hidden behind adornments from another bygone era.

She snapped the schematics into the lower-left corner of her heads-up retinal display, using the chart to track her movements through *Alabaster's* interior. Using a synchronizing algorithm, Rameez located the other people on the ship and tracked them. She overlaid this information against the schematics, too.

Jade had last been logged in at the infirmary, and Mesa decided to head there first. She rounded the corner, heading toward the elevator bank, then stopped, standing face to face with her friend.

Behind Jade, a cluster of five men appeared as their chamelonware suits shifted out of the invisible spectrum.

Her mind rebelled against the plain fact, and her final hope crumbled as it became apparent that her Jade was gone. Mesa's eyes burned with fresh tears, and her stomach dropped into a hollow pit.

"Hello, Mesa," Jade said. "My name is Alice Xie. You have something that belongs to me."

# CHAPTER TWENTY-SIX

MESA CRUMPLED AS THE FINAL cylinder of Alice's data packed unloaded and shot through her brain. The truth about Jade.

The realization hit as her knees struck the cold slate flooring, and blood spurted from her nostril as pain racked her skull. The feedback of the bio-fi loop was a banshee howling between her ears, a klaxon of a much-too-late warning. Jade was a data carrier.

Alice had known as much, but the secrets had remained locked away, buried deep beneath her shared memories with Mesa, until the final, necessary memory keys were in place to open them. The data packet unfurled, recognizing in Jade a common kinship, and reached out for a connection. She was denied, and the grasping tendrils of thought recoiled, turning back against the loop.

The soldiers flanked Jade. Two men peeled away to step forward. Their meaty hands curled around Mesa's biceps and hauled her forward, dragging her feet along the floor. They dumped her unceremoniously on the elevator floor and surrounded her. Jade stood over her, smiling.

Mnemonic overload paralyzed Mesa and fried her brain. Alice had blinded her, keeping her in the dark while letting her walk into a trap. Mesa realized, far too late, that Alice had never planned on leaving her mind. Her goals were far simpler and far more insidious. She was hell-bent on taking over, on drawing her fragmented self into a single core body and eliminating Mesa entirely.

Schaeffer's accusation had been more than she'd realized. Jade wasn't a spy—she was an organizer. There hadn't been only five data packets. There had been five *other* data packets, aside from hers. Jade made six.

*You lied to me,* she groaned. She curled up on the floor in pain, a sick feeling squeezing her torso tightly.

*This is wrong,* Alice said, a strain of panic vibrating her thoughts. *She blocked the file link.*

*What do you mean?*

*That isn't an archive packet in control.*

*Is Jade in there?*

*No. That is Alice Xie. She is complete.*

*How?*

*A copy of the original. The full original, from Los Angeles. The one who wiped your mind. The one who killed you.*

*So I kill her then.*

*I can't let you do that,* Alice said.

Something lunged deep inside her mind, tearing loose with maniacal pain. A seizure ripped through Mesa's body; foam curdled from her lips.

"Give her room," Jade said as Mesa's limbs twisted and flailed.

Mesa's back arched violently, and stars shot through the inside of her eyelid. The mems unveiling a kaleidoscope of pain as her throat seized, her heart hammering as she struggled to regain control. She was drowning, and she searched for something stable to latch on to, to stop the waves from crashing down atop her and forcing her under, farther and farther.

*Why would Schaeffer do this?* she wondered. *Why bring back Alice Xie like this?*

*A test market to prove that it could be done,* an echo of Alice said. *A fully blank slate, a cocktail of drugs, and a fully mnemonic load simply awaiting transfer. I'm sure he considered other alternatives, but this was much too easy for him to resist. There was a full control sample, and all the variables have been tested and eliminated. Using the original Alice Xie template was the only way to ensure a sound study.*

Mesa shifted toward Alice's voice, letting the tide carry her nearer to what seemed to be a small beacon of light in the recess of her mind—the *other* occupying the sea of her mindscape. She swam hard, but another tidal shift grabbed her legs and pulled her down. The pressure squeezed her body, choking her. The inside of her ears ached as if anvils were being pounded inside her skull, heating by the friction of violence.

She fought to return to the surface, her hands reaching, fingers stretching, flexing, probing, and trying to find something—anything—to grab hold of. The tip of a middle finger brushed something slick, and she strained to make contact. The ocean swirled around her, pulling her farther off course.

*This is why you killed Schaeffer,* Mesa said. *You pulled the trigger. You knew. You knew this Alice was here.*

*Of course,* Alice said.

Mesa locked on to the boastful pride in the other woman's voice and kicked hard. She was close. Her fingers wrapped around an ethereal edge, hooking through and sliding into nothing. She brought her legs up, curled herself into a ball, and quickly exploded forward.

*There!* she shouted. Her victory was entirely mental.

Her fingers grabbed onto the phantom hair and pulled the other presence close, drawing Alice's face toward hers. Alice smiled then slapped both palms against the side of Mesa's head, grabbing her ears, and pulled her face forward into a smacking collision against her own forehead.

Both women reeled back, but neither let go, two mental wraiths vying for control of a singular mind. Mesa was dazed and dizzy, her head lolling. Alice was much faster to recover, and she snaked forward, sinking her teeth into Mesa's throat.

Mesa's legs cramped as she kicked, and her hands fought to unlatch Alice from around her throat. She brought up a knee, striking at the nerves in the inside of the woman's thigh, but the kick was weak. She punched at her, twisted, and flailed.

Then she realized her error.

The problem, as it had been all along in her dealing with Alice Xie, was in thinking linearly. She couldn't confront the problem head-on. She needed to take it from the sides and behind. Alice had been using Mesa's mind against her, in the vain hope that Mesa would be struck off guard and forget one essential fact—they were in Mesa's mind. All she needed to do was take it back.

*Get out of my fucking head!* she roared then bucked and... vanished. She made a simple decision—to take control. Her mind. Her ethereal plane. Her weapon.

The waves crashed down against Alice, impossibly fast, with the weight of collapsing steel. The girders of Mesa's mind crumbled upon the invader, burying her.

Alice was caught off guard. Cords tightened around her throat as fists pulled at her ankles, dragging her down, farther and farther into the recess.

Mesa chased the beacon, homing in on the light, following it toward the bottom. Lightning danced through her mind as neurons fired and fired and fired. The ram's horn of her hippocampus flared painfully. The agony shot through the entirety of her mind, and she ground her teeth against the pain. Still, Mesa followed her quarry with an unrelenting determination.

*You can't do this to me*, Alice screamed. Lightning struck out at her, wrapping her in nets of electricity, setting her ethereal body aflame.

Mesa lashed out at her—an arc of light sliced down, bisecting the virus, hollowing its code. Reveling in the agonizing cries of the other woman's pain and fury, Mesa watched as Alice's belly blackened and burned.

Dragged down into the cluster of Mesa's mind, Alice was forced into a void of nothing more than primal instinct and flashes of insight. Trussed and bundled in the sheaths of lightning, Alice was helpless.

*If you kill me, you'll never recover your memories. You'll never know who you were.*

*I know who I am*, Mesa said. She stood in what had once been Alice's abode, a corner of her own mind cut off from her and twisted toward the bent artifices of a foreign data packet.

In the elevator, a red warning prompt blossomed against Mesa's retinal display.

UNAUTHORIZED ACCESS DETECTED

A churlish grin spread across Mesa's face, surprising herself. She gave a command that was both simple and freeing.

PURGE

Alice screamed as the light engulfed her, twisting about her form and pulling. Her limbs darkened and snapped, melting into the ether. Her screams deepened into an electric shrill as her code was destroyed.

Mesa rose slowly with the tide carrying her back to consciousness. She floated there a moment, dazed and lost. Opening her eyes was a struggle, and her body was a catalogue of pains, aches, and soreness. Her eyelids fluttered, and her vision turned from a milky haze to crystal clarity.

A face, familiar and welcome, hovered over hers.

Mesa smiled. "Jade," she whispered.

Jade frowned, and her expression soured. Then she reeled back an arm and rifled it into Mesa's face hard enough that the back of Mesa's skull bounced off the elevator floor. Mesa's eyes sank shut as the darkness welcomed her home once more.

# CHAPTER
# TWENTY-SEVEN

THE THRUM OF THE MAGNETOMETER lifts slowly drew Mesa back to wakefulness. Her eyes adjusted to the dim lighting, and she recoiled at the images transmitted along her optic nerves.

She was surrounded by corpses. The five guards that had been with Jade all lay still, their throats opened wide. In the dim glow of the accent lighting, their blood was black and oily.

The schematics snapped back into place, along with the real-time tracking algorithm. Opening a new socket, she sifted through the interior security camera views to confirm the reason for the lack of motion of the individual blips. All of the crew members had been slaughtered and were lying in their own slick, still-widening pools of gore.

The ship's systems detected pulses belonging to three

individuals—her, Jade, and a third individual housed in a medical facility in the vessel's bowels, near the engine room. There were no security feeds, and she scrubbed through *Alabaster's* logs, seeking information. Other than the standard listing of "med bay," she was unable to glean any other intel about the room's occupant.

Her hand slid in the blood as she tried to stand, realizing she was still in the elevator. She swatted at the controls, trying to get the doors to open. While she waited for the elevator to get over the hiccup in processing time, she studied the bodies at her feet then crouched to pat them down.

No guns. No knives. They'd been stripped of anything useful. Even her black tote bag was gone.

The elevator doors parted, and she stepped into a brightly lit hallway the color of sweet cream. She hesitated briefly at the sight of the woman splayed across the floor, her head chopped in half at a steep angle as if it had been nothing more than a melon on a butcher's block. She wore a dark-blue button-down and a pinstripe black skirt. She was dressed like a secretary, and even in death, her hand seemed to be reaching toward the shattered remains of a data pad.

*What did you do here, Jade?* Mesa wondered, remembering the much more painful truth. *Not Jade. Alice.* That name alone was enough to topple Mesa right into a migraine zone.

Following the bloody footprints to the end of the hallway, she glanced at the live-tracking results overlaying the map. Jade—Alice was right on the other side of the door, which was marked Lido.

Detecting her presence, the doors slid open with a quiet shush.

Alice was sitting at a table, facing the door. More secretaries and crew lay scattered around the deck, clearly deceased. A long bladed *dao* lay across her lap, and she sipped from a small teacup held gently in both hands.

"Ah, good. You're awake." She gestured to the open chair across from herself. "Please, sit."

Mesa was weary of following the woman's orders, but her odds of going up against the woman unarmed were not good, particularly not when said woman had a sword in her lap.

"I'm surprised you've kept me alive," Mesa said, sitting on the seat's edge.

"Killing you would have been rude and premature. I first must thank you for all that you've done."

"I'm sure if I hadn't killed Schaeffer, you would have."

"Yes, in time. Thank you for expediting that process," Alice said.

"Now you're free—is that it? I did all your dirty work, and now it's time for me to piss off, huh?"

"My, but you are like your father."

"Stop telling me that," Mesa said.

Alice raised an eyebrow, curious.

"Right, sorry. Other you. You know, there really are way too fucking many of you."

Alice conceded the point with a soft tilt of her head. "It seems you have helped remedy that problem, as well."

"Oh, yeah," Mesa said, knocking a fist against her temple. "It's all me now, bitch."

"You do need to learn how to curb your rudeness."

Mesa was taken aback, her face screwing up in shock. "Excuse me? *I need to...* like, seriously?"

Alice smiled softly around the porcelain cup as she drank.

"And where the fuck did you get a sword?"

"Schaeffer is a bit of a collector, particularly of antiquities." She slid her fingers across the curve of the hilt and down the handle in an oddly sensual gesture, as if she were tracing the lines of a lover's body.

"Neat," Mesa said, feigning disinterest.

"We did not have a chance to talk before," she said, waving her hand in the air as if to indicate the past, "before all that unpleasantness in Los Angeles some years back."

"I wouldn't remember one way or the other."

"No, of course not. Still, it was a shame. I had hoped things would turn out better for each of us."

"Yeah, you kinda fucked the doggy on that one, huh?"

Alice shrugged, the heat of her gaze turning briefly inward. "Crude, but, I suppose, not inaccurate."

"What's your deal?" Mesa asked.

"After your father killed me, Daedalus harvested my memory. I've been conscious post-death in white-room confinement."

"Schaeffer turned you into a fucking AI," Mesa said, scorn dripping from each word.

"My entire history was mined and reconstructed for his amusement. Daedalus is planning on weaponizing the body-shifting protocols. It would be quite the advancement for military strategy."

"Forgive me if I don't get all excited and quiver."

Alice smirked. Mesa hated how Alice's nerves drove that ugly smile onto Jade's face, disfiguring the body of her friend, soiling her corpse.

"You cut a deal with them," Mesa guessed. "Volunteered to be their guinea pig."

"Have you ever been imprisoned? Cut off from society entirely and stuffed in a box? Imagine not even having the luxury of your own body, of existing purely as a mindscape. Something to be probed and studied, pulled apart and reassembled, dissected and examined. You will never know that particular brand of torture. You look around and see all those I have killed, and you think me a monster. You have absolutely no idea what monstrosity is."

"Why you?" Mesa asked. "Why would Schaeffer pick you to implant?"

"There are various reasons, of course," Alice said. "I was a familiar subject—one who, thanks to his arrogance, he believed could be controlled or broken, if necessary. I was a willing volunteer who could suffice as both a control and a variable for his little science project."

"You played him."

Alice conceded the point with a subtle tilt of her head.

Mesa fumed. "You sold out the memorialists you delivered your data packets to. You put targets on all their heads and had them killed. Entire enclaves, wiped out. You killed my friends and my family and tried to have me murdered. You had Jade abducted, had her mind erased. You killed her so Schaeffer could play scientist and stuff you back into a body. Hell, you even cut up a woman's head like a cantaloupe," Mesa said, hooking a thumb over her shoulder toward the hallway behind her.

"Don't pretend that your hands are any cleaner, Mesa, dear. You've killed, as well."

"Yeah, I did. And I can't help but think your lovely guiding hand was a part of that, too. A part of you being stuck in my head and all."

Again, Alice smiled with snake-like unpleasantness. "That was an unexpected outcome. Your redeveloping mind triggered a file cascade, effectively merging our disparate consciousnesses. I'd love to hear more about it."

"I'd love to shove that sword up your ass for all of it."

Alice choked on her sip of tea, gagging behind a cupped hand, and worked to regain her composure. Her coughing fit turned into a spat of laughter. "Like father–"

"Don't even finish that line."

"Of course," Alice said. She set the cup upon a saucer and slid it to the side of the table.

"What now? You going to become a corporate cash cow, the spokeswoman for body-shifting?"

"Daedalus—Schaeffer, in particular—always

overestimated my ambitions in utilizing this technology. I'm afraid there are far grander imaginations involved now than my own. I only ever wanted to escape, Mesa. To start over."

"Oh, I see. The whole big act-three reveal of the villain who's just a misunderstood kitty cat after all, and not some raging megalomaniac. Fuck off with that noise, Alice. This isn't a cheapo kiddy holovid, and I'm not buying it. I don't care about your ambitions or your goals or how you are or aren't represented. You're a fucking crazy-ass killer at the end of the day, and I'm putting you down for good."

Alice snorted with bored derisiveness. Then she leapt forward, the *dao* in her hand, lightning-quick and stabbing toward center mass.

Mesa had been waiting for Alice to move, prepping herself for the inevitable attack. She dropped off the chair, fell beneath the table, then rocketed upward. Putting her shoulder into the underside of the metal frame, she charged forward, ramming Alice in the chest and plowing her down under the furniture.

Alice lashed out. The edge of the blade sliced across both of Mesa's shins in a shallow, upward arc.

Gritting her teeth against the pain, Mesa let the table fall on top of the other woman. Then she grabbed a chair and swung it by the legs as Alice shoved the table aside and tried to stand. Mesa clocked her in the side of the head, hard enough to daze the woman. She raised the chair again for another swing, and Alice kicked out, burying the heel of her foot in Mesa's solar plexus. Wind shot out of her lungs as she doubled over.

Alice charged forward, tackling Mesa to the floor. She grabbed Mesa's hair, pulled her head up, then rammed the back of her skull against the ground, over and over. Mesa screamed as the skin split, sending a bone-deep ache cascading across her entire head. Using the side of her hands, she struck at Alice's midsection, punching at her kidneys and ribs, trying to work her feet up between them to kick her off. When that failed, she slammed her palms against Alice's ears.

Mesa freed herself from under Alice and scrambled back. The *dao* was on the other side of Alice, out of reach.

"I thought you wanted to thank me," Mesa said, tasting gore at the back of her throat.

Standing, Alice appeared as unsteady as Mesa felt. "I never said I wasn't going to kill you, child. I owe you a good death."

"Hey, you're the one who dumped yourself into my head. Trust me, that wasn't my idea of a good time."

"And yet you were able to resolve that issue on your own quite satisfactorily. Still, it is rather hard to take that gesture for anything other than an insult. You killed me, Mesa. I felt a twinge of myself drown in your thoughts."

"You. Put. Her. There. Own up to your own goddamn responsibilities, would you?"

"That is a slight that cannot go unpunished."

"Dipshit, you tried to kill me. You remember any of that? You tried to kill that fucking little fragment of you that you put in my head. I did your job for you."

"And now I must finish cleaning up my mess, Mesa. That is my responsibility. I have made multiple mistakes. I own that, as you say. Now, I will resolve the problems that have arisen as a result of those mistakes."

"All so you can run away and hide."

"So I can live," Alice said, her voice an edge of steel. She grasped the hilt of the *dao*, extended the sword before her, and charged.

The attack was sloppy and clearly telegraphed, but Mesa realized too late that Alice had intended as much. When Mesa stepped aside to avoid the blade, Alice snapped her arm up and elbowed Mesa in the cheek. The blow rocked her on her heels, and she stumbled back, her hips knocking into the railing and preventing her from falling off the starboard side of the ship. Alice, though, saw the opening and pushed. Her palms connected solidly with Mesa's shoulders and tipped her over the rails.

Mesa scrambled for purchase, grabbing hold of the bottom-most rail with one hand, painfully stretching the tendons in her wrist and shoulder as all of her weight fell out beneath her. The pain alone was jarring enough to nearly cost Mesa her grip and send her plummeting to earth.

Alice stood above her, that ugly, foreign smile slowly spreading across Jade's face. Mesa's eyes darted between her and the cityscape blurring past below. Her vision tracked back up toward the monster overhead, then she caught sight of a possible way out of the situation.

She spotted a balcony below, kitty-corner from her. She wasn't sure if she could make it, and she didn't believe she had any other viable options. To miss the shot would mean death. To stay there any longer, with the crazy bitch with a sword looming over her, meant death.

*No, not really an option at all.*

Alice raised the blade.

Mesa planted her soles against the side of the ship, twisted her body at the waist, and sprung sideways, releasing the rail. The wind rocketed at her, tearing at her skin with a deafening rush. The ship continued to sail forward as she tumbled to the lower decks, keeping her eye on the prize.

She had thought to grab the railing and haul herself overboard, but luck—both good and bad—favored her. She didn't have to pull herself up another rail, but as the ship passed, the top part of the railing snagged her foot. She banged into the balcony floor, and her knee twisted painfully as her foot hooked and turned against the railing when she fell.

With a groan, she rolled over and caught a quick

glimpse of Alice staring down at her, plainly impressed. After taking a moment to regain her breath, she hobbled toward the sliding, opaque Dura-Plast door and pulled. She was surprised that it opened but not surprised to find the occupant nearby. The man had been stabbed through the belly but had fought for his life long enough to make it to the door, unlatch the lock, and perish against the glass.

Alice had clearly played with the man, tormenting him in ways she hadn't with the others. The victims Mesa had seen so far had been relatively straightforward murders. The man before her, though, had been stabbed and cut multiple times. Numerous slashes had opened his face; one cut through his eye.

Walking alongside the dresser, using the furniture for support to offset the pain and imbalance of her wounded knee, she recognized the e-papers tossed about the room as medical reports. She stopped briefly, unsurprised at the name of the subject. Alice Xie. Mesa crumpled the electronic paper into a tight ball and pitched it aside.

In the hallway, more of the unarmed dead waited. She stopped at the door's threshold, checking the 3-D schematic relay. Alice was riding the elevator from the lido deck down to the third deck, where Mesa was.

*Figures*, she thought.

Alice would be approaching from the opposite end of the floor, so Mesa moved to put even more distance between them. The elevator bay was out of the question, but she could escape down a nearby stairwell to the engine room directly below.

She tried not to ignore the pain in her leg, but two steps down, the agony was all she could think about. She wasn't about to buckle, though. *Not now.*

She gritted her teeth and tried to balance her weight on the balls of her feet while she gingerly tackled the next step with her good leg. Every time she stepped or bent her knee, a grinding pain bit its way down the top reaches of her calf. Her head ached, and she found herself stopping to blink away the flashes of double vision.

At the base of the stairs, she stepped through the entry and into a stripped-down hallway. The contrast between this floor and those above was startling. The artsy décor was lost to exposed piping, sheaths of cabling, wires, and ductwork.

The schematics said a maintenance room was nearby. She also noted the pulse registry at the opposite end of corridor, in what appeared to be a sealed room designated as an alternative medical bay.

She was curious but had no time to investigate at that moment. Alice was quickly approaching.

Mesa set off for the maintenance room, but the door refused to budge. She jiggled the handle a few times, disbelieving. The corners of panic folded over her until she forced them away.

*Damn it*, she roared, pushing at the door one last time.

She looked around, hoping for a stash of tools left in the open—a wrench or a hammer, anything. She found nothing.

She opened a comm line. "Rameez, I need you to shut down the central elevator corridor and engage any emergency compartmentalization ops."

She watched Rameez working furiously, keeping an eye on the schematic. Alice was in the elevator, and Mesa held her breath until it stopped between floors. *Perfect.*

"Thank you," she said.

"What is going on? Did you find Jade?"

"Jade's dead."

Rameez's concerned expression turned crestfallen.

"Alice Xie is in control of her body, and she's coming to kill me. She's on the elevator."

"Mesa, there's something you need to know. I did some digging and—"

"Hang on a minute. I'm outside a maintenance closet.

Can you pop the lock?"

"What? Yeah, yeah, of course."

She listened to the metallic click as the lock sprung free, then she flung the door open wide. She limped inside, scanning the walls for an appropriate tool she could use for defense and offense.

"What's the deal? You find something?"

"It's about Alice. She's still alive. They're running some kind of tests on her."

"Um, yeah. Kind of aware. Think back to how I said she's fucking trying to kill me."

"No, no, no," he said, rapidly. "That's what I mean. Her files say she's bedridden. Her memory was dumped into some quadriplegic. The host body was completely paralyzed, belonged to some coma patient until her family voted to end life support. Daedalus owned the hospital where medical treatment was being conducted, and once the family signed off on her..."

"They started using her as a guinea pig. Got it."

"These medical reports read like an Auschwitz experiment. Lots of physical tests, psychological tests. Crazy stuff."

"If she was a quad, why torment her physically?"

"That ties into the psychological stuff. They'd cut her up, break bones, let infection or sepsis or gangrene set in, then amputate. She'd be awake and forced to watch pieces of her body get cut away. That's fucked up even if you can't feel it, that sense of powerlessness."

"Yeah. OK, I get that." She scanned the wall, studying the collection of random tools.

The elevator was still stalled, but Jade's pulse tracker showed Alice was still mobile and working her way closer. The emergency doors had sealed her between sections of the floor above, but if she had any decent lock-hacking skills— and Mesa was sure she did—that wouldn't stall her for long.

"I think she's nearby," Rameez said.

"Which one?" Mesa asked, with more venom in her tone than she'd intended. She hoped Rameez knew the vitriol wasn't directed toward him.

"Both. One above, and the other is on the same floor as you."

"I saw the pulse tracker on this floor. It's been stationary."

"The area is marked off as a medical lab space. That's where you'll find Alice Xie Number Two."

"Oh, goodie."

"Are you OK?" he asked.

"No," she said, disconnecting the net. She'd spotted the instrument she had in mind. With a faint glimmer in her eye, she picked up a twenty-four-inch long-handle pipe wrench. She admired the cherry-red finish and gave it a few practice swings.

"All right, bitch," she said, "let's do this."

After prying open the elevator doors she muscled herself halfway up the shaft to the floor above, then rushed down the stairs two at a time. Alice was growing increasingly annoyed. Hacking through the electronic locks of the emergency doors did nothing to sooth her agitation. At one point, simply to relieve the mounting pressure of anger, she'd banged the base of her sword against the wall several times, swearing loudly.

Killing Mesa Everitt was going to be nothing but absolute pleasure.

She worked her way to the stairwell at the opposite end of the floor, then as she descended into the bowels of the ship, the realization of what lay below dawned on her. The girl would be there, certainly, as would one other soul—Alice Xie, or at least one of the other copies of her. *The quad,* she recalled.

Schaeffer had taken no small amount of pleasure in replicating Alice's memories into multiple hosts and disfiguring and dismantling them for her benefit. He got off on it—sexually, she assumed, but he certainly enjoyed the power over her that he was able to demonstrate. He lorded it over her constantly. The quad had been the most successful of the implantation experiments, and Schaeffer had taken much pleasure in breaking her, slowly and continuously over the last few years. He had taken even greater joy in sharing the results of her degradation with the Alice Xie that inhabited Jade's body. Stuck in the white data room, that Alice had vowed to kill him by any means possible. Each thread of sanity that had snapped in the quad's mind had strengthened her resolve to escape the white room.

Over time, though, the isolation ravaged her. Her strong backbone and defiance eventually gave way to platitudes and bargaining. That, then, led to enormous regret and self-recrimination, which, in turn, fueled her constant desire to eliminate Schaeffer.

Killing him was a long, drawn-out process, and it had cost her considerably. The data archives she had loosed into the wild had become nothing more than pawns in her elaborate game for revenge. She had been willing to sacrifice them in order to achieve her own goals. Some, like Mesa, would call her a monster for it. She thought of herself as shrewd.

She bargained and cajoled, always thinking of the next step, planning in layers. Schaeffer was afraid of outside complications and demanded complete validity in his testing. Controls, trials, and tests continuously probed for faults in her stolen methods and extrapolations toward achieving body-shifting. Eventually, he had consented to implanting her in a functional body—Jade.

In the end, Jade was no more of a loss than the archivers

had been.

She slowly marched down the industrial walkway, keenly aware of Mesa's presence and wary of potential traps. She reached the end of the hall and stood before an open door.

The interior of the room was so antiseptically white she wanted to scream. Instead, she smiled.

Mesa stood before her, clearly favoring one leg. Bruised, battered, she held a long, red wrench beside her leg.

"*Nî Hâo*," Alice said, raising the sword before her.

"*Nî Hâo*," Mesa said, returning the greeting and raising the wrench.

Both women strode forward, weapons at the ready, weighing each other's intent and seriousness.

While Mesa was hardly a proficient duelist, she knew enough to avoid the blade. She also knew she could not afford a long, drawn-out battle. She had no time for thrust-and-parry bullshit.

She sprang forward, taking Alice off guard, and swung the wrench low as she stepped in too close for Alice to be able to swing. She knocked the blade away and used the head of the wrench to club Alice in the knees.

Alice raised a leg, catching the blow along her shin and calf.

Mesa used the shock of pain to grapple the woman in her arms, jabbing violently at her with the metal butt, bringing it up beneath her chin. Teeth rattled, then Alice was working to get a free arm between them. She used the base of the *dao's* hilt to strike at Mesa's face.

Mesa raised both arms, pushing Alice's arms away, and reared back her head to deliver a powerful head-butt. The bone's in Alice's cheeks and nose fractured, and she stumbled back, slumping.

Standing over her, Mesa readied herself to finish it once and for all. She lifted the wrench, set to cave in Alice's skull. She tried as hard as she could to disassociate, but all she saw was Jade. Her friend.

She knew Jade wasn't in there. Her form had become nothing more than a shell hiding a monster, but killing her was still difficult. Killing Alice meant desecrating her friend, a woman who had been her companion, if only briefly, once upon a time.

Her moment of hesitation was all Alice needed, though. Alice's foot swept out, kicking Mesa's feet out from under her. Then Alice was on top of her, her hands scrabbling at Mesa's face, seeking a soft, vulnerable area.

She craned her neck, straining her face away from probing fingers while she tried to crawl out from beneath her attacker. Soft hands smelling faintly of jasmine pressed against the sides of her face while thumbs jammed into both of her eyes.

Mesa screamed as the points of Alice's nails dug into the corners of her eye sockets and an immeasurable painful weight pressed down against the soft jelly orbs. Tears flowed as a thumbnail punched through the sclera, and Mesa screamed, trying to get her arms up, to break away from the pain.

Alice's nail stabbed deeper into her eye and tore across her cornea. Blood flooded the sclera as vessels ruptured and exploded, turning her world a hazy red.

Mesa roared, sending a tight, powerful fist into the side of Alice's face, rocking the woman enough to relieve the painful torquing. She rolled, cradling the ruined socket in the cup of her palm, her hand turning slick from the carnage.

She needed to find the wrench, or the *dao*... something, anything, before—

Alice was on top of her again, sending a flurry of kicks

across her spine and hips, stomping hard against her bones with her heel. It hurt but was not nearly enough to distract from the hammering throbs in her skull.

A part of her, a small, quiet voice full of fear, spoke in the back of Mesa's mind, telling her to let go, that she had lost the fight. She recognized the voice as her own, and she wondered how much of it was true, if she believed any of it at all.

Friends gone. Family gone. She had nothing else. She could let Alice Xie have her little victory, end all this suffering, and go on to whatever she had planned for herself next. She could let it be somebody else's problem. Mesa was sick of running—and sick of losing.

*No,* she told herself, *no, not like this.* She lay there, broken and half-blind. Nearly everyone she knew was dead—and for what? So she could roll over and say, "Fuck it all," and let their killer—her killer—walk away untouched?

*Fuck that.*

She took a sharp blow to the kidney and knew she would piss blood for the next few days, but she didn't care. She kicked herself forward. The pipe wrench was a hair's breadth away. Alice was too distracted with stomping on Mesa's spine to notice her seeking fingers brushing against the wrench. She crawled again, reaching for the handle.

Alice grabbed at the disheveled hair hanging off the side of Mesa's shaved skull and pulled. She yanked Mesa's face back, standing on her spine, straining her neck.

"Where's the fun in that, now?" she asked, glaring at her with baleful bloodlust.

Alice reached out and grabbed the pipe wrench and held it as she kicked Mesa high in the belly, knocking the wind from her. Then she swung the wrench in a high, violent arc, slamming it down on Mesa's arm. The force of the blow tore through the radius and ulna, splintering bones and pulping the flesh and muscle around them.

She never seemed to tire of hearing Mesa's screams. But then Mesa twisted, rolling aside. With her good arm, she grabbed the silk-wrapped handle of the *dao* hidden behind her body.

In the throes of violence, Alice's world had narrowed to tunnel vision. When Mesa had reached for the pipe wrench, the wrench had been all Alice saw. She hadn't even noticed the *dao*, so near, just behind Mesa.

Mesa rolled back toward Alice, driving the sword up, impaling her through the stomach. The wrench clattered to the floor as Alice stumbled backward, a primitive echo in her mind demanding escape. The blade slid from her belly as her knees went weak. She fell, her hands staunching the wound, pressing hard to keep her insides contained.

Regaining her feet was no easy task, but Mesa used the *dao* as a support. Cradling her shattered arm against her waist, she stepped forward. The blade carved a shallow groove behind her as it dragged against the floor. Jade–*No*, she told herself, *Alice*–knelt before her, blood running through her hands.

Mesa swung the sword, her aim slightly off. Her depth perception was ruined, but she still got the job done. The blade sliced through Jade's neck and into the crook of her shoulder. The woman went deathly pale, and seconds later, she was no more. Her blood loss was too severe and much too rapid for the medichines to do any good.

Alice Xie, like Jade before her, was gone.

"Kill me," the old woman begged. Her eyes followed Mesa as she fell into a nearby chair.

"Kill me," she said again, her plea an electronic whine.

"I'm done killing," Mesa said, her voice hollow. Her throat ached from the anguished screams that had been ripped from her lungs.

"Please," Alice said.

Mesa didn't respond. Instead, she sucked on a bloodied tooth, distracting herself with the coppery taste while avoiding Alice's eyes.

The old woman seemed to understand that her groveling fell on deaf ears and gave up. Still, she watched, alert and focused.

Navigating the Somnambulist hub, Mesa went through the process of creating a new thread and organizing her thoughts. She wanted a clean, easy-to-follow upload.

Before sitting, she had extracted the memory chip from Jade's skull. The project had been a grisly, painful affair. The task was difficult with only one good arm, and the guilt over violating the corpse of her friend had taken a toll. Mesa had told herself it was necessary and dug in.

The mems held useful information, and she plugged Alice Xie's sequences into her minor convergence web, along with Kaften's. Her own memories of Schaeffer were homicidal, but those chips would fall as they may.

A second ping from Rameez struck the DRMR dashboard. She'd been too engrossed in compiling her post to respond to the first. She debated answering the second attempt.

"Oh, thank God," he said as she accepted the channel.

"What is it?"

"I've been trying to reach you. I was worried. Is everything...?"

"Almost finished."

"What are you doing?" he asked.

"Getting ready to burn them," she said. "Burn them right down to the fucking ground." She filled him in, watching his face grow crestfallen.

"Are you sure this is wise?" he asked.

"People need to know," she said. "What Daedalus is

doing, what they've already done—this is huge, Rameez."

"But if you send this out, then everybody knows. Everybody has access to this technology, it could be—"

"It could be a nuclear deterrent," she said. "Or at least something similar. I'm not naïve enough to think this all ends here with a push of a button, but there needs to be an awareness of this. This isn't something that should be confined to the dark corners of secrecy. People need to know. We need to figure out how to prepare for all of this. Ethics committees, new rules, whatever. Just fucking awareness, you know?"

"They'll arrest you," he said.

"I know. This is going to be big," she said. "Too big for Daedalus to risk coming after me again. This my safeguard, my last chance."

"Go nuclear and level the playing field."

"As I said, this is all I've got left."

"I tried hacking into their white rooms, but they've got incredibly strong mojo."

"Alice?"

"She's definitely in there. Or at least some form of her."

"Well, then, I definitely have to do this. Send me the uploads?"

He paused for a long moment then gave a heavy sigh. "Sure," he said. "Mesa, I..."

"What?"

"Be careful, OK?"

"Careful is not really an option for me anymore."

She disconnected the feed and waited for his information to come through. One more data point to feed into the web.

A half hour passed before she felt finished. She ran through the data twice more, ensuring that everything was solid and ready to go. The distraction was a welcome change from the roaring pain in her arm and face.

She gave the entire splice one last run-through, a third

chance to convince herself she was making a terrible mistake. Then she pushed it all through, dumping the entirety of the web into the public domain.

Imagining drone strikes sent to take down *Alabaster*, she disconnected and waited. The ship stayed true to its course. No missiles exploded against the hull.

Alice Xie, crippled and bedridden, lay silent, watching her.

"Rameez," Mesa said, pinging him through the neural commNet. "Where the fuck am I?"

A momentary panic graced his chubby features, then his eyes hardened. "What do you mean?"

"Sorry. The ship, *Alabaster*. Where am I?"

"Jesus, you scared me." His eyes darted across his own retinal displays. "Still in California airspace, heading north toward Sacramento."

"Can you land me there?"

Whatever internal conflicts were raging inside of him began to surface. His entire face darkened, and the corners of his jaw ticked. He wanted to argue; that much was clear. Instead, he said, in a clipped tone, a single word. "Yes."

She disconnected then shut her eye. Nothing left to do but wait.

Pain rolled over every square inch of her body. Her psyche felt as ruined as her form. Her life was an open, festering wound.

Alice said no more, but Mesa felt her eyes pressing against her as if her stare were a solid weight. She ignored her, welcoming the aches and pains of her injuries instead.

After what she estimated was an hour, she felt a noticeable shift in the constant thrumming that rumbled through the body of the ship as *Alabaster* began its descent toward the capitol.

An hour after that, a small squadron of soldiers flanked her, guns leveled in her direction, barking orders at her. She raised her one good arm in surrender.

Passing her friend, she gave Jade a silent apology for being too late to help her. The phalanx of soldiers led her off the ship and took her into custody. As she was placed into the back of a waiting vehicle, state media vied for a good shot of her face.

Mesa kept a live feed running on Somnambulist to ensure her safety, until the PRC caught wind of it and slapped a dampener into the port behind her ear.

She let the pain wash over her, waiting for the darkness to swallow her whole.

328  MICHAEL PATRICK HICKS

# CHAPTER TWENTY-EIGHT

Mesa lost track of time during the drive. The dampener disconnected her from the world, turning her head fuzzy. Thinking was too difficult. And for that, she was grateful. It made it impossible to think of either Jade or Alice, two new hollow points in her life that she did not have the energy to reflect on.

She found a certain joy in losing herself amid the dulling static. Her mind was completely empty, maybe for the first time since she'd awoken three years ago.

She stared blankly out the window. Neither of the PRC soldiers in the front of the vehicle spoke to her—one more thing to be grateful for.

Time ticked by, then she dully complied as the men pulled her from the car and led her into a building. She took no notice of the design, and the world washed by in a numb haze. At some point, her brain adjusted to the dampener and the world resolved. She found herself sitting alone atop a thin mattress in a small prison cell. Her skull ached, and the skin surrounding her ruined eye felt taut and swollen. The gauze that had been taped over the wound felt stiff and crusty beneath the pad of her exploring fingers.

In the morning, more guards came for her and took her to the prison infirmary. A man who spoke broken English said, "We numb you. You sleep. Wake up, new eye. Yes?"

Still dazed, she nodded. She hadn't slept at all, and she felt at least three steps behind everyone else. Or maybe the world was spinning faster around her, upsetting her balance. She was led to another bed, where she watched as a needle pierced the vein in the crook of her elbow.

"Count three," the man said.

She made it to two before her eye closed of its own accord.

When she awoke, a new layer of agony had replaced the pain in her face and skull. Fresh gauze covered her eye, and she was too weak to sit up. She lay still, bored and uncaring. After an hour, the doctor returned and hovered over her. He flashed a penlight into her good eye.

"You see?"

"Kinda hard to miss," she said, wincing against the bright, white glare.

He handed her a mirror and went about pulling away the gauze. "Good, yes?" he asked.

She adjusted the mirror, still too narcotized to feel shock. The skin was purple and swollen. A thick black bruise ringed the implant and stained the corner of her good eye. The implant itself was completely bottom-shelf tech, the kind tech corps gave away to impoverished developing nations to bolster their PR spins. A metal cup had been grafted to the bone, and in the center, where her human eye had once been, was a plainly artificial cybernetic replacement. The doctors hadn't even made any attempt to match iris colors.

"It's fine," she said, passing the mirror back to him. In truth, she didn't actually mind. The ocular implant would serve its purpose, even if it wouldn't win her any beauty awards. But even that was unimportant. She found herself simply not caring. Not about the eye. Not about her forced confinement. Not about anything.

"Good," he said again, taking the mirror, then turned his back on her.

Through the medicinal fog, she realized one arm was in a cast. "What's this?" she asked, slowly remembering the pain of her shattered ulna and radius.

"Metal rods," the doctor said, pointing at the cast. "Had to put in. Very damaged."

After what felt like at least an hour, she tried to sit up and realized her other wrist was handcuffed to the bedrail. She lay back down. *The hell with it.*

There were no privacy curtains and no other patients. She saw no doctors or nurses. Nothing to do but sit and wait. She was allowed two days to recuperate then injected with medichine boosters to speed up her healing process. On the third day, she was led back to her cell.

She passed the empty beds, wondering if she was the solitary prisoner in this building. She tried to ask a guard, but he only grunted at her.

"Do I get a lawyer? What am I being charged with?"

No answers. He motioned for her to enter her cell.

"Can I at least get some books?" she asked, standing on the other side of the bars. "In English," she specified, realizing her request might be a specialized one among the native Chinese speakers.

Time ticked by very, very slowly. She felt alone and realized she very possibly was alone, maybe trapped in a PRC black site or at least a black hole.

The next day, the guard returned with her morning meal.

When she was finished eating, he opened her door and led her outside to a small yard fenced in by massive electric fences and guard towers. A handful of other prisoners lingered in the yard. Most were Caucasian, but a few were Asian.

She strolled the grounds, keeping a wary eye on the other inmates and the guards. Then an older white man with silver hair approached her, but he kept his pace languid enough to demonstrate he was not a threat.

"You're new here," he said. "I'm Malcolm."

"Mesa," she said, watching him carefully.

He left a respectful distance between them.

After a moment of silence, she asked, "What is this place?"

He shrugged. "Political detainment. A place to keep us politically dangerous chaps out of their hair while they figure out what, exactly, to do with us."

She recognized his British accent. "You're not from around here."

He laughed. "Not originally, no."

"How long have you been here?"

He put his hands in his pockets, keeping a few polite feet away, outside her personal space. His brow crinkled, and he said, "Three years, maybe, give or take a few weeks. Kind of lost track of time."

A whistle blew, and Malcolm nodded toward the solitary door.

After that, Mesa didn't see him again. She was kept segregated from the others for reasons she never understood. Back in her cell, she found several thick, beat-up volumes of classic English literature. Thumbing through the books, she realized they'd been heavily censored. Thick black lines ran through the text, and entire pages were missing.

A month crawled by. The cast on her arm had been removed, and her physical wounds had healed. She got used to the eye and the subtle alteration to her depth perception, as well as being disconnected from the world at large. She missed the constant access to information and the data flow. She also realized that whatever emotions had roiled within her before her confinement had been replaced with an apathetic dullness.

At the start of her second month, the routine she had grown accustomed to was suddenly disrupted. The guard came for her, but instead of leading her toward the prison yard, he pulled her in the opposite direction.

The plain steel door opened into a bare concrete room with another door opposite. In between were a scarred metal table and an empty chair near her. The chair on the other side was filled by a blond man. A briefcase stood on the floor beside him, and he was dressed in a sleek shiny suit and black dress shoes.

"Ms. Everitt?" he asked. He spoke with a heavy accent that she couldn't place.

"The one and only," she said. Her throat was dry, her voice gruff.

"How are you feeling?"

"Sublime," she answered.

He offered a wan smile, as if he had grown accustomed to the sarcasm of inmates. "My name is Matthieu Frutiger. I am an investigator with the United Nations Security Council."

Mesa waited for the other shoe to drop. She crossed her arms over her chest, crossed her feet at her ankles, and waited it out. Let him make the next move.

Frutiger scooted his chair back and crossed his legs. On the table between them were a tablet and a pad of e-paper that transcribed their discussion with a talk-to-text algorithm.

"You've caused quite a ruckus. I'd like to ask you some questions."

"I'm not going anywhere."

"Your Somnambulist posting has become quite a sensation. Everyone is talking about it. It's on all the newsfeeds. Very impressive. Even after a month."

"Where are you from?"

"Switzerland," he said. "The content of your now-quite-viral mnemonic uploads caused quite a stir. The UN has opened investigative panels, and we are working quite closely with our member nations and local law enforcement agencies to put Daedalus under a microscope."

She gave Frutiger a long, appraising look. He was very prim and proper, his hair short. She had little trouble understanding him, but she was still deeply confused by this visit.

"Are you charging me? Am I a war criminal or something now?"

He let out a deep, boisterous laugh. "Quite the contrary. In fact, I am hopeful you will be our star witness."

Frutiger spent several minutes explaining the initial barebones layer of the case that had been quickly assembled following her Somnambulist post.

As Frutiger explained, "What you've stirred up has prompted the Security Council to form an International Criminal Tribunal, since Daedalus was a global corporation. They are assembling a team of counter-terrorism officials, the Sanctions committee, the Economic and Social Council, and its Commission on Science and Technology and Commission for Social Development. Specialized agencies are beginning to fold themselves into the investigations, everyone from the World Health Organization to the World Intellectual Property Organization.

"We are all very interested in Daedalus's activity regarding body-shifting and their targeting of you. There are also other considerations, such as the imprisonment of Alice Xie and the assorted, shall we say, *messiness* of all that. All of the dogs and ponies are on show, and everyone wants their time in the spotlight."

"What is all this, then?" Mesa asked. The thick rope of scars under her forearm shined in the overhead lighting as she waved one hand at the small room and the larger warren of cells behind her.

"A bit of safekeeping, I suppose," Frutiger said. "The PRC are very much aware of how volatile things are, and they are treading lightly. They are prepared to release you into my custody."

"Am I being charged?" she asked again.

"No," he said plainly, and for the record. She watched as the e-paper etched his words into the micro-thin screen. "In fact, after combing through your Somnambulist posting and interviewing your friend Rameez, we are only seeking your testimony. In the meantime, we are offering you safe haven until all this is over."

"You can promise me a free pass on everything? Elko, Seattle–I'm sure they have questions for me."

"They do. I can assure you that everyone is treading lightly. Nobody wants to make a misstep or get roped into our already-wide investigation. The PRC, Washington, all of them are quite happy to pass the buck, as you would say. We will take care of it. And you. You can work with us, and then you begin putting the pieces of your life back together."

"How is Rameez?" she asked, a large lump forming in her throat with the words. She hadn't realized how sorely she had missed him.

"He's well. He has been an enormous help."

"When the ship landed, there was copy of Alice Xie aboard. A few, actually."

Frutiger looked down at his tablet for a moment then took a deep breath. "The elderly woman housed a copy of Alice Xie. This is true. Unfortunately, she died soon after *Alabaster's* landing. We believe that Daedalus activated safeguard protocols and detonated a small explosive implant that was inserted into her cerebral cortex. Our forensics team has been busy piecing it all together. I'm afraid we haven't gotten terribly far.

"Aside from that woman and your friend, Jade, we found the primary data core containing the central intelligence of Alice Xie. Dealing with her has been difficult, as well."

This had Mesa's attention. She leaned in closer to the table. "What do you mean?"

"By all rights, we are dealing with a full-fledged and legitimate artificial intelligence. An exploratory committee is being formed to determine her legal standing and how to proceed with her. There is quite a lot of debate on the ethics of how to proceed and what kind of rights she is entitled to. She is not human, but she is not merely software. It is a puzzle, you see."

"Can't you just delete her?" Mesa asked. Hiding her scorn was impossible, and she felt her cheeks flush. After all she had been through, after all she had done, and after all that Alice Xie had been responsible for, to have that woman still ably manipulating the world in one form or another riled her.

"We could, certainly. But there is a reticence to do that. Some quarters are arguing that that is not quite fair. That it would be tantamount to an execution, and that there must be a trial to determine her culpability."

Mesa was stunned. She gripped the edge of table with both hands. "Fuck fair," she shouted. "That woman is a murderer, a killer. Do have any idea what she's done? To me, to my friends, to my family. You want fair? You—"

Frutiger help up his hand, attempting to quiet her. "That is why I need your help, Mesa. This investigation and Alice's role in it—you led us down this path. This started with you. And it will end with you."

Her jaw clenched, and she slowly let the tension release. Her shoulders deflated, and she released the table, sitting back. She closed her eyes and took several long breaths, trying to find her calm center. She could feel the weight of Frutiger's stare, and when she opened her eyes, she met his.

"What do I need to do?" she asked.

# CHAPTER TWENTY-NINE

Mesa had never been to Switzerland, as far as she knew.

Seven months passed in a flurry of activity. She was put into a flat in Sécheron, off the Route de Lausanne, on the right bank of Lake Geneva. She didn't get to see as much of the city as she would have liked, and whatever travel she was allowed was under the guard of a protectorate detail. Aside from visits to a few nearby coffee houses and strolls through the Jardin Botanique and the closer, smaller Parc William Rappard along the lake, she spent much of her time in the safe confines of the apartment. She never tired of the view of Lake Geneva, though, or the snow-capped Alps beyond, and she enjoyed watching the boaters and the beachgoers when the weather was right.

Although she had been to the UN base several times,

most of the interviews conducted with Frutiger and other investigators from the various panels of inquiry were carried out at the flat or via secure virtual white rooms established through the commNet. Frutiger had allowed the DRMR dampener to be removed, and Mesa reveled in losing herself in the data streams again. Regaining access was like rediscovering a lost limb, and she followed the news closely, particularly the stories surrounding Daedalus.

A number of executives and Daedalus chairmen across the globe had been either subpoenaed or arrested, depending on the depth of their involvement with Schaeffer's operations. When Mesa asked Frutiger about the researchers who had been involved, he simply shrugged and told her not to worry about them.

"We have them in custody," was all he would say. A part of her suspected they had been dumped into some off-the-books black site.

The company went through a large restructuring, and despite the controversy, it appeared to still have garnered a swelling of public support. Several countries that relied on the multinational conglomerate's financial support and bevy of income taxes from its workers had deemed Daedalus too big to fail. PR spin doctors and the new chairmen and executive, who only months earlier had witnessed their predecessors jailed and the center of UN investigations, promised to do better and established new rules for oversight, particularly in terms of emergent technologies. The company established partnerships with a number of other tech firms, law firms, and public relations firms, and Daedalus seemed to be on the verge of winning itself a shiny new coat to gloss over its hellacious involvement with Schaeffer and his rogue researchers.

With her permission, a data forensic team combed through Mesa's mind, downloading and examining every bit of data her brain stored. The process took several months.

The REMIND software engineered by Daedalus was removed and studied.

Every Sunday evening, she was allowed to make contact with Rameez over the commNet, and they spent several long nights talking, though neither of them were allowed to speak of the investigation or their involvement in it. Instead, they spoke of mundane matters, like the weather and new software apps, or TV shows.

"You're still in Geneva?" he asked.

She said she was. "Where's home for you these days?" she asked.

"I'm back in Washington," he said. "I have a new apartment. You should come by."

"I throw a hell of a housewarming," she said, and for what felt like the first time in ages, she laughed. She couldn't stop laughing, and it grew contagious. Rameez began laughing, too, which only made her laugh longer, until her ribs ached and she was left gasping for air.

"God, I needed that," she said.

"Me, too," Rameez said, wiping away tears. "I miss you, Mesa."

"I miss you, too, buddy." She wiped the tears from her good eye and disconnected.

In the weeks and months since they had reestablished contact with one another, Rameez had never asked her about the artificial eye. She knew it was a rather apparent alteration to her appearance, and she knew that he wasn't that oblivious to how she looked. The closest he had ever gotten was asking how she felt and if she was OK, and he had left it at that.

The eye didn't bother her. Neither did the scars that ran along her forearm. The PRC had not been delicate in their surgeries, and Frutiger had offered her a round of corrective surgeries to repair the deformities. She had turned him down, unable to see these changes as deformities. She was different, and different was good.

When she looked in the mirror, a simple thought bloomed: *This is who I am.* The voice was warm and smooth. It was her voice, she knew, and nobody else's. She was whole.

Her hair had been shaped into a pixie cut, and she felt good about who she had become. Not just good, but sure. The more she talked with Frutiger and the other investigators, the more she realized how little control she'd had of herself before. She could more clearly analyze her actions and separate them from those of Alice Xie. She was in charge, in control, and assured. Nobody was going to take that away from her.

After a year, she delivered her testimony to the International Criminal Tribunal via a secure white room. For more than a week, she testified before the Third Trial Chamber of five judges from Uganda, Korea, South America, France, and Italy.

Three months later, the Court handed down numerous indictments, with Schaeffer's researchers bearing the brunt of the punishment. Deemed a part of his inner-circle by the Office of the Prosecutor, the researchers were sentenced to life-long imprisonment to be served in Mali. They were found guilty of a litany of charges, including both physical and mental abuse, disregard of human life, abuse of science, ethical and amoral behavior, and crimes against humanity. Lighter sentences were given to individuals higher up on the chain. Department heads and corporate executives were charged largely with contempt of the Tribunal. Only three of a dozen executives charged were formally brought to trial by the Tribunal, and only one was found to be complicit in Schaeffer's dangerous experimentations. That single executive was given a twenty-five-year sentence and imprisoned at a UN detention facility in the West African republic of Benin.

She live-streamed the sentencing via a DRMR app, and

when the day was finished, Mesa felt more exhausted than satisfied. If anything, she felt more confused and questioned what, exactly, she was *supposed* to be feeling. She had expected a greater level of closure.

At nine, Frutiger knocked on her door, clearly drunk and carrying a six-pack of Heineken. "We did it!" he shouted, his cheeks flushed red and eyes bloodshot. She let him past, and he set the beer on her kitchen table. "This is for you."

She had never seen him like that before. She was used to the buttoned-up, professional Frutiger, not the loose, inebriated, cheerful man before her. He spun the cap off one of the emerald bottles and passed it to her. The beer was wonderfully cold and provided a sense of satisfaction that the day's earlier verdicts had not.

"What will you do now?" he asked her, falling onto the sofa.

She'd given that some thought in the intervening hours, but still found herself at a loss. Aside from Rameez, she had no one and nothing else. All of her closest friends were dead, her father was gone, and Kaizhou had sacrificed himself so that she might live. She owed both him and Jonah a decent life, and she found herself in the peculiar position of starting over from scratch, with no history to tie her down. Her life, her future, and whatever came next were all up to her. Her choices and her decisions were hers alone. Talking all of that over with a drunken Frutiger, though, lacked any sort of appeal.

Leaning against the breakfast counter, she answered truthfully but succinctly: "I don't know. I've got a few ideas, though."

Frutiger seemed to consider her words then shrugged. "That's good. Take a few days. Figure it out."

"What happens with Alice Xie now?" Mesa asked, pinpointing the source of her anxiety. The woman was still out there, if only as a collection of ones and zeros. Even that form of existence was deadly, a pathogenic danger that she didn't think either the UN Tribunal or Frutiger properly recognized. And by the time they figured it out, it would be too late.

"Daedalus kept her stored in a white room. We've taken similar precautions and shunted her off to a disconnected server. She's basically imprisoned, denied any type of access. Nobody will get to her, and she will not be able to get to anyone. She's grounded."

"That isn't good enough," Mesa said.

"It's all we can do," he said, clearly deflated. Whatever good buzz he had worked up before coming to her apartment, Mesa had effectively killed it. She didn't care.

"You need to take that hard drive and fucking burn it. Do you understand that? Delete her. Wipe her out. Kill her."

Frutiger took a long drink, but it lacked any of the enthusiasm that he'd displayed moments ago. "My hands are tied," he said, his voice softened with regret.

Three days later, Mesa and Frutiger shared a final beer at an airport bar. She had discussed her decision with him the day before, and he had approved.

"Everything's taken care of," he told her. "You're all set."

They clinked the necks of their beer bottles together, and she said, "Cheers."

"You're very brave, Mesa. You deserve a good life, a good home. Do your best, eh?"

She promised she would, both to him and to herself.

The flight was long and uneventful. After a year of what felt like standing still, she finally had a destination in mind. A goal. A chance to restart her life and to rebuild.

The following afternoon, she boarded a passenger ship leaving Seattle. When they had talked on Sunday, she had not told Rameez she would be in town, and she felt somewhat guilty. She had promised to call him again soon, though. She would have time to schedule a visit with him later, but she needed some time to herself. She inhaled the salty air and enjoyed the flecks of sea spray against her face as the ferry crested a wave.

Because she was traveling in the middle of a weekday, the deck was sparsely populated, which Mesa was grateful for. She'd had enough attention to last her a lifetime. She'd been inundated with questions and interrogations and had her mind invaded, investigated, and torn apart. She deserved some privacy and reveled in sitting alone in the middle of the Pacific.

Prior to boarding, she had caught the attention of a man standing alone at the pier. He gazed at her openly. When she turned to face him directly, showing him the damaged side of her face, he blushed and turned away. That was another bonus courtesy of her cybernetic implant. The eye and the thick network of scarring surrounding the orbit turned away a lot of gazes.

The damage could all have been corrected, of course. A brief round of reconstructive surgery would wipe out the scarring, and there were certainly many other better options for ocular implants than the generic brand she'd been stuck with. She enjoyed her status as an outsider, though. Fixing the damage meant being engaged, and she wasn't ready for that.

She had too many things to do.

Waves jostled her as they crashed against the hull. Somewhere along the way, a pod of dolphins had joined the ferry, and she watched the animals breach along the port, diving and racing. She cherished the simple pleasure.

Mesa raised her cup to them in mock salute, letting the scent of bergamot mingle with the salty sea air. She took a long pull of tea, not coffee, and let it slide down her throat, pulling down her worries. A chill in the air made her eye ache and sent a dull throb down the length of her arm, from wrist to elbow. Still, she drew comfort from the hot tea and let the drink soothe and relax her.

She shivered as the wind picked up, brushing across her, and zipped the brown leather jacket. The dolphins jumped again, squeaking in the air before disappearing beneath the waves, and then they were gone. In the distance, the ocean crashed against the breaker walls. White caps crested the height of the walls surrounding the seasteads and broke apart in the air.

The channels grew crowded as the ferry slowed to pass through the outer rings of aquaculture farms and maneuvered toward the debarkation points. She watched the fishermen, farmers, and workers go about their daily tasks, hoisting nets filled with mussels and clams. The pleasure boaters and yachters were out in full force, taking advantage of the day's ripe beauty.

Off in the distance, the shining spire of the center state rose from the ocean. The sun glinted off the solar arrays, turning the black panels into brilliant golden-white displays against the clear rich-blue sky.

She basked in the freshness of sunlight and ocean spray, watching the floating city-states of the seasteaders unfolding around her. She couldn't remember the last time she had felt at peace.

Then she remembered her promise. She pinged Rameez on the commNet, and he responded instantly, his face appearing on her retinal display.

"It's good to see you," he said, all smiles.

"Hi, Rameez," she said, returning his contagious smile and warming.

"You made it OK?"

"Yeah," she said, tucking her hair back behind her ear, suddenly self-conscious. She watched as the seastead drew closer. The bustle of activity drew her eyes, and she refused to look away, entranced by the promise the small collective of nation-states held for her.

"Yeah," she said again. "I made it. I'm home."

# A NOTE FROM THE AUTHOR

Thank you for choosing to read my book – it's greatly appreciated, and I hope you enjoyed the journey!

If would be willing to spare a minute or two, please leave a brief review of this work and let other readers know what you thought. Reviews are incredibly helpful, particularly for an independent author and publisher such as myself, and can help determine the success of a novel. They do not need to be long, twenty words or so should suffice, but their impact can be enormous.

I look forward to your thoughts, and thank you, once more, for taking the time to read this work.

If you would like to know about my future releases, and even get free advanced reader copies prior to their release, you can sign up for my newsletter at http://www. michaelpatrickhicks.com.

# ACKNOWLEDGEMENTS

Although the actual writing of this book was a solo effort, it took a team effort to get the story elements properly aligned and to produce the novel itself.

I owe no small amount of gratitude to my team of editors at Red Adept Editing for their support and for their fine efforts. Many thanks to Lynne McNamee for putting together such a terrific stable of editors, proofreaders, and content editors. Laura Koons helped shaped and refine the scope of this story, and Stefanie Spangler Buswell helped keep it all from falling apart. Both offered tremendous insight and their suggestions were invaluable. There would not be any sort of a book here at all if not for their aid and rescue efforts! Thanks, also, to Virge Buck for her keen eyes and attention to detail during the proofreading phase.

Eight Little Pages was commissioned by James Anderson Foster to design the audiobook artwork for his weekly Serial Audio production of *Convergence*, narrated by Travis Baldree. I liked Claire's work so much, I asked her to help me refresh the look for *Emergence*, as well, in order to keep the visual style consistent across both books. Her updated artwork now graces both the print and digital books of this revised and updated edition of *Emergence*. I am very, very happy with the results!

In the year since the release of *Convergence*, I've had the pleasure of becoming acquainted with a number of indie authors. In addition to producing fine work in their own right, they've also become a tremendous resource, a fine source of support, and, yes, even friends. Thanks to Lucas Bale, J.S. Collyer, S. Elliot Brandis, S.W. Fairbrother (who also read an earlier draft of this book and provided so much awesome feedback!), Harry Manners, Nadine Matheson, and Alex Roddie. Earlier this year, I was able to work alongside them in the production and release of a science fiction anthology, *No Way Home*, and their stories are each top-notch. We'll all be working together again very soon! I'd also like to give a shout out to Nicholas Sansbury Smith, author of the terrific *Orbs* and Extinction Cycle series of books, for his support of my debut and for frequently asking about the sequel. So, here you go Nick! These authors have become brothers and sisters in arms in this thing we do, so please support them and their work, as well.

And, of course, a tremendous amount of appreciation and love to my beautiful wife, Maureen. I couldn't do this without her. She is the heart that drives all this along. Thanks, also, to my friends and family for their words of encouragement, praise, and support along the way.

# ABOUT THE AUTHOR

**Michael Patrick Hicks** is the author of *Broken Shells: A Subterranean Horror Novella*, *Mass Hysteria*, an Audiobook Listeners Choice Awards Horror Finalist, and *Convergence*, an Amazon Breakthrough Novel Award Finalist. He is a member of the Horror Writers Association and the Great Lakes Association of Horror Writers.

In addition to his own works of original fiction, he has written for the online publications Audiobook Reviewer and Graphic Novel Reporter, and has previously worked as a freelance journalist and news photographer in Metro Detroit.

Michael lives in Michigan with his wife and two children. In between compulsively buying books and adding titles that he does not have time for to his Netflix queue, he is hard at work on his next story.

To stay up to date on Michael's latest releases, join his
newsletter at: http://bit.ly/1H8slIg

**Website:**
http://michaelpatrickhicks.com

**E-mail:**
mphicks@michaelpatrickhicks.com

**Facebook:**
http://www.facebook.com/authormichaelpatrickhicks

**Twitter:**
http://www.twitter.com/MikeH5856

"Hicks writes like Philip K Dick and
Robert Crais combined... He focuses on
the story and never lets go."
- Lucas Bale, author of the
award-winning *Beyond The
Wall* series

PRESERVATION

A DRMR SHORT STORY

MICHAEL PATRICK HICKS

KARI AKAGI SAT IN THE crook of a massive baobab tree, a rifle in her lap, roughly twenty meters above the low-lying plains of the Kruger National Park.

From her perch she could see the Olifants River, which divided the southern and northern regions of Kruger. The north was elephant country, and she watched as a herd bathed in the shallow depths and grazed along its banks.

There was a simple joy in watching the massive creatures live their lives, in seeing the young ones play.

Their life expectancy was too short for her liking, but the luckiest among them could live for fifty years or more. If the poachers didn't get to them first.

Her morning had started with news of another rhino killing. The reserve had less than one hundred left, and there was a countdown hanging over the heads of the survivors. Each one dead drove the black market prices of their ever-scarcer horns higher and higher into the millions.

The news had woken her like a kick to the gut, and she'd wanted to rage at the rangers and volunteers who had fucked up and let this happen. Unfair, certainly, but her anger was palpable. Instead, she retreated and cut off her commNet, fuming.

She zoomed in on the Olifants, increasing the resolution of her blink-powered retinal upgrades and recorded the lackadaisical scene playing out below. This was a memory she wanted to keep.

Standing to stretch her torso, she set the rifle aside and raised her arms above her head, holding the pose for several deep breaths. Then she bent at the waist, stretching her spine, shoulders, and the muscles of her one remaining thigh, the flex deep enough that she was able to touch the two long blades that had replaced both feet.

Her legs had been lost to an IED years ago. Her left leg, from the hip down, was a mechanized limb replacement system. Both high-grade prosthetics were equipped with hundreds of ultra-fast quantum-load microprocessors, hydraulics, rotors, flexions, actuators, and sensors. A neuronal interface allowed her to control each limb as if it were the real thing, and the built-in multi-directional response coordinators allowed her to move with ease and grace in virtually any environment.

With her chin practically touching the tough Kevlar shell of the artificial knee joint, she could feel the absorbed heat boiling off the deep blue fabric.

Although she was warm and hadn't eaten real food in several days, she had little concern for dehydration or starvation. The military had seen to her well-being both before and after her mandatory four tours in Afghanistan and Syria. Keeping her in-country in such harsh climates that ranged from desert tundra to colder mountain terrain had required significant modifications to her meat suit.

Akagi's innards had been replaced with artificial

organs to regulate her body's water loss, and nasal cavity inserts and heat exchangers implanted atop her jugular veins and neck arteries inhibited water loss that occurred through exhalation and perspiration. There were even filter systems installed in her bladder and large intestine to capture, concentrate, and store any water lost through digestive waste. In her rucksack was a three-month supply of hard-shelled, egg-shaped candies. Each one contained a liquid center and provided her with her daily requirement of nutrients and calories.

While the military had designed her to be an optimized soldier, she had found a more satisfying niche working as a wildlife ranger. The truth of it was, she had merely traded one war for another, exchanging a cause for a cause. Her cause, nowadays, just happened to have four legs and tusks or horns.

Rising from the stretch, she again lifted both arms over her head and pulled her torso first to the left, then the right, stretching her oblique abdominals.

Her body felt looser, her mind more composed. Until the ping hit her commNet with an urgent alert and a geotag.

Another kill.

She felt her cheeks warm in anger, then quickly cool as her implants triggered a temperature regulation control and systolic dampener. The physical stressors were muted, but they didn't do shit for her emotional state and only made her feel that much more pissed off.

"Has anyone heard from Gerhardt?" Command asked.

"Negative," she said. "What was his last status?"

"He checked in for morning debriefing, but no updates since."

"Roger that, Command."

Another kill, and now a missing ranger. She swore

softly to herself, unsettled.

Clambering down a ladder the park rangers had installed more than half a century ago, the dual-bladed system that comprised her feet hit the soft grass below. She broke out into a run, maintaining an easy pace to the latest kill site, roughly forty-five minutes away.

Akagi knelt before the butchered rhino, resting her hand against its still flank and closing her eyes for a moment of quiet respect.

The massive herbivore's face had been brutally hacked apart, probably by an axe. The horns were missing, naturally. Dried blood stained the earth around the creature.

She cursed the lack of resources and the bribed politicians who abetted in this gruesome horror. The reserve covered more than eight thousand square miles of land, and it was impossible for the small squad to cover all of it efficiently. In a fit of twisted logic, the politicians argued that the reduced population of near-extinct animals meant there was little need for increased funding and the hiring of more rangers. The reservation's budget was slashed and burned, leaving little more than twenty active field rangers to patrol twenty-two sections of the park.

Their duties had been eased slightly with the deployment of reconnaissance drones, but it hadn't taken long for the poachers and the syndicates they worked for to grow aware of the extra surveillance. One by one, the five drones were shot out of the sky and the budget for replacements dried up.

Poaching was ludicrously profitable, and the wealthy higher-ups in the syndicates spent good money buying

South African politicians and influence within the leadership of preservation agencies. Once upon a time, the reservation had implanted the rhinos and their horns with tracking chips to make life more difficult for the syndicates. As a result, the syndicates went on a spending spree to develop a smear campaign through third-party agencies about how the tracking chips made life more difficult for the animals, and how the reservation was mutilating rhino horns, destroying the vital essence of the rhinoceros. All it took were a few dozen parliamentary members in the syndicates' pockets to undo all the good the rangers were attempting. Even the rangers and veterinarians on staff were lulled by the big money the syndicates offered. Akagi herself had arrested one of the drone operators, who was tracking the preserve's animals for poachers, who were being supplied high-grade tranquilizers by one of the park's veterinarians.

More than six thousand miles away from Syria and she still found herself on the losing side of another desperate warzone, surrounded by corruption, turncoats, and failed leadership. She couldn't help but laugh to herself as the bitter resentment bubbled over.

Her partner, Okey Ekwensi, stood nearby with his canine companion, Dashi. The black-and-tan German shepherd panted lightly as he watched her movements.

Circling around the fallen rhino, she saw the mess of clumsy footprints from both animal and man. The rhino's cloven hooves left a large, rounded mark that looked somewhat like a bubbly W. There were five distinct boot treads as well.

Blood spatter along the ground led to the brush, where the trap had been sprung. The blood line along the ground left a clear trail, and she spotted red in the grass. Her mind's eye pictured, too clearly, the team of poachers surrounding the rhino and hacking at its flanks with their axes. Gore flew off the blades as they tore their weapons free from the animal's hide, raising them for another strong swing.

The rhino had tried to run, but the men — they were almost always men — had gone for the legs, severing its Achilles tendons. The rhino then collapsed, immobilized in the trampled dirt, where its face was hacked apart and dismembered.

"This is number eight-six for the year," she said.

"And it's only March," Okey said, nodding. He spoke softly, his black skin shiny from the layer of sweat covering him and plastering his fatigue shirt to his chest.

"They're not going to last the year."

Okey said nothing. The solemn look on his face said enough. He knew the score as well as she did. What else was left to say? They were standing there quietly in the middle of an extinction event.

"Let the dog loose," she said.

They followed Dashi into the tall grass fields as he tracked the poachers' scent, Okey keeping close. Akagi surveyed the terrain, seeking out the trail, looking for footprints, scanning the horizon with a variety of ocular magnifications.

Odds were, the poachers were long gone. They spent the better part of an hour following the trail before it went cold. The bent grass and boot treads gave way to flattened earth and the deep impression of tire tracks.

Dashi grew agitated, his panting becoming heavier as he sniffed at the air, straining on the leash. The sudden movements caught Okey by surprise and he nearly lost his grip on the leather strap. He recovered quickly and the two were off and running in a westerly direction.

Akagi followed close on their tails but came to a swift stop, her bladed feet sliding through the dust and briefly losing traction as the stabilizers fought to maintain her vertical equilibrium. The stench was enough to gag her, and she pulled her checkered shemagh over her mouth.

She recognized the soiled green fatigues as that of a ranger, but it was impossible to tell who it was. The man had been gutted, his innards spilled across the ground. His face was a pulpy mess, hacked apart by the poachers. He'd likely stumbled upon them or heard the sound of their vehicle and went to warn them off. Sorry fucker had been in the wrong place at the wrong time.

As she drew closer, she realized she knew the man. Not because of any physical features, but rather because of the lack of them.

"They took his arm," Okey said. "His leg too."

"Gerhardt," she said, refusing to look away from his splayed form.

Like Akagi, Gerhardt had been fitted with similar prosthetics following war injuries. He'd been caught on the wrong side of friendly fire when his troop had come under attack in Iran. They'd been forced to withdraw into a meat-packing facility and radioed for backup. Drones had been dispatched, and if the operators had bothered to discern the differences between hostiles and friendlies, the payload sure as hell didn't. A rain of hellfire missiles pounded the surrounding area, eliminating the Iranian Army and laying waste to the surrounding commercial zone. Gerhardt had been too close to an exterior wall and it had cost him.

Always in the wrong place at the wrong time, she thought.

The poachers had had a good day, it seemed. Black market bionics had a nice resale value. Not as much as rhino horns or elephant ivory, both of which had become more valuable than gold and oil combined in certain Asian markets, but still, they fetched a hefty price tag.

Another rhino lost. Another ranger killed, their seventh of the year.

We're all going extinct, she thought. We're the last of a dying breed.

She scratched at the scars along the side of her neck, shooing away a mosquito.

"Call it in," she said. "Get some trucks out here."

She thought, not for the first time, that this was less of a preserve and more of a graveyard.

# REVOLVER

## MICHAEL PATRICK HICKS

"A classic example of social science fiction"
*David Wailing, Author of Auto*

## FOREWORD BY
## LUCAS BALE

"A sharp, crackling, exploration of man's hubris, and science gone wrong. This is Frankenstein for the new millennium."
HUNTER SHEA, author of We Are Always Watching and The Jersey Devil
MICHAEL PATRICK HICKS
BLACK SITE

# THE MARQUE

MICHAEL PATRICK HICKS

# THE MARQUE

## MICHAEL PATRICK HICKS